BETRAYED!

Dart's guard melted under the relentless battering. He sagged against the roof post, unable to defend himself. The wooden sword was useless in his limp hand. Once again Dart felt himself spinning toward the abyss which he knew was his own death. The punishment they'd given his ribs was nothing compared to the firestorm brewing in his own skull. . . .

THE WOODEN SWORD

With acclaimed author Robert Asprin, Lynn Abbey coedited the popular fantasy series *Thieves' World*™, a remarkable shared-world anthology set in a mythical city of magic and mayhem. Abbey is also the author of several fantasy novels, including *The Black Flame*, *Daughter of the Bright Moon* and *The Guardians*.

THE WOODEN SWORD

LYNN ABBEY

ACE BOOKS, NEW YORK

This book is an Ace original edition,
and has never been previously published.

THE WOODEN SWORD

An Ace Book / published by arrangement with
the author

PRINTING HISTORY
Ace edition / September 1991

ISBN: 0-441-90866-7

Ace Books are published by The Berkley Publishing Group,
200 Madison Avenue, New York, New York 10016.
The name "ACE" and the "A" logo
are trademarks belonging to Charter Communications, Inc.

PRINTED IN THE UNITED STATES OF AMERICA

10 9 8 7 6 5 4 3 2 1

THE WOODEN SWORD

INTRODUCTION

Walensor's world was older than mankind. Its older gods were as old as the world, though they began as phenomena, unconscious of self or power, as mindless as the forces that engendered them. Mankind discovered consciousness; mankind awakened the gods.

Magic was born when the gods looked upon their worshippers. The Compact of magic was gradually revealed during the long dawn of history. Mankind awakened new gods as it grew, learned, and spread across the world. New languages arose as distance and circumstance divided mankind's first tribes. Magic found new vocabularies, new expressions, but the Compact endured: Gods created and gods destroyed; mankind lived and died. The gods were more powerful, but mankind could always awaken a new god to drive out an old one.

In Walensor, on the Inland Sea, magic expressed itself through *basi*, the life gift. All creatures received *basi* at the moment of their birth, and acquired more each passing day. Men and women in whom the life gift was most generous became sorcerers. Because the life gift was not equal, and because *basi* increased with age, there was no threshold for sorcery. In the long dawn of history, this was not important, but as societies carved their civilizations, sorcerers banded together. Thresholds for the teaching and use of magic were imposed.

The Walensor sorcerers came together at the confluence of three great rivers. They raised the basilica of magic called Eyerlon. They learned how to store *basi* in objects and they created an object that was pure *basi*: the Web of Walensor, which sheltered the land like a huge domed roof. A Walensor sorcerer could use the Web to communicate with any other sorcerer, and with the Walenfolk gods.

The threshold for joining the community of sorcerers was simple: If a child had sufficient *basi* to reach the Web before he or she became an adult, the child could come to Eyerlon, or a satellite basilica, to learn formal sorcery and take its place in the community. An adult might accrue enough *basi* to reach the Web late in life, but adults never joined the Eyerlon community. They became hedge-sorcerers communicating with the Web when necessary for the commonweal of Walensor, performing intuitive magic, and generally sparing the increasingly sophisticated Eyerlon sorcerers from the onerous task of dwelling with the commonfolk in the countryside.

The Walensor Web, rising out of the Eyerlon Basilica, gradually became the focus of civil life as spiritual life. It bound the Walenfolk not only to their many and generally harmonious gods, but to their lords and king, who employed sorcerers to communicate with each other. A chosen few among the sorcerers became basilidans, who conveyed messages from the gods to commonfolk and noblefolk alike. Every time the Web was used, it accrued more *basi*. It was not alive and it was not awakened to godhood. It was the greatest achievement of the ancient Compact: cooperation between mortal mankind and the gods it had awakened.

Mankind, whose fate was and remained mortality, equated godhood with immortality. The gods knew this was wrong: Nothing was immortal. The world had an absolute beginning and would have an absolute end. None of mankind's awakened gods recalled the world's true beginning. The gods dreaded the world's end as every conscious man or woman dreaded mortal death.

And some gods dreaded mankind. Even when mankind did not move from one place to another, leaving ancestral gods behind and awakening new gods where it resettled, mankind wrought change. Forests became fields; streams were dammed; hills were gutted for city walls. The immortal death of a quarried mountain or clear-cut forest was abrupt as any man's.

As mankind grew in number and cleverness, the Compact itself was subtly altered. Cities engendered their own self-interested gods; larger polities looked to the sun, moon, and stars, which could be seen and worshipped throughout a kingdom. Someday a god might awaken in mankind's shape from mankind's consciousness.

Far to the east of the Inland Sea the process had already begun in the mind of an ambitious mage. In harsh, arid Arrizan magic grew in fire, the spark of life; and the Pyromant Hazard discovered how to usurp its power. He learned how to bind the spirits of mortal men; he stole the flame from the Arrizan gods, but, try as he might, Hazard could not shed his mortality.

Then the Pyromant Hazard of Arrizan looked across the mountains and saw the Web of Walensor.

CHAPTER

—— 1 ——

Berika's head hurt as she walked to the fallow field. The warm morning sun, usually welcome this late in the year, was much too strong for her sensitive eyes. The bells dangling from her crook and the sheep in her flock were discordantly loud. Her mouth felt like the wrinkled peelings at the bottom of a cider keg—which was hardly surprising, considering how much of Rimp's apple brandy she'd guzzled the previous night.

Drinking had seemed like a good idea at the time. When Auld Mag, the village hedge-sorcerer, got the Brightwater mist into her and spouted King Manal's proclamation of victory over the Arrizan Imperial host, unbridled celebration seemed the only proper response. The war every Walen secretly feared would end with defeat and annihilation had been won. Rimp, the richest and most miserly man in the village, rolled out the keg of cider he'd bunged almost a decade ago, when the war began.

While the potent, cloudy brandy flowed freely, no one remembered the cost of those ten years: the men who would not return, including Berika's father and her eldest brother, Indon. The scars were born by those who fought, and by those who waited. Mag sat in the Brightwater mist, reciting one proclamation after another, and the villagers drank themselves stiff. (The old woman had

4

more *basi* than many Eyerlon sorcerers, but she was too frail to reach for the Web more often than once a month, when the moon was waxing full. King Manal's victory proclamation was old when she plucked it down.)

A burr found its way into Berika's wooden shoe. Her next step crushed it. The spines pierced her woolen hose like a swarm of stinging insects. Coming on top of her hangover, the itching was more than the shepherd could ignore. She sprawled in the high, dry grass, took off her hose, and removed the wicked little hooks one by one. The flock surrounded her, nibbling her dark blond braids, her clothes, and anything else they could reach. Berika gave the nearest rump a solid *thwack* with the crook. The noise made her cringe, but it got rid of the flock. She rubbed her aching eyes and let her thoughts wander.

It had been midnight, maybe later, when she had dragged her stool to the hearth where the Brightwater mist rose from a cauldron. Mag's eyes were closed; her voice was a cracked whisper. Berika gave the old woman a sip of brandy, then listened while the hedge-sorcerer recited another proclamation. A magga-trained sorcerer, a sorcerer who learned the art from the Eyerlon masters, could pick and choose among the Web's messages, but a hedge-sorcerer had to take each precisely in its turn.

The week-old proclamation Mag recited with Berika's brandy on her tongue commended the beguines for their selfless service during Walensor's ordeal. Berika thought some special providence had brought her to the hedge-sorcerer's side.

Berika revered beguines not for their nursing and nurturing— the twin missions mentioned in the king's proclamation—but as the only refuge for women who could not become sorcerers and would not become wives. Berika's dream of reaching the Web and thereby leaving Gorse for a sorcerer's life in Eyerlon was not idle—Auld Mag was her great-aunt, and her mother, Ingolde, was certain to become the next hedge-sorcerer when Mag died. But she was birth-betrothed to Mag's son, Hirmin, and if she did not reach the Web before her seventeenth birthday, her betrothal would be consummated unless she escaped to the beguines.

Sorcery remained the cleanest way out of her dilemma. No betrothal could stand between a child-sorcerer and the wonders of Eyerlon. The Basilica would compensate both families with fresh-minted *gold*. But try as she might, Berika had not reached the Web. By the time she was fourteen, and the other girls her age were marrying, Berika's efforts were tainted with desperation; she began to think more seriously of the beguines.

The unwelcome betrothal was the result of a bargain that Berika's mother had made with Auld Mag long before Berika was born. Ingolde never admitted what she'd gotten in return, but her first daughter was irrevocably promised to Mag's only child, Hirmin. If Hirmin were handsome like Berika's brothers, or gentle like her father . . . If he'd had any merit whatsoever—but Hirmin Maggotson was ugly without and brutal within. When she was little, Berika feared him; as she grew, her fear solidified into acid hate.

A girl needed a dowry and her family's permission to become a beguine. Ingolde got surly whenever her daughter raised the subject: An oath was an oath, she'd snarl, always adding that she kept hers. An unmarried woman—a girl became a woman by decree on her seventeenth birthday—could join, without permission or dowry, if she crossed the beguinage threshold as naked as she'd come into the world. The nearest beguinage was in the Donitor's city of Relamain, a place almost as far from Gorse as fabled Eyerlon itself. Berika didn't know how many days' walking she would need to reach Relamain, but if she hadn't reached the Web by dawn on her birthday, she was determined to find out.

Then King Manal's words in Mag's voice shattered Berika's hopes:

> For all that we are thankful to the beguines, and we commend their selfless devotion to the sick and injured of Walensor, we cannot overlook the empty hearths and silent nurseries of our kingdom. We decree it is time to replace the generation we have lost. We hereby release each beguine from her vows.

> Moreover, to each man who fought for Walensor against the Arrizi scourge, we bestow the inalienable right to take two wives, by marriage or freehold, and he shall pay no poll tax on his second wife, nor on her children.

> Further, shall one or both of these wives be a beguine released from her vow, the crown treasury shall pay him a gold mark for her dowry. And finally, we decree that for ten

years hence, no woman shall be given refuge at the be-guinage unless she be proved barren.

Bright welts rose where the burrs pricked Berika's skin. They burned, but they were not the cause of the tears rolling down her cheeks. She lacked the *basi* to reach the Web in time, and last night she'd learned that her king had bolted the beguinage door. Worst of all, Hirmin who had fought for Walensor, did not even have to marry her. He could take her in freehold as if she were chattel property like the sheep—

The sheep!

Shuddering, Berika realized she couldn't see—or hear—them. Gods willing, they would have stayed on the high path to the fallow field, but sheep were godless. Shapeless Au, creator of all things including the gods themselves, made shepherds for sheep and decided nothing further need be done.

With her hose dangling around her neck, Berika thrust her foot into the shoe and stumbled along the low path. The bell-ewe, the boldest of the flock, was up to her belly in mud and churning determinedly toward the swift stream. The rest—bless their empty heads—dawdled on the bank. Berika charged at them, wailing like a demon and cringing inwardly each time the bells hit the crook. When she had them intimidated she plunged into the mud after the mired ewe.

She walloped the ewe with the long crook. Its rearend jumped in the desired direction, but the front kept churning. It was thirsty, it smelled water, and it was going to stick its nose in that water.

"Stupid, gods-forsaken sheep," Berika cursed as mud filled her shoes. "Good for nothing—" Except sheep weren't good for nothing; in her house, sheep were everything.

If, by some miracle, the ewe did reach the water, it would promptly drown—since sheep were too stupid to hold their breath when they drank, or lift their heads when they swallowed. Steadying herself with the crook, Berika slogged deeper into the quagmire. She lunged; she lost both shoes, but got a solid grip on its fleece.

"Stupid . . . gods-forsaken . . . good for—"

With her shoulder against its shoulder, Berika shoved the ewe toward the bank. The sheep squirted onto firm footing; the shepherd got a mouthful of muck. Spitting and cursing, she looked up in time to see the filthy beast test the mire again.

"Don't you dare!" Berika grabbed the crook and jangled its bells.

Square-pupil eyes blinked solemnly; the ewe took another step forward. Berika shrieked. The ewe shook itself and scampered toward the rest of the flock. Berika made a quick, futile search for her shoes.

Once Berika had the flock in the fallow field she could relax until it was time to take them back to the village. The fields of Gorse grew more rocks than grain; there was a waist-high wall around the fallow field. She rinsed the mud from her legs and the stale cider from her mouth. Her headache was gone; she could be thankful for that at least.

The shepherd searched for a spot where she could watch the flock, dry her skirt, and yet not see too much of the wild forest. King Manal, on the day of his coronation some fifty years earlier, had granted an assart charter to a handful of peasants, Berika's grandfather among them, who swore that a lightning-fire had already burned the trees on the forest edge. It was always in the king's interest to increase the size of the kingdom. The Compact prohibited men from destroying any ancient tree, it said nothing about the rights of mortal men when some nonmortal power did the killing for them. And so the village of Gorse was founded, as other villages had been founded by assart charter. The charred, skeletal snags were chopped up for houses and firewood. Plowed fields replaced the wild woodlands and in a few years Gorse looked very much like any other hamlet on the remote Fenklare border.

Gorse was, however, different from its distant neighbors in several ways. It belonged to King Manal, himself, for the length of his personal reign, not to the donitor of Fenklare, and for this the folk of Gorse were duly grateful: The king had more important things on his mind than collecting the customary dues of a solitary and struggling hamlet while the donitor's nosy taxmen could not set foot on the assart land.

But there was a darker side to Gorse's assart rights. The forest goddess, Weycha, understood the Compact differently. She regarded the cultivated lands of Walensor with considerable suspicion and she hadn't forgiven the village for plowing the soil where her trees had grown since time immemorial. But Weycha was not a powerful goddess, not at least in Eyerlon where the Web plunged through the Basilica's golden dome. King Manal did not fear her, but Berika and her neighbors knew better.

They left the largest snag among the fire-killed trees untouched. They built a roofless fane around it, so its lifeless branches might continue to feel the sun, the rain, and the wind. Where other villages cluttered their fanes with the votive images of every god and demigod connected to the Walensor Web, Gorse directed all its devotions to Weycha. When greenwood sprouted from the charred bark, they would know they were forgiven. Until then, they were wary of Weycha and her forest.

Berika found a place on the wall with the right vantage on both the flock and the forest. After drying her feet with her hose, she spread them and her skirt out to dry. There'd be hell to pay for the lost shoes, but nothing compared to the greeting she'd have gotten if she'd lost the ewe. As bad luck went, Berika was doing pretty well.

It was, she reflected, the story of her life: precious little good luck, and the best bad luck for days around. Even Hirmin. Bad as he was, he was also the sole heir of two village founders, with unentailed rights to half the orchard and an eighth of the plowed land. The Arrizi hellfire poison had taken a mean-spirited man and transformed him into a crippled monster, but it still continued to fester in his lungs; eventually it would kill him.

Ingolde knew to what kind of a man she'd promised her daughter. When she saw how his hellfire wounds lingered, she made no secret of her relief. *Four years, five at the most. He'll be dead by the time you're twenty-two. Live with him a few years. All that he has will come to you—stay with you if his children are taken to Eyerlon. It's a small price.*

Widowed Embla would leap at the chance to be Hirmin's wife. Ingolde had taken the young widow and her children into the shepherd's house last winter after Embla's husband died. Embla wouldn't go cold or hungry, but she had nothing to call her own. Heldey, who was closer to Berika's age, and the childless widow of Berika's oldest brother, Indon, would gladly leave the shepherd's house for Hirmin's bed.

There simply was no better situation for a woman, noble or common, than unentailed possession of her dead husband's property.

"I won't do it," Berika shouted to the uninterested sheep. "I hate Hirmin. I'll kill myself first—" Her voice trailed off. That

was an empty threat: Her hate was too potent for self-destruction,
and killing him was no better. Berika had never seen anyone
stoned, but she knew she didn't want to be executed for her
husband's murder.

"Two more months: The rest of Gleaning, all of Slaughter, and
seven days of Greater Hoarfrost, that's all I needed." She looked
at the sky, where the great gods dwelt within and beyond the Web.
"Forty days and I'd be seventeen. I'd be in Relamain. I'd have
pledged myself to the beguines; I know I would have—" Her
voice faded again. Pledging wasn't enough. King Manal's proclamation, which cancelled vows, would certainly cancel a new
beguine's pledge. The beguinages were lost as a refuge.

Eyes tightly closed, Berika raised her face to the sun. She
poured her soul into the effort, but the Web, as ever, remained
beyond her reach. Her eyes began to water and she returned to her
bent-over misery.

"Dear gods, help me. Some one of you, hear me and help me.
I'll do anything, I swear it, but don't make me marry Hirmin. Give
me the *basi* to reach the Web. Show me another path. *Please?*"

She got down from the wall and began to twirl around.
Walenfolk did not ordinarily spin like tops to attract the attention
of their gods. They made offerings in their fanes, or had a sorcerer
place their plea in the appropriate nexus of the Web. But once,
when Berika was a little girl who had lost the brightly colored
bead that was her most prized possession, she said a private prayer
just this way, whirling until she collapsed. When she opened her
eyes, the bead lay beyond her outstretched arm, under a piece of
firewood. She still had the bead; she still spun when she prayed.
There was always a chance it might work again.

The hangover wasn't quite gone; the shepherd fell sooner, and
harder, than she expected. She rolled onto her back and waited for
the ground to stop moving before she tried to sit up. When she was
certain she knew up from down, she opened her eyes. Praying
brought her face to face with Weycha's forest and a very strange,
shimmering *something* on the far bank. She blinked, slowly and
deliberately.

"Bright shining water . . . " she murmured.

The apparition did resemble the Brightwater of sorcery, though
its colors were all golds, ambers, and reds, with only a twinkling
of green and no blue at all. Berika's heart leapt to the conclusion
that the gods had heard her prayer; her mind held back. If the

shimmering object was an answer to her prayers, then she did not understand it. This was not like finding a lost bead. The gods had granted Berika—a girl who could not reach the Web—a gift they seldom gave their chosen basilidans.

"A fetch," she said aloud. "I fetched!"

Her voice carried across the water. The apparition raised its head. It didn't have a proper face; its eyes shifted and glowed. Berika opened her mouth, intending to scream. She whimpered instead. A dark hole appeared beneath the burning eyes. It sprouted a hand, raised it, and pointed an unnaturally long finger at her.

Berika understood: There was only one way to escape Hirmin. The gods, hearing her prayer, had sent a fetch to kill her. Death, she quickly decided, was not an improvement over marriage. She grabbed a stone from the wall and threw it. The fetch scrambled for cover, and so did the shepherd. By the time Berika lifted her head above the wall, the fetch was perched on a partly submerged rock.

"Are you the hazard my lady fears?"

The girl's terror melted into confusion. He—the fetch had a raspy, deep voice—seemed afraid of her.

"I've come to find the hazard that threatens my lady. Do you threaten my lady?"

Rheumy-eyed Mag, with her knobby fingers and whiskers, was more dreadful than the fetch, who was quite small and shivered each time he spoke. Berika was emboldened to stand erect. She jangled the crook. The little creature vanished behind his rock.

"Go away. You don't belong here."

The fetch darted toward the bank. He lost his footing on the slick stones and tumbled into the frigid stream, where he floundered. Berika's first impulse was to rescue him, as she'd rescue her sheep or any other living creature. But the fetch wasn't any living creature. She bit her knuckles and was relieved when he clambered out of the water on the forest's side of the stream.

The fire was gone from his eyes. His bright, shifting colors were muddied. The fetch could easily pass for a dirty, scrawny toddler. He wrapped his arms about himself and shivered violently.

"Go back to your own kind," Berika told him. "Go quick! They'll take care of you. Stay away from the stream. You're too little. It's too deep and you can't swim. It's dangerous."

His hands stopped moving. "Dangerous? Danger? Hazard? I must protect my lady from hazard. I must protect my lady from danger. Are you danger?"

Berika sighed. "The water . . . you godless sheep. The water! Go back where you came from. Tell them I don't want to die."

The fetch knelt. He dragged his hands through the water. He smelled his fingers and licked the moisture from them. "The stream will not harm you. It is not danger. It is not hazard. My lady says hazard will come from outside. You are outside." He shoved his foot into the water.

He hadn't killed her; Berika suspected the fetch couldn't kill her. She was calm enough to appreciate the irony: an incompetent fetch sent to an incompetent sorcerer. "It's all a mistake," she shouted. "There's no danger here. None at all. Go back to your lady and tell her there's no hazard."

He cocked his head, listening to something Berika could not hear. "Hazard is on your side of the water. Far beyond. A lady died with hazard. Not my lady. I protect my lady from hazard."

Berika's throat tightened: not hazard, but Hazard. Her fetch knew the name of Walensor's defeated enemy. The last thing Berika wanted was to interfere with the Arrizan Pyromant, dead or alive. "You can go back to your lady." She chose her words more carefully, and slipped one hand behind her back to search for another loose stone. "Hazard's gone. He and his army were crushed at Tremontin when our sorcery brought the mountains down. You tell your lady. The war's over; the men are already on their way home."

"Tremontin . . . "

Was that fire flickering in her fetch's eyes, or some trick of sunlight reflecting off the water? Either way, Berika's terror returned.

"Tremontin. Tremontin died, not hazard. I must protect my lady from hazard."

Berika hid her trembling fist in the folds of her skirt. "If Hazard's not dead, he's on the far side of the pass with no army. The war's over. Go home." Her voice lacked authority; the creature didn't move. "There's no way for an Arrizi army to get into Walensor now that Kasserine and Tremontin are both gone. And anyway, this is the Donit of Fenklare; there's never been any fighting here."

"Donit. Fenklare. Fenklare Donit . . ."

The fetch seemed enthralled by the sounds he made. Berika judged it was time to try to escape. She had a leg over the wall before a breeze rattled the crook bells.

"Wait! Wait for me!"

Common sense suggested otherwise, but a lifetime of being Ingolde's daughter reminded Berika that catastrophe wasn't a fetch, or his lady, or even Hazard, Pyromant of Arrizan; it was the back of her mother's hand if she showed up without the sheep. Still, Berika knew sheepherding better than she knew anything else, and she had the flock moving before she heard the splash.

"Wait for me! Wait! I need you."

Berika prodded the bell-ewe into a trot; the rest followed. The flock was noisy, but not noisy enough. Splashing was replaced by the snap of dried grass. She cursed Ingolde for not marrying the pigkeeper. Pigs were worth more than sheep, and pigs didn't need anyone's protection. They stood their ground. A half-grown boar could kill a man. Sheep just got sheepish.

She knew she was doomed when the ewe's nose went up. A moment later the whole flock was jammed together, staring at the sky.

"Why do you run? Do you know this hazard?"

Berika spun around with the crook braced. The fetch was barely a step behind her. She cracked the hooked end against his head, then reversed her grip on the stick and rammed the iron-wrapped ferrule into his gut. The fetch collapsed with a groan. He was much bigger than he'd seemed from the wall, and clothed in rags instead of leaves. Berika didn't waste more time wondering how she'd been so mistaken about his appearance. She ran for the village, leaving the flock behind.

Beyond the fallow field was a hill; beyond that, the apple orchard. Beyond the orchard was the millpond and the fish weir; and beyond the weir was home. Berika had never needed much of a head start to beat her brothers home. Near the crest of the hill, she dared a glance over her shoulder.

The fetch was at the bottom of the hill. He was man-sized, man-shaped, and not at all scrawny. There was a red smear on the side of his face, but it wasn't slowing him down. Berika tossed the crook aside and lifted her skirt to her thighs. His pace matched her own; his stride was surely longer. Her lungs burned. The fetch's breath—she could hear it as he got closer—was even and easy. He'd catch her before she reached the orchard.

Berika screamed when he caught one of her braids. She lunged forward and, for a heartbeat, was free of him. Then a hand closed over her shoulder and they both crashed to the ground. The shepherd writhed like a snake. She kicked and scratched. She bit whatever flesh came near her teeth. The fetch yelped and scrambled away.

Boys and men could leap directly to their feet; girls and women had to get untangled first. Berika didn't need much time—she'd worn an ankle-length skirt since she'd learned to walk—but she took more than she had. The fetch came forward in that time, and staying away from Berika's face, he twisted her arm and planted his knee between her shoulders. The fight went out of her with a sigh.

"You say you are not danger, are not hazard—but I think I should not trust you. You draw my blood. What would you do to my lady?"

"You're hurting me—" Berika could do nothing but plead—and to her astonishment, pleading worked. He let her roll free. She would have rolled all the way down the hill, but he snatched her wrist before she got away. This time she moved with him when he twisted her arm, and found herself looking into an ordinary face.

"If you are not hazard, why do you run? Why won't you help me?"

An almost ordinary face. The wide eyes shimmered with the red, gold, and amber she remembered all too well. The pupils weren't round; they weren't hard-angled like a sheep's. They were star-shaped, and deeper than a starless night. Berika shielded herself with her free hand. She knotted her fingers in the traditional gesture against evil.

"Help me!" the fetch cried. "Help me—I beg you. I must protect my lady. Don't you understand? I'm all she has—" He shuddered; he released Berika's wrist. "It's dark. I can't see. I can't see anything! My lady—Where are you?"

Against all caution and reason, Berika lowered her hand. His eyes no longer shimmered. The star-pupils grew round and huge. He called for his lady again.

"What *are* you?" she demanded, easily eluding his flailing arms. "Where did you come from?"

His breathing was shallow.

"What do they call you? What's your name?"

A guttural, inhuman sound erupted from the fetch's throat. He covered his face with his forearms and rolled in the grass. Berika made certain her skirt was untangled. Whatever he was, man or fetch, she wasn't going to stay anywhere near him. Then, with obvious effort, the fetch spat out a single intelligible syllable.

"Dart? What kind of a name is *Dart*? No mother would name her son Dart—that's a dog's name."

The fetch was exhausted. He lay on his back, chest heaving, arms still thrown over his face. "No mother—only my lady. Only my lady. I'm falling. It's dark, and it's cold, and I'm falling. Help me—"

Berika could escape. The fetch—Dart—was in no condition to stop her. She would have turned on her heel, but the sheep were scattered across the hillside. By habit she counted them. If she would not abandon the godless sheep, then she could not abandon the creature her prayer had fetched.

"Do you hurt?" she asked, feeling foolish before the words were out of her mouth.

Dart said, "Fine-marp," which meant nothing to the shepherd. Then he fainted.

"I don't think I can help you," Berika whispered when he continued to lie there without moving. "I think I should go home and tell Ingolde—maybe Auld Mag. But first I've got to get the sheep. Ingolde won't help either of us if I come home without the sheep."

She had better luck than she had any right to expect. Her crook rose straight out of the grass, and the sheep flocked together without protest. She tapped the last straggler with the crook, and stubbed her toe. A gentle *thrum* rose from an impossibly large acorn at her feet.

Find my harp. The meaning of the fetch's garbled words came to Berika.

All sorcerers had touchstones. Auld Mag had a gnarled stick that gave off sparks when she struck with it. Bards were sorcerers with an extra gift for music; their touchstone was often a valuable harp. Only one bard had visited Gorse during the war: a woman whose sharp tongue offended her noblefolk patron and completely intimidated Ingolde. Berika remembered her well. She carried her harp in a carved-wood swan. Dart's harp case—assuming it was a harp case and belonged to him—didn't *look* like an acorn. It *was* an acorn, seamless and perfectly formed except for the tooled-leather strap where a stem should be.

Curiosity got the better of Berika. She stroked the smooth golden shell. Vibrations numbed her fingertips. She looked at Dart, who hadn't moved. Mag's stick worked for Mag alone, but anyone could play a harp. Was this Dart's touchstone, or had he stolen it? A touchstone might well have the power to drive its misuser mad—and Dart was surely mad.

The next, inevitable thought formed in Berika's mind as Dart let out a chilling scream. She jumped away from the acorn.

"I wouldn't—not really. Honestly. But I've got to pick it up—if I'm going to bring it to you."

Suddenly wary, Berika covered her hands with her apron before lifting the case out of the grass. She carried it up the hill with her arms stretched out in front her.

"I'm not hurting it. I'm hardly holding it at all. I'll put it right here beside you." She braced it against his side. He did not seem to be breathing. Berika could not make herself search for a pulse.

"I'll get Ingolde."

CHAPTER

2

The sheep milled about in the undercroft. Berika heard footsteps on the path behind her. She fumbled with the rope latch, not daring to turn around.

"Back early, aren't you? What happened to your shoes?"

Berika sighed. She began with the bell-ewe wandering into the mud where she lost her shoes. She didn't end until Dart was lying at her feet.

"A fetch, Beri? Your shoes for a fetch? And you expect me to hie myself to the fallow field? All you should expect is the back of my hand—"

"If you won't go, then I'll go. I gave my word. He—The fetch needs help." Berika bolted, but her mother snagged her arm.

Ingolde's expression was as dark as the clouds piling up on the horizon. "Girl—if you're lying—"

"I'm not. I swear it, Ingolde." A tremor added sincerity to Berika's voice. "He came out of the forest. His eyes glowed like coals on the fire, and when I asked him his name he curled up and started moaning."

"He?" Ingolde muttered through her fingers. Berika's imagination had always been too grand for a quiet village, but this was different. Any mother—any woman—could see something had happened. It didn't take hedge-sorcery to ken the confused emotions on Berika's flushed cheeks, but Ingolde had the *basi* for hedge-sorcery.

"There's an old pair of Braydon's shoes in the wood box. I'll be on the hill beyond the orchard."

By the time Berika found the shoes, and wadded fleece to make the toes tight, Ingolde should have found Dart, if he was where she left him. There was no point to running, but she did. Ingolde was on her knees and too busy to notice her daughter, who was as winded as she was relieved.

Ingolde wasn't alone. The other women of the shepherd's house, Embla and Heldey, knelt beside her. Old Larsov, who was too old for fighting when the war started, hovered nearby talking to himself. With their dark homespun clothes and hunched shoulders, the quartet reminded Berika of crows. She wanted to run at them, shouting and waving her arms.

Ingolde turned around before Berika had a chance to embarrass herself. "He's not from around here, I'll grant you that, Beri." The caustic compliment made Berika blush. Ingolde pressed her thumb against Dart's eyelid; Berika held her breath. Only the white showed. The glowing iris with its star-shaped pupil—if Berika had not imagined it—was hidden.

"He's alive, but not by much," Ingolde concluded. "Mother Cathe knows what he's got . . . or if it's catching."

"You couldn't tell he was a *man*?" Heldey inquired archly.

"He came out of Weychawood," Berika retorted.

"What would a man be doing in the forest?" Embla asked.

"Hiding out until the war was over, by the look of him." Heldey was always the quickest with a sharp answer.

"A coward?" Embla continued.

"No—not a coward, you fools," Berika retorted. "A fetch. My fetch." A tirade formed between Berika's ears, and remained there. She'd scream at Heldey, if the sable-haired girl embroidered the insult, but not Embla. No one ever yelled at mousy, little Embla who asked outrageous questions with a child's innocence. Heldey smiled like a well-fed cat; she knew better than to say anything.

Embla didn't notice the glances her friends exchanged, or the scowl growing on Ingolde's face. "Do you think he has a family someplace? A wife? Children?"

Heldey could contain her amusement no longer. "A wife?" she sputtered, looking at Berika. "That's rich. Married to a coward in the forest! Who'd want that?"

It wasn't what Heldey said that stung, but what she carefully implied. Who had been making such a fuss over her betrothal? Who indeed?

Ingolde saw her daughter's lips getting thin and pale. She interceded. "Don't think about who he is, or *what* he is," she advised in a tone that allowed no debate. "Tell yourselves he's trouble and keep your distance."

The young women were silent—all the opportunity old Larsov needed to add his own interpretations. "Trouble? Worse than trouble! Look at him. Parti-haired. He's mad, you know, with hair like that. No wits at all."

Dart's long matted hair had been uniformly dark and damp when Berika left him. She hadn't noticed its color, or colors: gold, red, brown, and all the shades between them. He might be mad, then. The wisdom of hedge-sorcery linked addled *basi* with two-colored hair. Dart's hair was many more than two colors: What did that say about his *basi* and his wits? His eyebrows were an unremarkable brown. His face was scraped smooth; Berika couldn't guess what his beard might be like.

Odd that he would have shaved, yet left his hair uncut and uncombed. . . .

"—might as well throw him back in that stream. That's what I say. Just another mouth to feed when we don't need one." Larsov would prattle until someone told him to shut up. "And what will the men think? Here they finally get home, after winning the war. Thinking how their womenfolk have missed them—and here their womenfolk have found themselves a parti-haired man. A fine thing—that's what I say—a fine thing to come home to."

The old man wasn't easy to ignore, but the women had had a lot of practice over the years. Ingolde pushed him gently aside as she untied her apron and spread it on the grass. The younger women imitated her, knotting the garments together until they had a sling strong enough to carry the stranger. Larsov was chattering about parti-haired men and parti-haired bastards when Ingolde began wrapping a corner of the sling around her wrist. Embla and Heldey chose their corners, but Berika's arms were filled with the huge acorn.

"We can't leave this."

The cloth unwound from Ingolde's wrist. "Bright shining water," she swore softly, then recovered. "We *can* leave it. And we *will* leave it. Pick up your corner," she commanded, retrieving her own.

"It belongs to him," Berika protested. "He asked me to find it for him, and he stopped moaning when I put it next to him."

"Well, it wasn't anywhere around him when I got here, and he isn't asking for it right now. It's not natural. It doesn't belong. Maybe it's what's turned his hair and left him moaning in the first place. Did you think of that? Did you think that maybe he stole it?"

A blush of memory flooded Berika's cheeks. "Mo-*ther*—"

"We're leaving it here. Come back for it—if you think it's so important. But if you do, don't put it beside him. Put it in the fane, nowhere else, or you'll be the one on the other side of the stream."

Berika glanced at the sky. "Storm'll be here before I can get back."

"If a little rain could hurt it, your hero's ruined it already. Now—*Lift!*"

Berika hesitated until her mother moved. Then she dropped the nut and grabbed the empty corner. The knots slipped, then tightened, and Dart rose from the grass.

"I didn't say he was *my* anything. I said I *fetched* him."

Ingolde stopped short. The sling swayed precariously. "What did you say?"

"*Nothing!*"

By the time the four women lugged the heavy sling to the shepherd's house on the far side of the village common, they were breathing too hard for conversation. Embla made a straw pallet by the hearth with the help of her children while Heldey and Ingolde stoked the fire and put a kettle on the hook. Berika hovered at the threshold. The women still reminded her of crows, and Dart—now that he was lying on the floor of her mother's house, did not interest her.

The acorn they'd left on the hillside interested her. Ingolde had said she could go back for it. She got as far as the embankment behind Mag's cottage before her mother called her back.

"There's a bloody lump on the side of your *fetch's* head, and a bruise in his gut. I'll wager he got both from a shepherd's crook.

Do you want to tell me what truly happened, or shall I wager the rest?"

Berika tried to stare her skeptical mother down. She failed, as she always did. "He changed when he fell into the stream, and he changed again when he crossed it. He's man-shaped, but he's a fetch, Mother. I saw him." Ingolde's expression didn't change. "I ran away when I realized he was going to cross the stream. He chased me, and I hit him with the crook."

"Was that before, or after, he asked you to find the acorn?"

The younger woman stared at her feet. "Before."

"And did you think he was man or fetch when you struck him?"

Berika would not answer.

"Don't you be forgetting that. He's trouble, Beri. He'll be trouble for you the moment Hirmin finds out you found him. You're promised, Berika: betrothed. He can have you stoned if there's no blood on the linen—and your fetch, too."

The advice was well meant, and nothing Berika wanted to hear. "If that rutting bastard ever gets me in his bed, it won't be maiden's blood that stains the gods-be-damned linen!" Her rage was more powerful in a hoarse whisper than it would have been in a shrill scream.

"Be careful," Ingolde warned herself as much as her daughter.

"Don't tell me about careful, Ingolde. It's too late for careful—it was too late for careful long before you noticed." Berika remembered the first time Hirmin caught her and she failed to fight her way free. She was oblivious to the tears that began to stream down her face. "I can't reach the Web. I've tried and I've tried. I can't stretch far enough. I begged the gods to give me a way out—"

Ingolde slapped her daughter and dried her hand in the silence. "He's a man, Berika—just like Hirmin, maybe worse. Go in there and look at him again. Look beyond his mad hair to those rags he's wearing. Your *fetch* wore velvet and suede when he started his journey. Look at his boots. *Boots.* Not wooden shoes like you've always worn, but high leather boots, worn and shiny on the inside of his leg. Who wears boots like that? Look at his belt; he wears it *over* a shirt and dalmatic. It's no good for holding up his breeches, but those buckles dangling from the left side—those *silver* buckles—what do you suppose he needed them for? That man, Berika, rode a horse and carried a sword—not some overgrown oak-nut—"

"The acorn!" Berika interjected. The storm hadn't broken—if anything, the sky was brighter than it had been. "That's what the gods sent me. Dart doesn't matter. Just the acorn. Ingolde, please—I've got to fetch it back."

Her mother's shoulders sagged. "You aren't listening, are you?" She looked across the weir to the orchard and the hill. "Go on. Go get that acorn, if that's what you want. I'll water the sheep. Experience isn't the best teacher, Berika, only the hardest."

Berika said nothing as her mother walked away. Beneath her apron, her fingertips made a wardsign. She tried to remember the last time Ingolde offered to tend the sheep: not this year, nor last year either. For a moment Berika forgot Dart and the acorn; there were a dozen questions she wanted to ask her mother. Then common sense reasserted itself, and she ran down the path to the weir.

Larsov sat on a bench outside the mill house, enrapt by something in his lap. Berika crossed the log bridge before her mind made sense of what her eyes had seen.

"You brought it!"

The old man did more than carry the touchstone back to Gorse; he mastered its secrets. The cap was off. The cup was in three pieces beside him, and his lap cradled a small wooden harp. It was a rugged instrument, primitive in its mystery. The pillar was bark-covered; the sound-box was naked rootstock. The neck between them was neither branch nor root, but a gnarled mixture of both. There were no tuning pegs; woody fibers simply grew from the box to the neck.

"He could not have made it himself," Berika whispered, not quite ready to touch it. "It could not have been *made* at all."

"Weycha's wood," Larsov agreed. "Just like the snag in the fane."

She touched the rough bark. There was a sound like greenwood bursting in the hearth. The short hairs on Berika's arm stood up. Larsov couldn't see through her sleeve, but Berika quickly tucked her arm behind her back anyway.

"Snapped at you, eh?" he grinned. "Motherwood—it *knows*."

Motherwood, Weycha's wood, the charred snag—they were one and the same: wood from a tree so old the forest goddess moved within it. The harp was much more than a bard's touchstone.

An image of Dart with his wild eyes and hair—the agony

overwhelming him when she asked his name—flashed in Berika's mind. She banished it, and touched the harp with both hands.

"I can feel it."

The tingling became stinging, and the stinging became the outright pain of sparks burning everywhere into her flesh. Berika confined her discomfort behind a tight-lipped smile.

"I can hold it."

She jerked it out of Larsov's lap. The pain flared—she thought she might drop the harp—then faded, and she clutched the instrument against her breasts. New, welcome, aches spread into her shoulders. Berika feared that the harp would be lifeless when she held it. What good was a gift from the gods if she could not use it?

Moving carefully—her knees were wobbly and her feet were as wooden as her shoes—Berika carried the harp to a nearby wall. She held the harp as the exiled bard had held hers, and her shoulder began to feel the way her brother Indon looked the day he fell from the roof. Indon had fainted; Berika spread her fingers. She slapped the thick strings.

The shepherd could sing and beat out the rhythms of the village dances on a beaded drum; she had no idea how to play a harp. The instrument yielded its first sound when her stiff fingers hooked a string by accident. She gasped as vibrations raced up her arm and down her spine. Larsov hurried to take the harp.

"No! Don't touch it! I'm going to play it."

Larsov's hands dropped to his sides, and Berika closed her eyes. *Get me to the Web!* She plucked a handful of notes. Her stomach churned. *Lift me up! Lift me up until I can reach the Web!* she commanded as if the harp were sheep.

The voice of the fetch's harp was almost rich enough to create music from the shepherd's aimless plucking. It dampened the worst of the dissonance, but it did not lift the young woman to the Web or anywhere else. Vibrations reinforced themselves to make each note more difficult than the last until Berika's hands were splayed and shaking.

"That was foolish," Larsov chided her when the last note faded. "Playing a harp that isn't yours."

Berika wrapped her arms around the pillar. "It is mine. It has to be mine; has to be. I can play it, and it will get me out of here."

The old man nodded. He'd never aspired to the Web but he'd been to the sorcerer's city. "I went to Eyerlon once. One each from Flayne town and the other market villages—I'm the only one left. We went to Eyerlon to see Prince Manal crowned king—and to tell him of the lightning-fire that cleared the land here. We were gone four months: one going, one coming back, and two in the city of Eyerlon! Your grandfather was with me. A good-looking man, your grandfather. You take after Ingolde's folk, but your father's father—now he had his choice of the women—"

Berika knew all of Larsov's stories, and his amorous tales were not among her favorites. But harping had left her too weary to protest, and there was a chance he'd talk about Eyerlon, rather than his, or her grandfather's, conquests along the way.

"—We were near the front, because King Manal would grant his assart charters right after he was crowned. We had to be in the verge before dawn. There was no place to sleep. It rained, and your grandfather got drunk—"

The old man could have left that part out—but he never did, and he was leading up to the only tale Berika liked: a handful of commonfolk marching with the glittering noblefolk through the alabaster gates and along the metalled streets of Eyerlon to the golden dome of the Basilica.

"—You could put Gorse in that place ten times over. Not that there was a Gorse just then—only our petition, signed by old Benit sorMeklan, the Fenklare Donitor himself. *Midons* Benit was too sick to come. He was dead by the time we came back to Relamain—"

"Tell me about the Basilica," Berika pleaded. "What did it look like?"

"I could see the Web plunging down in the Brightwaterfall. It started so far up that I couldn't see if it came through the dome or from somewhere else. And the baths were all gold basins suspended in the air. There was a basilidan in each one, changing the Brightwater as it spilled down. All blues, greens, reds, golds. I couldn't see the Brightwater for the colors in it. And all the great sorcerers arranged in their disciplines standing in the pool underneath. The magga masters right in the Brightwaterfall—"

Berika built the scene in her mind. She dressed herself in grey robes and placed herself out of the pool in the ranks of the lesser, undisciplined sorcerers. There were limits to her ambition. She didn't expect to be a magga sorcerer of one of the disciplines, much less a basilidan. All she wanted was a simple grey robe, a silver torque around her neck, and Eyerlon.

Feeling returned to her fingers. She plucked a single string. "Please take me?" she whispered, but the note was lifeless.

"Not on another man's touchstone," Larsov chided.

Berika glowered; she hadn't meant to speak aloud. "It's the only way. I can't reach the Web on my own yet. The harp's here to help me."

"The harp can't take you to the Web. You must take it to Eyerlon."

Everything seemed to stop, including her heart, while Berika absorbed the new possibility. The gods heard her prayer and understood her need. Her *basi* wasn't strong enough to reach the Web, and her king had closed the beguinages to repopulate his realm, but there was still a way out for a girl birth-betrothed to a monster. She could run away to Eyerlon, where some magga bard or noble patron would surely pay enough gold for a Motherwood harp to keep a common shepherd in comfort for the rest of her life.

"I could. The men walk from here to Eyerlon, and beyond, every spring—" A cold thought shattered her fantasy. "The men have a muster flag. They're welcome at the charterhouses. They don't have to pay for their food. How will I get to Eyerlon without coins? I won't have any money until I sell the harp—"

Larsov recoiled as if Berika had completely misunderstood him, but before she could ask another question, the village was aroused by a woman's scream of terror. The shepherd's head snapped around; the sound had come from her mother's house.

"His eyes!" She shoved the harp into Larsov's arms. "Dart's opened his eyes!"

Berika passed her mother in her headlong dash to reach the threshold first. She tried to get in front of Heldey, but the dark-haired girl had too much of a lead. As Berika leaped over the wide, raised stones of the threshold, Heldey handed her a squalling, terrified little boy.

"Get Roben out of here," Heldey explained, giving Berika a shove as she did.

"Do it yourself—" Berika countered, nearly losing her grip. But the answer was obvious: Heldey's arms were filled with Embla's other two children while Embla herself had hysterics. Outside the house Berika looked for someone else to saddle with the toddler, but the only empty pair of arms belonged to Ingolde, whose flinty eyes issued no invitation whatsoever.

Heldey straddled the threshold. "Come on, Embie. Don't look. Put your back to the wall and—"

There was a heartbeat of silence; then both women shrieked. Heldey caught her heel on the stone; Ingolde caught her and the children.

"He's on fire! *Fire!*" With a child clutched tightly in each arm, Heldey thrashed free of Ingolde's support and raced for the fane.

Embla burst through the doorway a moment later and pulled her eldest son from Berika's arms. "Run away!" she whispered with childish urgency, and took her own advice.

When something large and heavy crashed to the floor within the shepherd's house, and the sheep in the undercroft could be heard battering against the lower door, several other villagers followed Embla's path to the open-roof fane. Ingolde wasn't among them. The shepherd's house was hers by right, and no mad forest-demon would drive her out. Berika hitched up her skirt. She crossed the threshold a half-step behind her mother.

The straw pallet by the hearth was empty, as were all the corners they could see in the late afternoon light.

"He's in the loft," Ingolde concluded, indicating the three steps to the storage area directly above the undercroft.

Berika nodded. "Watch out for his eyes," she suggested without moving toward the stairs.

"*E-e-yup!*"

Mother and daughter were startled, but it was only Auld Mag ordering Hirmin to lift her over the stones into the shepherd's house. The hedge-sorcerer and her son were an odd pair—she a frail crone holding her stick with both skeletal hands, Hirmin a burly giant. He was accounted a handsome man once, before he caught a blast of Arrizi hellfire in the Norivarl highlands. Now his left eye wandered and his right eye was lost beneath a crust of weeping scars.

Mag scuttled to the hearth. She prodded the straw with her stick. "Brought the wrong harvest to your fire, eh?" She hawked into the smoldering embers. "Should've brought him to me."

Ingolde regarded her aunt with all the considerable disdain she could muster. "Your son said you'd exhausted yourself last night and were not to be disturbed by 'women's twaddle'."

The old woman glanced quickly at her son, but Hirmin's hellfire grimace never changed. She was the only one who had ever loved him, but even she knew his flaws. "Eh? Well, maybe I was. I'm here now, and I'll take him."

Her hands disappeared into the bulky sleeves of her smock. When they reappeared, droplets of water flew from her fingertips to the hearth. The embers hissed; an unaccountably large plume of silver-blue steam rose toward the roof vent.

"Come here!"

Dart crept slowly to the edge of the loft. His eyes were wide open and black with wariness; they did not glow or shift. His parti-colored hair was dry and stiff with snarls. Man-shaped or not, he looked like a wild, and frightened, animal.

"Here!" Auld Mag thumped the hearth with her stick.

The fetch balanced on his fingers and toes, as he had when Berika first saw him on the far side of the stream. He glanced quickly at the door, and the frowning people between him and it. He looked up at the vent. He did not leave the loft. Mag dropped her sleeves again. She approached Dart slowly, crooning as she did. When she was within arm's reach, her hand flashed out and she touched his forehead with a dripping finger. The fetch blinked once and toppled onto his rump, with the hedge-sorcerer still touching him.

Auld Mag closed her eyes. The shepherd's house was quiet, except for the sound of her breathing. "He's as mad as his hair. I've touched newborn babes with stronger *basi* than he's got. He does not belong on this side of the stream." Her arm fell. "He could not cross it without help. Who helped him? Who brought him across?"

Berika answered. "I didn't bring him across. He came himself. I knew he shouldn't—"

"Eh?" Her damp fingers stretched before her, Auld Mag took a step in Berika's direction. "You knew? You knew what? You knew how?"

Hirmin moved to his mother's voice. Berika saw them both coming at her and retreated. "I was with the sheep, in the fallow field. I looked up, and there he was on a rock . . . on the forest side. He said things that made no sense, and then he fell into the stream. He couldn't swim. That's how I knew—he couldn't swim. I told him so when he climbed back out." Mag stopped moving and so did Berika. "I told him to go back to his own kind. When he wouldn't listen, I was frightened and ran away. He followed me. I struck him with my crook—I guess I hit him too hard—so

I came back to the village to get Ingolde." All of which was true, as far as it went, so long as Dart was silent and Mag didn't touch her with Brightwater.

"Embla said he grabbed her. He's got demon's eyes," Heldey said from the doorway, startling everyone except Dart, who had not moved since Mag touched him.

"He's not a demon. He's a fetch," Berika insisted, regretting her words at once.

Mag clamped her hand over Berika's wrist. "Did you fetch him? You didn't touch the Web—I'd *know* if you reached the Web, girl. Don't lie to me. Don't you dare lie to me." Her cloudy eyes peered up at the shepherd.

There were differences between a demon and a fetch, even if no one—including the greatest basilidans—could agree on what they were. Both reeked of *basi*; neither belonged in the world of mortal men. The basilidans said a fetch was a god-chosen demon, as they were god-chosen sorcerers. A fetch was, therefore, bound by the Compact; a demon was not. Common sense said commonfolk were best off without either.

Berika twisted the laces of her smock, but it was her soul that was naked. "No . . . I don't know. I *prayed*, and there was something on the rocks. Not him—not like him—except for his eyes." She couldn't lie with Brightwater circling her wrist. "I swore I'd do anything not to marry Hirmin—to be gone from Gorse before my seventeenth birthday."

"Did you?" Mag's head bobbed. "Maybe it's *you* should go in the fane for Weycha's judgment, not him, eh?" She released the young woman's hand. "You know what happens when you try to cross your oath—"

"It's not my oath!" Berika felt the walls curling in around her. "I never promised. No one ever asked *me*." The room began to spin beneath her feet, growing dark and losing color until all Berika could see were the hedge-sorcerer's expressionless eyes.

She lunged for the door, shoving Ingolde and Heldey aside. She bolted around the house to the undercroft. Her gut churned, and though she'd had nothing to eat since breakfast, Berika fell, retching, to her knees. Thin, burning bile, a token of her pain and hatred, mingled with the mud beside the water trough. She staggered toward the gate.

"Berika!"

Hirmin.

He didn't know the area behind the house as well as he knew the rest of the village; he wouldn't enter the pen or the undercroft. Berika worked frantically on the rope holding the gate shut, but Ingolde had watered the sheep, and Ingolde made snarls instead of proper knots.

"Berika!"

She held very still. Pyromant Hazard's conjured hellfire hadn't left Hirmin completely blind. He knew light from shadow and was quick to follow movement. Sometimes she got lucky—but not this time. He trapped her against the gatepost. His fingers squeezed between her ribs; his thumbs dug into her breasts. She longed to vomit her bile into his face, but her gut was empty and her mouth was coated with paste.

"You spread your legs for him." It was not a question.

Hirmin's breath reeked. Auld Mag said it was the hellfire; Berika knew it was his soul. A demon's embrace could be no worse than his. She longed for the crook, but it was out of reach in the undercroft. She tried jabbing his belly, but the angle was bad.

"You're a whore, Berika, but I don't care. You're mine and you'll never get away." He wiggled his thumbs.

Berika's cheeks burned with anger and shame. "Let go of me," she hissed, punctuating the demand with a kick to his shins, though she'd been aiming a bit higher. He clouted her across the face. Berika's mouth filled with blood and, finally, she could spit in Hirmin's face. He lost what little restraint he had. His hands closed around her throat.

"Leave my daughter go." Ingolde struck him with an iron pothook from the hearth.

Hirmin cowered. He feared his cousin as much as he lusted for her daughter. Berika clung to the gatepost, gasping for air. With blood smeared across her chin, she met her mother's stare.

"By all the gods above the Web—you made the promise. *You* marry him. I'll kill him if he touches me again—or die trying—and it will be on your soul. You made me do it."

Ingolde shielded her eyes from the sun, but it wasn't light that made her eyes glisten. Her voice wavered when she spoke. "We'll see—"

"It's too late, Ingolde. You've said so yourself."

"There's forty days yet. A lot can happen in four weeks." She smoothed her daughter's hair. "Your . . . Dart collapsed after you ran out. Mag wants to put him in the fane. Will you help us?"

Sympathy and kindness were rare enough in her mother's voice; deference was unprecedented, and too late. Berika chose not to respond until Ingolde retreated. Then she led the way up the path. She'd help them carry her fetch because she wanted to, not because Ingolde asked.

CHAPTER

3

Until the goddess Weycha forgave or forgot the clearing of her land, the octagonal fane of Gorse would honor one deity to the exclusion of all others. If a woman wished to entreat cow-headed Mother Cathe for an easy birth, she had to make the daylong journey to the market town of Flayne and back again. It was no easier for the men when they hunted, fished, or raised a new roof. Where other Walensor fanes overflowed with effigies and offerings, in Gorse there was only a forbidding fire-scarred snag reaching through the open roof. After two generations without an approachable god beside them, the villagers, though faithful with their prayers, had grown fatalistic and self-reliant.

Without thought, Berika and the other women kissed the blackened bark and anointed themselves with Brightwater from a hollow in the snag.

"Blessed be the trees of the forest. They are the life of the world. Forgive us, Weycha, that we till the soil where your trees once lived free and wild. We beg you to forgive us, and watch over us, and bless our king with life."

When greenwood burst through the charred bark, Gorse would know it had been forgiven. Until then, the villagers lived on the goddess's sufferance and the king's mercy. In daily life the king's

31

mercy was more important than a goddess's sufferance. Not until
a new king was crowned could Fenklare's sorMeklan donitor
make one of his vassals or relatives the village's lord or include it
in his tax collector's twice-yearly circuit. No one had expected
Manal to reign for nearly fifty years. If the Arrizan war had not
intervened, the charter families of Gorse would be indisputably
rich. As it was, though death touched Gorse during the long war,
hunger and poverty had not.

Ingolde replenished the hollow from a barrel which collected
rainwater through the gap between the eaves and the snag.

"We leave this stranger with you. Watch over him. Look into
his soul. Weigh him and judge him. We beseech you, Weycha,
goddess and guardian of the forest." She shook the excess water
onto Dart's face. "He'll be safe enough here," she added.

Dart didn't stir as they arranged him on the hard ground beside
the well where the overhang of the eaves would protect him if it
rained. The threadbare dalmatic he wore in place of a common
man's tunic or smock, split along the seams and across the grain;
its embroidered orphrey bands around the neck and along the open
side crumbled to dust when the women touched them. They were
careful not to disturb his equally threadbare breeches.

"Weather's changing," Embla said, chafing her forearms. "He
might catch cold—"

"It was cold last night, too," Ingolde replied, reopening the
single door.

Embla heard Ingolde's mood and hurried through the door with
Heldey close behind her. Berika stood alone beside her unconscious fetch. She untied her apron and tucked it around his bare
shoulders.

Ingolde returned to the snag. "Leave him be—it's for Weycha
to take care of him." A piece of bark broke off in her hand: not a
good omen. "We didn't need this, Berika. We don't need gifts
from the gods."

"I thought you didn't believe me. You said he was a man—just
a man. You didn't even say that he was *mad*."

"I see a man. I *feel* trouble—for you most of all."

The shepherd lifted Dart's hair from his forehead. She rolled it
between her fingers. Parti-colored or not, it did not make her flesh
tingle the way the harp did. He wasn't the fetch. He wasn't the
boon-gift, merely the madman who brought it to her. She tucked

the strands behind his ear. Limp and unconscious, Dart's features were pleasant, but forgettable.

"I don't feel anything like that. I almost wish I did. I wonder who he was before he lost his wits and his hair turned colors."

"Hush—" Ingolde said, and Berika followed her mother out of the fane without another comment. Ingolde lowered a weathered beam into rusty brackets and began lashing the beam in place. The thongs tangled in her hands. "You do it." She made room for her daughter.

"Wait—his harp—" Berika undid the knotwork as her mother's eyebrows asked an eloquent question. "The acorn. There was a harp inside the acorn. Larsov brought it back. He had it on his lap when I walked by. It's very old and strange. Larsov says it's motherwood. I can guess the trouble *he'll* make if he tries to play it. And you know he will. I think it should be inside the fane, don't you?"

Ingolde winnowed Berika's words carefully: the likelihood that her daughter, and not Larsov, had already tried to play it, and survived, against the likelihood that the old man would, indeed, try and be less fortunate. "Well enough. Put it beside him and bind the door tight when you leave. I've got to help Donali fill the cauldron. Mag says she's got to reach the Web again tonight."

Berika started down the hill before her mother finished speaking. She'd heard all she wanted: permission without too much suspicion. Larsov was inside the mill house, bestowing his unwanted advice on the women preparing the hedge-sorcerer's bath. He had left the harp on the pieces of its acorn case and did not notice Berika gathering everything in her skirt.

The combined *basi* of the acorn and the harp made Berika dizzy. She had to sit down before she'd gone a dozen steps— careful to look at the women by the well and to smile reassuringly at her mother. She saw how the four pieces of the acorn fit around the harp.

They snapped together before she'd discovered the mechanism which would unlock them again. She tried twisting the cap. She tried pulling on the leather strap. By then her mother was coming from the well with Donali, each of them bent under a water yoke. Berika scrambled to her feet and hoisted the acorn by its strap.

Donali stumbled when she saw the huge nut.

"Hurry it to the fane, then," Ingolde said, "and help us with the water."

Less than two dozen people lived in Gorse—not counting young children—and all of them had been jolted by the events of the last day. These few who hadn't watched Ingolde and her household trudge across the common with a *stranger* slung in their aprons had heard Embla scream. They all knew there was a *demon* locked in their fane, and that Auld Mag would brave the Brightwater two nights running to pass the word to Eyerlon. Notwithstanding the start of the Arrizan war, or its ending, the village had never known such excitement.

Berika overheard their conversations as she travelled the length of the village from the mill to the fane.

"Better if someone rode into Flayne and had their Eyerlon sorcerer use the Web." "Ride what—Gond's ox?" "Cost a silver mark to get that Flayne sorcerer to do a hedge-sorcerer's work—" "Look you there— What's *she* got?"

"Suppose *they* say we've got to keep him here till they come for him? We've hardly got enough in store to get us through the winter." "And suppose they tell us *not* to keep him? Have you thought of *that*, Camra?" "Suppose they say: Kill the demon!" "Suppose they want proof?" "Berika will— Now what's that she's got?" "Brightwater! It looks like an acorn—"

"It's too much for Auld Mag. Twice in as many nights. It will be her death. We shouldn't allow it." "But those eyes—Heldey said *hellfire* shone in his eyes." "We can't be having that here and not tell Eyerlon. They'll think we're to blame." "We won't be assarted forever, that's true, King Manal's going to die one of these first days." "With Mag doing our Web-work we'll be lucky—" "Look what's coming up the hill—"

Berika heard each conversation fade as she passed. She squared her shoulders, held her head high, and pretended not to care about the wagging tongues.

"She thinks she's too good for the rest of us. Just like her mother."

"More pride than sense—but nowhere near the *basi* she needs to reach the Web, no matter how hard or often she tries."

"Hirmin will straighten her out."

"Aye, and then some—right across his bed."

Berika wanted to run. She walked slowly instead, feeling the harp shift and vibrate with every step. There wasn't any love lost between her and her neighbors. They weren't saying anything she hadn't heard before. She might not have enough *basi* to reach the

Web, but she'd escape them, and Hirmin, and everything else she hated. The gods had heard her prayer. They gave her a demon harp to take to Eyerlon to sell for a lifetime's worth of gold.

Berika had a plan. There were other fallow fields behind the fane. She didn't usually take the flock there until after frost hardened the ground, but no one would ask questions if she took the sheep there tomorrow. No one would notice if she paused to paw through the bramble bushes surrounding the fane except where they were pruned back around the door—there were still berries among the thorns. By the time anyone did notice that the sheep were alone, she and the acorn would be on the far side of Flayne, headed for Eyerlon.

She undid the knots binding the door and shoved it open so anyone looking up from the common would guess that she and the acorn were inside, then, after assuring herself that no one was, in fact, looking up from the common at that exact moment, she ran around the outside of the fane to its back where she intended to leave the acorn in the protection of the brambles. Thorns snagged Berika's sleeves as she wrestled through the brittle branches; they gouged her hands. Great, cold drops of rain with the sting of ice began to fall from the dark grey sky. A particularly nasty branch whisked past her face, barely missing her eye.

Berika decided she did not have to get the acorn all the way to the wall. She could leave it right where it was with a scattering of leaves to protect it from the rain—if it needed protection.

Then she heard moaning on the other side of the wall, inside the fane whose door was no longer bound.

Could a fetch feel pain? Demons came from another world. They didn't belong in this world. Were demons as afraid in this world as she would be in theirs? Dart sounded miserable enough, though it could be deceit. All demonfolk deceived; it was their way. If Dart were a fetch, then he was a demon. If he were neither fetch nor demon, then he was a man.

Berika could not imagine how anyone, man or demon, survived in the forest, but she could imagine waking up behind a barred door without the one thing in either world that mattered. All she had to do was imagine that moment, forty nights hence, when Hirmin locked the door.

She took the acorn from its hiding place into the fane.

"I hope it makes you happy," she muttered sourly.

Dart hadn't noticed her. His arm was limp when she wrapped

the leather strap around it. He made a peculiar raspy sound with each shallow breath—the way infants did once death filled their lungs. Berika tucked her apron around his shoulders again.

"What were you doing in Weychawood before I called you to the stream? Did the war make you mad? Is that why you babbled about Hazard? The war's over now. But you wouldn't have left the forest if I hadn't fetched you to the stream."

His skin was clammy. There wasn't any need for Auld Mag to risk herself in the bath. Weycha was making her judgment clearly and quickly. Whatever they said in Eyerlon, it wouldn't matter. This poor mad creature would be back in the forest, buried in a stone-ringed shallow grave, by tomorrow night.

Berika arranged his arm so it cradled the acorn. "You can hold it tonight. I need it more than you, but I won't need it until tomorrow. I'll remember you. I'll make offerings for you—when I get to Eyerlon."

Dart moved, and Berika sprang away from him. There were two glowing spots where his face would be.

"Ber-ri-ka?"

The spots vanished and reappeared; they rose. Berika slammed the door shut with a bang that echoed off the fish weir.

"Ber-ri-ka?"

The door began to open. Berika threw her weight against it. Feet and shoulders braced for dear life, she groped for the beam, all the while searching her memories of the morning and afternoon. She'd never mentioned her name; she didn't think anyone else had. How had he known it was her? And how, when he'd been fighting for every breath, had he gotten to the door so quickly? And with such strength?

How had he . . . ? No—how had *it*. Dart might well be mad, but he was not a man. She'd fetched him to the stream; that made him a demon, and like all his kind he was full of mystery and deceit.

"What were you doing in there?" Camra, a woman a few years older than Ingolde, demanded. She, Rimp, and Larsov were hurrying up the path.

Berika was glad, for once, to see her nosy neighbors. "Ingolde said I should put his touchstone—he has a harp within an acorn—beside him. I did, and he woke up," she said without a quiver of deceit.

"Harp? What's this about a harp?" Rimp labored up the hill,

leaning heavily on his crutch. "No one told me anything about a harp."

"Such a beauty as you've never seen." Larsov offered the younger man his help. "Motherwood for sure, all dark and shiny with age."

Rimp waved Berika away from the door. "I should have seen it. I'm alderman here till there's a new king and we get a lord. I'm responsible. It's only right that I know what goes on here." He shouted at Berika, but she wasn't his real target. "Ingolde isn't the one to be making all the decisions." Rimp and his kin judged themselves better than their neighbors; they owned the mill. When the war began, Rimp rode his own horse and carried a sword while the other men walked and carried pitchforks. The Arrizi gutted his horse, stole his sword, and severed his heel-cord, but he still had the mill. He was an important man, even if he could not walk without a crutch.

Then Rimp realized he was alone beside the door. He made a decision. "We'll leave it where it is until Mag's off the Web." He lowered the beam into the brackets, restored Berika's knotwork, and led a very slow procession back to his house, where the Brightwater bath was brewing.

A cloud of mist roiled through the door when he opened it. Water focused a sorcerer's *basi*. Cold, running water worked best, but for a frail old woman like Mag, fragrant, inefficient steam was a necessary substitute. A handful of women, Ingolde among them, had the hedge-sorcerer bound into a sling and hoisted above a simmering cauldron. The old woman was halfway through the invocation, but the steam hadn't changed to Brightwater yet.

Hirmin stood stock-still on one side of the pit hearth. One of the ropes to his mother's sling was firmly tied around his waist. Ingolde snubbed the other end behind her. She caught Berika's eye.

"Did you get that nut into the fane . . . and bind the door well? I heard the commotion."

"I gave you my word," Berika replied, gesturing to take her mother's place. "Go see for yourself, if you don't believe me."

Ingolde replied with the thinnest of smiles: "I believe you. Now take your place with the others."

If life passed for Auld Mag as it passed for most hedge-sorcerers, she'd die with her *basi* linked to the Web and there'd be a reflux. An unlucky person, a person without sufficient inherent

basi to master the Brightwater and reestablish the link to the Web,
might be reduced to drooling idiocy. But a lucky person would
inherit Mag's *basi* and replace her as hedge-sorcerer. Ingolde had
been ready for years; Hirmin thought that if his mother had a
choice, or chance, she'd pass her mastery to him; and Berika
never stopped hoping.

"*Now*," Ingolde repeated. "There's no room for you here."

Berika's skirt swirled around her ankles as she escaped her
mother's lingering smile.

"Don't go giving yourself airs, Berika," Heldey chided, making room for her all the same. "You're no different from the rest
of us stuck out here in an assart. You're not the only one who's
turned blue in the face trying for the Web and Eyerlon."

The shepherd's eyes widened. Until that moment she'd never
suspected that she was not the only one who strove and practiced
endlessly in secret. She kept her face impassive, but that very lack
of reaction gave her away.

"Twenty-five years your mother's been waiting to take Mag's
place. She's not going to make room for *you*. You know what they
say about her—"

Berika did, but she was spared hearing it another time when
Auld Mag arched her back and spread her arms wide.

"The Web embraces me! I embrace the Web!"

Plumes of lavender, blue, green, and pale yellow shot through
the steam. Ingolde braced herself against a wind none of the other
villagers could feel. She got no help from her partner, who, as
always, imitated his mother's gestures.

"King Manal sits securely on his throne in this, the forty-
seventh year of his reign, the seventh day of the month of
Gleaning in the Greater week. The Web shines bright in Eyerlon.
The Communicant watches from within." The voice was Mag's
but the words belonged to the Web and Eyerlon. "Dust still hovers
over the ruins of Tremontin. Nothing stirs. Nothing lives. The
soldiers have been sent home knowing the war is over. All is
well."

The invocation was over. If there were no proclamations
waiting for a hedge-sorcerer's recitation, Mag could try to tell the
Communicant about Gorse's fire-eyed guest. There were no
proclamations, but there was a message:

"From Gannet, with the returning army, words for his wife and
sister—"

A cadre of sorcerers accompanied the magnates and the army. Bad news travelled fast, and free, but for a price any sorcerer could place a personal message in the Web. Personal, but never private. There were no secrets when a hedge-sorcerer did the retrieving. Gannet's sister gasped; his wife put her arms around their children. Neighbors shifted nervously and tried not to meet anyone else's eyes.

"I've won a promise from an adjutant of Midons Driskolt, Sidon sorMeklan. When we reach Relamain he'll present me to the Donitor himself. If I can win another twelve silver marks, I'll have enough to buy our way into his service—"

Gannet's son pressed his hands over his ears and ran from the steamy mill room. The most lethal weapon in the Arrizi arsenal was not Pyromant Hazard or his hellfire, but the dice game, iron-in-the-fire, which spread from the Arrizi prisoners, through their guards, to the common soldiers, who carried it across the kingdom like a plague. Gannet claimed he was lucky with the five colored dice, but, somehow, the campaign season always lasted a few weeks longer than his luck. He came home owing his neighbors—when he came home at all. Last winter he had been compelled to work off his debts with the slaves in the Donitor's stables.

There was a second message as well:

"From Braydon Braydson. Named to prince's guard. Winter with Eyerlon garrison."

Berika's surviving brother was the opposite of Gannet. He wouldn't buy a second word if one would suffice, not even to say which of the two, Rinchen or Alegshorn, had taken him into personal service. It wouldn't matter to Braydon and, after a few tense moments, it didn't matter to Berika either.

Dart was mad, fetched, and a demon—but he *wasn't* a mistake. Everything *had* been planned. The demon's fate was nothing to Berika. She'd take the harp to Eyerlon—where her brother would have connections in the royal garrison. He would tell his prince what she'd brought, and his prince would see that she was properly rewarded. She'd remember Dart at the Basilica, and then he could be safely forgotten.

There were no more messages. Auld Mag sagged against her restraints. Amber fingers wandered aimlessly through the steam. Mag had the *basi*, but the question was: Did she have the strength to focus it? Years had passed since she'd inserted a message into the Web.

"Hear me! Hear me, O Eyerlon!"

A sickly green mist enveloped the hedge-sorcerer. Ingolde braced herself against a new surge, and even Hirmin had to shuffle his feet to keep his balance.

"Hear me! Help me! A stranger has come. A stranger out of the forest with eyes that *burn*!"

Wind rattled the shutters. Rain poured through the vent hole in the thatch, blending with steam until it made a seething cloud above the rafters.

"Hear me! Help me!" Mag's voice came from the thick center of the steam. "What must we do?"

Her voice cracked, but the Brightwater steam retained its color and focus. Hedge-sorcerers were, by definition, the least important members of the sorcerous fraternity. The Communicant in Eyerlon might leave a hedge-sorcerer hanging for hours. Waiting wasn't a problem unless Auld Mag lost her grip, or the cauldron boiled dry.

"Help me! Hear me!"

Berika gazed at the cauldron, then at the growing cloud. How much trouble, she wondered, would she cause if she added another bucket to the huge pot? How much might she prevent? Three full buckets sat beside the circle: Someone had considered the possibility of adding water. She tried, and failed, to catch Ingolde's attention. She tugged on Heldey's sleeve.

"I'm going to add that water to the cauldron. Want to help?"

"Cathe's horn—you're mad! You could crack the cauldron. You could stop the steam from rising—"

"It's in my mind. I think I should do it, if it's in my mind."

Heldey took Berika's hand and would not release it. "It's that demon making you talk so. Fight it, Beri. Fight it or you'll doom us all."

But Berika fought Heldey instead.

"Hear me!" Mag's voice was louder than it had been, and clearly desperate. "Help me—I beg you!"

Berika jerked her hand free. "I'll help you, Mag." She reached for the buckets.

Half the village joined Heldey in demanding that Berika stop. If Ingolde had been among them, Berika might have obeyed, but Ingolde was staring straight at her daughter and her expression was one of concern, not disapproval. Berika lifted two buckets. She stepped on the hearthstones. The colored mist curled around her face, and a voice filled her mind.

I have lost him. I cannot find him. My champion has been taken from me.

The buckets slipped through Berika's numb fingers. Miraculously they did not overturn. She felt a hand clamp on her shoulder, and withdraw. Her neighbors could touch her, but they could not hold her.

I kept him to protect me from Hazard. Who has stolen him? Has Hazard stolen him?

Weycha. The enormity struck Berika like a fist; she dropped to her knees. She'd fetched, all right; she'd fetched herself a goddess's pet.

I fetched him out of mankind to protect me from mankind.

There was a certain logic to that: If a man's prayers fetched a demon, then a goddess might fetch a man. But to the extent that Berika could understand Weycha, horror overwhelmed both logic and curiosity. Her thoughts flew straight to the goddess:

You changed a man into a demon? What about the Compact? Men are born; men die. Gods can't—

My sister-self in Tremontin is dead. Do not speak to me of the Compact!

Berika was assaulted by swirling winds. She found herself within a forest but it was not Weycha's forest. There were sheer mountains soaring above the trees; the mountains of Fenklare were lower, rounder, tree-covered. She became part of that other forest. Roots did their work through her feet, storing the sap that flowed down her body. Sunlight shone on her face. She was sleepy. It was autumn, as it had been countless times before. And then, without warning, it was nothing. She was not within the forest; she was kindling wood and snags waiting for fire. No pain. Nothing.

The forest of Tremontin was gone. Weycha's sister-self, the goddess of Tremontin's forest, was dead.

The shepherd could censor her tongue, but not her thoughts. *Walensor had to win the war.*

Hazard wins! Hazard takes my sister-self. Hazard takes his army. All to fire—Where is my champion? Where is the one I made to protect me?

I don't—but Berika did know, and the goddess saw through her.

*You stole him! Walensor breaks the Compact! My sister-self
gone. My champion stolen away by . . . by you!*

Berika did not have to say she was sorry, or think it. She reeked
sorrow and regret.

You.

Never had Berika felt so insignificant, or so unable to hide. She
relived her life as the goddess sifted her memories. Her pain and
joy were flayed until only her hatred remained, and it was nothing
of which she could be proud, although it did sustain her in the
cold, cruel light.

Hazard lives—and you *have stolen my champion.*

The goddess withdrew. Berika felt herself fall from a great
height. She grabbed at the quicksilver threads of the Web. They
slipped through her fingers. Darkness swallowed her before she
struck bottom.

CHAPTER

—— 4 ——

"Are you all right?"

Piercing blue-grey eyes crystallized from a swirl of dull colors. "Ingolde?"

The almost familiar face disappeared as acrid fumes rose into Berika's eyes. Instinctively she pushed the dish of ugly yellow crystals away. Her vision cleared, and remained that way. "Ingolde—"

Her mother nodded. "You'll be fine." She stood up.

"Ingolde . . . Mother?"

A goddess's touch left bruises on the soul and mind. Berika remembered that Weycha was angry, and that she was the focus of that anger, but the rest was a mixture of pain and shame.

The overturned cauldron lay a body's length away. The fire itself was a soggy wreck. Water puddled in the hearthstones. Auld Mag's swing was reduced to two hacked-off ropes hanging from the beam. Auld Mag was missing—unless she was at the center of the knot of women Ingolde had now joined.

With her back against the centerpost, Berika pushed herself upright. The floor tilted, and the room spun, but the post supported her, and the lightheadedness passed. She slid one foot forward, and when that didn't send her toppling, she walked slowly to her mother's side.

Auld Mag lay on the rough planks of a hastily erected table. Though the old woman fought for each breath, she was losing the battle. Her skin was a bloodless, waxy grey. While Berika watched, her eyes opened. One pupil was tiny, the other was blown wide. Camra, who had watched her husband die the same way, pricked Mag's arm with a spindle.

"Godstruck," Camra whispered, returning the spindle to its slot in the belt beneath her apron. "*Basi*'s flown." She folded Mag's arms. "Nothing to do but wait."

Berika turned away. Godstruck. Sometimes the life gift returned and the body recovered, but not when the victim was a hedge-sorcerer and her *basi* passed through the Web to her successor. The shepherd looked around the room. Hirmin was sitting on a child's stool with his hands circling the hellfire scars on his face. He had not inherited the reflux.

Donali, Rimp's young, pregnant wife, interrupted Berika's reverie. "Let Mag die under her own roof, where she belongs. Her spirit will linger here if she dies here. She won't go quietly—everybody knows *that*."

Cold rain still beat against the thatch. Mag wasn't heavy—and the women could keep her dry with an oiled-wool cloak—but it seemed an unnecessary ordeal for them and the godstruck crone.

The village midwife took Donali's hands between hers. "The child's not due till midwinter. There's no danger in letting Auld Mag breathe her last under your roof. She'll be gone long before then. Don't worry—"

Donali's lips trembled; she withdrew from the other woman's comfort. Donali was an outsider in the village, a refugee from the Norivarl highlands, between Kasserine and Tremontin, where the war began and ended, where the customs had always been different. As a child Donali had witnessed Hazard's hellfire conjury which turned the Kasserine Pass into a swift blood-red river of slag. She knew death in a way no woman from Gorse knew it. Still, Donali would always be an outsider here, and the Fenklare women would have prevailed if Rimp hadn't come to her aid.

"Carried or dragged, Mag dies under her own roof." He balanced on his good leg and hid his crutch behind his back. "I'll not risk my wife, and my heir, on the passage of *her* spirit."

If Ingolde had argued, Rimp might have backed down, but Ingolde did not care where, or how, her aunt died. Camra got a cloak from the pegs by the door. Berika thought she knew what was expected of her. She stood opposite Heldey at one corner of the table planks, wrapping her apron over her hands to protect them from splinters.

"Someone bring Hirmin along." Berika affected not to hear Rimp's clearly spoken words.

Heldey reached over Mag's feet to give Berika a poke in the ribs. "He's your betrothed. *You* bring him. We can carry Auld Mag without you."

Berika gave Heldey a black look. She continued fussing with her apron until Ingolde's voice echoed through the room.

"Tell Hirmin what's to be done—and help him across the common."

She hunched her shoulders and stubbornly refused to move.

"*Berika!*"

When Ingolde mastered Auld Mag's reflux, she would stabilize it in a touchstone. When she mastered it. In the meantime, her voice cut like a thorn switch. Berika unwrapped her hands. Hirmin heard Berika approach and held his hands out for her.

"I'll stand in front of you," she told him, "and a little to one side. I'll tell you when to step up, and when to step down—" She flinched when he touched her. "We're going toward the door."

Hirmin pulled her closer. She stood between his knees.

"Not yet," he objected. "The storm might kill her. Her *basi*'s gone. Ingolde stole it from me. Mother tried to give it to me, but Ingolde took it instead. The pain's coming back, Beri. The hellfire pain Mother took from me with her *basi*. If I were hedge-sorcerer, I could drive the pain away myself—but I'm not. Ingolde is. I won't bear the pain, Beri. I won't bear it *alone*. I heard Ingolde today, taking your part against my rights. Your pain or mine, wife—which way will the new hedge-sorcerer choose?"

Bile surged through Berika's throat. She did not know which way Ingolde would choose, or if her mother would have the power to leach away Hirmin's pain if she chose that course. Hirmin lived through hedge-sorcery, he'd die without it. Berika knew she'd share his agony, no matter what Ingolde did.

"I have forty days left before you dare call me wife."

"Tomorrow," he hissed. "You'll stay with my mother and me

until she dies—no one will take your place—and then I'll hang the bloody linen to say you've become my wife."

Berika's throat was raw when she swallowed. It was small comfort to know that Hirmin would hang their nuptial linen on the outside wall of the cottage, thereby giving her full marriage rights rather than the lesser rights of a freehold woman.

"Take me to my mother's side, wife."

Berika's hatred and fear both failed her. She lacked the strength of will to disobey him before witnesses. The last shreds of hope evaporated. She'd angered a goddess with her prayers, and now Hirmin had her trapped like a fly in amber.

Heldey and the others gave Berika plenty of room when she led Hirmin to the plank table. She guided her betrothed's hand to his mother's face. Hirmin held the shepherd's smock, lest she try to connive with Ingolde, but Berika's spirit had foundered. She might as well have been godstruck like Auld Mag. She was oblivious to Hirmin pressing his ruined face against Mag's withered breasts.

But Donali was not. The awful parody of a child's love moved the pregnant woman to hysteria. "Get them out of here! Get them both out of my house!"

Ingolde's powerful stare pierced Berika's apathy and she became aware that the whole village was staring at her, willing her to take Hirmin away and suffer his mistreatment in silence, as every wife was expected to do. Her apathy was burned away by a new hatred. She hated Ingolde and the rest of Gorse for their sheepish complacency. She hated them more than she hated Hirmin for being what he was. She promised herself that after this neither they nor Hirmin would ever hurt her again. Then she forced herself to stroke his wispy ginger-and-white hair.

"I'll be with you, Hirmin. I'll take your pain away."

When he was young, Hirmin had escaped many well-deserved beatings with a bright-eyed, winsome smile. He still had the habit of cocking his head, but the hellfire had left him with a lipless mouth and a single eye of gemstone blue within a weepy crater. When he winked, Berika nearly fainted, but she ground her teeth together and led him woodenly into the storm.

By the time the women got Auld Mag onto her pallet and covered with all the blankets they could find, her breath was louder than the wind whistling through the thatch. Not one of the women, not even Embla, met Berika's eyes or wished her well before leaving. When she was alone with the dying woman and her son, Berika dragged Hirmin and a stool to the pallet.

"Hold her hand, not mine," she told him.

She twisted her wrist the way Dart twisted hers on the hillside. When she was free, she stepped quickly out of reach.

"Beri! Stay beside me, Berika! You *must* stay beside me."

Shaking her head and smiling with her teeth, Berika backed silently toward the door. It was much darker in the dirt-walled cottage than it had been behind the shepherd's house. The rain confused Hirmin's ears. Another step and she'd be gone to the fane and the harp, but Ingolde blocked the doorway.

"Someone must stay with them," she said softly enough that Hirmin did not hear.

"You do it."

Ingolde's face showed the strain of absorbing the reflux. Despite the *basi* surrounding her, Gorse's new hedge-sorcerer looked, and was, exhausted. "One night, Beri. You can do this, Beri. It will be over, like a nightmare, and behind you. Do you think I would take the hellfire pain into myself—even if I could? He's going to *die*, Beri, long before your child is born."

"I'll rut with the pigs before I bear his child. I'd take that fetch in the fane for a lover, and grow a demon in my womb—" Berika watched the blood drain from her mother's face. She had done the impossible; she'd left her mother speechless, but it was a hollow victory. "He's noble compared to Hirmin."

"You didn't hear, did you? All the while you stood before the cauldron, you were dreaming, weren't you?"

Not hardly, Berika thought as she nodded.

"Weycha threw her basilidan from the Web. Then she came to Auld Mag swearing that Walensor had broken the Compact. Mag was too weak to repeat everything the goddess said, but Weycha's got no use for mankind now, and she's sworn to take back her fetch—your fetch. When I took the Web from Mag, it was empty. There'll be no greenwood in the fane while I live—and we'll be lucky if that's the worst of it. We'll be lucky if we don't find some basilidan telling us to give our land back to Weycha, assart charter be damned."

Berika listened to everything her mother said and heard none of its greater significance. She didn't care what happened to Ingolde, to Gorse, or to Weycha. Only one thing mattered to her: "What about the harp, mother?"

"What harp?"

"The acorn—that huge acorn I found with Dart, with the harp inside. The one you told me to put in the fane with him. Did Mag say anything about it? Or the goddess?"

Ingolde stiffened. She'd forgotten the touchstone completely. "No. No, nothing at all." She massaged her forehead. "It must not be important, Beri." Her arm dropped heavily to her side.

Berika stared at her feet; it was the only way she could keep herself from staring past her mother to the fane. *It's mine. It was meant for me. One thing so special, so valuable, that it could solve all my problems.* She took a deep breath and raised her head. "You're tired, Ingolde. So am I. Go home. I'll survive."

Any other time Ingolde would have been suspicious of her daughter's amiability, but just then she was simply grateful. She caressed Berika's cheek. "We all survive. A girl who wants to marry is a blind fool, but we all survive."

Berika bit her tongue.

"I'll come over in the morning. Pray that Weycha takes Mag along with her fetch."

The door closed. Berika leaned against it.

"Berika? Where are you? Come to me. Berika? Are you still here?"

Hirmin let go of his mother's hand to spin on his stool, looking for his betrothed. He cursed her and swore it did not matter whether she hid herself or not. He'd use his own blood to stain the linen, then proclaim she'd fled her rightful place. He'd proclaim her an adulteress, then have her branded rather than stoned, so they'd look the same.

A steady drizzle leaked through the rotten thatch of Mag's cottage. It fell on Berika's hair, collected in her eyebrows, behind her ears, and finally found its way beneath her smock. She endured it all, lest Hirmin hear her move. The oil lamp hanging from the centerpost hissed, sputtered, and finally went out. Berika marked time listening to the rain outside, the rain inside, the wheezing of the dying woman and her son. She gasped when a mouse scurried across her foot, but Hirmin did not react.

Hirmin fussed with Mag's blankets twice before his snoring drowned the sounds of his mother's breathing and the storm. When Berika stretched the cramps out of her stiff limbs, her knees and back creaked. Hirmin snorted. She froze, with her fingers nearly touching the floor.

• • •

The open-roofed fane was dark—but not as dark as Dart's memory. He remembered waking up. It was the only memory he possessed. He was cold; that became the second memory. He was wet and shivering; those were the third and fourth memories. He was the sum of physical discomfort and isolation. The color of the memories he had acquired since opening his eyes was scarcely brighter than the abyss in which his mind was suspended, but it was bright enough to tell him one thing: he *was*.

He did not know who he was, or where he was, but he *was*, and for the moment that was sufficient. He dragged his aching body away from the cold and wet to the hard and dry. He made a discovery: The abyss was impenetrable, but it was not empty. It emitted knowledge. The cold and wet was rain. The hard and dry was dirt, or wood, which was also wall.

His mind could remember what had happened since he opened his eyes. He could recall nothing from the past with his will, but through experience the abyss would yield its secrets to recognition. He explored his prison, recognizing what he could, building a tiny bastion of self in the vast, black abyss.

He touched his face, recognizing his eyes, nose, mouth. There was a crusty sore on the side of his head; there was a smooth, hard *scar* beneath his jaw. From the scar and the sore he recognized time: present and past, distant and recent.

He moaned.

The abyss was the memory of his life before he opened his eyes. He was a man—he could recognize that easily enough—but he could not recall his name. He could not imagine how he'd become a man without a memory. He moaned again, and warm, salted water came from his eyes.

He wallowed in his misery and discovered he enjoyed it no more than he enjoyed wallowing in cold, wet mud. Moving slowly on his hands and knees, he explored the dry portions of his world. He found a smooth object sprouting a loop of different texture—considerably larger than his head, though small enough to fit easily in his arms. He found a piece of cloth, more coarsely woven than the tatters he wore.

After rubbing it against his face, smelling it, and tasting it, he wrapped it around his shoulders.

"Ber-ri-ka—"

The abyss exploded. When he breathed again, he remembered

sunlight, grass, and Berika. He was not alone. She was woman to his man. His joy was fleeting. Berika raised her arm; he recognized the hooked stick with bells at one end and a metal cap on the other. He touched the crusted sore on the side of his head.

"Ber-ri-ka."

Yes, my champion, Berika.

The darkness vanished, replaced by an otherworldly light at once recognizable and indescribable.

"My lady?"

She stole you away from me. I have searched myself for you, and find you here—calling her by name. You would abandon me for this Berika!

"I would not abandon you." He did not know who—what—his lady was, but he could not have abandoned her for Berika. He was neither a fool nor mad.

You were at the water. Did I not tell you to protect me while I slept? Did I not tell you to protect me from Hazard as I protect you from all else? Why were you at the water's edge? Berika could not steal you from my heart. Why were you in the verge of mankind?

His lady was angry, like Berika. In all other ways, though, she was not like Berika. She had no face. He could not recognize if she was the cause of the abyss, but he knew that she was the entire reason for his existence. All that his lady said was true. He had strayed from her heart. He had not been where he belonged when he first saw Berika, and now he was mankind. He had *returned* to mankind, but he had not abandoned her.

"I looked for Hazard. I found myself at the stream. I do not know"—his voice dropped to a whisper—"how I got there." A shiver raced the length of his body from feet to head. Something very strange migrated from the abyss to his mind. "My lady, I thought you sent me there—"

You thought! A swirl of wind whipped icy raindrops against his face. Berika's cloth fell from his shoulders. *I did not fetch you for thinking.* As suddenly as it began, the wind became a gentle breeze. *I did not make you for thinking.*

"I thought I had found Hazard. I thought Berika was Hazard. She said there was no hazard. I—I believed her, even though she struck me. Did Berika lie? Is she Hazard?"

The breeze touched the place where Berika had marked him with her crook. *Hazard*? his lady sighed, as she took his pain away. *Hazard rides a hot wind through Arrizan's heart. He is no*

*sheepherding girl but a pyromant with enough hellfire in his soul
to steal the Web. Hazard is a man with a god's lust—and I am a
fool to take man as my protector when man is already my enemy.*

He did not understand half of what the lady said, but he
understood her despair. With the aid of thought or memory, he
unlocked the smoother object in his lap. He began to play. The
presence within and around him brightened, then became omi-
nously still before addressing him again.

*Hellfire and Brightwater, they are one and the same in the
hands of man. Who will be gods when all the forests, rivers, and
beasts have been brought to mankind's yoke? What will mankind
awaken when he has betrayed his own life?*

"I have not betrayed you!" he shouted, letting his harp slide
into the darkness. His memory had grown since he began to play.
"You said to protect you from Hazard; I swore that I would protect
you from hazard. I asked you *how*; you said I would know what
to do. But all I know is my oath: protect my lady from hazard. I
don't know anything else, my lady. All that I did, I did because of
that. You said nothing of hellfire or Brightwater. You did not say:
Hazard is a man.

"If I have done wrong, my lady, I will undo it. Without my oath
I am nothing—truly I *am* nothing if I have failed you."

He found the harp. The music he made was harsh and defiant.
The lady stilled his fingers. He shuddered, but not from cold. He
could not be certain what his lady was, but, as she caressed him,
he could not doubt that he was a man.

No, you did not abandon or betray me, she conceded. *I chose
you to be my champion. You were a willful, stubborn, and clever
man, and I foresaw that I would need such a man to protect me.
You are ever willful, ever my champion, my dart against a fate
larger than myself. I am the one who betrayed and abandoned
you. I made you a tree without roots. It is not your fault; fate
fetched you back to man. When mankind can move mountains, a
forest goddess must accept her fate. It is time to sleep and not
awaken.*

The presence retreated; he called her back. "Dart—is that me?
Is that my name?" He recognized it. It was his name when Berika
struck him with her noisy stick, but it was not the name he had
when he got the cut that became a scar under his jaw.

She paused, but she did not return. *It is what I have called you
since I fetched you, but it is not your name.*

"What is my name?"

The wind caressed him, but it was not his lady's wind. He thought she had vanished, then heard her faintly in the distance. *You had no name when I found you. I could not fetch a man who had a name. I could not make a champion from a named man.*

She was gone, returning to her stronghold in the forest. Dart explored one wall after the other in his effort to follow her. He found the door and threw himself at it. The bar and knotwork held. He gathered himself for another attempt, and the presence returned.

"I'm coming back to you," he told her. "It will be as it was: the two of us, my lady and her champion. I will protect you from Hazard."

What you have done cannot be undone, Dart. If you returned to the forest now, you would starve or freeze. Your tree must have roots; you must make your way among men now. I shall sleep through the cold, as I have always slept. I chose you as I slept; I made you my champion as I slept. Berika called you as I began to sleep. It may be that you shall protect me, my champion, but I cannot protect you. Do not follow me. Do not return to the forest. Fate gave Berika the power to steal you away from me. Follow her. Protect her.

She was gone. Dart was alone, blinking back tears and rubbing his shoulder. He was cold. He was hungry. He hadn't been hungry since . . .

There was no way to measure the time—except that it was unthinkably long. He staggered until he struck the snag at the center of the fane and recognized it. He sank to his knees. His forehead came to rest on the damp ground. He was the forest's champion. He had lived with her—within her—and been her lover. There was no reason to doubt the obvious. He had promised to protect her from her enemies, and he had renewed that promise.

Your tree must have roots.

Roots. Men did not have roots. Men ate with their hands, not through them or through their feet.

He set his hands to finding something edible in the darkness. Men did not eat dirt, or charcoal, or wood. Men drank, but not when they were nauseous from hunger and not from barrels left open beside dead trees. It took him a while to recognize a barrel with his hands. He almost forgot how hungry he was—almost, but not quite. His stomach made a sound all by itself.

"Breakfast," he whispered worshipfully as a steaming bowl hovered just out of reach in his mind's eye.

Dart wondered how long it would be until dawn, and tried very hard not to think about the door he could not open. He quickly decided it was easier to do something than to ignore his hunger. He found the harp and began to play.

The rain had stopped. The winds died down to a sporadic breeze mingling with the plaintive music rising from the fane. Berika cursed vigorously, but silently, when she heard the harp's voice. She'd hoped the end of the storm meant the goddess had reclaimed her champion. The last thing she wanted to hear was him playing *her* harp.

She lifted the latch of the cottage door. She was finished here—finished with Hirmin, with Mag, with her mother, and with Gorse. There was no turning back, she promised herself, even if Hirmin heard the latch move. But the rhythm of his snoring never faltered.

The common was treacherous when it was muddy, but the clouds were thinning and there was enough moonlight filtering through to guide Berika safely to the shepherd's house, where her winter cloak should be hanging beside the door. She feared her mother might have bolted the door, but the latch worked. Despite every precaution, the hinges gave a very loud creak.

"Berika?"

She pressed the door shut. In her mother's house, with the sheep penned in the undercroft, strange noises were often heard in the night. If she was quiet, and lucky, Ingolde might go back to sleep.

"Berika? Is that you at the door?"

Using her fingers as she would with the flock, the shepherd counted the flock in her mind three times. Ingolde didn't say another word; Berika thought she was safe. She felt through pegs for the cloak she'd woven the previous winter. Berika was a shepherd, not a weaver. Her warp threads were uneven; the weft was marred by knots and vagrant loops. Her cloak was easy to find, even in the dark.

The household's coin hoard was cached beneath one of the pegs. Some of the coins were older than the house, older than Gorse, for that matter. Others she'd earned herself, raising orphaned lambs, but most of the coins were new. Ingolde had earned them since the war started, weaving a heavy twill cloth fine enough for a nobleman's riding cloak. Berika needed money to get to Eyerlon. She'd planned to empty the cache, but—confronted with the act, not the thought—her resolve weakened.

Berika wouldn't stand in Ingolde's debt, but she would take a wedge of blue-veined sheep's cheese and a loaf of bread from the larder. She tiptoed past the corner where Embla slept with her children.

"Berika?"

Ingolde was still awake and not bothering to whisper. Embla could sleep through anything, but Heldey was a light sleeper and certain to be awake. Berika stopped trying to be quiet. Whatever Heldey knew, the whole village would know before the sun rose above the rooftops.

"Berika?"

The rounded loaf bread slipped through Berika's fingers. She struck the table chasing it across the floor, making enough noise to awaken at least one of Embla's children. There were no secrets in a village, she reminded herself as she shoved the bread into a long, coarsely woven scrip that looped over her belt.

"Are you leaving, Berika?"

There might be no secrets, but Berika didn't have to answer her mother—at least not with words. The hinges screamed in protest as she yanked the door open.

"Take the hoard from the post, Beri. It's a long way from Gorse; you'll need money."

Berika slammed the door behind her. The latch didn't catch; the shepherd's house filled with a damp breeze. Embla thrashed under her blankets, trying to keep warm; Heldey didn't twitch, proving that she was pretending to sleep.

Ingolde got up. She stuck her hand into the hollow post and frowned when she felt the coins. If the cache wasn't empty, then Berika had taken nothing. Ingolde closed the door with a sigh. What did it matter if her daughter left home empty-handed? The coins in ten such hollow posts wouldn't get her to safety.

Ingolde knew more about impulsiveness than her daughter imagined. She knew what happened when a woman tried to escape her fate. A lifetime ago Ingolde had been betrothed to a journeyman weaver in her father's cloth-works. Chlodrin was twice her age and half as smart, but he was the man her father chose for her, and she hadn't questioned the course her life would take, until an overcast day in the autumn of her sixteenth year.

Strangers thundered into her town: six handsome, rowdy young men from the Donitor's castle at Relamain, with their tail of lackeys, horses, and dogs. They'd come to hunt stag in nearby Weychawood, to amuse themselves away from the watchful eyes of their fathers. The clothier's house was the finest in the town; it was the one they claimed as their own. Ingolde and her younger sisters were exiled to attic workrooms while the noblefolk ate and drank everything in storage. No one dared complain, not even the master weaver, Ingolde's father. Their uninvited guests were rich, but more important, they were noble. They had *rights* no commoner could resist.

Young Ingolde noticed none of that. Her ears were filled with titles; her eyes were full of fur-lined cloaks and brightly dyed velvets. Though her father meant to keep his already-promised daughter hidden, Ingolde exchanged places with a kitchen wench and poured apple brandy into noblefolk goblets. She caught the eye of a golden-haired lordling. She blushed when he teased her, hiding her face behind her apron, but he had the eloquence Chlodrin lacked and all the predatory inclinations her father rightly feared.

So many years had passed—but from her bed in the shepherd's house Ingolde Braydswidow remembered her lordling's kisses, the smell of his skin, the taste of his passion. He sought her each night thereafter. Her father frowned, Chlodrin glowered, but neither dared stop her, or him.

Her lover made promises her head knew better than to believe. He said he'd bring her to the walled castle at Relamain. He said he'd get his father's permission to marry her by rights and she would be called Lady Ingolde. He said he'd be back in the spring. He gave her a ring of burnished gold, and a belly that began to swell and harden as soon as he was gone.

The master weaver beat his daughter till every part of her was bloody save the one that mattered. He turned her out of his house both barefoot and without her cloak. Ingolde was very sick and weak by the time she got to her aunt Mag's door in Gorse. The hedge-sorcerer gave her a potion to slow the growth of the unborn child; she found her niece a willing husband, a shepherd who appreciated the advantages a weaver-wife could bring. And she extracted a single promise as payment: a daughter-bride for her son.

Ingolde didn't hesitate.

Brayd was always a bit in awe of his better-born wife, especially when she set out to make him a rich man. His son was born a month earlier than expected, but not so early as to raise any questions in the minds of Gorse. They called him Indon, and he never suspected he was anything but a shepherd's son.

Ingolde never saw her lordling again—never knew if he came back to her father's town for her. She kept the gold ring for many years, until bloat killed half their sheep. Brayd never asked how she came to have such wealth. He was gone two months, returning with a dozen ewes, a walleyed ram, and a plain bronze ring. She still wore *that* ring.

Ingolde remembered everything about her lordling except his name. She had never called him by his birth or family name. She called him "Midons" and nothing more because she was common and he was not. His birth name might have been Ean—that name seemed familiar. It *was* familiar. Ean sorMeklan became Fenklare's Donitor while Indon was still at her breast, succeeding his father who was also named Ean. It didn't matter, not after all those years.

There was music floating down from the fane again. Ingolde's tears vanished into the coarse linen bedclothes as she listened, and remembered. Despite her tears, Ingolde had no regrets. Except—possibly—a newborn one, that she'd lied to Berika each time she told her daughter to accept Fate's path without a struggle, each time she told her that love was a woman's enemy.

CHAPTER

5

The woolen winter cloak of Walensor's commonfolk was a simple, efficient garment. A rectangle made from four lengths of cloth, the pieces were seamed at the shoulders, center back, and, below an opening for the wrist, along the outer selvedges to the hem. A thong was drawn through the warp and weft below the neck opening to form a hood. It was warm, waterproof, and windproof, when it was held shut, but it was bulky, and in the least bit of wind it billowed like a sail. Berika's cloak twisted around her shoulders and, despite her shrugging and tugging, would not hang straight. Giving up on it momentarily, she tied the hood thongs into a careless knot. There'd be time enough to fuss with her cloak once she and the harp were beyond the village gate.

Haunting music floated down the hill from the fane, though it was so attuned to the dying storm that Berika was scarcely aware of it. The moon was behind the trees, the air grew colder as it dried, and the steep, muddy path to the fane was slick and treacherous.

The bindings on the fane door were hidden in the shadows; they were also swollen and slick from the rain. Berika went after them with her teeth and nails. Her cloak slipped away from her shoulders. Its full weight hung from the thong that pressed against her neck. Berika ignored the knots on the door and worked on the one at her throat.

"Ber-ri-ka? Ber-ri-ka?"

The leather thong slipped off Berika's fingers. "First the rain, then the flood." She clamped the leather between her teeth and went back to working on the door. The fetch knew only one name; it was just her luck—her typical luck—that hers was the name he knew.

"Berika? Berika, Berika . . ."

The fetch was practicing. Each time he called her name it was harder to believe he did not know her. Berika's fingers had minds of their own: ten silly minds which would not cooperate. The leather thongs cut her mouth. With half a thought, she yanked them out of her mouth, and, naturally, the knot dissolved. Her cloak slid from her shoulders into the mud before she could react.

A moment later, the fetch crashed against the door from the inside. The jolt did everything Berika had been trying to do. The knots broke, the fire-hardened bar flew out of the brackets. The door swung open. Berika's mouth hung open, but no sound emerged. Pain, surprise, and anger negated each other.

And no sounds emerged from the fane.

Berika was convinced that the harp was her gods-given property. No matter that she hadn't suspected it existed the day before. No matter that its owner was a fetch—a demon—or a madman. No matter that a sheep could ken the ill omens everywhere. Berika intended to leave Gorse with that harp under her cloak.

She strode into the darkness. A gust of wind closed the door, leaving her cloak on the ground outside. Berika held her breath and listened. Either the fetch wasn't breathing, or he had resorted to the same trick. She flailed her arms through the air. Her fingers felt the cold wall, the charred bark of Weycha's snag, and—at the limit of her right hand's reach—flesh. The young woman pulled her hand back as if she'd touched a hot coal.

Berika expected the worst. When that didn't happen, her confidence soared. "I need the harp. It belongs to me now."

No answer. No sounds at all.

She reasoned that the fetch would have left the instrument by the snag. Eyes wide open and useless, the shepherd took a careful step in that direction.

"I'm taking the harp with me to Eyerlon."

"Eye-er-lon," he echoed.

Duck-walking around the snag, Berika groped amid the surface roots for the harp. She was halfway around when a tingle raced up her arm. Success! With one hand on the neck and the other on the pillar, Berika gauged the distance between herself and freedom: two bounds and a pause to open the door. She tried to lift the harp; it wouldn't budge.

"Tell me about Eyerlon."

She hadn't heard him move closer, but she could feel his breath on her forehead.

"Eyerlon is the ancient place of Walensor. The Web's strung from Eyerlon. All the magga sorcerers are there—the ones with the most *basi* and the skill to use it—basilidans, inquists, menders, bards, communicants—the best of all the disciplines. And King Manal's there, since before I was born, because the menders couldn't fix his legs after his accident. It's the most important city in Walensor, with marble walls and paved streets. Everybody's rich in Eyerlon. I'll sell the harp to a bard or lord, and then I'll be rich, too." She gave a sharp tug but nothing happened.

"It's my harp," Dart said. "My lady gave it to me. If it must be sold to a bard, then I will sell it."

"You're a fetch. Nothing belongs to you; you belong to the goddess. You brought me the harp because I need it and you don't. You weren't supposed to cross the stream or leave the forest. You can't go to Eyerlon because you've got to go back to Weycha. And you better go now, 'cause there's going to be hell to pay around here tomorrow."

The fetch's grip on the harp seemed to waver. Berika tried again.

This time he pulled back. "I cannot go back to the forest. If you are going to Eyerlon, then I will go with you."

Berika fell, and discovered she had better leverage from her knees. "You don't even know where Eyerlon is. You wouldn't know Eyerlon if it grew out of the ground in front of you."

"I lived in Eyerlon."

Dart's voice softened as he recovered from another explosion in the abyss. He had lived in Eyerlon—whatever, wherever, Eyerlon was. Eyerlon was a bright speck in the abyss; it did not link up with anything he recognized or remembered. The abyss was larger than he'd imagined.

Berika took advantage of his distraction. She gave the harp a vicious twist; it was hers. She took one step to clear the snag, then lunged for the door. There was no way the fetch could catch her; she could beat either of her big brothers in a ten-foot sprint.

But the fetch wasn't Indon or Braydon. Berika ran into him, not the door. Somehow she held the harp; the fetch held her.

"Let me go," she hissed, marking each word with a determined attempt to free herself.

The very manlike fetch responded by confining her more tightly in his arms. "Let go of my harp."

Berika didn't argue; she kicked his shin instead. It was a glancing blow, deflected by her heavy skirt, but it stunned the fetch long enough for her to scoot free. She expected the fetch to look for her, but he was cannier than she and would not be baited from his position near the door. Berika turned the harp so the sturdy pillar was aimed at his chest. She charged. The gambit almost worked.

The fetch staggered sideways, dragging Berika and the harp with him. Berika felt herself falling. She reached for something—anything—and let go of the harp. Her fingers closed over a tatter from the fetch's shirt. It ripped loose, and both she and the fetch fell like drunkards at the midwinter feast. The fetch landed on his back; Berika collapsed across his chest.

Their faces touched. She could hear his heartbeat. Her arm was beneath his neck and a braid was caught beneath his shoulder. Her skirt was hiked above her knees. It was worse than Hirmin ripping her laces.

Berika moved an inch, not more than two, before the fetch locked his arms around her.

"If you broke my harp—"

The shepherd recognized that tone. It had been dangerous coming from Braydon after she shattered his best knife by throwing it at a rock. It wasn't likely to be less dangerous coming from a fetch. So Berika did what she'd done to Braydon that afternoon many years before: She opened her mouth wide and bit his nearest piece of flesh with all her strength.

In the shambles of his memory Dart recognized a direct relationship between Berika and pain. She'd struck him with a stick, kicked him, bitten him on the arm when they were in the grass, and now she was biting his neck. He could not, would not, endure it. He willed the pain away. His muscles tensed, exploded, and Berika vanished.

He sat up slowly and massaged the aching place at the base of his neck. The flesh was moist and sticky. He touched his fingertips to his tongue.

Recognition—knowledge glimmered in the abyss—blood, his own, and anger. When he bled, he did not bleed alone. If he hurt, someone else hurt worse. His right hand slapped against his left hip; he wondered why—there was nothing there. He lost interest in his pain, in Berika, in vengeance. What did his hands remember that he did not?

A muffled sob broke Dart's reverie. He remembered a sound he had ignored: her body slamming against the wall. Another flash of recognition in counterpoint to the first: shame. He was a lady's champion and protector. A man of that ilk did not wreak vengeance on a woman.

"Berika, are you hurt? Did I hurt you?"

The woman shivered when he touched her. He shivered because he was cold, but Berika shivered because she was hurting and frightened. Dart held his hand steady until the trembling stopped.

When she bit him, Berika expected to be thrust to freedom; she hadn't expected to be hurled across the fane. She struck the wall near the eave-line, but it was her knee-first encounter with a root that left her sobbing. The knee was numb to her fingers, but it burned inside. She could not unbend it, dared not try.

In her mind's eye Berika saw Rimp returning to Gorse in a cart, his crutch sticking up beside him. Rimp would never leave Gorse again; neither would she.

"Berika? Are you hurt? Did I hurt you?"

She shuddered when the fetch touched her.

"Did I hurt you?"

"Yes."

"You bit me. You hurt me. I wasn't hurting you, and then you hurt me."

"I'm sorry." But Berika's sorrow was all for herself. She wouldn't have bit him if he hadn't held onto the harp. She'd lost her freedom for a few drops of demon's blood—as if demons had real blood or real pain. "I can't walk."

"I'm sorry."

The fetch sounded sincere—though who was to say what

sincerity was to a goddess's pet. He began to stroke her arm, slowly and gently. Berika thought she could escape if she tried, but she didn't try. Why escape Weycha's pet when she couldn't escape Gorse?

"I—I don't know what happened to me. I was angry. I thought the harp was broken. . . ."

His hand was still. Berika guessed he was looking for the harp with his other hand. A thump, a wandering chord, and then he was stroking her arm again.

"When I felt your teeth . . . everything went red. I'm sorry. I wanted you to stop hurting me; I didn't mean to hurt you instead. A man should not hurt a woman."

Berika smiled bitterly. Only a goddess's pet could think that men didn't hurt women. Braydon had given her a split lip and a black eye when she broke his knife, and he was as gentle as their father. Then there was Hirmin—

A sigh shook its way out of Berika's breast, and took some of the pain with it. She sighed again, surrendering to the numbness that followed the pain.

"Where does it hurt?"

Berika slipped her arm from beneath his hand. "My knee." The pain and anxiety returned. She rocked from side to side.

"Which one."

"It doesn't matter. . . . My right. It's broke; I can feel the pieces. I can't walk. I'm never going to walk again."

Dart hadn't suspected he possessed the strength to hurt her so badly, just as he hadn't suspected that crossing the stream would betray his lady. The relentless ache of a guilty conscience, he discovered, was intensified, not lessened, by innocence. He placed his hands over Berika's knee. There was knowledge in his body. Knowledge to hurt a woman against a wall; knowledge to play a wooden harp; and, mercifully, knowledge to loosen spasmed muscles.

"Don't," Berika pleaded when he unwound her hose.

Dart hesitated. His lady had told him to follow Berika and be her champion, but Berika was very different from his lady. She cowered when he caressed her. He could not comfort her the way he comforted his lady.

"I will not hurt you," he insisted, cradling her leg in his lap. "Can you move your . . . toes?"

Berika insisted she could not; he moved them for her. She did not react.

"I don't know what's to come of me. I can't leave. I can't walk. Mother Cathe's mercy, I won't even be able to tend the sheep. . . . I'm crippled. O gods—a cripple wed to a beast!"

Dart cupped one hand behind Berika's ankle and the other over her knee. "Does this hurt?" He straightened her leg. She flattened her back against the wall. He reversed the process. She writhed in her efforts to be free of him, and moved her knee far more than he would have dared. "It's broke! Leave me alone. Haven't you done enough?"

He released her. "You've bruised it badly, but there is nothing broken."

"How do you know?"

"I just . . . *know*."

"How? Do you think you're a mender too?" Berika shook her skirt back to its accustomed length. She ran her hands along her leg, assuring herself that the knee still hurt and that she could not move it. "Who taught you? Your lady who lives in the forest? Weycha? What does the forest-goddess know about knees?"

Dart could not summon his own name from the abyss, but it appeared that when he was distraught enough, other names might surface:

"Hors-ten. Horsten." Dart coughed. When his throat cleared he spoke with an accent Berika did not recognize. " 'The spooks will tell you to pay them to set a bone or seal a cut. But you won't find a spook on the battlefield or running with the hounds. What will you do when it's your boon-friend lying there bloody in the mud and the spooks have packed up their towers and run?' "

The name had a face: an older man with a patch over one eye, a puckered scar on his cheek, and gold disks in his ears. But who or why or when or where remained a mystery. A clammy sweat bloomed on Dart's palms.

Berika forgot her knee. "Who are you—what is your *true* name? It's not Dart, is it?" No answer. "Horsten. Is it Horsten?"

Dart made a sound that was painful to hear. Berika felt him trembling.

"You're special—even for a demon—because Weycha fetched you. That's why you changed when you crossed the stream, isn't it?" Suspicion colored Berika's question. "A goddess prayed—to what, I wonder—and fetched you. You're godchosen—you've got to be a demon—but you were something before she fetched you. A man? A madman with parti-colored hair?"

Dart recoiled from her questions. He wished she'd leave him alone. Her questions drew him deep into the abyss and threatened to sever the shining thread binding him to his mind and memory.

When Berika understood that Dart was unaware of her, and everything else, she tried to put some distance between them. With her right leg still stiff and crooked, she hauled herself up over her left foot. The movement brought Dart back from the brink.

"Careful. It's—"

Berika's breath caught in her throat. She would have fallen had Dart not caught her.

"—going to hurt."

Without thinking, she clung to him. "Mother Cathe, no," she moaned, invoking the goddess of the hearth, birth, and—in her darkest aspect—death. "No . . ."

"A few days," Dart reassured her, even as he considered that he could remember clearly less than one day.

"I don't *have* a few days! It was tonight or never—Can't you understand that? I have to leave tonight, after coming here. It's not just the harp."

Dart guided her back to the ground. "I cannot let you take my harp."

"I said it wasn't just the harp!" Berika clutched her sides with all her strength. Pain added intensity to her voice. "Auld Mag is dying. I'm betrothed—more than betrothed—to her son Hirmin. I should be *there*, but I'm not; I'm *here*." She made a growl of frustration deep in her throat when the fetch did not seem to understand. "My mother, she thinks you're a *man*!"

"I am."

"You're a *demon*. Weycha's demon. Weycha fetched you, then I fetched you because I *need* the harp. You're a fetch and you don't understand anything. If you were a man, you'd know why I can't be here with you. A woman—a girl, a betrothed girl—who is *found* with a man who isn't the man she should be with. Well—she's punished. She's run out—"

"If you want to leave anyway, what difference does it make?"

Words caught in Berika's throat. She couldn't repeat Hirmin's threat to have her mutilated. She trembled with silent screams.

Weycha's fetch knelt and put his arms around her. He found the big knots at the base of her neck, and the others along the tops of her shoulders. She resisted in her mind, but her muscles heeded the motion of his fingers, not her will.

The gods in the Web knew what might happen next, but Berika was spared that knowledge when another piece of his shirt turned to shreds in her hand.

"You'll be stark naked by morning!"

Dart peeled the last of his sleeve from his arm. No wonder he was cold. How long had he been wearing these clothes? A shiver that had nothing to do with the damp air shot down his spine.

Berika guessed his thoughts. She recalled the observations Ingolde had made about his clothing, but the image that came to her mind was Auld Mag in a winding sheet. Dart's clothes weren't worn out, they were rotten—as if he'd been buried in them. As if Weycha had fetched a man from his grave and made him her pet.

Resurrection was a violation of the Compact—but hadn't Weycha also insisted that the Compact was broken?

She found his hand in the darkness and held it tightly. "Try to remember, Dart. Where were you before you saw me? Where were you when you put on the clothes you're wearing?"

He groaned the way he had in the meadow. He pulled his hand from Berika's grasp and covered his face—but not before she saw glowing red pools where his eyes should be. The shepherd screamed. She scrambled away on her hands and knees, completely forgetting her injury, as she had forgotten—for a moment—that he was not a man.

"I command thee, fetch, by Brightwater and the Web, go back to the forest!" She clutched the charred bark of the snag. "Weycha—take back your demon!"

"I am no demon. I am my lady's champion. She came to me in my harping to say that I am a man and that I cannot come back to the forest. It is not my will to hurt you, Berika, but my memory is dark and empty and I will not let you send me there with your questions." His breathing slowed and strengthened. "Please do not be angry with me—Without you, I am alone."

Berika's terror waned. She could not maintain her fear of him. The sound of his voice, the rhythm of his words, lulled her into a comfortable trust she had rarely, if ever, felt before. The urge to comfort him grew like a sneeze within her, and was even more difficult to suppress. She sat on her hands and bit her tongue to keep from saying she was not angry.

Dart's stomach ruptured the silence. Recognition flowed through his nose to another part of the abyss within. "Do I smell . . . bread?" he asked, as hunger pushed all other thoughts and concerns aside. "And cheese?"

Berika's hands shot to her belt. The scrip had come loose, and the aroma of food was thick in the air. "I dropped my scrip. If you can find it, it's yours. I guess you haven't eaten for a while, have you?"

The abyss loomed as Dart searched for the scrip. He did not want to know when he had last eaten. He touched the coarse fabric of the scrip. His hands shook when he tore the loaf in half. Then his mouth was filled with the sweet taste of bread, and the danger passed.

Berika listened to him devour the food she thought would take her halfway to Eyerlon. He wasn't particularly noisy about it, and she could distinctly hear him tear the bread into morsels before putting it in his mouth—which was more delicacy of manners than she was accustomed to—but he filled the fane with a presence that fairly screamed *hunger*.

"I was hungry," Dart explained as he licked his fingers clean. He searched for Berika. She jerked away when he found her. "I ate all your food, didn't I? Everything you had for Eyerlon."

Berika warned herself anew not to be deceived by his manner. He was a demon; it was his nature to deceive. The warnings proved useless. "It's all right, I'm not going to Eyerlon." Her voice stuck between sincerity and bitterness. "It was only a dream. I'm never going to get out of Gorse. I belong to Hirmin; Auld Mag and my mother decided before I was born."

"Is Hirmin—?" Dart sought the necessary words, but comparisons were difficult with his limited memory. "Is he like me?"

Berika snorted. "I guess he's as much a man as you are . . . from the other direction. He reminds me of the ram sheep."

"He's woolly?"

"He's only got two thoughts: eating and rutting."

Dart blushed. Rutting. Now he had a word for what he felt when he touched her leg. It was an ugly word, but it took its rightful place in his memory. "I'm sorry," he said, for himself, and for Hirmin whom he did not know.

"It's not your fault. I'd never have made it to Eyerlon, anyway, even if I had taken your harp. It was all a foolish dream. The road to Eyerlon's no place for a shepherd travelling by herself. I'll stay here and hope that my mother's right. She usually is."

Dart was uncomfortable in the lengthening silence. That which comforted his lady the most was least acceptable to Berika. Finally he tried the other way in which he comforted his lady when she despaired. He retrieved his harp and purged his feelings through its music.

"You can go to Eyerlon—if you can't go back to Weycha in the forest," Berika said. "The way you play—no one will suspect you're a demon and not a bard. You could earn your trencher by any fire."

The music stopped. "Earn my trencher?"

"Trencher bread . . . your supper. I don't suppose you ate supper with the other demons. You have to have coins—black grit and silver flakes—to stay at the king's charterhouse on the way to Eyerlon. You'd earn your place by the fire by singing songs."

Dart played an isolated arpeggio. "My music has no words; I play what I feel. I know no songs. I could not sing for my trencher. How would you 'earn your trencher'?"

There was lengthy silence before Berika whispered: "I hadn't thought about it," and then another silence. "You're not a fool, Dart—whatever else you are, you're good at thinking. You could learn the most popular songs."

Dart scratched his chin. "Getting to Eyerlon grows more complicated. Trenchers and places by the fire. Learning and singing songs for charterhouses—when I do not know what a charterhouse is. Yet every time I say the word, I am more convinced that Eyerlon is where I must go. Where *we* must go. I to protect my lady; you to escape Hirmin. Do you think I could sing for us both?"

Berika sat up straight. Her knee twinged and her shoulders sagged. "You'll only need one."

"But I need . . . a *friend*." The word brought a starburst of recognition: faces that vanished as quickly as they appeared and left him with the aching knowledge that once he'd had many. "We must travel to Eyerlon together, Berika."

"I can't."

Her voice was muffled; Dart guessed she had turned away. "Not tonight. Later, after your knee's strong, and you've taught me these charterhouse songs. And I've earned myself some clothes that don't fall off." He pulled the sleeve off the other arm as he spoke.

"It'll be too late. Hirmin."

"I'll protect you from Hirmin."

Berika shuddered as she drew her breath. No one could protect her from Hirmin. She struggled to her feet. "I've got to get back. I can't be found here." She'd crawl to Mag's cottage if she had to.

"Don't you want to go to Eyerlon? Don't you want to escape Hirmin?"

"No," she whispered, hoping he couldn't hear.

CHAPTER
6

Gorse awoke with dawnlight. Cocks crowed and the cattle lowed impatiently. Curls of smoke rose from the vents of thatched roofs. Rimp's mill, with its high stone walls, was the only house with a chimney.

Embla opened the door of the shepherd's house. She shook the rainwater from the yoke propped against the wall, balanced the beam behind her neck, and headed for the cow byre, yawning and rubbing her eyes. She glanced up the hill to the fane as she crossed the common yard. If the roof had blown off, or the door had been opened, she would have sounded the alarm herself, but the door was shut, with the bar in its brackets.

The sun was two hands above the valley before Embla's eldest, five-year-old Roben, splashed through all the puddles between the common and the fane.

"The binding's off! Mamma! Mamma! The binding's off the fane door!"

He came down the hill with his arms outstretched like wings, and his voice high enough to pierce the soundest sleep. The common was full before Embla had him quieted. Ingolde, shielding her eyes with her palm, studied the quiet fane, then looked across the common to Mag's cottage—Hirmin's cottage.

No stained square of cloth hung from the wattle-and-daub walls. Had her daughter gotten safely away? Was her aunt still alive?

The new hedge-sorcerer could wait all morning before curiosity compelled her to open that door, but the rest of the village lacked her patience.

"Shouldn't we do something?" Camra asked. Her tone implied that *we* meant the new hedge-sorcerer.

Ingolde swallowed a scowl and a caustic remark. She squared her shoulders and started up the hill. There was a rustling behind her, and she glanced back, ready to freeze anyone with the audacity to follow her. *Anyone*. All of Gorse was flocking behind her like the sheep. Ingolde reached for the Web. The reflux had faded during the night; she'd need months of practice before she'd catch the Web with a distracted thought. If anything lingered in the fane, she'd face it with her neighbors close behind her and nothing more than her own intelligence to guide her.

Roben's footprints were clear in the mud, close-spaced headed to the fane, wider coming back. They weren't the only readable tracks. Here and there, but pointed uphill only, were the marks of wood-soled shoes, Braydon's shoes, now Berika's. Ingolde felt a splinter of anxiety. There was a third set of footprints in the mud; above her daughter's, beneath Roben's. They were deeper on the downhill journey than they were on the uphill return. Ingolde examined one of them more closely, knowing what she'd find: a sharp-edged heel ringed with nailheads.

Rimp owned boots with nailed heels, but the crippled miller did not leave an even stride in his wake. There were no horses in Gorse, no saddles, and no need for boots with nailed heels to lock against a stirrup.

The hedge-sorcerer stopped. She massaged an intangible lump in her throat until she could swallow again. The footprints could only belong to Berika's stranger. He'd carried something down from the fane and returned without it.

She wanted to follow those deep, downhill tracks, but the eyes of her neighbors were hard on her back. Instead she lifted the bar from its brackets and cracked the door open.

Nothing reacted to the shaft of light reaching from the doorway to the snag. Ingolde shoved the door so it banged loudly against the inside wall. Something rustled across the floor, staying in the shadows.

"Come into the sunlight."

Nothing. Then, a young man's voice saying: "I can't."

Ingolde moistened her lips. The stranger hadn't spoken at all when Mag confronted him. "So be it. Weycha has made her judgment. If you cannot enter the light, I shall bolt the door and *burn* it all, with you inside." She wouldn't—or she didn't think she would—but he wouldn't know that.

The stranger came blinking into the light. One hand held Berika's apron string, the other held shreds of cloth. Ingolde subjected every part of him to her fiercest scrutiny, ending with the cloth pulled tightly around his hips. His cheeks turned scarlet, also his chest, his neck and the rims of his ears. His eyes widened and glazed, but they did not burn. He looked at the ground between his feet, and Ingolde relaxed.

"It seems you are a man of ordinary parts after all."

He swallowed with evident difficulty. The blush began to fade. "Are you Ingolde?"

"I am the hedge-sorcerer of this village. Who are you?"

"My lady calls me Dart."

The hedge-sorcerer rolled her lower lip between her teeth. She'd hoped that Berika had not told the truth. Dart recovered from his embarrassment, meeting her stare with one of his own. His speech was too refined for this part of Fenklare, but unaccented—which was more than could be said of Donali's Norivarl twang.

"Dart is the name my daughter gave a witless creature from the forest. She is no lady and Dart is not a man's name. What is the name you had from your mother and father?"

"My name is Dart. My lady said I had lost my name before she found me. Berika is *not* my—" Dart's stomach interrupted him with a protracted gurgle. "I am very hungry," he admitted.

Dart—the word, the *name*, echoed in Ingolde's thoughts. She'd seen him feral and wary in her own loft. He was not a demon, but neither was he an ordinary man. As Larsov said—his hair was parti-colored, and though he seemed sensible enough in the morning light, he'd been witless when Mag touched him with the Brightwater. Did anyone in Gorse, including herself and her daughter—if she were still in the village—need to know who he'd been before the gods and fate addled his *basi*?

"If you please"—the madman dropped the shreds of cloth and extended his hand toward her—"I mean no harm to you or yours. I have lost all that a man might remember, but I have had a long night alone in this place to learn that honor lies deeper than memory. I need food, clothing, a roof over my head. I will repay you honestly for them. You will not regret your trust."

"Don't make promises you can't keep," Ingolde warned him. "Until I know who you are and how my daughter came to find you, there can be no trust between us. There is no *lady* in the forest, only a goddess, Weycha, and last night she threw her basilidan and our hedge-sorcerer from the Web. I only know one thing: You don't belong here." She was pleased to see that Dart looked anxious, but she could not savor the sight: Her neighbors were clamoring for reassurance. "Stay behind me," she told him. "Don't say anything."

Ingolde noted that Dart was obedient—an unusual quality in noblefolk, if he were noble. More likely he was mortified to appear before commonfolk wearing nothing but a woman's apron.

"Weycha has left a man with neither memory or name," she proclaimed as they left the fane. "He's forgotten who he was and where he came from. He calls himself Dart—"

"That's just what Berika said—" Heldey babbled until Ingolde's acid glance froze her tongue.

"Berika spoke of a fetch. This Dart is a *man*. I judge that Weycha has lifted the madness that changed the color of his hair. When the time comes"—Ingolde meant when Mag was dead and gone—"I'll use the Web to seek his kin. He speaks too prettily to be one of us. Some lord—"

Heldey could not contain herself. "A lord—Berika's fetch is a nobleman!"

"Enough!" Ingolde brandished her fist. She did not want to hear Berika's name again until she, herself, had traced those footprints. "He's heard their speech, and now he uses it. He could be a nobleman's son or he could be a nobleman's slave"—though Ingolde doubted it. "He doesn't know who, or what, he is. As this is *Weycha's* judgment, we shall not question it."

Her eyes followed the tracks which led to, and emerged from, the threshold of Mag's cottage. A private war began and ended in a single heartbeat. Whatever had happened between her daughter and the stranger, it had already happened and would keep until she had him decently dressed.

The villagers followed her along the common.

"Have you nothing better to do?" she shouted when they followed Dart across her threshold.

One by one they hurried away, except for Heldey, Embla, and her children—none of whom, it seemed, could stop staring at the blushing stranger.

"You've seen a man before," Ingolde scolded as she flung open the clothes chest.

A wedding dress was on top, hemmed to the length of Berika's legs, and a length of berry-dyed cloth for her dowry. Beneath these were winter clothes for all the women and children of the shepherd's house. Ingolde burrowed to the bottom layers before touching men's clothing. Two sons and a husband remembered themselves to her fingers. One son and her husband moldered in separate, foreign graves. The third man of her life, Braydon, wouldn't need anything from the shepherd's house now that he was taken into a prince's service.

Any shirt or knee-length breeches would have fit the stranger. Weavers wove one width of cloth. Scissors were rare and difficult to use. Even the noblefolk reinforced their clothing with embroidery and fitted it with belts and laces. Garments were worn until they were reduced to tatters and patches.

At the very bottom of the chest was a suit of men's clothes that had never been worn. Ingolde wrestled them into the light. She'd made them for Indon the summer he was killed, but they did not remind her of her love child and she could give them away with only momentary pain.

"Those're Indon's," Heldey accused with all the bitterness an eighteen-year-old widow could muster.

Ingolde recast the argument: "And why are you hovering there, Heldine? Isn't there something you should be doing instead? Have the sheep been let out of the undercroft?"

Heldey ignored the sheep—no easy task considering their noise and aroma in the undercroft directly beneath her feet. "If you're going to bring a man into this house, I should have some say. I was Indon's wife. He was the oldest son. The house would have gone to him. I have rights."

Ingolde pushed herself up with her knuckles. "Rights, Heldine? Did you give my Indon heirs? Your first child never quickened, your second died hours after it was born. If I brought a man into this house, who is to say I would not marry him myself?"

"I'm not afraid of you, Ingolde Braydswidow." Heldey's declaration had no effect on the hedge-sorcerer. The younger woman glanced at Dart, then retreated toward the door. "All right—I'll tend the sheep. I'm not going to be a shepherd's barren widow the rest of my life. You'll see." Dust-demons swirled around Heldey's skirt as she stormed out of the shepherd's house.

Ingolde nodded. She tossed her son's clothes at her guest without warning. He lunged forward and caught them cleanly. Another mote of knowledge for them both: His reflexes were quicker than thought and independent of his damaged memory.

"Dress yourself. I'll not have a naked man in my doorway."

Dart scrambled into the shadow, but he could not escape his host's flinty eyes. The clothing was maddeningly familiar. He could almost dress himself without thinking, and then found himself staring at the length of hose, not knowing what to do next. All the while, he felt Ingolde watching him, measuring him.

The hedge-sorcerer judged that despite the length of his unkempt hair, he had not been mad for very long. When he balanced on one foot and struggled to bind the hose around his leg, muscles rippled smoothly across his back and shoulders. He could do a solid day's work in the fields, but he had none of the leanness that marked the commonfolk for the rest of their lives after the harvest failed and they survived on famine foods. There was a pale scar running arrow-straight along Dart's ribs. With the war, it wasn't unusual to see a common man with steel scars, but it was rare to see one that had been carefully sealed by a skilled mender.

The room became quieter as Heldey shooed the flock from the undercroft.

"You're wearing your debts, now," Ingolde said when Dart knotted up the fullness of Indon's shirt. "There's a straw-fork in the undercroft. I think you'll know what to do with it."

"If you please, I'm hungry." Dart looked at the empty bowls of whey and bread crusts on the sideboard.

"Work's best on an empty belly."

Dart met Ingolde's eyes. The hedge-sorcerer braced herself for the onslaught which she was sure would come if she were wrong about him. His face hardened and it didn't take *basi* to guess his thoughts, but the stranger bent to her will.

"As pleases you, Ingolde. I am in your debt. But I am no demon, and I must eat something."

"Roben." Ingolde pried Embla's son from her skirt where he'd taken refuge. "Help Dart clean the undercroft, and when that's done take an apple each from the root cellar to hold you until supper."

Disbelief and disappointment were plain on Dart's face, but he said nothing. Smiling at Roben, he allowed himself to be led from the house.

Ingolde controlled her doubts until the door closed, then released them with a sigh. She'd know what to do if Dart were a demon: keep him bound in the fane until an Eyerlon sorcerer came to claim him. Eyerlon wouldn't help them deal with a madman, even a nobly born madman. She could almost wish Gorse had ended its assartage and had its own nosy, greedy lord into whose lap Dart could be dumped. Almost, and no further: The time for taxes and tithes would come soon enough. Meanwhile, she'd cope with this stranger with the parti-colored hair.

The undercroft door opened. Light poked up through the planks by the bed.

"Iser's iron whiskers—this place reeks!"

"Mistress Ingolde says there's no god-swearing in her house, or under it, either."

"It still reeks."

Ingolde scooped up the empty bowls from the sideboard. Chuckling softly, she dropped them in the bucket for washing. So he swore by the warrior's god; that was no surprise. The straw-rake scraped with a strong, regular rhythm. He was working; she could control him. That was a very pleasant surprise indeed.

Larsov, Bourge, and Camra watched Ingolde walk across the common to Auld Mag's cottage. Gorse's new hedge-sorcerer had many good reasons to visit her predecessor, so with a little luck no one would ever notice or suspect the bootprint trail she followed. The door was unlatched. She entered a dark, forbidding house already filled with the cloying scent of death.

Gradually Ingolde made out the shape of Hirmin balanced on his stool and that of the pallet where Mag lay and—one hoped—had died during the night. There was no sign of her daughter.

"Hirmin?" No response. "Hirmin?" A little louder. It wasn't prudent to jolt the scarred man from his dreams. He, too, had parti-colored hair. He'd gone raving more than once—and that was when his mother was there to shoulder some of his pain. Stomping her feet with each step, Ingolde advanced into the cottage.

Mag still lived. Her breathing was shallow; her eyes did not respond to movement. Hirmin was only a little more responsive.

He grunted when Ingolde uncurled his fingers from his mother's wrist. She tried to tuck his hand into the crook of his other arm without disturbing him, but his balance was more precarious than she'd guessed. She backed away when he thumped to the floor, but the disfigured man merely coughed, smacked his lips, and quickly settled into a peaceful sleep.

Ingolde waited until Hirmin's snoring was steady before touching Mag's forehead. The old woman's mouth gaped open like a baby bird's. Ingolde looked away. There'd be no mercy in feeding her. Better to wait until the soul flew out to its next home.

"Berika?" she called out, softly so as not to awaken Hirmin.

"Behind the door. I—I can't get up. My knee's broke."

Ingolde knelt down by her daughter. She directed her thoughts and *basi* upward, to the Web, and this time she caught it. Sorcery and, more importantly, knowledge, flowed to Ingolde's fingertips. She laid her hands on either side of Berika's knee. Ingolde was not a mender; she would never be able to bring order to the chaos of ravaged flesh. On this, the first morning of her hedge-sorcery, she was overwhelmed by the onslaught of images. She lifted her hands; the torrent ceased. Not knowing how broken, shattered bones kenned to a practiced sorcerer, Ingolde could not discern between injury and health. Gritting her teeth, she touched Berika's other knee. Then she raised her hands and released the Web.

"I ken the same from both knees, Beri," she said breathlessly before she, herself, had recovered from the Web's power. "How? Why? What happened to make you think it *was* broken? Why did Dart bring you here?"

That question had enthralled Berika through the dead of the night, past dawn, and into the morning. When her mother asked it, the spell was broken; a torrent of words began to flow, along with sobs and tears. Ingolde embraced her daughter and strained her ears to understand the answer.

The fetch would not surrender the harp, Berika said between the sobs, sniffles, and heart-rending gasps. He offered himself instead: He would travel with her to Eyerlon. He was kind and gentle; he spoke to her heart, and her heart wanted so desperately to listen—until he asked how she would get to Eyerlon without him.

Ingolde hugged her daughter and rocked her in her arms. She knew how the rest would go, and did not want to hear. But Berika could not stop until she had finished.

"My heart said: Go with him, whether he's man or demon. My heart said he'd take care of me and keep me safe. But the heart lies. If I gave myself to Dart, where would I find myself tomorrow? If I give myself to Hirmin, I know where I'll be tomorrow and every day. I'll have my sheep. I'll have my rights—"

Ingolde held her breath.

"All men are alike. A woman endures men; she survives through her children and her labor. Love is the enemy—isn't it?"

Ingolde could not answer.

Camra and Bourge stood in the doorway.

"Mag lives," Ingolde told them while her daughter's tears soaked through her smock.

But the women weren't interested in Mag. "The sheet," Bourge demanded. "Where's the bloody sheet? Berika—you spent the night with him—tell him he's shamed you until he hangs out the sheet!"

Pure misery pumped Berika's tears and made her shoulders heave. Ingolde smoothed her daughter's braids and kissed her lightly on the top of the head. She told herself it wasn't too late, then got to her feet.

"The shame's yours," she snarled at the women. "Thinking of marriage while Mag fights for every breath!"

Ingolde herded the women out of the cottage and shut the door behind her. She strode to the fane. The hedge-sorcerer tended the fane. It was the one task Mag never surrendered, and suddenly, Ingolde knew why: No one would bother a sorcerer, even a newly made hedge-sorcerer, in a fane. She beat her fist against the snag.

"What else should I have done?—could I have done?" Prayerful thoughts came naturally in this place. "What can I do now? Send them both away? Eyerlon's no place for a madman with noble manners or a girl who knows sheep and nothing else. Eyerlon's no place for anyone without *basi*, gold, or patronage. . . ."

Braydon. She'd forgotten her second son, and the tantalizing message Mag brought from the Web before disaster struck. He was a sarjent—the lowest ranking officer in the army. But the lowest rank was a marked achievement for a shepherd's son. Braydon would have some money; he certainly had patronage if he'd been accepted into the Eyerlon garrison.

Ingolde released Weycha's charred snag. Her spine crackled as she stretched her arms.

• • •

Dart cleaned the undercroft and ate his apple. He carried straw onto Dietta's roof, thickened the thatch near the smoke vent, and got himself a crust of dark brown bread. He waded out among the eels in the fish weir to check the strength of the dam, and shared a withered sausage with Larsov.

Gorse had been without a healthy man since the end of Lesser Sowing when the muster order came through the Web. There was little the women could not do, but much they considered men's work and left undone all summer. Dart reckoned they were taking advantage of him: Walking through the muck of the weir, not to mention letting the eels wriggle between his legs, should have been worth two or three trenchers. But he was a wise man—or his lady had given him wisdom—and he did not begrudge the labor while his wits collected themselves. He was getting accustomed to the quirky way in which his memory restored itself, and he was waiting for Berika, who had yet to emerge from the miserable cottage where he'd left her.

When Ingolde ladled their supper into wooden bowls, Dart picked up two and held them out.

"One's enough," she said.

"I thought—If you please, Mistress Ingolde, shouldn't I take them to the cottage? You sent me after extra turnips because you had to feed Berika and Hirmin."

Ingolde scowled. "I said my daughter and her betrothed, if I said anything at all—which I don't remember doing." She filled the second bowl, then took them out of his hands. "Roben—take these across to the cottage."

They glared at each other. "I carried her there because she asked me to. I'd rather have carried her all the way to Eyerlon. She was afraid of him—afraid for her life. But she was more afraid of *me*, because she believes a man who won't hurt her can't be a man at all."

Dart retreated to a corner, where he ate quickly and in silence. He found the harp case where Ingolde had put it, and opened the door.

"You can play here, if harping's what you mean to do." Ingolde's soft-spoken authority stopped him in his tracks. "You'd be very foolish to go anywhere else."

She was right, though the knowledge stuck in Dart's throat and would not be swallowed. He was not ready to defy the customs of this place, and he did want to play his harp more than anything else. Music remained his most familiar language, even if his lady no longer listened. He continued the song he'd begun in the fane, embellishing the simple melody of loneliness and isolation with the strident chords of frustration. Household by household, the villagers came to the shepherd's house—except Berika and Hirmin. Every time Dart looked at the door he saw Ingolde as well. His fingers blurred over the strings of his instrument and his frustration spread like straw-fire through the room.

The villagers left the shepherd's house bickering at each other.

"I'm going outside." Dart reconstructed the acorn around the harp.

"See that you stay outside, then." Ingolde sensed he was a few breaths short of total defiance and did not try to stop him.

Heldey followed Dart, despite Ingolde's warning. She caught him a few steps short of Mag's cottage. "I know about last night—Beri went to you in the fane. But you can't go in there. That's Hirmin's house, and she's his wife, or she will be soon enough. You'll get her killed, or worse, if you touch her again."

"I didn't—"

Dart was stunned and outraged. He gestured aimlessly at the closed door. Heldey took his hand, and brought it to her breast. "Beri's always wanted a shining nobleman to ride into her life and carry her away. She wanted that even more than she wanted to reach the Web—even when she wouldn't admit it. Nobody in Gorse was good enough for her. Hirmin *loves* her, in his way. She wouldn't have to be afraid of him if she'd accept that. He'd do anything for her if she stopped chasing him away."

Dart did not pull his hand back when the sable-haired girl released it. The love he remembered with his lady seemed to have no place in Gorse. "I don't know you at all," he murmured, more to himself than Heldey.

"You haven't tried. I'm not like Berika." Heldey had absolute faith in her mother-in-law. If Ingolde said the stranger was a nobly mannered man who'd lost his memory, she meant to help him regain it and his noble rights. She guided his hand across the front of her smock. "I'm a widow and I'm not house-bound."

"House-bound?"

"Yes, house-bound. Once a girl's *grown*, if she spends a day and night alone with a man who's no kin to her, he's got freehold over her—unless her own kin come and take her back by force.

With Beri—since she's spent a day and night with her betrothed—she's house-bound until he hangs out a bloody sheet to show he's made her his rightful wife."

For the first time, Dart did not welcome the fireworks of recognition. Heldey spoke the truth: This was the way of the world he'd forgotten while he was with his lady in the forest. "And if Berika had spent the night with me. . . ?"

"You are a man, aren't you? You're not a demon, even if your hair is parti-colored?"

Dart balanced his weight on one hip. He raked his hair with his fingers. The gesture brought an unexpected burst of memory, which, for the moment, he must ignore. "She'd be my wife by freehold?"

Heldey gave a short, ugly laugh. "She's betrothed to Hirmin, fool. She's been betrothed to him since before she was born. He's been waiting all her life to make her his rightful wife. If Hirmin knew you'd touched her, he'd have you bound and left for wolves in the forest, and he'd have her branded or stoned—but she'd still be his wife."

Dart looked away. He had no fear of wolves, the forest, or even death; his fear was for Berika.

"But he won't know," Heldey said in a softer, gentler voice. "He's going to have to open a vein to bloody their linen. Berika won't tell him. Ingolde certainly won't. And I won't either. But, you best look somewhere less dangerous from now on." She traced a line from his temple to the hollow of his neck.

Dart snatched her wrist with a speed that surprised them both. "You're no way different from Hirmin. You've marked me as something you'll have, whether I will it or not. With you and him around, I understand why Berika is so desperate to be away from here."

Heldey slashed him with her fingernails. He dodged easily, releasing her wrist as he did. She ran across the yard and vanished into the night beyond the houses. Dart's shoulders sagged; he rubbed the back of his neck again. He recognized the tension in his muscles and the anger in her eyes: He'd made himself an enemy.

Yet Heldey was right in one thing: There was nothing he could do to help Berika, whom his lady had told him to protect and champion. He walked away from the cottage. The sky was clear; moonlight showed him the path beyond the millpond to the orchard. He considered everything Heldey told him, and the fragments of his past that her words unlocked.

He'd had enemies before, and friends. They had no faces or names, but there were many of them. There had been women, too, and he guessed from the vague feelings surrounding vaguer memories that they were more like Heldey than Berika.

Dart paused by a tree. There was now, which was a piece of memory made up of two days and the night between them. There was the past of the forest and his lady, which he suspected would remain dreamlike. And there was the past of a time when he lived in this world they called Fenklare, a world which he was beginning to recognize and dislike intensely.

How much time all together? He had a young man's body. How long had he lived in Fenklare before his lady found him? How much time had he spent with her in the forest? A week? A month? The whole summer?

Dart was suddenly shivering. The shaking spread to his gut. He collapsed in the wet grass. It was more than a single season. He didn't know how he knew, but he knew. He'd been in the forest longer than Berika or Heldey had been alive—possibly longer than Ingolde, or even that old crone Mag.

CHAPTER

7

"Oh, my lady—What have you taken from me?" Dart did not call his lady by her name, Weycha. "How long did you keep me within you in the forest? Had Berika been born? Ingolde? Auld Mag, the crone? When did I start living in your rhythm, sleeping in your arms when the air was cold, making music for you, love to you, when it was not?"

Weycha would have answered him, had she been awake. She would have told her champion that she had taken nothing from him. She had found the husk of a ruined, dissolute young man, whom she restored and filled with purpose. But her answer would not have satisfied the young man in Gorse's orchard.

"A single month." Recognition again: "Two weeks, Lesser and Greater; twenty days together—nights . . . Twenty days, weeks, months . . . Twenty years . . . "

Dart plumbed his memories of Weycha. There was nothing precise about them. Weycha herself was a presence; when Dart sought her face he found Berika. If he could not remember her face, why did he try to remember anything? Yet the longer he pondered, the longer it seemed, until twenty years felt more accurate than twenty months, weeks, or days. But if it was twenty years—how could he account for his young man's body? Had he been a child—an infant? Then, how to account for the scars on his chin and along his ribs?

"Why me?" he demanded. "What have—had—I done?" He stifled those thoughts with a vigorous shake of his head. He did not want to know. He did not want to know as much as he already knew. In Walensor a boy became a man at the age of twenty-two, and a man reckoned himself worn-out at fifty. If he had spent twenty years—or more, maybe much more—anything, anyone, he had loved or hated would be changed beyond recognition.

He pummelled the tree with his fist. "It is not *fair*! You took me out of my life. I could be as old as the trees. I could be . . . *old*—"

Dart didn't need memory to realize that he would not trade the young man he found himself to be for any other age. All the same, there was a deep anger in him that had not been there before. He watched the sun rise for the first time, then followed the path to the stream.

"You took my natural life from me." Dart stood on the cultivated side of the stream, addressing the wild forest. "You said you found me and made me into your protector; that was all well for you. You needed a champion and a protector, but you did not need *me*. A tree without roots, my lady—a tree without roots cannot stand, is not alive. You told me that fate moved me from you to Berika. You told me to follow her—but I cannot follow her. You told me to protect her—and I could not protect her.

"Now I tell you, my lady—I can do nothing for anyone until I know who *I* am. I will go wherever I have to go to learn who I was before you found me. I will do anything I have to do. And if Hazard comes while I am gone, he can be no worse for you than Hirmin is for Berika."

A child's defiance, a child's threat—a child's plea absorbed by the murmuring water. Weycha was asleep, beyond her champion's anger. Dart waited until the sun rose above the trees, then trudged back to Gorse.

Several people wished Dart a good day as he came through the yard. If he'd wanted to, he could have remembered their names and returned the greeting. If he'd wanted to remember—which he did not. He scarcely noticed the unadorned wall and closed door of Mag's cottage. The door to the shepherd's house was open; he crossed the threshold silently.

"Heldey swore you'd run off."

"Where would I go?"

Ingolde looked up from the dough on the kneading board. She had a fair notion of what had passed between Dart and Heldey. "Anywhere. There's nothing here for you."

"Doesn't the undercroft need cleaning again, or the fish weir?" He gave the nut case a desultory nudge into the corner with his foot—a gesture which was not lost on Ingolde.

"You're not meant for mucking out pens and stalls."

"What do you know?" Dart retorted as he turned around.

He pulled the door shut as he left. The short hairs on Ingolde's neck tingled. She shrugged until the coarse cloth of her gown dulled the sensation. Auld Mag would have hobbled after him, but Auld Mag hadn't tended her own hearth for many years. Ingolde still had to put bread on the table. There was no time to pry answers out of a strange, sullen youth who might be more than he seemed, and might be much less.

The supple rake bowed as Dart attacked the soiled straw in the undercroft. His shoulders were tense, his knuckles were white, and his jaw jutted forward. He plunged into his anger, but labor relaxed his shoulders, his hands, even his face. He left his shirt hanging on a post and thrust the rake deep into the shadows Berika had not cleaned since springtime.

By his lady's grace, Dart was a strong man in the prime of his life. He shrugged off the effects of a sleepless night. Ingolde kneaded her bread to the rhythm of wordless melodies rising through the floor planks.

When he was finished in the undercroft, Dart exchanged the rake for a sharp-tined fork. The motes of recognition rising from the abyss of his past did not differentiate between what he had done and what he had merely seen done. The manure pile in the paddock needed to be turned. The fork, not the rake, was the proper tool for turning it. The sun circled over the shepherd's house; shimmering vapors rose from the open pile. The only moving shadows were the one he made for himself, and a second one whose approach he did not notice.

"You're not fooling anyone."

Dart lost the melody he'd been humming. Clots fell from the fork when his concentration wavered in mid-arc. He kicked them toward the new pile and thrust the fork into the old one without acknowledging Heldey's presence.

"You don't belong here. You can't stay." She looked down on

him from the highest rail of the fence, next to the place where his shirt was hung.

Dart couldn't find another melody. He lost the rhythm of the work, too. More clots littered the mud than made their way to the new pile. Sighing and wiping his face with his arm, Dart rested against the fork, but he did not turn around.

"Mag's dead."

He left the fork standing. "It was expected."

"But you killed her."

Sweat stung Dart's eyes. He turned then, and reached for his shirt to dry his forehead. Heldey didn't flinch when he stared at her.

"You've got *demon's* eyes," she said evenly. "Not round like a man's, but star-shaped and shifty. No one will believe you if I say you enthralled Berika and Auld Mag."

A lump hardened in Dart's throat. There was no reason to think the hedge-sorcerer was wrong; there was no way he could see his eyes. It hadn't occurred to him to question Ingolde's judgment that he was in all ways a man. He swallowed. "Nobody thinks I enthralled Berika or killed Auld Mag."

"They might—if I tell them about your eyes, and what you did to me last night."

Laughter erupted from the darkest corners of Dart's mind. He had, indeed, known many women like Heldey without knowing their names well enough to forget them. "I did nothing to you last night—or is that what's got you bothered?" He braced his arms on either side of her, trapping her on the rail.

"No," Heldey insisted, trying futilely to escape.

Dart was caught in a current that was neither recall nor recognition. Words came to him the way music did. He teased her with a lopsided grin, and when his instincts said the moment was right, he swept Heldey up in his arms. She squealed, and locked her arms behind his neck as he carried her to the fresh straw in the undercroft.

"And what do you think of me now?" Dart heard himself ask when they were both sated and comfortable in each other's arms. His voice was both sweet and venomous.

Apprehension shook the woman beside him. "I—I do not know." She reached for her smock. "You are not like any man I know."

"But a man?"

Heldey nodded. "A man. Surely a great man—a noble man." She pulled the smock over her head.

"See that you remember." Dart kissed her one last time before releasing her.

Laces and sleeves flying, Heldey ran from the undercroft. Dart lingered in the shadows. Heldey might well think him a noble man; she, however, could not compare to the elusive memories of his lady. Nor did she compare well with Berika.

I must be more careful. Dart shrugged into his shirt. Long, matted hair fell the length of his head to his chin and would not be tamed. He tore one snarl out by its roots before recognizing a better solution in the large sheep shears hanging from a nail. He'd whacked off the worst of the rat's nest before realizing that in making it easier for his eyes to see, he'd made it equally easy for his eyes to be seen.

Leaving the job half finished, he sneaked around to the front of the shepherd's house. Heldey was feeding the chickens. She recoiled when he flashed a smile at her—but that was likely a reaction to his sheared hair as anything else. The sound of women wailing came through the open door of Mag's cottage; there was no sign of Hirmin, Berika, or the damned bloody sheet. Dart guessed that Ingolde, as the new hedge-sorcerer, would be among the wailers. He was wrong: She stood by her own hearth tearing old cloth into long strips.

"Heldey tells me that Auld Mag is dead."

Dart startled Ingolde. Her hands jerked up, and the cloth fell into the ashes. The look she gave him when she turned his way was not at all friendly. He wondered if she'd heard anything from the undercroft. His face grew hot and prickly.

"She says my eyes are star-shaped and shifty, and that the village will believe her when she says I enthralled Berika and killed the old woman. I suppose she'll say I enthralled her as well."

Ingolde slowly picked the cloth out of the ashes. "Come over here—where the light comes through the vent."

He did, and she frowned when she held his eyelids apart, then looked away.

"Are they a man's eyes?" he asked.

"They are not," Ingolde replied without looking at him.

"But you said I was a man. You swore to the whole village—"

"I was wrong. Beri said you had fire eyes when she first saw you; Embla said the same thing. I saw no fire; I looked no further."

"What do they—I—look like?"

The hedge-sorcerer managed to face him; he could see the fear in *her* eyes. "Your eyes are very dark. In shadow they are . . . No one could tell they are not a man's eyes. But in the light . . . the pupil is not round like a man's nor angled like a beast's." She blinked and turned away again. "Star-shaped and shifty, that is as good a way to describe them as any. And the color . . . it is not brown."

"What color, then?"

Ingolde folded the cloth with a snap. "I don't know. Particolored like your hair, I suppose. I don't know what you are, and, right now, I don't much care." She took a stride toward the door, but Dart was quicker and blocked her path.

"Did I kill Auld Mag? I know I didn't enthrall Berika, much less Heldey—but I don't know about the old woman."

His grip was firm, but in no way painful; Ingolde did not doubt that she could wrest free. Dart was not frightening, not, at least, in the general way of men. He gave no sign of the brutal rage that simmered in common men's hearts. Only Ingolde's one-time lover, the noble youth who had abandoned her, shared Dart's self-confident strength and control. Berika might well have resisted him; Heldey—Ingolde knew—hadn't tried. Another notch on the counting-stick, then, to say Dart *was* noblefolk, despite those strange eyes bearing down on her.

"Do *you* think I killed Auld Mag?" Dart recast his question in the lengthening silence.

Ingolde shook her head. "She was old and weak. For the last year we've held our breath every time she reached for the Web. It was the excitement that killed her—but you were the cause of the excitement."

Emotion bypassed the emptiness of Dart's memory, and was thereby more trustworthy than any conscious thought; the emotion making his heart pound was anger both righteous and futile. "Heldey is wrong about me, but she will win because Weycha lifted me out of my life to make her her champion. I think I'm as old as the trees, Ingolde. Older than you, older than Larsov or Mag." He released Ingolde's arm. "What will happen to you? You said I was just a man. I'm not a demon, but I'm also not *just* a man, am I? Will they turn against you, too?"

The hedge-sorcerer's head jerked up; she had not expected him to think of her. "I am new to my tasks yet. I will admit I made a mistake. That will satisfy everyone."

Dart nodded. "But, will it be the truth?"

Ingolde recoiled; he did not need weapons so long as he had his tongue. "Go back to where you came from. Leave us in peace. Go back to your lady." She paused by the door, fearing, and hoping, that his eyes would betray him.

"I cannot go back to her. That part of my life, as long as it was, is over. Since I met your daughter I have become a man again. I'm learning how from all of you—even Heldey."

The hedge-sorcerer fled her own house. Dart watched her disappear into Mag's cottage. A wry, fleeting smile lifted one corner of his mouth; then he looked for the acorn and his harp. He braced his back against the doorjamb and began to play.

Shielded by his effortless music, Dart waited, watched, and learned. The old folks, led by Bourge and Larsov, took the children out to gather food for a funeral feast. From what he overheard, the villagers ate famine food after someone died: The oldest showed the youngest where to find the wild things that sustained life when the crops failed, as they almost always did at least once in every generation.

Knowing how like a child he was in so many ways, and that he was likely to leave Gorse unprepared for the journey, Dart considered going with them. He set that notion aside when Berika and the other women emerged from the cottage bearing Mag's shrouded corpse. He tried to catch her attention as they started up the path to the fane, but caught Heldey's instead. Their eyes met and Dart's fingers momentarily lost their way among the harp strings.

Berika was the only woman to leave the fane. She returned to the quiet cottage, closing the door behind her without once looking at the music-filled threshold of the shepherd's house. The sun passed over the common. Embla went after the sheep, then returned to the fane. Wisps of smoke rose from the millhouse chimney and vanished in the grey clouds of twilight. Berika reemerged from the cottage. She picked her way across the common as stiff and round-shouldered as Auld Mag had ever been.

"Are you ready to leave for Eyerlon?" Dart asked when she was close enough for soft speech.

Berika looked at him with red-rimmed eyes. Her skirt swung against his shoulder as she crossed the threshold. She said nothing until she was well inside the shepherd's house. "It's too late."

Dart glanced across the common, watching Hirmin feel his way along the outer wall. There was a heavily stained cloth draped over his arm.

"It doesn't matter. My memory is empty. Yours can be, too, if you will it so. Your life begins in Eyerlon—"

The lid of the clothes chest slammed shut, and Dart nearly lost his grip on the harp. When he had it firmly in hand again, Berika was standing behind him.

"Blind and crippled, there's no place he couldn't follow me. Hellfire isn't *basi*, but it's close enough. I tried—I had the knife in my hands, but I could not kill him."

Berika carried an armful of clothing out of the shepherd's house and into Mag's cottage. She left the cottage door open; Hirmin closed it.

A high-pitched wail pierced the twilight. Dart started from the threshold, dumping his harp, but the wail, and many more like it, came from the fane, not the cottage. Dart retrieved his harp and put it away. There'd be no other music while the women of Gorse keened themselves hoarse. When he could stand the sound no longer, Dart made his way to the millhouse and knocked on the door.

"What do men do while the women shriek and the old folks take the young out hunting for worms?"

Rimp opened the door. "Tomorrow we cook what the reavers collect. Like as not, you'll dig a grave." He looked at the fane with a sour grin. "Tonight we drink. They'll be going until dawn, if I knew Mag. That old buzzard won't slip her coil without a protest. Don't suppose you know iron-in-the-fire, living mad in the wood and all."

Dart shook his head. "Is it a song? Will you teach me?"

"A game. Five dice in a cup. A betting game. Don't suppose you've got any money?"

Dart shook his head again, and followed Rimp into the house.

It was not a difficult game. There were five six-sided dice. Four had pipped faces—two were black and two were red. The fifth die was black on one face, red on another, mixed on the remaining four; it determined whether the point throw was *iron*, *fire*, or a combination. There was some skill required—which of the two black dice or red dice to choose for a combination—but the game was mostly luck: The thrower won if the iron of the next throw was equal or higher and the fire was equal or below his point. The thrower could pass the cup if he didn't like his throw, and lose nothing worse than his ante. It was simple enough to be played by a drunk, and spread like a rumor from the Arrizi prisoners who played it constantly.

Rimp taught Dart the basic rules in a few demonstrations. The hamstrung veteran fancied himself an expert and regretted that their stakes would be kernels of unmilled grain swept off the floor. Then Dart, with no proper strategy, called a worthless point and proceeded to win with his next three throws.

"Uncanny," Rimp said, getting his brandy jug from the sideboard. He filled a mug to overflowing and shoved it across the table to his companion. "Have a sip—it might not be Brightwater liquor, but it's sweeter than anything you'll have drunk in the woods. Try again, and mind the rules. Never bet high iron sixes or sparking aces. You'll get nowhere without knowing the rules."

Dart took a hearty swallow of the cloudy liquid. He didn't taste anything; didn't feel anything either—his lips were numb and his tongue. He coughed and his eyes began to water profusely.

"You'll get used to it." Rimp laughed, pounding between Dart's shoulders. "But sip, boy, never gulp."

"Never," Dart croaked, but he did, emptying that mug and two more like it before Larsov came through the door to say they'd gathered enough for the funeral meal—considering how little folks ate at a funeral.

The old man would have joined them for another round of drinking, if not gambling, but a yawning spasm overtook Dart and he announced his intention to return to the shepherd's house. He felt taller than he'd been when he sat down, and his knees no longer worked quite the way he thought they should. His feet certainly had developed minds of their own. The women were still caterwauling up a storm in the fane, but, mercifully, Dart found his ears were as numb and fuzzy as the rest of him.

He tripped over the threshold and crawled the rest of the way to Ingolde's great, empty bed.

Dart awoke suddenly. Dream-silk clung to his eyes; he neither recognized nor recalled the grim woman with the grey-streaked hair who had awakened him.

"I have chosen you."

Dart shook his head; it throbbed in protest. Light was turning the dream-silk to heavy glue, pulling his eyelids together.

Ingolde grabbed the blanket. "I see you spent your evening with Rimp's jug. So, you're man enough to get drunk."

"Go away." He groped blindly for the blanket.

Ingolde caught his hand and held it firmly. "If you were not in *my* bed, I'd throw a water bucket over you. As it is, if you don't get moving, I might well anyway."

Dart followed his hand out of the bed. He knew the woman now, her home, and the restless sheep milling about in the undercroft. Ingolde gave his wrist a final pinch before releasing it. Dart lurched in the direction she pointed him, stubbed his toe, and staggered to the water bucket into which he plunged his head. His balance returned; his legs straightened, and he was wide awake. "I'm ready."

"Take the bread and the sausage." Her eyes showed him where to look. "And we'll be on with it."

The common was much brighter than the house. He stood on the threshold stone feeling much-observed and foolish, shielding his eyes until they adjusted to the light.

"Well, pick her up."

Dart blinked. He looked from one end of the common to the other before looking down on the cloth-bound shape at his feet. He blinked again and took an unwitting step backward into Ingolde.

"Don't tell me you're afraid."

Pride stiffened him. "Just surprised," he assured her as he got his arms under Mag's shrouded corpse and hefted the awkward bundle to waist height. "You'll have—" The words stopped when he saw Berika in the half-circle of women. They were all haggard, even Ingolde. Auld Mag, it would seem, had not gone quietly to the afterlife. But Berika was more than haggard; she was almost unrecognizable with a bruise that darkened half her face. Her right eye was almost swollen shut and there was a crust of blood along her upper lip.

Dart turned to Ingolde. Auld Mag nearly slipped from his arms. The scowl on Ingolde's face kept him from asking untimely questions, but it didn't keep the anger out of his voice. "This is not right," he said so only she could hear.

"Do as you're told," Ingolde shot back in the same low tone. "Unless you want things to get much, much worse."

And, against his better judgment, Dart obeyed her. He was careful not to look at Berika again, but in avoiding her, he wound up looking at Hirmin. The scarred man's one eye narrowed. His lips twisted into what might have been a smile, or simply the result of his injury. Everyone said Hirmin was nearly blind, but Dart jutted his chin and shook his head once, just in case.

"Where are we going?" he asked as they went over the millpond bridge. "How long will we be gone?" Ingolde hunched her shoulders. She took the log-and-dirt steps to the orchard two at a time and Dart was hard-pressed to keep up with her. His arms began to burn. Auld Mag had gotten heavier, and short of tossing her over his shoulder, there was no other way to carry her. He headed for an apple tree with an inviting sweep in its lower branches.

"I've got to rest," he shouted and braced the corpse against the tree. His hands began to throb with the next beat of his heart.

"Not here!" Ingolde came toward him. There was no fire in her eyes, but there should have been. Dart jammed his numb hands together. "You can rest on the other side."

"The other side of what?" Dart grunted as the weight came into his arms again. He gritted his teeth and covered the distance between himself and Ingolde at a bone-numbing run. "Damn your eyes—the other side of *what*?"

Ingolde hissed like a serpent. "You will be quiet! And you will be patient!"

Dart felt an invisible web settle over him. Outrage vanquished the aches and fatigue; he reached deep within himself. He would *not* be quiet, and he would *not* be patient. Ingolde's composure wavered. She seemed about to break and run. Dart reconsidered. Now that his arms weren't being ripped out of their sockets, he judged that he could continue. The web was gone as well. He took a step forward in silence. A pale and trembling Ingolde continued toward the stream.

CHAPTER

8

Ingolde's legs bent like withies. Her head throbbed and the colors of sunlight faded to twilight grey. She was astounded by her own behavior—astounded and appalled. Whatever had possessed her to fling her unpracticed hedge-sorcery at a demon?

Nothing *possessed* her, nothing more than blind arrogance—and that made her rashness harder to swallow.

Dart's eyes glowed just as Heldey and Embla claimed they did, but he didn't know his own power. Ingolde was certain of this because she was certain she'd be dead otherwise. He'd swirled up a storm of *basi* in the blink of an eye. Moments later it and her poorly made compulsion were gone; but she was unharmed. Ingolde considered the sorcery that could cut with such precision, then vanish into a façade of a newborn's innocence, and was not at all reassured.

They reached the stream that separated Weychawood from the cleared fields.

Brightwater! Ingolde shuddered. Tendrils of milky opalescence floated within the current; she'd seen them by moonlight for many years, but never before by sunlight.

"Do we cross?" Dart asked as he joined her on the bank.

His hair was slick against his face; his breathing was louder than his words. How odd, Ingolde thought, that he cast his *basi* to break her compulsion but had not restored his own strength.

"We cross," Ingolde agreed. She did not look back to see how the stream with its Brightwater current responded to Dart's presence. She did look down, and despite everything, felt a surge of satisfaction that the pale tendrils curling around her ankles were noticeably brighter when they moved downstream.

"Uh-oh!" Dart stumbled.

A jet of icy, incandescent blue swept through the stream like a scythe. Ingolde leaped to the bank before it could touch her.

Dart churned desperately. He heaved the shrouded corpse to the bank, then fell backward into the current. Ingolde watched silently while he clambered to dry ground, shedding streams of clear, colorless water with every gesture.

"Are you angry with me?" he demanded.

Cold droplets struck her face when Dart shook his dripping, uneven hair. She wiped them away as if they were stinging hot, and retreated from him and the stream. Ingolde did not trust herself to answer.

Dart wrung the hem of his shirt, then sat down to wring out his breeches and hose. "Is there something you're not telling me? Are we racing against something? Should I be afraid?"

Ingolde's answer was the crunch of her shoes in the dry leaves as she turned away. Dart slung Mag's corpse over his shoulder, where it balanced with greater ease and less dignity.

The forest was quiet and cool, and only vaguely familiar. Perhaps if Dart had paused to look at the leaves as he trampled through them, he could have recognized them. Once he saw flashing red feathers disappear in a pine tree; he recognized the bird's song and remembered imitating it with his harp. The hedge-sorcerer kept moving; the recognition remained an isolated jewel in the darkness of his memory.

Ingolde surprised Dart when she stopped. "Is this a good place?" she demanded.

Dart let the corpse slide to the ground. "Good for what?" This grove looked no different from the others she had passed through without hesitation. He was thirsty. There was a kink in his neck that no amount of twitching and stretching would help.

"Will Weycha, your lady, be pleased if we leave Auld Mag here? She was so wroth last night—I don't want to anger her further."

He swung his arm in circles until his neck snapped and the kink became a fading ache. "Cold-steel whiskers, Ingolde, how would I know?"

A grin tugged at the corners of Ingolde's mouth. "Cold-steel whiskers": Her noble lover had said that when he shaved each morning with his knife. Brayd had said shaving was a waste of steel and skin and let his beard grow. Dart's chin had a three-day stubble, but he'd never be a man like Brayd. Ingolde swallowed her smile. "I—I assumed you could tell. I've never done this before. One place seems—feels—no different from another."

Dart could not imagine his sensual goddess caring where they left a withered old woman's corpse, but he closed his eyes and asked anyway. *My lady? Can you hear me? I'm with you in the forest. Is this a good place?* Nothing. Nothing at all—except the certainty that in all their time together he had never shouted for her with his mind like this.

"I can't ask her, or answer for her."

Ingolde's shoulders sagged. "Then this place is as good as any." She measured the angle of the sunlight streaking through the branches, realigned the corpse so Mag's head was to the east, and offered Dart the shovel. "We'll pile stones over the grave once it's finished. The grave itself does not need to be deep."

Dart hesitated before taking the shovel. "I haven't had any breakfast."

"I've had neither food nor sleep."

He snatched the implement from her hand and rammed it into the dirt, striking the first of many ground roots. An axe would have been more useful than the shovel, but all Dart had was a belt knife with a thick, dull blade. Ingolde searched for stones; Dart thought about going back to the village and rejected the thought without quite knowing why. Three times the hedge-sorcerer came back with a waterbag instead of rocks and let him pause long enough to drink. The fourth time, the grave was as deep as Dart was willing to make it. They lowered the corpse into the grave together.

"Rest now. I'll finish it."

Dart was cool and rested well before Ingolde had the cairn arranged to her satisfaction. She muttered a few words over her handiwork, then led Dart to another grove.

"My daughter, Berika, meant to leave the village the other night," Ingolde began without warning. "I always thought she might—she was determined to fight what fate arranged for her."

Dart weighed his words carefully. "She didn't seem to think that *fate* had arranged it."

Ingolde flinched. "I saw her footprints going up to the fane, and another's—yours—coming down. She confided in you, then, and you . . . convinced her to stay in Gorse? You convinced her not to leave . . . ?" The hedge-sorcerer's voice trailed off into silence, which lingered until Dart realized he'd been asked to tell his side of the story.

"She meant, as you say, to leave. She also meant to take my harp with her. She had some notion of selling it in Eyerlon. I could not let her do that." Dart rolled up his sleeve to reveal the livid bite marks on his arm. "She did not want to give the harp back, so I had to take it, and, in taking it, I made her fall. She hurt her knee, not badly, but enough that she could not start her journey just then. I said a day could not matter—"

"But you took her to Hirmin?"

Dart's eyes did not glow, but his voice took on a finely honed edge. "I did what she bid me to do. I knew much less that night about a woman's life in Gorse. I did not know you counted yourselves, or your daughters, so cheaply."

Ingolde was properly shamed. Her voice was ragged and she looked through her wringing hands to the ground between her feet. "I was younger than she is now, and I needed my mother's sister's help. To be betrothed at birth is not so very bad, when a woman must marry anyway. Better to know what lies ahead than to risk the knives of love."

Dart knew nothing of Ingolde's story, nor did it interest him. "Hirmin is a monster."

"He was a boy! How was I to know what he would become— what Arrizan hellfire would do to him?"

Ingolde could absorb only so much guilt and shame before lashing back. "Hirmin worshipped my daughter from the moment she was born. He lived for the day she would be his, and she ran from him. Even now, if she would not fight him, he would bow down to her. It is not so great a price to pay."

"Heldey said the same thing. It's a pity Berika can't lie to herself so easily. She'll have the truth, and have it her way, or not at all."

"You know her well." Ingolde's voice lifted slightly. "Do you—?" She let the thought dangle. Dart had fine manners, gentle wisdom, and a demon's burning eyes. Was he any improvement over Hirmin?

Dart understood the unfinished question. "Where women are concerned, you may be certain I'm a man," he acknowledged with a self-conscious smile.

They stared at each other. Dart looked past Ingolde's grey-streaked hair and saw the rich brown it had once been. His imagination removed the weariness from her eyes and the wrinkles from her skin. In her prime, Ingolde would have turned any man's head. For one disconcerting moment he wanted to take her in his arms, but that passed and he was left with a familiar question: Was he Ingolde's age? Was that why he found her attractive? Or was he as old as the oak tree at his back?

Ingolde shivered, though sunlight fell on her shoulders and the day was warm for the time of year. "You must not stay in Gorse."

"I cannot remain in the forest. I have no other home."

"You are right about Heldey; she means to accuse you. Heldey fears for her soul because of what she did with you; she cannot believe she did it of her own will. You are a man, a nobly born man I think, but you've admitted yourself, you're not just a man. The part of you that is not a man we must call a demon. I will not be able to defend you. You must leave the village."

"What will happen to Berika? I swear to you, Berika has no guilt or shame where I'm concerned, but Heldey doesn't believe that. Is she going to save Berika's soul by accusing her, too?"

"Berika has a brother, Braydon. He's just been taken into the prince's guard in Eyerlon garrison. Which prince, I do not know. I have the silver flakes and grit to see you both to the city if you're careful. If you're the man I think you are, you'll do well in Eyerlon. I only ask that you give my son what's left of the purse and tell him to see her set up someplace . . . respectable."

"What if she won't come with me?"

"Then you must convince her. Or not. Either way, you will have to leave before Gorse becomes a danger to you and you become a danger to it."

Dart considered his choices carefully. "It's not fair!" he shouted.

A small band of birds took flight from the tree above them. A squirrel chittered from a lower branch, having dropped its dinner in surprise. A grumpy owl swooped past, hooting as it sought a quieter perch.

"Nothing in this life is fair," the hedge-sorcerer replied, no happier than the owl. "Go back to the village; the coins are in a hollow post next to the door. Take Berika, if you can, but go before I get back. I must reach for the Web tonight. The Communicant will have questions, even if Heldey doesn't. He was probably nosing around the Web last night trying to find Auld Mag. Brightwater—he was probably trying to find Weycha's basilidan. I will be compelled to answer truthfully and I will be your enemy after that." She closed her eyes. Her breathing slowed.

Dart scuffed his feet through the crunchy leaves. He scratched his ear and his nose, and cleared his throat—knowing that Ingolde had said all she would say. His thoughts churned after he left the grove, and the forest. He got to the middle of the stream, where he stood and fretted until his feet were cramped and numb. Then, limping, he returned to Gorse.

As Dart guessed, the entire village was gathered around the pit hearth where the funeral feast was cooking in the open air. Hirmin's distinctive profile was absent. The bloodstains on the sheet nailed to the wall of his cottage were rusty brown and the door was open. Dart had hoped to slip unnoticed into the shepherd's house, but his wish went unfulfilled.

"Ingolde?" Berika asked, intercepting her fetch at the threshold. Her eyes were swollen and red; the bruise on her cheek was larger and darker than before. "Isn't she with you?" There was a cut on her lip. She tried to talk without reopening it and her words were difficult to understand.

Dart retreated into the house. "She said she wanted to be alone. We were both tired—" He compared his exhaustion to Berika's. "Ingolde said she'd have to reach for the Web tonight. She said she had to prepare herself. Heldey is going to accuse me as a demon. Ingolde said she could not defend me; my eyes are wrong. She told me to leave Gorse, Berika; that after tonight she'd be my enemy. She told me where to find coins for the journey. She told me to leave without being seen, and she said to take you with me to Eyerlon. . . ."

The battered expression on Berika's face did not brighten at all. "For a demon, you know nothing about stealth. Everybody saw you cross the bridge. Come to the feast—you can try again while they prepare the bath for Ingolde."

Dart's stomach reminded him that he hadn't eaten all day. He followed Berika eagerly to the fire pit, and sat down beside the others. But his enthusiasm dampened when he saw the thin, lumpy gruel she ladled into his bowl. There was, no doubt, great wisdom in Fenklare's mourning customs. The rough, uncultivated foods of the scrub and forest could mean the difference between death and survival in the famines that from time to time struck even the lushest cropland. But nothing short of starvation could make a funeral feast look appetizing. Dart felt his throat constrict before Berika placed the bowl in his reluctant hands.

A rounded, pearly thing floated to the surface.

It had legs; they moved.

Dart set the bowl down behind him.

"Not good enough for you, eh?"

Dart pretended that he did not hear Heldey.

"What did you eat in the forest? Raw meat? The souls of children. Oh, I forget—you didn't live in the *wild* forest. You lived with a *lady*. What did you eat with her? Ambrosia and nectar? Tell us how gods-food tastes."

Heldey flipped Dart's steamy bowl over with her foot. He jumped up when the repulsive contents touched his breeches.

"Leave him alone," Berika snapped when Dart said nothing in his own defense. "He doesn't remember—"

"He remembers."

Heldey scooped up the almost empty bowl. A coiled grub stuck to the rim. Pinching it between her fingernails, she brandished it inches from Dart's face. He knocked her arm aside with sufficient strength to send her sprawling. He reached for her, fingers hooked like claws; his eyes simmered.

"There!" Heldey shouted, triumphant even as she scrabbled for safety. "Look at him! *Demon's eyes! Demon!*"

Dart closed his eyes; the glow vanished, but Berika had seen it. "It's just the light," she argued, unconvincingly.

Heldey was on her feet again. She made a many-pointed star in the air. The simple cow-horn gesture to invoke Mother Cathe might not be enough; she sought the protection of Noisary, the sun god of Walensor's royalty. "Demon be gone from here." Her eyes would have shot lightning had she herself been a demon. "Go back where you came from!" She ran away.

Berika picked up the discarded bowl and wiped it with her

apron. "Don't give Heldey any mind. If Ingolde said you're a man, you're a man until she says otherwise."

Searing pain nailed Dart where he stood. He was blind when his eyes betrayed him. Vision returned slowly as the pain ebbed. He could see his feet. Was he a man? He was no longer certain himself.

"Berika!"

Heldey hadn't gone to the shepherd's house, but to Hirmin's cottage. She had a tight grip on the scarred man's sleeve and towed him across the yard.

"Wife!" He could see Berika then, and shrugged Heldey aside.

There was no mistaking the fear, or the hate, on Berika's face, but she did not flee.

"No man. You talk to no man!" Hirmin emphasized his command with a roundhouse blow that staggered his defiant bride. He snared her wrist and, using her arm like a whip, propelled her toward the cottage. "Inside!"

"Enough!" Ingolde, who obviously knew a good deal about stealth, surprised them all by catching her daughter in a necessarily brusque embrace. She released Berika after a moment to confront Hirmin. "What you do inside is a husband's right, but here in the yard you answer to me."

Such were a hedge-sorcerer's unchallengeable rights. Ingolde could stop public brutality, but she was powerless when he circled her and herded Berika into his cottage with silent threats. Dart strode after them until Ingolde called his name.

"It is his *right*."

There was desperation, not *basi*, in the hedge-sorcerer's voice, and doubt on her face when Dart turned slowly to look at her. The door slammed; then the smaller sound of metal against metal was heard as a bolt slid into place. Dart had missed his chance, and for a heartbeat his eyes glowed at Ingolde. He could see through the pain when his anger was pure.

"See? See his eyes?" Heldey cackled. "He's a *demon*. You can't deny it now."

Ingolde was trapped between them. Her shoulders sank, and she sighed. "Dart is no danger to us."

"He threw me halfway across the yard, and you saw how he was going after Hirmin. What could poor Hirmin do to him?"

Not what was Hirmin doing to Berika behind the door which blocked sight but not sound—but what could a mortal man do to a demon whose eyes glowed? Dart could tell them that the fire brought pain, not power, but he could not promise that he was not a demon as well as a man.

"Dart is a demon," Ingolde agreed flatly. "He cannot remain free among us." She looked at Dart without seeing him. She'd told him what would happen if he was still in the village when she got back. "Bind him and lock him in the fane."

Despite her words, Ingolde did not try to stop Dart when he began to run. Nor did anyone else, including Heldey. He took the shortest path from the yard toward the forest, abandoning Berika and his harp as he'd already abandoned his lady. The simplefolk of Gorse feared demons too much to chase them.

"We'll make wardings. That will keep him from coming back," Heldey suggested, warming to the authority she'd usurped.

A scream escaped from Hirmin's cottage. It ended with a crash that loosened daub from the outer walls. Ingolde roused herself then, turning toward the sounds. No good came from fighting fate head on—that was her daughter's mistake. One attacked fate on the flank with small nudges, and smaller victories.

"I'll do better than that," she said, asserting her usual confidence. "Ready the bath—I'll make *basils*. Rimp, open the sluice gates! Make me a proper bath in cold water—from Weycha's stream to stop Weycha's demon."

Rimp hurried to do Ingolde's bidding. Only Heldey failed to follow him.

"Well, what are *you* waiting for? Go make scraps for the *basils*. It's your idea, isn't it? This is no time for second thoughts, Heldine. You make him into a demon, now reap your reward."

"Will *basils* truly keep him out—"

"If he is a demon."

Heldey ran to an abandoned cottage where scraps of cloth and leather might have escaped earlier scavenging. A scowl tightened Ingolde's face. Brightwater talismans wouldn't keep Dart out of Gorse, if he came back for her daughter. If he came back at all. Ingolde strode to the millhouse; she refused to pray.

CHAPTER

9

Dart ran across the fish weir bridge. He ran past the orchard and all the fields that had been cleared and planted before the war. He plunged into the scrub where the pigs foraged. The luck of fools and desperation protected him: He flushed none of them from their barrows and eluded countless snaring roots and branches. A self-made wind dried his tears before they reached his chin.

He ran until a balance was restored between timeless emotional agony and his straining lungs. Then he collapsed in the frost-dried grass. The sound of Weycha's stream came to him between his ragged breaths.

He judged himself a despairing, isolated failure of a man—but not for long. He could not know, and did not guess, that he had those singular qualities necessary to any champion: the unwavering faith that what he wanted to do was the right thing to do, and an equally stubborn belief that he could survive anything.

The gasping stopped. His lungs no longer hurt. Dart rose to his feet. A twig broke on the far side of the stream, and, after a moment, two specks of light appeared at the water's edge. Did his own eyes glow that way? He'd never know, so it didn't matter. The specks disappeared, twigs snapped, and Dart was alone again, but no longer lonely.

He walked along the stream bank, following the current back to Gorse. He was on his hands and knees more than once, because the grass was dew-slick and treacherous, not because of carelessness. He was satisfied with himself when he came out of the scrub near the sluice gate above the mill and the fish weir. The gate was closed; the water wheel was turning. Doubling his caution, he crept along the foundation of the mill house.

The room where Dart had played iron-in-the-fire the previous evening radiated noise. He could hear Ingolde's voice without understanding what she said. Thinking he'd hear better from the other side of the wheel, he crept out onto the narrow foundation ledge, only to stop abruptly when he got a good look at the pond below him.

Luminous tendrils of greens and blues spread across the quiet surface: the Brightwater by which everyone swore. The flow was quicksilver brilliant where it plunged out of a wooden gutter pipe. A rainbow spread where it struck the pond's surface. The reds and golds were the most intense, and the shortest-lived; only the cooler colors survived to weave into the current flowing under the bridge.

For one mad moment Dart wanted to dive into the luminous water and lose himself forever beneath the surface. Then he remembered Berika. He made his way back to the bank. The whole village had to be up there, including Berika and Hirmin; they wouldn't miss Ingolde's first immersion in the hedge-sorcery bath. And though Dart was unafraid of hedge-sorcery, he did not plan to scoop Berika out of her misery with all Gorse for witnesses. He'd wait until the water was lifeless and the village was asleep.

Belatedly, Dart remembered his harp, still in the shepherd's house, and the coin horde Ingolde had given him leave to take. He made his way silently to the house and found the door unsecured. He had the acorn and a purse of many small black grit coins and a few of the irregularly shaped silver flakes tucked under his arms, when the doors of the mill house opened. Racing across the common, he reached the high grass on the hill between Mag's cottage and the fane just in time to see Heldey coming his way with a torch.

Let your enemy use torches, a raspy voice whispered from the abyss. *You'll see him clear enough and he'll never see you.* Dart had given the memory-voice a name the first time he'd heard it: Horsten. Whoever Horsten was, whatever he'd been, his advice was worth taking. Dart stayed low and quiet behind a blackberry bush. He closed his eyes—just to be safe—and waited.

"There's a good spot—" Heldey said, no more than an arm's reach away.

The whole bush shook. Thorns snagged Dart's clothes and scraped the vulnerable flesh of his face and hands. He endured them all—and went unnoticed.

"If Dart holds any evil intent toward us, he shall not penetrate the *basil* ring."

Ingolde's voice, close by and still rich with sorcery, made Dart shiver. He feared discovery, but risked opening his eyes to see what they were doing and whether it could affect him, regardless of his intent.

"Are you sure?" Heldey knotted a strip of cloth to the bush.

Icy water sprayed the fresh scratches on his face, making his breath catch and numbing the sting of the thorns. He thought of Berika and the golden dome of the Eyerlon Basilica. Ingolde's *basils*, which Heldey was so busy tying to every branch she could reach, reminded him of Berika. Surely that was no accident.

The two women circled the village with the dripping *basils*, then hurried down the path to the yard where the villagers waited. Dart studied the gathering closely and realized he'd been wrong from the start—Berika and Hirmin had not been with their neighbors in the mill house. Their cottage door never opened as the villagers went to their homes and beds. The door to the shepherd's house was the last to close.

Dart waited a few moments longer. He pushed the dripping branches aside. Those that were bound with the dripping *basils* seemed less apt to snag or scratch. He did not want to think what they might have done if Ingolde had truly meant to keep him away.

Moonrise tinted the eastern sky. Dart hid himself on the western side of Hirmin's cottage. He pressed his ear against a bark-covered post.

Berika was crying.

Berika clung to a rough beam spanning the width of the one-room cottage. It was a precarious perch. There was no room between the thatched roof and the beam so she hung upside down with her arms and ankles thrust into the straw. Grit, dust, and worse fell into her eyes; she could see no better than her husband.

But she was safe, for the moment. Hirmin hadn't heard her clamber onto the shelf above the box-bed or shinny along the beam. Eventually, when he'd torn the cottage apart beneath her, he'd look up but, for the moment, she was safe.

The war was over: Berika didn't know why she kept fighting. She hadn't tried to kill Hirmin while he sat beside his dying mother—when it would have been easy. She hadn't been able to when he came groping for her after Mag died. She was a rightful wife under a husband's hand now—though Hirmin's hands were far from the worst part of him.

It was only a matter of time until he looked up. Or until she was so numb and weak that she fell from exhaustion and her own weight. The shepherd hadn't slept in two nights. She was bruised, battered, and bloodied in so many places the aches blurred together.

Another speck fell into Berika's eye. She couldn't wipe it away. Her tears ran through the channels of her ears and out again. Not knowing which god or goddess might take mercy on her, she entreated them all:

Let it be over. Please gods—Cathe, Iser, Noisary, Weycha, *any god—let it be over!*

"There you are!"

A jolt of fear put new life in Berika's limbs. She flattened herself against the beam. Hirmin jumped and caught the hem of her skirt. Berika screamed and tugged the cloth free. His scarred arms had no strength when he raised them above his head. He jumped again and missed.

"You're mine, Beri," he roared.

Arrizan hellfire may have crippled Hirmin, but it hadn't made him stupid. He rummaged through the jumble of poles and tools behind the door until he found a long-handled scythe. The blade was too rusted to threaten grain at harvest time, but it was wicked enough when Berika glimpsed it slicing toward her.

"You'll be sorry you weren't nice to me when you had the chance."

Berika screamed again when he shoved the blade between her hips and the beam.

Dart ran at the cottage door twice before realizing Hirmin had barred the door as well as latching it. Berika continued to scream. With the bar in place, the door was the strongest part of the cottage. The walls were more vulnerable, as was the thatched roof with its neglected, soot-scorched vent.

The whole roof sagged each time Dart shifted his weight or took a step. He was cautious until he reached the vent. Then he tore at the charred straw. He'd already lowered his leg through the hole when he considered that he might be landing in a fire. By then gravity had him and it was too late. The hearth was as cold as Mag herself, and considerably softer.

"Leave her alone!"

Hirmin and Berika were equally dumfounded by the apparition. Hirmin gave one last yank on the scythe. Berika's legs scraped along the beam. She hung by her arms without the strength to lift herself to relative safety. Hirmin could have caught her, if his narrow vision had not been fixed on the hearth.

He feinted with the scythe. "Get out!"

"Do you still want to go to Eyerlon?" Dart shouted.

Berika's arms gave out. She crashed to the ground, but her head came up almost at once. There was only one sensible answer to that question, regardless of who, or what, asked it: "Yes."

"Get the door open."

With Hirmin's attention diverted, Berika made her way to the door, unbarred and unlatched it, and fled into the yard.

Hirmin feinted again. This time the handle struck Dart in the midsection; he retreated, staggering, from the hearth and the ashes. Hirmin cocked his head and squinted. "*You!*" He changed his grip on the scythe. "Weycha's demon. You don't frighten me; I've seen worse than you in hellfire."

Dart dodged Hirmin's swing. He caught the long wood handle and was surprised to find that the maimed man was both strong and agile within his limits. It was impossible to fight the rusty scythe barehanded. Dart looked for another weapon. All the other farm tools were by the door—if he could have reached them he could have escaped without fighting. On his side of the room there were empty shelves, a box-bed, and Mag's thornwood stick.

He grabbed the thornwood stick and tested its balance. As Mag had used the stick—with the heavy knob in her fist—it gave her the strength her legs lacked. With it reversed, the supple staff could be used as a long-handled mace. Dart swung it once and liked the sound it made.

"Give it up, Hirmin. She won't be bound by her mother's promise." Dart made a tentative backhand pass at Hirmin's shoulder as he spoke. The knob glanced off Hirmin's neck. Dart prepared for another, harder strike, but he hadn't reckoned with the sensitivity of hellfire scars.

Hirmin dropped the scythe and bellowed like a gored ox. His fingers hovered over the scar tissue. He could not touch his own flesh or soothe the pain. His good eye was squeezed shut, and it was unlikely he'd hear the end of the world through his groaning.

Dart escaped to the yard, where Berika awaited him.

"Did you kill him?"

Dart threw the cane aside and took her hand. "He's not going anywhere. Come on." He led her up the hill to the bush where he'd left the harp.

"That's not the—"

Another bellow of pain and rage coming from the cottage ended Berika's protest. Hirmin knew she was gone. There was no time for argument: She followed her rescuer.

"He's taken my wife! The demon's taken Berika!"

Dart released Berika and squandered precious moments pawing through the bushes. He lost more time knotting Ingolde's purse through his belt and adjusting the strap of the acorn harp-case. By the time he took Berika's hand again, there were several torches burning in the common and one moving toward their hill. With Horsten's disembodied voice still echoing in the abyss, Dart was confident they could move without being seen; Berika was not.

She knew where the paths were and how the moonlight would fall across them. Horsten was correct in theory, but the shepherd was right about Gorse.

"There they are! On the hill. Heading for the orchard!"

The torches moved en masse. Dart was transfixed. He had expected Ingolde to restrain Hirmin and the others, yet he could hear her voice among the others. She *was* his enemy.

He stood flat-footed as the wrought-up villagers assaulted the hill. A stone that landed only a few feet away finally roused him from his trance. The moonlight that had revealed them revealed the path as well. They ran along the edge of the orchard, and so did their pursuers.

Dart caught Berika's arm again. He led her off the path into the grass. In daylight, the weeds offered no protection. At night, despite the moon, there was a slim chance they would not be seen. Berika struggled to keep up, but her legs ached from clinging to the beam. She was barefoot as well, having left her hose and ill-fitting wood-soled shoes beside the door of her mother's house when she moved the rest of her clothes across the yard to the cottage. She had her cloak, at least, and clutched it tightly around her shoulders. When it snagged on an unseen stalk, she lost her footing on the dew-slicked hill. She tumbled forward with a yelp, taking Dart with her.

"Too late," she gasped, striking Dart with her fist because there was nothing else to hit. "Too late."

Dart gathered her in his arms, not to comfort her but to keep her quiet. "Shh—the torches." He turned her head so she could see. Hirmin held one; Heldey the other. "They think we're still on the path."

"Too late," Berika insisted, much more softly. "Hirmin will find me."

"They can't see us. The grass will cover us all the way to the stream. Just stay low—crawl."

Dart had gone a little way before he realized Berika wasn't behind him. He put her out in front. She tried, but it wasn't long before she collapsed again.

"I can't," she whispered.

He lifted her up. "It's not much farther. Once we're across the stream we'll be safe—"

Berika became deadweight in his arms. "The stream? No . . . I can't cross the stream. Just leave me here. Go. He'll find me. The hellfire guides him."

Dart didn't bother arguing. Berika was heavier than Mag, but endowed with a vital disinclination to be dropped once she realized she was being carried. The stream was low at this time of year; its banks were waist-high above the water. Dart set Berika on her feet momentarily while he jumped down. Berika scrambled beyond his reach.

"I want to go back."

Dart caught the hem of her skirt; he pulled her toward him. "What about Eyerlon?"

"There's nothing for me in Eyerlon."

"The high towers and the wide streets . . . "

"It was a dream. A girl's dream. I must go back."

He could reach Berika's wrist by then, and once he had it, she could not escape. "Hirmin's beaten your body. Has he beaten your spirit? Is that your difference between a girl and a woman—her spirit?"

Berika sniffed once, then lapsed into quaking sobs. Dart shifted anxiously. There had been no sign of pursuit since they eluded the torches along the crest of the hill, but they wouldn't be safe on the civilized side of the stream. The despairing girl protested feebly as Dart grappled her into his arms, until she felt the icy water swirling around them. She did not move at all when he set her down on the Weycha-side bank. He carried her into the forest.

The moonlight did not penetrate to the forest floor, and Dart's eyes were no better than another man's in the darkness. The sharp tines of invisible branches scratched them both. Roots looped out of the fallen leaves, fruits, and branches to catch Dart's feet.

My lady—where is a good place? He repeated Ingolde's question this time for himself. *We need shelter.*

Dart listened. He heard Berika shivering, and put that behind him. He heard the bone-crackle of an owl eating dinner, and set that aside. He heard the air in his lungs and blood pulsing through his heart. He heard the sound of moonlight slipping through the branches, and finally, the slow beat of a goddess's heart.

My lady?

Weycha did not rouse from her winter sleep, but she did answer. Her presence lured Dart through the undergrowth to a great fir tree whose roots reached her heart and whose dense branches made a clearing in which nothing else grew. The tang of resin promised safety—even to tired, sore, and frightened Berika.

She shook the water from the oiled wool of her cloak. "He won't come this far by night," she said as she spread the woven fabric over a pine-needle mattress. Berika's cloak was impervious to any foul weather; it would last her lifetime and beyond. She folded it around her, as her shepherd father had taught her, to make a nest large enough for two.

Dart, who had his heeled boots but no cloak, was grateful. He pulled the corners in behind him and was asleep before he was warm. He dreamed no dreams, but woke suddenly with every muscle tense. Berika's head rested comfortably on his shoulder; whatever roused him had not destroyed her rest. He raised his head through the folds of the cloak. The stars were gone; the sky was a misty purple and the forest was utterly quiet.

There was no guessing what had awakened him, and no hope at all of going back to sleep.

Berika opened her eyes as Dart eased out of the cloak. He

brushed his hand across her brow, gently closing her eyes. "Go back to sleep. It's nothing."

She struggled weakly. "He's coming. . . ."

"Go back to sleep." He folded the cloak over her.

It was just her fear of Hirmin, Dart told himself, and did not waste time listening. He stretched the damp from his limbs. He was ready when a flock of birds rose noisily from their night roost.

The long-handled scythe had been Hirmin's weapon of choice since he was tall enough to swing it. He carried it to war. He used it as a crutch when he came home the last time. It had grown rusty in recent years, but during the night he'd honed the rust away.

Dart left the clearing to meet him. "You cannot possess by right or property what was never freely given," he told the disfigured man.

Hirmin hawked; the spittle struck Dart's shirt. "That for your demon's eyes and noblefolk tongue. Run, or die where you stand."

Dart did not run. He dodged as he had in the cottage. He had agility and speed, but nothing—not even a thornwood staff—for a weapon. He feinted into the brush, hoping the branches would slow the curved blade enough for him to get inside its sweep. But the scythe was meant for cutting brush. The blade ripped through the twigs and along the length of Dart's forearm.

Weycha's champion yelped, then beat a retreat. The sound awakened Berika, who screamed hysterically when she saw the two men. Hirmin dropped into a smiling, bowlegged straddle; Dart was distracted between his injury and Berika's terror. He barely avoided Hirmin's next slice.

Away from the tree. Away from the girl. Over here.

A third distraction—at a time when he needed none—erupted in Dart's mind. He looked over his shoulder and lost his balance. With his bloody arm tucked against his waist, he turned his fall into a rolling dive, and once again, eluded Hirmin's scythe.

Over here. Here. Take my heart.

Flat on his back, Dart was looking out for Hirmin when he saw the ancient skeleton tree. He rolled again and scrambled to his feet. Dart was faster than Hirmin, but Hirmin might not follow—not while Berika was helpless with terror. It was a chance he had to take.

Take my heart, my love!

Weycha's commands booming within Dart's skull might kill

him faster than Hirmin's scythe. She took control of him and drew his injured arm away from his body, toward the tree— Into the tree—

The *basi* of a goddess flowed through the tree, into her champion. The sensation went beyond fire or ice, beyond any mortal pain. It eclipsed Dart's strength and swallowed the tree. It reached out for Hirmin and flung him into the air. Fifty paces away, Berika stopped crying and covered her eyes.

Dart's heart stopped . . . and started. The pain was gone, his strength returned. He raised his arm above his head, brandishing a sword that glimmered with life and light.

He was outside of time, with his lady, and with the weapon she made for him. The sword balanced perfectly in his hand, awakening countless memories in the darkness. Dart leaped for joy: Weycha's weapon, his lady's gift, a sword, a missing piece of himself. He landed on the balls of his feet, laid one hand above the other on the roughened hilt, and advanced toward Hirmin.

The shock wave passed. Berika peeked between her fingers. The tree was gone—or was it? Was that a tree looming over Hirmin? She blinked, and lowered her hands in time to see Dart bring his strange sword down on her husband's neck. It was over between two beats of her heart: A seething crimson blade sliced easily through flesh and bone. Hirmin's head struck the ground before his body tumbled.

She couldn't see Dart's face—and for that small mercy Berika was thankful.

The rule of time restored itself. Berika saw blood spraying from the blade as her protector swung it clean. The weapon was etched into her memory. It was wood, and that, all things taken into consideration, was no surprise. The blade was a deep burnished red: heartwood, seething *basi*. The hilt was dark and mottled like bark.

Bile flooded Berika's throat. She gagged and gasped. Dart turned slowly toward her. He didn't look any different—the same open regular features, shaggy, parti-colored hair, stubbled chin, and eyes that seemed, at this distance, completely ordinary. He smiled and came toward her.

"Are you all right? The tree . . . Are you hurt?"

Berika buried her face in her apron.

"Are you frightened? Don't be afraid. The sword is my lady's gift. There is nothing you should fear."

Dart touched her hair. He knelt beside her. He forgot about the sword. The blade glanced off Berika's shoulder.

"Please don't kill me," she whimpered, extending her arms in submission.

She collapsed as the blade skidded harmlessly down her back.

CHAPTER

— 10 —

"Give me your hand—"

Berika stared dully at her companion. Then, disdaining his help, she scrabbled up the crumbling slope in the boots she'd reluctantly taken from her rightful husband's corpse. Dart's extended arm drifted to his shirt, where it twisted the cloth covering his breast. He could not breach the wall Berika held around herself. She chose their path; set their pace. She accepted that he walked with her, but would not speak to him. Frustration and despair simmered in Dart's mind, but the pain grew from his heart.

They walked east, which Dart understood was the proper direction for Eyerlon. They broke through fields that had been fallow since the terrible defeat at Kasserine, where four thousand Walenfolk men died in a single morning. They passed croft-cottages that were roofless and vine-covered. Dart expected they'd come to a path as clear as the one which meandered east from the fane in Gorse, but the only trails he saw were made by deer and led back to the forest stream they'd waded at noon.

Midway through the afternoon Berika marched through the overgrown yard of another abandoned croft. Dart saw the ruin of a path beyond the southern wall. He called it to Berika's attention.

She acknowledged the path with a grunt, but she kept to her own course. Dart had no choice but to follow her.

The afternoon had been warm, but as the sunlight turned ruddy, the air cooled. When Dart saw a hill rising above the fallow fields, and considered the vantage it would offer, he resolved to climb it with her or without her. At the very least, they must find shelter from the night frost. Berika climbed behind him, sullen and silent.

If nothing better presented itself, they'd be wisest to return to the abandoned croft, but something better did present itself. Eastward of the hill, fields had been plowed for the winter planting, and a bare-ground track ran through them to jumbled rooftops: the market town of Flayne.

"We would not have seen it otherwise. You didn't mean for us to find shelter and food in Flayne, did you?" Dart's tone was that of a child betrayed by its parents.

Berika stiffened as if she'd become part of the stone on which she sat.

"Speak to me, Berika. Tell me what's wrong."

Silence.

Dart raked his hair. "Would you rather that Hirmin had killed me? Or you?"

"No."

"Then, what? What have I done that I ought not to have done? What should I have done differently?" Dart had asked these questions many times already; he did not wait for an answer. "I dug his grave and made a circle for him, as Ingolde did for Auld Mag. I covered the grave with pine boughs and weighted them with stones. What more than that—or was that too much? Should I have left him to rot?"

Berika shuddered. "You struck his head *off*! Your *sword* shone like a bloody sun. You're everything he said you were. Everything Heldey said."

"I—I—" he stammered. His hair became more disordered as he sought the proper words. "When the sword came to my hand . . . I *knew* it was my sword to protect my lady and you. Something flowed back into me. Not memory. Something else."

"Something came out of you," Berika corrected harshly. "You showed another shape: your true shape, a demon's shape."

"I did not."

"You did. Just like the first time I saw you, on the other side of the stream, when I thought you were covered with glowing leaves.

Only this time there were no leaves, only dark, twisted branches. A demon's skeleton: filled with *basi* and cursed!"

Dart reached but did not touch her. "Berika . . . look at me." His skin tingled. He could compel Berika to turn; the power existed within him. He had only to move his fingertips to confirm Berika's accusation and fear. Instead he made a tight fist and hid the fist behind his back. "I am a man, Berika—always a man. What I have been given by my lady, I only use for you, never against you."

" 'Pray for others, not yourself. . . . ' " Berika wiped her face with her sleeve. "I never listened. I prayed for myself and you came for me."

"I am not an answer to anyone's prayers," Dart insisted. "My lady prayed for me to be *her* champion against Hazard of Arrizan. If I could not answer my lady's prayers, how could I answer yours? By my own will I shall learn who I am, and then, if I can, I shall champion my lady Weycha, and you. You need never fear me."

Berika stared at the splotches on her patched smock. "I'll never live in a city." Tears rolled off her chin, adding more dark spots to the rust-colored cloth. "All I know is sheep, and who needs a shepherd in a stone-walled city? I can't cook. I can't sew. My spinning's all slubs and gaps—"

"You can sing," Dart interrupted. "You were going to teach me your songs, so I could play while you sang—"

"Not for noblefolk, Dart—just common songs for commonfolk. Noblefolk'd die before they sang a common song."

It occurred to Dart that Berika claimed to know a lot about the noblefolk she also insisted she'd never met, but he kept this insight to himself for the moment. The sun was some three handspans above the horizon. "We can go back to the croft or forward to Flayne, but I think we shall freeze if we stay here. I say we should go on to Flayne."

"Not Flayne," she said, looking away again. "Ingolde will have our names outcast through the Web by now. You murdered my husband, and I'm an adulteress now because I left him and went with you. That's why I've shunned the track and the town."

Her words stirred the abyss with recognition: He knew something of Walensor's law. "I killed Hirmin in self-defense, Berika. That is not murder. And, for the other, if you are so sure I'm not a man, how can there be a question of adultery?"

Berika would not answer. "Not Flayne," she repeated. "There's an Eyerlon sorcerer in Flayne who'll be waiting for us. Ingolde will make sure of it."

Dart shrugged. His shoulders and back ached from carrying the acorn and the sword. He had no interest in another night on the cold, hard ground, and could not imagine that Berika, whose bruises were much worse, truly desired it either. "You know Ingolde best, Berika," he said with deceptive meekness. "But I cannot imagine Ingolde admitting to the Web and the world that she'd lost a daughter, a son-in-law, and a demon in one night unless she were forced—and I cannot imagine anyone in Gorse with the will to force her. I think we may go where we like, so long as we do not go back there. So—let us spend the night in Flayne rather than a roofless crofter's cottage."

The truth pierced Berika's heart. No one in Gorse would go looking for trouble. She was as free as she'd ever dreamed, and freedom was empty, not exhilarating. She followed Dart down the slope.

Berika was a clever girl—too clever by half, Ingolde said. The spinning her hands could not do well was wonderfully done by her mind. Before they reached the rutted track she spun the warp of a new fantasy: the exiled shepherd fated to travel with a shape-shifting demon. It held enough truth to make it strong, enough romance to keep the emptiness at bay.

"Teach me a song," Dart requested, once they were walking again.

Berika obliged with a morbid ballad about doomed lovers. He cut her off before she sang the refrain.

"No one will offer us hot food or a place by the hearth with that. Larsov sang about a widow and a big iron pot. That's the one I would learn."

The shepherd's cheeks flamed. "I can't sing *that*."

"You won't have to after you teach me the words."

Berika's fantasy required a melancholy, doomed demon, not one who was as insufferably practical as her mother. She began off-key and without rhythm. Dart found the proper melody despite her. By the third verse, he was whistling, and by the fifth, Berika was singing at the top of her lungs.

The track became a high-crown road after one from the south merged with it. The road became wide enough for two wagons. In the afternoon, however, Dart and Berika had it to themselves, save for the dung collector and his donkey.

Flayne was a small town, as the market towns of prosperous Fenklare were measured, but several times the size of Gorse. Though Berika came to Flayne at least once a season, she had never been on its streets after sunset. No wonder, then, that the shepherd-girl pared the distance between herself and Dart— demon and murderer though he might be. No wonder that nothing seemed familiar and she was lost once the gate disappeared from view.

By the week of Lesser Gleaning, Walensor's nights were much longer than its days. Commonfolk worked until sunset, when they closed their doors, shuttered their windows, and ate their suppers by lamplight. Amber glows leaked from every covered window, but only one door was open and beckoning strangers.

"It's a hostelry—I think," Berika said.

"The White Ram—Do you know it? Will I be able to play for our meal, or will we have to pay for it?"

Berika saw the signboard above the lintel. She would have guessed the name to be The Ram's Head, since that was the only part of the animal the artist had emblazoned on the wood. She noticed the angular scrawls above the horns. Writing—as useless a notion as ever came down the road from the cities, and an utter mystery to the likes of her.

But not, apparently, to Dart.

Ingolde could have told her innocent daughter that *all* noblefolk knew their letters and their numbers, too. How else did they know how many silver flakes to wring from each common household? Then, if the mood were right, Ingolde might have whispered that noblefolk and merchants invented writing so they need not entrust their secrets to the Web—and all their kind had secrets. But Ingolde was not there, and Berika had only a moment's wonder before Dart brushed aside the leather curtain with the calm assurance of a nobleman, or a fool.

The hall of the White Ram was crowded and noisy. The air was thick with smoke from the hanging lamps and the fireplace where two huge pots steamed on their hooks. Berika clutched her heavy cloak and refused to take another step.

"Where is the best place for me to play and sing?" Dart asked, assuming this was the reason she stood gaping just inside the door.

Silencing her companion with a dark stare, Berika scurried to a bench—empty because it caught the draft every time the curtain shifted—and strove to make them both invisible. She succeeded only too well. The girl with the pitcher of ale and a fistful of mugs took no notice of them, nor did the lad with the coarse trencher loaves.

Dart's gut growled mournfully; Berika's betrayed her by replying in harmony. Neither of them had eaten since Mag's funeral feast. When the hosteler lifted one of the kettles from its hook and his wife began to ladle out the thick stew, Dart lost patience with his guide.

"Everyone else is eating; no one's singing. What must we do to change this?"

But before Berika could admit that she did not know, the lad with the bread appeared before them. "Have you come from Tremontin?"

The Arrizan war had ended at Tremontin. The princes of Walensor and their sorcerers brought the mountains of Tremontin down upon Hazard's army, destroying it. Had enough time passed to disperse Walensor's victorious army back across the kingdom?

Walensor's commonfolk soldiers mustered in their everyday clothes. Berika could not tell if the hall was filled with townsfolk or soldiers. A surge of panic kept her voice bottled in her throat.

"We lagged behind a bit," Dart answered cautiously when he realized Berika was mute.

The lad saw the sword rising above Dart's left shoulder. In the uneven light, it was simply a sword. No one carried a wooden sword, and only men of some importance carried swords at all. "Did you see Prince Rinchen and Prince Alegshorn?" he asked eagerly. "What was it like when the Arrizi were crushed?"

A battlefield rose from the abyss. It had no name, and was certainly not Tremontin—but Dart had been there. He saw himself holding a gore-caked steel sword. "Carnage," he said with a grimace. "Carnage everywhere."

The lad was surprised. "Everyone else says they didn't see nothing. When the dust cleared, the whole Arrizi army was *gone*—buried at the bottom of the pass.

The mangled corpses in his mind's eye became splintering trees—and he was there, in Tremontin, as each of them died, as his lady set him free with the commandment to be her champion and protector. Dart began to tremble, and that freed Berika from her paralysis. She remembered what she herself had seen when Auld Mag fell from the Web.

"The ground shook and the sky turned dark. The thunder was loud enough to make your belly shake." She guessed right about the ground and the noise, but Tremontin fell at midnight and the sky was already dark.

"It was carnage enough—if you happened to be one of Weycha's shattered trees," Berika concluded. The words tingled in her ears. Notions came together like lightning: What if Weycha were right? What if the Pyromant Hazard had not been crushed with his army? What if the war was not over? What if Dart, with his wooden sword, were truly a champion?

The serving lad was not convinced that a carnage of trees was the same as a carnage of men, but he was satisfied that the strangers came from Tremontin. "Did you see the princes?"

"We'll sing and play of it," Dart replied, "to pay for our supper."

"No need tonight. My mother's so glad to have the war over and our Alf back safe, she says she'll feed the whole army."

Soldiers had a nose for a free meal—which accounted for the crowd. Dart accepted the bread and broke it open. The boy continued around the room.

Dart held out the bread to Berika and pointed to the hearth where the stew was being served.

"I can't go up there," Berika hissed, refusing to take it.

"I can't *get* there with all this bound around my shoulder."

"There might be someone from Gorse. Coming home, recognizing me, and asking questions . . ."

Dart sighed and piled his belongings on the bench. Even without the sword or harp to distinguish him, his manner was different from the other, common men in the hall. The mistress smiled when she saw him with the trencher in his hands. She swirled her ladle through the pot, giving him a portion that was more meat than dark gravy.

"I haven't seen a meal this meaty in . . . in I don't know how long," Dart said with such sincerity that the mistress crowned his trencher with a thick, shining slab of fatback bacon. Ingolde's meals were larger, but red meat—salted, smoked, or fresh—was rarely served.

Dart came back to the bench with a smile and a bit of a swagger. He tried to catch Berika's eye, but she had her shoulders hunched and her face hidden. For a moment Dart thought he'd shamed her and Ingolde with his appetite. Then he realized she'd draped her cloak over the harp case and the sword.

"Have you recognized someone?" he whispered as he mimicked her posture on the bench.

"Worse."

She jabbed her bread into the stew. Hot gravy splashed onto Dart's breeches. The hollow bread wobbled on his lap.

"What could be worse?" His fingers pinched her wrist.

"We're being watched," she snarled, twisting free and taking the bacon as reparations.

She did not intend to tell her companion *how* she knew—not after his explosion in the forest. There was no guessing what her demon might do if he knew someone in the hall had kenned his sword and harp with sorcery.

Not a mere hedge-sorcerer, either, but an Eyerlon sorcerer with *basi* to spare. Dart's belongings reeked *basi*, the blood red wooden sword even more than the harp. Berika could feel them herself. She didn't want to think what an Eyerlon sorcerer might feel, nor was she certain her woolen cloak hid anything at all. But she had to try, just as she had to try to keep her thoughts contained, and her eyes—the portals to her soul—downcast.

Unfortunately, Berika didn't tell Dart to do the same. He didn't know about kenning, but he did it instinctively. There were a dozen men sitting at a nearby table; one looked up from his meal as Dart examined the room. He was a youngish man with mud-colored hair and a sparse beard. He met Dart's stare for a moment, then went back to his meal.

Dart scarcely tasted the meat and vegetables he gulped down. Something about the mud-haired man set the abyss churning. Dart threw everything into the blackness with a question attached. A joke made the rounds at the large table; the mud-haired man laughed. A glint of silver winked at the nape of his neck and was gone again.

Dart recognized the silver as a torque filled with Brightwater.

"A sorcerer. Berika, we've found a sorcerer! I'll tell him what's happened to me—what I think happened to me. Maybe he'll help me find out who I am and what I must do to uphold my oath."

Berika shook her head sadly, afraid to say that after what she'd seen in the forest, no one, especially a sorcerer, should know what happened to Dart. Maybe when—if—they got to Eyerlon, where the basilidans of Walensor's various gods kept their sacrams, they could seek help from a magga-sorcerer, but not in Flayne. She was still shaking her head when a shadow fell across her lap.

"You're strangers here, aren't you?"

With the sorcerer smiling in front of her, Berika held her breath and prayers lest he ken them. Dart suspected nothing. "We've just arrived from Tremontin." Tremontin, after all, had just gotten them a more than decent meal.

"Were you with the Mareshal and our Donitor?"

Berika dared to look at the sorcerer's face. *Everyone*, even a shepherd from Gorse, knew you could serve Walensor and King Manal with Ean sorMeklan, Donitor of Fenklare, or Jemat sorLewel, the king's Mareshal—but never with them both because there was blood feud between their families. Everyone except Dart, though his answer was less deadly than it might have been.

"We were not far from them, and the princes, when Tremontin fell and the trees died."

The sorcerer nodded thoughtfully. Berika noted that his glance, when it wasn't fixed on Dart, was drawn to her cloak and what it covered.

"Yagrin," the sorcerer announced, thrusting his hands forward in a formal greeting.

Berika thought she might faint as her demon calmly placed his hands between the sorcerer's as if he'd performed the ritual a thousand times before and had no fear of it.

"Dart."

"Dart? That's an uncommon name hereabout. Are you from Fenklare?" Yagrin smiled as Dart's hands closed over his.

Invisible wisps of spider silk brushed Dart's cheek and wrapped around his thoughts. He cocked his head, remembering how Ingolde had tried to constrain his will with a similar cobweb. The cobweb weakened but did not break when he shrugged his mind. Dart was not surprised: Yagrin wore a sorcerer's torque, Ingolde did not. "My lady beside me is from Gorse."

Yagrin looked at Berika's patched, homespun clothes, the toes of Hirmin's huge boots sticking out beneath her skirt. He said nothing, but Berika blushed all the same; a common shepherd was no one's lady.

"May I do something for you?" Yagrin asked.

"We're on our way to see the basilidans of Eyerlon," Dart

replied, not recalling that all routes between Tremontin and Flayne would have funneled through Eyerlon.

Berika's groan was lost as Yagrin repeated the word: Eyerlon. "Come with me to my sacram in the fane. I'll let Eyerlon know you're coming." The sorcerer allowed Dart to rise. He took Berika's cloak and held it for her, as if she were the lady they both knew she was not. "That is an unusual sword you have there," he said to Dart. The heavy material fell unevenly over Berika's shoulders. "As unusual as your name . . ."

Berika distrusted the smiling sorcerer, but her upbringing in Ingolde's house prohibited her from leaving a meat-laced meal behind. Dart and Yagrin got ahead of her as she wrestled the sopping bread into her scrip. If her suspicions proved true, cold greasy morsels might be more valuable than time. Then as the leather curtain in the doorway slid off her back, she saw Yagrin examining the wooden sword in moonlight.

"A wonder and a marvel," the sorcerer whispered. He ran his fingers lightly along the blade.

Cut off his fingers—Berika prayed, but the dark red wood had no edge in the moonlight.

"Who is your lady, and where did your lady get this?"

A sorcerous imperative tightened around Dart's throat, commanding him to answer Yagrin's questions. He yielded to it—he had nothing to hide, nothing to be ashamed of—but Weycha's imperatives were much stronger and the goddess had lost her trust of Walenfolk sorcery. Dart's tongue could form no words. His breath came in explosive, incomprehensible gasps, and for a moment Berika thought he might faint as he had when she first asked his name in the meadow by Weycha's stream, but he mastered himself. "I may not speak of that," he explained, wiping saliva and sweat from his lip. "She is my lady and I have sworn to protect her."

He reached for his sword; Yagrin retreated, holding the sword crosswise in front of him like a fighting stick. Puzzled, but not yet angered, Dart advanced. Yagrin changed his stance from guard to threat. For a moment no one moved, giving Berika time to wonder what would happen if Dart took his demon shape while someone else held his sword.

Luck was on the shepherd's side for once. Another shepherd had left a crook leaning against the hostelry wall. Berika was not foolish enough to use it against the wooden sword—she knew it had an edge somewhere. Instead she swung the borrowed crook into the cleft between the sorcerer's neck and skull with all her might. Yagrin crumpled silently to the ground.

"Was that necessary?"

"If you want to keep your damned sword it is." Berika hesitated, then put the crook back where she found it. "Pick it up and let's get out of here."

"Why?" Dart asked, all innocence and ordinary eyes. "He was a sorcerer. We were looking for a sorcerer."

"Dart, he wasn't going to give it back to you. If you'd gone with him to the sacrum, he'd have drawn upon the Web's power to force you into your demon shape and keep you prisoner until Eyerlon decided what should be done with you."

"I don't have a demon shape, Berika," Dart countered, sliding the sword into the sling he'd improvised from Hirmin's belt. "I've done nothing wrong. My enemy is Hazard, not Eyerlon. I have nothing to hide from any sorcerer. I could not let him *keep* my sword—"

"That's what I was afraid of." Berika tugged on his sleeve. "Come on, we don't have time to argue. Do you have any idea what would happen to us if you cut off a sorcerer's head the way you cut off Hirmin's?"

Dart shrugged. "Is that worse than killing a sorcerer with a shepherd's crook?"

Berika's reply was a grumble from the back of her throat. She hadn't killed Yagrin, at least she hoped he was still alive, but this was no time to argue the finer points of law. She let go of Dart's sleeve and started running, not particularly caring if he followed or not.

CHAPTER

11

Fear kept Berika moving along the King's Road out of Flayne until long after midnight. The fear had less to do with Yagrin than with the alarm he was certain to send through the Web as soon as his head cleared. Berika wanted to believe that Yagrin remained alive. The murder of a man or woman whose *basi* did not reach the Web was a crime under the king's justice; the punishment was execution on the gallows. But he, or she, who murdered a sorcerer stood before a tribunal in Eyerlon and faced a punishment that transcended death. The thought of losing her *basi* and her soul was so horrible that Berika convinced herself that Yagrin was in his sacram filling the Web with the images of his attackers.

Each time they paused to rest, Berika stared at the stars, the silver-velvet clouds, and the invisible fibers of the Web. Then she'd raise the cowl of her cloak and pace until Dart was ready to move again.

She was, in fact, as invisible to the Web as it was to her. The Web spun thought from one mind to another, not images which, though they could be placed in the Web, were generally too complex and individual to be retrieved. Yet the Web *was* in the night sky above them. The greatest sorcerers could see its shadow on the brightest day. The least hedge-sorcerer was an integral part of it. And to live in fear of it was the loneliest exile Berika could imagine.

"Since we struck down Yagrin, we cannot expect another sorcerer to help us, can we?" Dart generously did not say who struck him down.

Berika continued her pacing, which was answer enough.

"Should we surrender? Should we go back to Gorse?"

Berika turned toward him, though her face, and expression, remained hidden in the cowl. "That's the last place we can go. If Ingolde *didn't* outcast us, she's in trouble now. And if she did, no one in Gorse would risk helping us or hiding us."

"Surrender, then?"

"I don't know."

Dart weighed the despair and bitterness in Berika's voice. The determined young woman who wanted to take his harp to Eyerlon by herself had become a frightened, stubborn child who knew no more about the larger world of Walensor than he remembered. Indeed, circumstances were proving that he knew much more than she, for all that his knowledge was hidden in the abyss of his past.

"We'll keep on our way then—We'll find the road from Flayne and follow it until we get to Eyerlon. All roads lead to Eyerlon, sooner or later, I guess."

"Not the road."

"Yes, the road. I'd go back to Flayne and beg for justice—except, as I think about it—you were right about Yagrin. He wasn't Hazard, but I was wrong to trust him, doubly wrong to let him hold my lady's sword. I won't make that mistake again."

"We're outcast from the Web," Berika said despairingly. "All Walensor knows what we've done. We'll be recognized. There's no place for us to hide. No place to go."

"Gently, Berika. If Walensor knows anything, it knows that a woman with a shepherd's stick struck a sorcerer senseless, and that she's travelling with a simple-sorted man carrying a wooden sword. If we are not seen with a crook or the sword, no one will recognize us."

Berika's shoulders sagged. "Will you leave that sword behind?" She could almost accept being outcast if it separated her from that *basi*-ridden wooden sword.

"No. But we won't be seen with it. Until I find something better, I'll keep it wrapped inside your cloak. When we come upon an inn or charterhouse, I'll hide it before we enter. I think it will be safe enough; and we will be safer without it to draw attention."

She wanted to say that nothing could hide *that* sword, but such a statement merely strengthened his argument. It was the wooden sword that caught Yagrin's attention, not Dart. Dart was, as he claimed, a simple-sorted man, not at all interesting until he started talking.

"What about the harp? I can feel it; so could any sorcerer. You'll have to hide it too—"

"What about 'playing for our supper'?"

"That won't work. The harp reeks *basi*; it's almost as bad as that sword. Just seeing the acorn would tell anyone it's not natural, and there'd be questions. We'll work in the stables, or steal—or starve, which is the most likely turn."

Dart chafed his arms and got to his feet. "We might freeze first." His breath was the same color as the fast-moving clouds.

The moon was nearly full and surrounded with a silvery winter's crown. Dart appeared ignorant of the crown's significance, and the shepherd did not tell him snow was likely. She could pad Hirmin's boots with straw, but Dart, without a decent cloak to keep him warm and dry, would freeze for certain. Assuming he was, as he claimed, a man and vulnerable to death.

A cold, heavy wind came up the valley to confirm Berika's dire thoughts. Clouds were gathering on the northern horizon where winter was always born. Wisps of hair escaped from her braids; they whipped across her cheeks and stuck to her eyelashes. The air smelled of snow, ice, and winter. She could almost hear her father's voice telling her to bring the flock in quickly, or make a shelter where she stood.

The shepherd surveyed her surroundings, seeking a refuge for herself and her companion, who, for the moment, she would accept as a man. The best of a poor choosing was a tumbled haystack at the edge of a field.

"That's as good a place as we'll find."

Dart affected a stiff, shoulders-up walk to mask his shivering. He reached the haystack before she did. He could smell the rot and the musk of the vermin who had already claimed it as their den. Without complaint, he began making a deeper nest in the leeward side.

"Watch yourself," Berika cautioned when she saw him haul an

armful of straw while she gathered smaller amounts with greater care. "You'll get yourself bit."

The sheaf fell to the ground when Dart considered the possibility. Then, with the barest sigh, he retrieved it. The moon was hidden and the field pitch-dark before they completed their crude bowl shelter. Wind and sleet pelted all around them, but snug in their hollow, beneath Berika's ample cloak, the travellers were dry and growing warmer. Neither Dart nor Berika spoke, though each knew the other was wide-awake and listening to the crackling of the straw around them.

Fenklare was not quite ready for winter. The sleet melted as it touched the ground. Berika removed a chunk of cold, greasy bread from her scrip. She placed half in her companion's hand. Dart whispered his thanks and put the whole thing in his mouth.

"No sense wasting good food," Berika said, letting her tone of voice remind him that he had not given the matter a single thought, and that he was foolish for swallowing the bread in one gulp.

Dart was chastened, but it was too late to do anything except lick his fingers thoroughly while Berika made a lengthy meal from her portion. A twig snapped; they both jumped, but the sound was not repeated.

"What sort of man would come along our way on a night like this?" Dart asked. He meant the question lightly, but the answers he gave to his own question were dark enough. "Outcasts, criminals, and fugitives like ourselves."

Berika was silent. Dart assumed that she agreed with him.

"We dreamed of going to Eyerlon," he said, "but we're off to a poor start for getting there."

"I should have stopped while I was only dreaming," she replied. "That was bad enough. I should have known better. I did know better. I told you I shouldn't leave Gorse, that I didn't belong anywhere else. But I stole you from a goddess; you're a demon in your heart. I couldn't resist a goddess's pet demon."

That stung more than all the sleet around them. "I am not a demon." His usually calm manner was rough at the edges. "No one stole me or fetched me—not you or anyone else."

"I prayed to all the gods in the Web to get me out of the rest of my life. When I opened my eyes, there you were. And you have gotten me out of the rest of my life. Your eyes glow. You admit you were in the forest with Weycha. She's given you a motherwood harp and a motherwood sword. What are you, if you're not a demon?"

"I am a man." This time Dart could not assume Berika's silence meant agreement. "My lady chose me to be her champion. She said my memory was already gone when she found me. She said I was nothing before she made me her champion—nothing but a man. Ingolde knew that, even after she saw my eyes."

"Ingolde never saw the sword; never saw what you did with it. You're no man, Dart. If you're not a demon, you're something worse. And you're the end of my world, either way."

Dart conceded defeat. "As you wish—but I was born a man, whether I remember it or not. I have scars, Berika. Why would a demon have scars? My lady chose me to be her champion—I do not know how, or why, or when, or where—"

He drew his breath in, and forgot to let it go. Another night grew in his memory, taking shape without the signal fire of recognition. Another night as dark and miserable as this one, when the air was raw and the rain was close to freezing. He remembered being cold to the bone, and cowed like a whipped dog. Then memory and reality joined together.

Berika felt him shiver beside her and knew instinctively that he was more than cold. "Dart? Dart? Don't change on me. Please, all the gods—your lady—don't turn him into a demon." Berika found the edge of the cloak and crawled into the rain.

"It was a night like this," he remembered aloud. "I don't know why I was outside—I must've been drunk or gotten lost. I started out on a horse—but I fell off, or got thrown, or both—and I kept going on foot, on my hands and knees. I knew I was going the wrong way, but I kept going until I could go no farther. Then Weycha found me. My lady. She took me to her home. I think I would have gladly stayed with her forever, but she made me her champion and sent me out to do her battles."

The rain striking Berika's face was icy and irrelevant. Dart was a demon, she frantically reminded herself. He was Weycha's fetch and could not be a man no matter what he remembered, no matter how sincere his raspy voice sounded, no matter how much his tale matched her own idylls of saving a dying nobleman who rewarded her with love, devotion, and a fine home far from Gorse and the sheep. Of course, she daydreamed of rescuing a prince—one of King Manal's grandsons, Rinchen or Alegshorn—and she would never have sent him away. Those imperfections aside, the shepherd realized, Dart's memories were nothing more or less than her own daydreams.

"No lady would do that." Berika chose her words with great precision. She did not want to lie. "No true lady could. But in a dream, Dart, anything can happen. In my dream. You have no memory because you were nothing at all until I put my dreams in the Web and fetched you."

"My lady is not your dream. She gave me the harp, not you, and the sword . . ."

There was no denying that the harp and sword were real, but Berika was serenely certain she understood what had happened. "What does your lady look like? Whose face does she wear? Doesn't she have *my* face?" She clenched her fist with her fingernails digging into her palm. "Whose face, Dart? Whose name? Any name. Your own name, if you're a man."

Berika heard Dart's breath grow shallow and rapid, as it had the other time when she'd demanded his name. Her fist was throbbing. She straightened her fingers and the pain ebbed. Unfamiliar compassion entered into Berika's thoughts: Dart was her fetch; she was responsible for his pain—not the other way around. She became aware of her soaked smock and the cold hair plastered against her face. Water enhanced all sorcery, and she'd broken so many laws already, another would scarcely weigh against her.

Demon fetch—my dream demon fetch. Go back where you came.

She shaped an invisible ball with her damp hands and tossed it over her head.

Go back where you came. It's my fault, not yours. Go back. Back. Back, back, back . . .

She felt nothing. She made another invisible ball and threw it with all her might. She put barbs on her thoughts and shot them at the imaginary ball. Nothing changed. The rain was rain, and Dart still labored for each shallow breath.

Am I going to have this thing—*this muddle-minded, stolen fetch attached to me for the rest of my life?*

That was the sort of impulsive thought that had gotten Berika in trouble in the first place. She tried to take it back. She tossed apologies like a marketday juggler, but they were worse than nothing. In her mind's eye, Berika saw herself become the stupid, godless, wall-eyed sheep and Dart become the shepherd. Shame held her for an instant, then left her limp.

"You're soaked through and freezing," she heard Dart say.

Berika hadn't felt the cold until Dart touched her; then she shivered violently. He pulled her under the cloak. It was neither warm enough nor dry enough; Dart held her tightly against his chest. The shame and shivering began to fade.

She closed her eyes and filled her lungs with the scent of safety. Commonfolk slept two, three, and four to a bed without much regard for age or gender, but there was little intimacy and less gentleness among them. If the warm touch of Dart's breath against her cheek reminded Berika of anything, it reminded her of an infant in its mother's arms, not of love, and certainly not of a woman and a man. Hirmin was worse than most men, with his leering and pawing, but not unlike them.

Nothing felt amiss when Dart kneaded the knotted muscles at the base of her neck. Nothing pleasant could trigger the revulsion Berika felt when Hirmin tore at her clothes. She was not aware that his lips brushed against her cheek until they pressed hard against her own, and even then she rallied slowly.

She caught his wrist, but did not push it away. She opened her mouth, but no rage burst out. The reflexes she had cultivated since her eyes perceived the power a man had over a common woman's life failed her. Worse, they betrayed her. Only the persistent belief that the arms around her belonged to a demon, not a man, gave her the strength to resist.

Berika knew she escaped because he allowed it.

"There's nothing to be afraid of," Dart assured her. He kissed each finger clinging to his wrist. Holding her was like holding the wooden sword: a skill honed by unrecalled practice until it was instinct, not memory.

"No," Berika whispered, not entirely certain herself what she meant.

"I'm not like Hirmin, or any of the others."

"No."

There *were* no others, only Hirmin. No other man had challenged Hirmin's right to a snarly, sour girl when there were willing lasses all around. They joked that Berika had her mother's taste, and laughed until she blushed or cried. Ingolde had told her daughter that love was the enemy of a woman's happiness and that a nobleman was the deadliest enemy of all, but Berika cherished her dreams. Then Hirmin came home, scarred in body and soul, and the dreams soured.

"No. I know what men do to women, and what comes of it. I would have chosen the chaste life of a beguine—but King Manal has closed the beguinages. I don't need a man and I've learned to live without love. I don't need a demon-lover for anything."

Berika's tone was not entirely convincing, but Dart twisted his hand free and swept his hair from his face with a loud sigh. He rolled onto his back, allowing a shaft of cold, damp air to come between them. "For the last time, Berika, I don't know why I can't remember my name or anything about myself. But *my* lady chose me because I was a man. We pleased each other well, and not at all chastely. By that, if nothing else, we can both know I cannot have been fetched, stolen, or called in any way from *your* dreams."

The earlier dreams—the idylls before Berika lost her private war with her betrothed—were not so pure, chaste, and bitter as the later one. If those old dreams could be reawakened, in any small way, this was the moment. Taking care to disturb neither the silence nor the drape of the cloak, Berika slid her hand toward him.

That would be twice as foolish. Such wisdom as Berika acquired in her nearly seventeen years spoke with a stern, disapproving voice. She cringed and confined her hand between her breasts.

What should I do?

Ingolde—the real Ingolde who had risked everything for her noble lover—could have told her daughter what to do, but that Ingolde was not the voice of her daughter's conscience. In the absence of anything she could recognize as an answer, Berika drew a familiar conclusion: She did not know what to do because she already had what she deserved. Her heart ached enough to squeeze a few hot, bitter tears from her eyes. Then it, and everything else, was numb again.

CHAPTER
—— 12 ——

The sleet and rain stopped before dawn, though lead-colored clouds obscured the sunrise, promising future storms. Berika's demeanor conveyed the same promise. Dart left her alone. He had the memory of another cold, miserable night to occupy his thoughts as they made their way along the slick trail back to the slightly less treacherous King's Road.

Each image Dart harvested during the previous night grew more recognizable as he pondered it. He had been drunk. He had been in the stews of someplace he could not yet name—but a place larger than Flayne. He knew the stews well, or so it seemed from the rich texture of the memories. Their gaming dens, doxies, and taverns were his former self's favored haunts. He was a city dweller, which made it more difficult to understand how he'd gotten from the stews to the forest beyond Gorse.

"I'll call you Ean from now on."

Berika startled him. He lost his balance and landed painfully on one knee. "Ean?" A face deep in the abyss showed itself for a moment, then faded without becoming a firm part of his memory. "Ean?" The vanished face belonged to Ean; Ean was not a friend. "Why Ean?"

"Dart's not a name. If we don't want to attract attention, you can't call yourself Dart."

"But why Ean? Why not Brayd?" Dart turned his eye inward; nothing floated to the surface of the abyss. "Or Rimp? Or Larsov—?" He gave all the men's names he knew, even Hirmin.

"Because it's a sorMeklan name and this is the Donit of Fenklare and half the commonfolk families think that just maybe they'll have a pinch more luck if they name themselves and their sons after their sorMeklan Donitor and *his* sons. Fenklare's lousy with Benits, Eans and even Driskolt—they're in every village except Gorse, because we've been an assart. No one will think twice if you say your name is Ean. If I had a son, I'd probably name him Ean."

"Benit? Ean? Driskolt?" Dart tried them in his memory; nothing stirred. "What about Horsten? At least I remember that I knew a Horsten once." He knew an Ean, too, but Horsten bore an aura of friendship.

Berika sighed. She took a long step to catch up with him again. "Not in Fenklare. Horsten's a Pennaik name. So are Manal, Rinchen, and Alegshorn." Berika wrinkled her nose. "In Fenklare no one, noble or common, would give a child a Pennaik name. The sorRodions may be the kings and princes of Walensor, but they're Pennaiks, not Walenfolk. You don't want to give yourself a Pennaik name. Safest thing is to name yourself after one of the sorMeklans. The last two Donitors have both been named Ean, so that's the safest of the safe."

"Safer to call myself after some Donitor, but not the king?" Dart was skeptical. Some of these names should have stirred the fire of recognition—unless Berika was, once again, wrong about the ways of the world beyond Gorse.

"Fenklare's older than Walensor. We've always had Donitors, but we didn't have a king until Rodion of Pennaik decided *he* wanted to be one. The Donitors of Fenklare, Arl, Esham, and the other Donits have to answer to the king, but commonfolk answer to their Donitor. In Fenklare that's always been the sorMeklans."

"Fenklare, but not Gorse. You're certain of this, Berika?"

"Not Gorse. Not yet. King Manal protects the Weychawood, and Gorse is a chartered assart in King Manal's gift—in Prince Rinchen's gift, really, 'cause he'll give Gorse to Ean sorMeklan when he gets crowned, and Ean sorMeklan will give us to someone else, until there's a noblefolk lord in Gorse squeezing everything dry. Unless King Manal doesn't die. Any maybe he won't. He's outlived almost everyone already. His son, Prince Vigelan, died at Kasserine—" Berika's voice softened when she thought of Kasserine, where her father lay with the cream of Walensor's ill-prepared army at the bottom of a hellfire lake. "Prince Rinchen's his grandson, so's Prince Alegshorn—"

Since he left the forest Dart had learned that the princes Rinchen and Alegshorn were rivals for their grandfather's throne. Rinchen was less than a year older than Alegshorn; they were both young men in their early twenties. But when Berika added their father's name, Vigelan, to the list, recognition sparked across the abyss. Dart remembered a bold, brilliant young man riding beside him, and he remembered a black-haired, leaky-nosed, sticky-handed toddler riding with him on a spirited grey stallion.

"I should have a horse."

Berika was nonplussed. "A horse? The last thing we need is a horse. I tell you that Gorse has it easier 'cause we don't pay sorMeklan's taxes, and you start talking about horses. The worst horse alive would cost three-and-six, silver, and it would eat that much again in a month. You don't even have a cloak, remember that?"

"I *remember* horses, that's all. I rode a horse; I didn't walk. I wasn't hungry. I wasn't cold, and my feet didn't hurt."

Berika stifled the retort on the tip of her tongue. There were moments when the things that Dart—now Ean—claimed to remember were almost as disturbing as the shining wooden sword. But then Berika remembered that radiant sword, those radiant eyes, Hirmin's head bounding toward her. Ean became Dart, and a demon again. He belonged to Weycha; Berika's dreams and prayers could never fetch a footsore nobleman.

The footing was easier after they reached the road, but the awkwardness between them did not improve. Berika untied her scrip. She gave Ean the best of the remaining morsels, and as she expected, he didn't notice the privilege she accorded him. When it was empty she headed off the road to rinse the scrip in the ditch beside it.

"That's the end of our food."

"You should have told me."

"You didn't ask."

Dart was standing at the edge of the road, hipshot and puzzled, when Berika finished. He offered his hand to help her onto the road; Berika preferred her hands and knees.

"So that's the way of it again," he mused, giving her a stranger's stare.

Berika shook out her skirt before meeting his eyes. "The way of what?"

"Nothing." He turned and started walking. "I won't forget again."

"Forget what? Dar—*Ean*, forget what?"

His over-the-shoulder glance made it clear he had nothing more to say. Berika scurried to catch up with him again. The shepherd from Gorse knew no more about noblefolk than she knew about fetches, perhaps less. Gorse's long winter evenings were full of stories, about demons, not noblefolk.

Dart was mystified. He accepted all the reasons Berika gave for his new name, and he certainly could not think of a better one. Yet, with the change that had come over Berika since she'd chosen it, he'd almost have preferred she'd called him Hirmin.

They weren't the only travellers on the eastern road from Flayne, though it seemed they were the only ones travelling east. At first Dart followed Berika's example, hunching his shoulders each time a cart or soldier came the other way. He grunted when friendly voices wished them godspeed, and greeted no one in return. By the time they'd had a half-dozen such encounters, he'd had enough of furtiveness.

"Maybe we should talk to people when they talk to us. We might learn something about Eyerlon, or the road. Maybe where we can get some food. As it is, we're acting like we've got something to hide."

"We do."

Dart caught Berika's arm. "But if we act as if we've got something to hide, then people will know we're hiding something, won't they? So if we act as if we haven't got anything—"

"If that's what you want to do." Her sigh started in her shoulders and left her face even darker and sadder than it had been. "You know best."

"When did *that* happen? My memory comes back to me in broken pieces, Berika. Whatever I remember, it leaves me more confused than I was before. You mention Prince Rinchen, who commanded the army at Tremontin, and I think of giving a snot-nosed boy a ride on my horse. What I remember makes no sense. I *need* you, Berika.

"Heldey said something when we were together in the undercroft—" Which was the first hint Berika had of what had passed between her erstwhile friend and her demon. "I can't remember what exactly—but I remembered a hall filled shoulder-to-shoulder with people. A great hall with gilt basins and marble columns and waterfalls—"

"The Basilica of Eyerlon—?"

Dart nodded. "I thought so—think so. And now I think—don't ask me how—that my lady found me not long thereafter."

"You were there—" Berika tried to get her balance back, but her feet and knees remained in another world. "O gods—" Her head fell forward; her empty stomach heaved. Dart eased her to the ground. "You don't know—" Berika rested her head against his arm because she'd lost the strength to hold it erect herself. "You don't know what that means."

"It means I've been in Eyerlon—I've said that all along—and if I return there, maybe I'll see something that will bring my memory back."

Berika shook her head weakly. "You're . . . You're . . ." Her fingers fluttered. "You truly are—were—noblefolk: a great man, a lord. You truly are an Ean."

"If you can't *fetch* a prince, you'll have me *born* one!" Dart's laugh was both short and forced. "Berika, believe me, what I remember is being jammed together so tight it was hard to breathe. Whoever I was—am—I'm just a man. A simple, ordinary man like Larsov, when he was there for the assart charter. Gods know, maybe I was there with him."

"Commonfolk don't ride horses. And commonfolk don't meet mysterious ladies who give them magic swords and magic harps and make them *champions*. Besides, you've never *acted* like one of us."

Dart sighed and got a firmer grip on Berika's arms, expecting an explosion to follow his next words. "Berika, Weycha said I was nothing when she—That's hardly noble, is it? Ingolde said I had the manners of a nobleman, but I might just as easily be a nobleman's slave."

Berika's eyes widened. The strength returned to her limbs. "Why didn't you tell me what Ingolde said? You said your lady had my face, and I believed I fetched you whole-cloth out of my dreams. Why didn't you tell me what Ingolde said? Why did you lie to me?"

Dart blushed in the dreary afternoon light, but that was all the satisfaction Berika got. "I didn't lie to you. My lady has your face. I told you my lady was angry with me; she's hidden herself behind your face, because yours was the face I followed across the stream." That was not so much a lie as a simplification, and his face began to cool as he said it.

"But if you'd told me what Ingolde said—"

"She also said that I had the wrong scars for a bard or a farmer, and the wrong manners. She said a lot of things, but mostly she said: *You're not one of us.* She said I'd cause trouble if I tried to stay in Gorse, because I didn't belong there. I guess it seemed more important to prove that I'm a man, not a demon; I never gave much thought to what *kind* of man I should be."

"It makes all the difference in the world, Dart—Ean. There's commonfolk and there's noblefolk. You should have told me what Ingolde said. I've seen you use a sword. I'd have understood, even if you didn't."

"And, Iser's fist, you'd be wrong."

Berika used his shoulder to lever herself upright. She tucked the stray hairs of her braids behind her ears and took extra care to brush the mud and dirt from her skirt. "Not hardly. Who taught you to swear by the warrior's god?"

It happened too often now to be unfamiliar or shocking; more like a muscle strain that spiked in a single, awkward position. A frisson rippled up Dart's spine, and when it passed into his skull Iser had always been his god.

Berika watched his eyelids flutter. "You remember now, don't you?" Her triumph was blunted slightly by curiosity.

Dart shook himself back to the muddy road and the mottled grey sky. "No." As both experience and memory grew, cheating the truth became easier. "Larsov swears by Iser; maybe I picked it up from him." Easier, but not easy. He got to his feet and started walking.

Berika was desperate to be helpful. She wanted to ask *the* question that would reveal everything. Dart was willing to listen, though his hopes centered more on forgetting his empty stomach than remembering his past. Berika's seeds in the wind were sincere; she ran through almost every proper name she could remember, blending truth and legend, mortal and divine, simple and noble, until Dark asked her gently to stop.

He might just as well have kicked her in the ribs. Rain was beginning to fall; she fluffed her cloak and hid within it. Dart refused to talk to a shadow and brushed the hood back from her face.

"Names and words that have no meaning for you won't have any for me—"

"I'm doing the best I can. I'm a common shepherd from an assart village. Forgive me, I don't know many words that would have meaning for a nobleman."

"I'm sorry." He reached for her hood, only to poke her in the face with his cold, stiff fingers as he did. "I don't think you're common at all. Anyone who thought you were, wouldn't be worthy of nobility."

Berika fixed the hood herself, letting it fall forward so she couldn't see more than the ground at her feet.

Dart sighed a cloud before daring to lay a hand across her hunched shoulders. "I said I'm sorry. Keep trying, please? What do I, of all men, know about knowing?"

"I think, *midons*—" Berika's voice was brittle, and the honorific was layered in sarcasm. "I think you know everything that you want to know."

Dart caught himself swearing to Iser Ironfist again and left the oath unfinished. He tugged his shirt up around his ears and pulled his hands turtlelike up the sleeves. The sword's straw sheath pierced the coarse cloth, allowing the rain to make streams down his back and under the roped waist of his breeches. With each step, the harp-case bounced between the prickling straw and yesterday's bruises. He wriggled his shoulders and hips in an effort to get it to lie flat again, and got a waterfall from his hair instead.

"This isn't fair!"

His protest carried a good distance, but Berika gave no sign of having heard it, and he splashed through the growing puddles to catch up with her.

The King's Road was the best road in Walensor. The soldiers followed it when they mustered. Carts followed the soldiers, bringing supplies to the army on the eastern frontier. But unlike the older roads, the King's Road did not touch every market town. Some, like Flayne, were on the road, but most were connected to it by lesser tracks. When night found them, there wasn't a cottage, much less a village or town, in sight.

There was a fire not far from the road, and Dart, who was soaked and chilled to the bone wherever he wasn't already numb, stared longingly at it. Predictably, Berika had a host of reasons why they should keep going.

"I don't care." Dart had his teeth clenched to keep them from rattling. "If they roast and eat me, at least I'll die warm." He strode off with great determination, only to lose his balance as soon as he left the relatively flat road. The world became black, then wet, then cold.

"Dart! Ean! Are you hurt?"

He heard Berika slide carefully into the ditch, clutching dead reeds to keep herself upright. The anger in her voice had been replaced by something that was almost concern; it gave Dart the will to untangle himself.

"Just dumb with cold." He wiped the mud from his face to his sleeve and got a mouthful of blood in the process.

Dart saw a waist-to-head silhouette, charcoal on black; Berika saw nothing at all. She groped for something manlike in the darkness. "You've got to get up. You can't lie in the water."

Their arms met, and Dart got to his feet with a gasp and a groan. Cramps seized both legs; the toes of his his left foot curled into a painful ball. Berika tried to bundle him into her cloak.

"No, let's just get to the fire."

Dart was in no condition to talk when they stumbled into the circle of light, so Berika made up the story, her teeth chattering more from fear than cold, though in simple truth she and Dart looked more disreputable than the men already huddled around the fire. They saw the sword hilt rising above Dart's shoulder. No one would ask a man to bare his weapon in such miserable weather, and a hilt might well be made from wood. They accepted Dart as a comrade-in-arms and Berika as the doxy he had picked up along the way.

The five had a little tent of pitch-seamed leather, which they propped over Dart until his shivering and bleeding stopped. They had two rabbits roasting on their fire, and though they would not share their meat, they had plenty of hard bread to soak in the drippings.

"How'd you come to lose your cloak and hat, not to mention

your food?" the man asked Dart, but his eyes were on Berika, and the answer he expected was clear on his face.

Berika played the part for discretion's sake. She slid an arm around her companion and leaned against his shoulder while he finished chewing. She felt him grow tense and thoughtful. A multitude of disasters paraded through her mind and she risked a little prayer to the unfamiliar Iser Ironfist.

Dart swallowed and flashed an idiot's open grin. "Don't really know. I was passed-out drunk when it happened."

Berika hid her face in his shirt.

"In Relamain?" someone else asked.

Berika dug her fingers into the small of his back and squeezed. *They're taking our measure!* she thought urgently, though Dart had shown no sign of that very rare talent for hearing what was not said. *They're trying to see if you've anything left to steal . . . anything left but me!*

"Relamain? Might have been Relamain. My memory's all a blur."

The plunge into the ditch had done more than bloody his lip and nose. Berika was certain it had addled the few wits Dart had. She squeezed and twisted, no longer trying to be the least bit subtle.

"Mayhap you'll try to win something back—for the rest of your journey?"

Dart pried Berika's fingers from his flesh. He held them firmly, but not half so tight as she'd held him. "I've nothing left to lose." He shrugged and tucked her hand flat against his hip. "I'm neither a drinker nor a gambler—or at least not a good one."

Berika was pleased that Dart could not be tempted; she was suspicious when the other men let his resolve stand. A moderate man was not necessarily an admired one. The ten-year war had done more than take the cream of Walensor's men—both simple and noble. Many a soldier came home with a greater taste for wine and dice than work. Gorse had lost most of its men to battle, but there were a few who simply never made it home from the cities along the way. These days the winter nights were more apt to be filled with the sound of five dice rattling in a cup than men taking their turn storytelling while the women spun and wove.

These men had a jug of Brightwater liquor, which they'd passed around more than once before Dart and Berika appeared. They included Dart in the jug's next circuit; he included Berika. Gorse's orchards yielded a fair cider and a potable brandy, which Berika had drunk all her life. Each year they sold a barrel or two in Flayne, but she had never tasted the distilled product of that trade. She expected it to be more fiery than Rimp's fermented brandy, but it was, in fact, very easy to swallow. She understood immediately how the liquor got its common name. After a second pull Berika passed the jug back to Dart.

Not much time passed, no more than four or five more swallows, before Berika found it much easier to list against Dart than to sit up straight. The fire, smoking and hissing in the light rain, entranced her while the warmth in her stomach burned away every ache she carried. Dart no longer took the jug, and Berika found her tongue too thick to request it. Her eyes had gotten heavy, too. Dice were rattling again—just another rhythm blending with the rain. Nothing to worry about. Nothing to keep her eyes open for.

The sky was bright when Berika opened her eyes again—bright enough to make her squint at least, though the clouds remained thick enough to hide the sunrise. She was warm; she was dry. She was alone—except for the sound of dice rattling in a leather cup.

She was up on her knees and gaping.

The men had gone, leaving the remnants of their supper behind. Dart crouched on the far side of the dying fire, an expression of rapt curiosity across his face. He scooped the dice into the cup and cast them down again. Berika cleared her throat, alerting her to the sour taste in her gut and the faint hammering in her head, but attracting Dart not at all.

"What happened?" Berika got to her feet, hoping to find something drinkable. The Brightwater jug lay on its side; she didn't check to see if it was empty.

"It's the game Rimp taught me the night Auld Mag died. He had no feel for it," Dart replied, recapturing the dice. "Our friends last night had more practice playing—if not winning. They called on the gods and luck each time they threw, but there's no trick to the throwing, just knowing when to bet."

"Ummph—That's what they *all* say." She found a clear puddle and splashed the cold water against her face before licking it from her hands.

"So you do know how it's played. They said my doxy would, and I recalled you didn't want me to play—" Dart's voice trailed off as Berika's shoulders stiffened and he realized he'd said something wrong . . . again. "You didn't . . . did you?"

Berika wiped her face on her sleeve, acutely aware that there was more hair flying from her braids than confined in them, that the too-large boots stuck out from the hem of her skirt like moldy turnips, and the skirt itself was torn and stained in a half-dozen places. "I'm no doxy," she insisted with a vigorous sniffle. "Not yours, nor anybody's. Hirmin took me for his rightful wife in the proper way, even though I hated him. I'm not some roundheels doxy. I'm a widow proper and not beholden to you. We're going to Eyerlon together—but that's the end of it. I'll go to the hiring fair or the beguines, and you'll go on your way alone."

Dart left the dice on the ground when he stood up. "I only meant I think that I could do something about keeping us fed and warm on the way to Eyerlon." He snatched a water sack from the branch of a bush and threw it toward her. "I remember muck-mouth, too."

Berika blushed to the ear lobes, turned, and ran to the scant shelter of a nearby thorn bush.

CHAPTER

13

Dart kept the dice, despite Berika's disapproval. He tried his luck with the five cubes and Ingolde's coins at a charterhouse on the King's Road the next night. He was cautious at first—too cautious—and lost all but a few. Berika watched the pile shrink with veiled eyes.

Fenklare's sorMeklan Donitor granted charters to inns along the King's Road for his own convenience, which meant they were inconveniently spaced for foot travellers. For every night that found them sleeping in a warm corner of a charterhouse hall, Dart and Berika spent at least one night huddled under Berika's cloak.

Once, they got lucky between charterhouses and shared a pitched shelter with a pair of veteran soldiers who were more interested in talking about the war than throwing dice. Dart soaked up their tales like fleece in a puddle, but Berika was achy and fell asleep before the stars came out. They had nothing for breakfast but the stale crumbs clinging to the inside of Berika's scrip, which bothered Dart more than her.

"Maybe we should risk bringing the harp inside at the next charterhouse. The men last night said we'd pass one today. We need a solid meal," Dart mused once he'd retrieved the acorn and the straw-wrapped sword from the hedge where he'd hidden them the previous evening, before they approached the veterans.

Berika said nothing. Dart slung his possessions over his shoulder without further comment. The cold and the damp, the days spent walking on the uneven road, and the nagging ache of an empty stomach were taking their toll on Berika. The bruises on her face and arms did not fade; the skin surrounding them turned yellow. Her cheeks became hollow. Her eyes were ringed with bruises as dark as any she'd gotten from Hirmin.

The moon marched from the month of Gleaning to Slaughter. From the gossip they'd gathered at the charterhouses and along the roads, they were two days' walking from the Donitor's city of Relamain and nearing the first of the great rivers that flowed past Eyerlon. They were also travelling much slower than they were when they left Gorse. Berika's eyes were bloodshot and bleary; the skin around them was a waxen grey. She called a halt frequently, and left the road for the muddy ditch beside it, where Dart could hear her clearing her throat with a dry hacking cough.

When they came to the charterhouse north of Relamain, Dart suggested they stop, even though the sky was clear and the whole afternoon lay before them. Berika did not object.

Dart used their last quartered flake of silver to get Berika a place by the hearth and a bowl of creamy soup. She stared at its steam awhile, then sipped it slowly. Dart took the remaining black-metal grit coins to another corner, where dice tumbled onto a polished wood plank. The pit was filled with odd-shaped coins as tarnished as his own. The men played from boredom, not bothering to clear the pit after each forging. They gladly made room for a stranger and passed him the cup straightaway.

The plank was old, and despite his earlier disdain, Dart rubbed it often for luck. Perhaps the wood was lucky, or perhaps he was the sort of man who played best with a shadow of desperation across his shoulder. Dart's little pile of black grit coins grew larger and brighter. The men with whom he'd begun the game surrendered their places to others with more silver in their purses.

Afternoon sunlight warmed the smooth planks; then lamps were lit and candles rammed onto the nailheads above the pit. Berika fell asleep by the hearth; Dart kept playing.

Dart's turn, called a *forge*, ended. He passed the leather cup sunwise to his left and absently drummed his fingertips on the plank. He had a good memory, when he had something to remember. He recalled which number showed on the dice most frequently, which points were the easiest to make and which were the hardest. In the life he did not remember, he'd gambled often, but never with the understanding he evolved that afternoon and evening in the sorMeklan charterhouse. What the other men called luck with the iron-black and fire-red combinations, he reduced to patterns and probabilities.

Dart's pile of coins grew steadily while others shrank around it. He concentrated on the dice and forgot where his winnings were coming from until every man at the table was glaring at him with suspicion.

His heart and stomach exchanged places. The dice rattled against the side of the cup, and he wasn't deliberately shaking it. They spilled across the plank. The fifth die was black-up: The two red dice were meaningless; the black dice showed a pair of sixes.

"High iron with nothing in the fire," someone whispered with ill-concealed satisfaction.

He could pass the cup, ending his forge but leaving the pit intact for the next thrower, or he could toss in another coin and try to throw high iron a second time. If he failed, the other men would divide the pit; if he succeeded, he could take it all before passing the cup.

The light that flashed in Dart's mind wasn't the brilliance of recognition. To the contrary, there was the distant sense of discovery, of a truth which he'd never understood before: There were times when a wise man made, and lost, a foolish bet to keep his path to the door cleared. Dart was calm when he scooped up the dice, but he didn't let it show. He pushed an unflaked round silver mark into the pit—the fool's bet. Four more skidded in to join it. Dart closed his eyes, and let the dice tumble.

"You're out. Your luck's gone bad, Ean." Dart used the name Berika had given him when he played iron-in-the-fire.

Dart opened his eyes. The coins clashed against each other as the other players took their share from the pit. He looked into a host of friendlier faces. Leaving eight grit aside, he swept his pile into Ingolde's leather purse.

"We need ale," he said when the purse was secure at his waist.

One of the older men who'd watched the game but had not played clapped Dart on the shoulder. "You had a good run, lad, but you don't know when to stop. Give it over on the high iron;

take the pass and let someone else throw—but never raise yourself."

A wench shoved a mug into Dart's hand. When the dark ale hit the back of his throat he realized how tense he'd been. He swallowed hard and waited a heartbeat for everything to settle in his stomach. "I'll remember that," he said with a slightly breathless nod.

"You lost half your winnings on one bad move."

Dart didn't fake unsteadiness getting to his feet. "I won't forget." He flexed his knees and winced as blood returned to his feet.

The deep-voiced veteran spoke the truth—Dart had squandered half his winnings on one foolish throw, but half his winnings was still a lot more than what he'd sat down with. It was more than enough to get himself a bowl of the creamy soup and to tempt Berika with a little steamed cake studded with dark fruit and sticky with honey. Berika licked the honey and pried out the fruit; the cake itself sat uneaten in her hands. The vacant stare returned to her eyes as quickly as it had lifted.

"Are you all right?" Dart asked, knowing she wasn't. "I can get you something else, if you need it. I've played well; we've got grit, and silver too."

Berika heard Dart's voice from the depths of an echoing cave rather than a warm, crowded room. Her head ached, her skin burned, and though she knew she was hungry, food turned to stone in her gut. She was sick, and after all she'd been through—from the sleepless night over Mag's corpse, the horrible days with Hirmin, to the wretched tumult of the journey out of Gorse—the only question worth asking was: How much sicker was she going to get? And that was a question Dart could not answer.

She inhaled deeply, pushing her lungs hard against her ribs, then let all the air out. A short breath, but not a painful one, and not—thank you, Mother Cathe—a wheezy one. Then she was wracked with dry coughing. The cake fell from her hands to her lap and from there unnoticed to the floor. Dart offered the dregs of his ale; that helped, but the pain lingered.

"What's wrong, Berika? Tell me. I don't know what to do."

Berika returned the mug and slumped against the warm stones of the hearth wall. Another spasm shook her; she folded herself forward until her head touched her knees.

Fever heightened Berika's senses. She heard Dart's hand touch her cheek and felt it gather the solitary hairs escaping from her braids. She expected his calloused fingers to smooth her hair against her temple and trace the arch from her cheekbone to her jaw. She was ready to be comforted rather than repelled. But nothing happened and the anticipation left her with a shudder.

"You can sleep here. I thought you'd rather stay here on the bench than sleep in the straw. I'll be back in the morning. I'll leave you alone now."

Can't you tell the difference? I don't want to be alone. . . . Berika's pleas were heartfelt, and lost in silence. *I want to be with you.*

There was nothing unfriendly about the hands that helped her stretch out on the bench, that tucked her cloak beneath her chin and around her ankles; there was nothing more than friendly, either—as if Dart had become a shepherd and she just another sheep to be tended.

Berika slept well, wrapped in her cloak on the bench beside the hearth, but she was no better in the morning when Dart brought her a bowl of barley gruel. Her throat seemed lined with hot coals. She could hardly talk.

"She needs a mender, Ean." The veteran who'd offered his advice at the gaming table offered a bit more. "And you both need a good rest. It you don't mind my asking, what sends the two of you pell-mell across Fenklare with a handful of grit and one cloak between you?"

The man's clothes were the finest Dart remembered seeing: a soft leather dalmatic over a finely woven shirt; thick wool breeches, high boots, and a plaid cloak in sunset colors. He carried a sword of patterned steel. And his tone was a breath short of threatening.

Dart looked to Berika, but she was no help, and he had to think of an answer by himself. He chose the truth because it was simpler.

"We've got to get to Eyerlon."

"Eyerlon, is it?" The veteran shook his head slowly and sadly. "Half the princes' army lingers in Eyerlon, lad. You're not the only one who didn't want to go home. The inns are filled, the streets are crowded, and nobody's hiring. Unless you've got friends there already—and I see that you don't—there's no reason to go."

"We've got to. Eyerlon's the only place we can go."

"I didn't take you for a fool."

Dart brushed the straw from his clothes as he stood up. He squared his shoulders and met the veteran's stare straight on. "I'm not; and we're going to Eyerlon."

The older man retreated a half-step. His eyes narrowed as he reassessed the man he called Ean. "A fool would know better than to travel with a sick woman. He'd leave the King's Road and hie himself south to Relamain. He'd take her to a mender's sacram in the fane, and he'd get himself proper clothes."

Dart moistened his lips and cast a worried glance at Berika, who was too listless to help him. "I don't know my way around Relamain."

"You don't know your way around Relamain, because you've never been there, or to Eyerlon either. You didn't muster did you? And you never fought. Have you, Ean? How old are you? You look old enough. Are you the last son of your line?"

Every instinct told Dart to run, but the veteran stood between him and the door, and he wouldn't leave Berika. He shook his head and shifted his balance from one foot to the other and back again. He said: "I have no family but my lady, and she held me back to protect her," which, though less than the truth, was not quite a lie.

"Not that lady." The older man tipped his head at Berika; Dart nodded. "You're not the first I've heard of whose mother took King Manal's exemption to heart and kept the last of her sons at home. It's over, Ean. Walensor's at peace now. Take the girl to Relamain. There's an inn inside the western gate, the Knotted Rose. I'm known there. Rest until she's healthy, then go home. There's nothing for you in Eyerlon."

"I don't know your name."

"Canter ruCanter barKethmeron avsorMeklan." He extended his sword hand.

Fever or not, Berika's head shot up, and even Dart knew he'd seriously underestimated the veteran's rank. *AvsorMeklan* meant Canter was related to the Donitor's family; the sheer length of the rest meant the relationship was not casual. The extended hand was as much a challenge as a gesture of friendship between equals. Dart grasped it firmly.

"My lady named me Dart when she made me her protector. It is a truer name than Ean."

The nobleman did not betray the suspicion he felt, but calmly completed the greeting ritual with his left hand. "You be careful, Dart." He pulled his hands back.

Dart watched the noble veteran leave. He was still staring at the door when Berika tugged on the hem of his shirt.

"How could you be so stupid?" she demanded in a desperate, rasping whisper. "Talking about ladies and protectors like that? Couldn't you tell he was a nobleman? Why did you have to go making yourself mysterious for him? You're supposed to be Ean! Just common Ean—you said that was what you wanted: to be a common man."

"I could not lie to Canter ruCanter. It would have been pundonor between us." Dart tried to hold her hand, but she wriggled free.

"*Pundonor*? What, by your lady, is pundonor?"

Dart blanched. "I—I don't know. It was just there—in my mind as I looked at him: I could not lie; it would be pundonor. I had to tell him as much of the truth as I dared."

"With what you dared, we're *doomed*." Berika untangled her cloak and struggled to her feet. "We've got to get out of here before he comes back with an inquist."

"We'll go to Relamain."

"Fool—that's the sorMeklan stronghold. That's the last place we should go."

"You need mending, and I need a cloak. We'll go to Relamain, to the Knotted Rose, like he said. We can trust him."

Berika sat on the bench with a thud. "We're doomed."

The point was moot. Berika was too weak to walk across the room without shaking. Dart waited until noon, when a farmer arrived at the charterhouse to trade eggs and cheese for the night soil. For a trickle of grit he agreed to take them to Relamain in his cart. The sun was in its downward arc by the time they reached the gates.

On any given night there might be eight hundred souls in Relamain. On this particular night in Lesser Slaughter, the city was swollen with veterans who were reluctant to return to their quiet villages. It was not merely that Berika had never seen so many people in one place; the people themselves were strange to her. She felt worse than common.

Rural folk, like herself and Dart, in patched homespun, were hardly to be seen. Relamain women wore long dresses laced tightly at the sides and sleeves. There wasn't a stained apron, gathered skirt, or smock in sight. The men wore their breeches long and tucked into high boots or wrapped with gaiters. Almost all of the men wore a long-sleeved, knee-length dalmatic which was slit in front and back—as if every one of them rode a horse.

Berika looked wistfully at the receding cart with its tall, noisome jugs. Dart took her hand and pulled her away from the gate. He seemed not the least bit disturbed by the city. Perhaps he could not appreciate how different it was from Gorse or Flayne. Perhaps the sights, sounds, and smells rang familiar chords deep inside him. Berika was past caring. She leaned against him with her eyes closed and let him lead her through the square, into the twisting streets.

The Knotted Rose stood where Canter ruCanter promised. His name and four silver flakes—a whole mark of the precious metal—brought the landlady out of her kitchen. She grumbled about renting a room to an invalid.

"Canter ruCanter said we'd find hospitality here. I would not want to tell him he was wrong," Dart said after introducing himself simply as Ean.

The landlady weighed their dirty, rustic clothes against Canter ruCanter's name and Dart's calm assurance. Dart fished another quartered mark out of his purse. There were eight irregular pieces of flake silver on the table, which was sufficient to swing the balance in their favor.

"The menders will have shut their sacrams by now," the woman told Dart as she swept the silver into her palm. "Takes a noble name or gold to get them off the verge after sunset."

Berika's head shot up when the word *gold* was uttered. "I don't need a mender," she insisted.

"I can brew up a posset as good as any mender's. Won't cost but another flake," the landlady offered.

Dart accepted. He had no gold, and Berika needed anything that might help her. A boy led them to their room. On the way, he showed them the hall where supper would be served at the start of the first night watch. Its walls were hung with tapestries, its wooden floors were swept clean, and its carved furniture was fitted with velvet-flocked cushions.

Dart said he'd eat in his room with the lady who could say nothing at all.

Their two-silver-mark room was tiny and tucked under the eaves at the end of a corridor that ran the length of the upper story of the inn. Berika knew, despite her fever, that they were being cheated. She summoned up an imitation of Ingolde's best scolding voice and told the boy to be quick with her posset and Master Ean's supper.

The boy ran down the corridor before Dart shut the door. Cheated or not, the least room in the Knotted Rose was grander than any in Gorse, with an iron brazier puffing away in one corner and a *glass* lamp on the shelf. The bed was a great box that must have been placed in the room before the roof was tiled over. A great empty box, however, since those who stayed in a city inn were expected to provide their own bedding. Berika looked at the ropes holding the bed together and succumbed to nervous laughter.

Dart was mystified.

"Eight silver flakes—two whole marks—for a room and we still have to sleep on the floor! There's not even straw for padding."

"I'll find the stables and get some straw. I didn't see any in the hall."

Berika swallowed her laughter. "You can't bring *straw* up here."

"What should I get?"

"Nothing. Nothing at all." She threw her cloak over the ropes in the bed. "We'll make do like this. O gods, Dart, don't do anything to make anyone ask questions. We shouldn't be here. Commonfolk don't stay here, and we're worse than commonfolk in this place. We're commonfolk from the countryside with mud under our fingernails. Two silver marks for one night's room and board. It takes a sheep the whole summer to make a fleece that's worth one mark and it's gone. I'll get well, Dart. I'll eat enough for three days, I swear it. I'll be better by morning and we can get out of this place."

"Canter said I've got to get a cloak, and proper clothes for the journey. I thought we'd stay here longer—"

"Can't you understand anything!" Berika's face reddened; her voice turned shrill and shrewish. Yelling hurt her throat and made her that much angrier. "We've only got this room for one night! It will take two more silver marks to stay here tomorrow night. Sometimes you're so slow I think you never were a man at all. Silver. *Silver!* Brightwater! You have one lucky night with the dice and you think silver's under every rock. Your precious lady didn't make you rich. You've got Ingolde's hoard—every grit and flake she ever, ever saved. What do you think is going to happen when that purse is empty . . . ? When you've gambled it all away?" She pressed her fists against her breasts and doubled over coughing.

Dart muttered apologies. He rubbed between her shoulders and swore that he would not upset her in the future, but neither the coughing nor the anger ceased until Berika was too exhausted to sustain them. The boy returned with a heavy tray. Berika drank the posset, whose prime ingredient was Brightwater liquor, because they'd paid for it; she forced herself to eat the food for the same reason. The combination put her to sleep quickly. Dart wrapped her in her cloak and left her sleeping quietly.

He *had* thought they could stay in the room as long as they wished and was truly appalled to realize they could not. He had a passel of angry questions for Canter ruCanter, but since the veteran was obviously nowhere about, Dart knew he would have to find his own way out of this mess.

The landlady frowned when Dart asked the way to the nearest gaming-house, and she demanded another night's rent as surety. Once she had that in the strongbox, she gave him the directions he needed.

"There's a dozen gaming-houses, but Canter ruCanter goes to the Golden Cockerel when he's here, so I imagine that's where you'll want to go too."

Dart knew he was a long way from the assart village of Gorse. He was a longer way from the empty-headed youth who left Weycha's forest by mistake. It did not matter that Relamain had not dazzled him with brilliant flashes of recognition—those shocks were now more disorienting than useful. Since he'd unlocked the secrets of iron-in-the-fire, he was beginning to be less interested in who he had been than in what he might become.

"You imagine correctly," he told the landlady.

His confidence flagged somewhat once he was outside the Knotted Rose. All the streets looked alike in the dark, and the Golden Cockerel, when he finally found it, was filled with men who looked nothing like Canter ruCanter. There were women with painted faces and bursting gowns; blood-soaked rings where cocks fought each other to the death; and a dozen or more gaming tables where gold glittered among the silver in the pits.

All of it, however, rocked Dart with recognition. He leaned

against the door frame, pinching the flesh between his eyes and waiting for the explosions to cease.

A young man sauntered over to the doorway. He made a show of looking around and sniffing the air before deigning to notice Dart. "Lost your way, bumflower." It was a statement—not a question.

Dart knew an insult when he heard one. He copied the other fellow's rakish stance and met his stare defiantly.

"I said you don't belong here."

The voice was louder and menacing. It cut through the din. Heads came up, eyes sharpened, and one or two people edged away from the tables. Dart was ready to fight, until the brilliance of recognition focused on his own reflection in a brass candle sconce.

The cold wind of reality swept away his rage. He'd heard Berika say they were worse than common in Relamain; they were *country*-common. He had dismissed that as another of her endless, and meaningless, distinctions. But no longer. Dart was the only one in the Golden Cockerel wearing homespun cloth and open leather shoes. He was the only one with naked knees and scraggly hair. He was—he recognized himself to be—country-common: a bumflower not fit to stand upwind of a nobleman.

He fled through the door. He ran down the street and then down an alley to a cul-de-sac where he hid in the shadows. He put his hands over his ears and closed his eyes. It was not enough to be a man. A man might be a common man. A common man might be a bumflower, but never a champion. A common man had no honor; he could not take exception to a point of honor: the pundonor Dart recognized between himself and Canter ruCanter, the one between himself and the nameless, but clearly noble, young man at the Golden Cockerel.

I am my lady's champion.

Dart clung to the thought. The coils of panic lost a fraction of their power. He remembered the harp, and the wooden sword, and discovered he could swallow again, and breathe. The harp and the sword were real, so his lady was real. And he was her champion. Dart opened his eyes and wiped his face on his sleeve. If he was his lady's champion, then he was a nobleman—there was no other way. He would never argue the point with Berika again. He acted like a nobleman because he was his lady's champion and champions were noble.

"Eyes a-fire!"

Dart got to his feet, tracking the shout to its source in the alley outside the cul-de-sac. It could only mean one thing. Dart squared his shoulders and headed toward the sound of dice rattling in a leather cup.

The alley led to a stable. The men gathered beside several clearings in the straw were common-dress soldiers, little more than bumflowers, with purses thinner than the one Dart wore at his waist. A flask sat in one filth-lined pit. The men there did not share the liquor but played for a chance to wet their throats.

A scrawny boy knelt behind a box at the entrance. His game was simple: three hollowed gourds and a nut which he hid and revealed with dazzle and dexterity. From where he stood, Dart could see the nut fall onto the boy's thighs. He shook his head and kept going; if the men throwing their grit on the box were too far gone to know they were cheated, they were too far gone for a stranger's help.

Back where the best horses were stabled, men who thought their luck might improve played a more traditional game for the silver that would get them inside again. They made room for a stranger and passed him the leather cup and the Brightwater flask. Dart took the one, but only pretended to take a swallow from the other.

Dart called his point and threw the dice. On the other side of the pit, the man stared bleary-eyed at the red and black cubes; Dart pressed his fingertips together. He sighed; at this hour in this place iron-in-the-fire could hardly be deemed a game of chance. He was raking in the pit when a fresh face sat down opposite him.

"Everything you got there for this."

A patterned cloak covered the pit. It had seen better days. The fur on its collar was bald in places. There was a hole in the back; the patch hung by a single thread. Berika's cloak was a work of art in comparison, but the man who wore this cloak would not be taken for a bumflower. It could be fastened over the left shoulder; a right-handed man could reach his scabbard without fumbling. Straps dangling above the hem would attach it firmly to a saddle: A billowing cloak was a danger to both horse and rider.

Dart smiled and passed the leather cup. "Call your point."

"I'll use my own dice," the other averred, offering them for Dart's inspection.

As a gambler, Dart was more appearance than substance. He

checked the little cubes to see if they were painted properly. He tossed them in the air, whirled them around in his hand, and had not the least inkling whether they were shaved or loaded. They were wood; he didn't need to know more.

My lady, I need a cloak like that if I'm to be your champion. It should be a better cloak to honor you—and Berika—but any cloak is better than no cloak at all. . . . He returned the dice. "Call your point."

A bloom of sweat appeared on the challenger's lip. He'd judged Dart by his appearance and taken him for a dullwitted rustic, but he felt a twinge of doubt. The dice rattled and sprayed across the dirt: null in fire, full of iron, and a pair of sixes.

"High iron," Dart said softly, in case the man had missed the call.

He hadn't. He stared at the dice as if they had betrayed him.

Dart cleared his throat. "Will you pass?"

The challenger licked his lip. He had a choice; iron-in-the-fire always left the player with a choice. He could leave the cloak where it was, pass the cup to Dart, and pray to all his favorite gods that Dart's luck was worse than his, or he could add something to the pit and try to rescue his bet with a second high-iron throw. "I'm empty," he admitted, and passed the cup to Dart.

"You've already laid down your cloak. What about your dalmatic?" Dart's question was unexpected. He should have passed the cup right back.

The man looked down at his chest. His dalmatic was a brushed leather the color of wine and hardly worn. It was worth more than the cloak. "What would a country boy like you do with it?"

Dart shrugged. "The same as I'll do with the cloak—unless you really think I can hit high iron. What's the risk?"

"No risk," the challenger agreed, loosening the laces and drawing the dalmatic over his head and shoulders. "No risk at all, if you agree it's worth four flakes."

Dart matched the pit with a silver mark and scooped up the dice. He'd played against men who talked to the dice as they rattled in the cup, and others who did a little dance. His ritual was no ritual at all, just a quick swirl and a toss.

He reached for the clothing.

The challenger reached for his dice. "A chance. Give me another chance. I'm good for it. I got coins under my bed."

Dart tugged the dalmatic over his shirt. Ingolde's marsh ocher dye was not the best match, but pleasing colors were far less important than simple possession. He stood up. The cloak unfurled and settled over his shoulders; it was a comforting and familiar gesture.

"Hey—you got to give me another chance."

Dart flipped the cloak over his left shoulder. The gesture was noble from start to finish. "You challenged me."

"Bumflower—"

The wooden sword was sheathed in straw beneath the bed where Berika slept, but that didn't stop Dart's right hand. And the movement alone was enough to make the cloakless man shiver.

"I am *not* a bumflower."

The better players did not linger in the stables. Some had sense enough to return to their lodgings; others returned to the fancy rooms as soon as they had a handful of silver. Dart followed a middle course and visited a half-dozen dirt-pit games before he was satisfied with the weight of his purse. It was past midnight. Sober men were few and far between, and not betting against each other.

Snow had begun falling after midnight. It covered the street with a sparkling silence. Mittens, a hat, and fleece leggings would be welcome additions to Dart's wardrobe, but for the moment he felt better than he could remember.

CHAPTER
—— 14 ——

Berika woke up when the latch clicked and someone entered the room without a lamp. She clutched her cloak tightly around her neck. She wished that she had a knife and wished even more that she felt strong enough to fight. Then the intruder swore as he collided with the steep roof, and she relaxed. Letting go of the edge of her cloak, Berika expected Dart to roll himself into its warmth.

The ropes creaked and sagged; his boots hit the floor, but the expected tug on her cloak never came. Dart's spine butted into hers. His breathing settled into the steady rhythms of sleep. Berika tossed and turned until they were facing the same direction and she could reach him. She wasn't *that* sick, and certainly not *that* angry—not anymore, not after spending so long by herself in a strange place.

She jumped when she touched the unfamiliar fabric of Dart's new cloak. She had taken their chaste intimacy for granted, not valuing it until, suddenly, it was gone. Even his smell was different, tainted with horse lather and oil smoke. Her first reaction was panic: The notion that the body beside her was not Dart made a fleeting appearance, then faded. He was different, but he was still Dart.

Berika reminded herself of that many times over before she fell asleep again, but the panic returned in the morning, before she was fully out of her dreams. She was alone in the bed; someone was watching her. She sat up, and woke up—in that order. Her eyes were full of sleep-silk and would not focus.

"Feeling better?"

Berika realized she was holding her breath. She exhaled, coughed, and found she could see clearly. She saw the patterned cloak and remembered touching its complicated weave earlier. She saw the wine-colored dalmatic, and everything she'd been about to say fled her mind as she absorbed the new and the old.

"Dart, you look ridiculous."

That was not the reaction Dart expected, much less hoped for. His eyes widened and his lips tensed. "I finally concede your point that I cannot be a common man, that I must appear, at least, noble—and you tell me I look ridiculous."

Berika cocked her head to one side like a perplexed dog. She rejected the next several thoughts that came to mind. "I never meant for you to look like you didn't know who you were."

"You're the one who said I must be nobly born."

"But—Brightwater—not like that!"

Her fever had broken; her head was clearer than it had been in days—clearer than it had been the last time they'd had this discussion—but Berika was still far from healthy. Dart wanted to know exactly what was wrong with his appearance—why he did not seem nobly born. The harder he pressed, the further Berika retreated, until her back was against the outer wall. Finally she held her hands over her ears and rocked from side to side.

"I don't know. I don't know," she repeated with increasing volume and despair.

Dart shed his cloak. He pulled off the dalmatic and threw it into a corner. "Is that better?" he demanded. "Now we can both be taken advantage of? *Bumflowers* don't get to Eyerlon, Berika. You were right about that, at least." He grabbed the cloak and stormed out of the room. The door slammed hard enough to shower Berika with dirt from the rafters.

The country-common shepherd was still pulling herself together when there was a gentle knock on the door.

"You can come back in." She wiped the moisture from her cheeks.

The door cracked open. The landlady's face, not Dart's, came into view. "He said I should bring you your breakfast and another posset." The city woman studied Berika with unsubtle thoroughness. She did not venture further into the room.

"I'm not hungry," Berika lied.

"It's bought and paid for," the landlady countered, thrusting the basket into view. Berika sighed and the door opened the rest of the way. "He's a strange one, that one of yours. Looks as poor as a leaky bucket, then he gives my Ownin a heap o'silver marks to keep in his strongbox—" She spotted the crumpled dalmatic and tried unsuccessfully to hide her curiosity. "A true strange one."

Berika took the tray and balanced it on the ropes beside her. "He's had trials," she acknowledged, praying the woman would not notice the huge acorn or the straw-wrapped sword.

The landlady dashed those prayers. "I could get you a feather mattress. There's more than enough in what he gave Ownin."

"No. I don't want anything with *his* silver." The words were too sharp. The landlady's curiosity was visibly pricked. Berika tried to blunt it before it reached the shadowed objects beneath the rope mattress. "We've got to get to Eyerlon," Berika muttered as she'd muttered before—as if it explained everything.

The landlady nodded before she closed the door behind her. It was impossible for Berika to guess what the old woman was thinking. She pierced the yolk of her bought-and-paid-for egg with a spear of bread and ate it glumly. . . .

The pattern was set. Dart was gone all day and most of the night. When he returned, he brought clothes—long woolen breeches, a pair of mittens, fleece gaiters, a brocade hat with a droopy brim and three huge, moth-eaten feathers—and, according to the landlady, more silver for her Ownin's strong box. Always more silver; nothing had been taken out, which intrigued the woman, who toted baskets of food up the stairs herself, almost as much as the growing mound of clothing—but nowhere near as much as those strange objects under the bed.

Berika's eyes lost their hollowness. Her bruises faded, and, for the first time in her life, she wasn't tired enough to fall asleep whenever she closed her eyes. There was no weaving to do, no spinning, no carding; the sheep were a fading memory like her bruises. Her room had a window, but it faced another wall. If she craned her neck around, she could see the sky, which was almost always grey.

Berika discovered boredom, which was amusing for about half a day, after which it was simply boring.

She didn't consider leaving the inn. Not with the landlady certain to be under the bed as soon as she set foot in the street. The street didn't hold much interest for Berika, anyway. She'd seen it once, coming through the gate, and it hadn't looked like the sort of place where she'd feel comfortable. By the third day she would have admitted—had anyone asked—that sitting on a platform of knotted ropes all day wasn't comfortable, either. Ingolde's disapproval was preferable to the landlady's curiosity, and weaving was preferable to doing nothing.

I'll ask him to take me with him, Berika promised herself when the room was dark. *There's no reason he can't take me. I'll ask him when he gets in tonight. He can't refuse me. I hardly cough at all.*

She filled her lungs to prove the point, and curled up in spasms that seemed to start somewhere around her knees. In her heart of hearts Berika knew she would be panting before she reached the bottom of the stairs, and that without Dart she'd be sick to death.

Without Dart, I wouldn't be here at all. I'd be safe at home in Gorse.

Berika pulled the cloak over her head and squeezed her eyes shut. She hadn't forgotten Hirmin, but he wasn't part of her boredom, and he'd never been a part of her fantasies. Her legs were stiff with inactivity; her back ached no matter how much she wriggled around on the ropes. Sleep seemed farther away than Eyerlon, farther than Gorse, but she found it eventually, and alone.

The sun shone at dawn for the first time since the start of Great Slaughter. Light made its way across the jumbled rooftops and down the air shaft, ending in an angular pool that included Berika's face. Dart was beside her and sound asleep. They weren't on the same schedule anymore. She reached for the edge of his cloak to keep the light from disturbing him. The heavy fabric fell from her fingers.

"Dart?" Berika whispered hoarsely.

To be sure, the man beside her wore Dart's clothes—as much of them as Berika recognized from the previous morning. He had been cleanshaven when Berika first saw him on the opposite bank of the forest stream, but his face had bristled and bearded since then. His hair had always been a wild, tangled wreath. It was a stranger's face that rested on a folded corner of a cloak—a bit ruddy and raw, as men were when they shed their whiskers and smoothed away the stubble with pumice. His hair had been whacked off even with his jaw and washed until it glistened. The overall impression was of a dark gold-brown, but looking close, Berika could see that no two strands were quite the same and ranged from sable to the palest yellow. She let a lock flow over her fingers.

Dart stirred and she pulled back quickly. His hand was visible now. The nails were trimmed, and grime no longer circled them or his knuckles. Berika sat on her hands.

In the corner, taking form as the light reached them, stood a pair of tall boots with sweeping cuffs and angled heels. Her father's shapeless shoes were nowhere to be seen. Berika looked at his face again. Some folk said nobility was in the bone—and commonfolk were made from a lesser clay. It was a flawed theory, given the tendency of young noblemen to constantly mix the clay. But no one would be likely to call Dart a bumflower again.

Berika eased out of the bed without disturbing him. She smoothed her skirt and attacked the worst of the stains with her ragged nails. The worst stains had appeared since she'd left Gorse, but there were others far older. She had never owned more than one of anything. Laundering was reserved for garments that met stinkweed or worse. It shrank the woolen weft but not the linen warp, and did nothing for a garment's appearance. And bathing was for babies and corpses. In Gorse, that was, but not in Relamain; Berika had seen the landlady wrinkling her nose when she picked up the food basket.

One stain was past lifting. Berika lapped it beneath another, cleaner fold. In Gorse, Ingolde was considered fastidious; not only did she own a wash basin, she used a chamber pot—with the sheep-straw right below. A hole in the floor was sufficient for everyone else in the village, including her daughter. At least Berika had known what the curve-mouth jug in the corner was *for*, though she found it awkward to use. Dart, she recalled, had neither asked what it was, nor hesitated to use it.

Berika sighed. Her mood demanded a long sigh from the pit of her stomach, but her lungs could not cooperate. Whatever relief the sigh would have brought was lost in the swallowed spasms of her coughing, confirming what Ingolde often said: No good comes from feeling sorry for yourself.

Berika wiped the tears from her cheek and pulled the thong from one of her braids. There was no excuse for the state of her hair—except that her comb and brush were still in Gorse. She grimaced as a leaf fluttered onto her lap. If memory served, she'd forgotten to move the comb and brush to Hirmin's cottage and they were probably still on their hook in the shepherd's house. She attacked her hair with fingers and vengeance; when the knots would not give, she used her teeth to loosen them and spat the snarls onto the floor.

Grooming might take the better part of the day—Berika could sit on her braids, and her hair, on those rare occasions when it was not confined in braids, touched the backs of her knees. It certainly took all her attention.

"You'd do better with a steel comb."

Berika froze with a rope of hair in each hand, and a third bobbling against her nose. "Don't have a comb." Crackling sounds added emphasis as she spread her arms and pulled another plait out. It was easier when she lowered her head, and she didn't have to look at him.

"I could get you one."

"Steel combs cost money."

"We have enough."

She tossed her loose hair over her shoulder. "What 'we'? You lost *my* money before I even knew you had it. It's all your money now."

"You don't believe that."

"What a man earns belongs to him, and I guess you earned it."

"We *share*," Dart protested.

"You never asked if I wanted to spend a fortune to stay here—while you're out spreading your silver as fast as you gather it." Berika's voice was as nasty as she could make it—despite knowing that what she said was not true.

"I must look like a nobleman, and you must get well so we can continue to Eyerlon."

"You've spent a fortune on looking like a nobleman."

Dart's jaw stiffened. "Only the boots, and last night at the bathhouse. I wagered for the rest, and won."

Berika knew no reason for her anger; it simply existed and she wanted to be rid of it as effectively as possible. Her hearing was, therefore, selective. "Those boots cost a fortune all by themselves. You like betting. Well, I'll bet that you could have gotten us a deck passage clear to Eyerlon for what they cost. And look at them!"

Color flooded Dart's cheeks. "The cobbler said Midons Ean sorMeklan himself had them made," he admitted. "But Midons Ean didn't like the way they fit and refused to pay for them. Everything else"—Dart gestured toward the heap of acquisitions— "was won and lost Iser knows how many times before coming to me, and all of it's worn and patched. But these were made for the Donitor and never saw worse. I know these are fitting for noblefolk."

"They're fitting for noblefolk, all right. You can't *walk* in those things. Or don't you figure to walk anymore? Maybe you figure you know how to ride a horse."

He turned with deliberately slow movements. Berika belatedly reminded herself of the dangers inherent in arguing with a demon. She stole a glance at his eyes, which were mercifully dark.

"Yes, Berika, I can ride a horse," he said in soft, measured tones. "I can ride any horse. I can play any game in any gaming-house. I can handle a sword, and I can handle a woman—if it comes to that."

Berika was reckless and past caring. "I'm sure you can. I'm sure you've handled plenty since coming to Relamain—and all of them better than a country-common shepherd from Gorse."

Dart opened his mouth, reconsidered, and began a thorough examination of his travelling companion. Berika imagined her clothing vanishing under his appraisal. She felt naked, wanting, and she pulled a curtain of scraggly hair over her face in shame.

It was, in fact, the first time Dart had ever put Berika and gaming-house corps of doxies in the same thought. Just as he'd left the forest without a memory of the differences between noble and commonfolk, he'd considered womankind as a single entity or as individuals without distinction. The morning light was brutal. Common life was brutal, valuing strength and survival far more than beauty.

"Different," Dart mused without changing his expression. "Very different, but, no, not necessarily better. *Friendlier*, but I don't think I'd want to spend the greater or lesser part of a month on the road with any of them. And it's known, by the way, that I have spent the greater and lesser part of a month with a single woman, that I've gotten her a room in the best inn in Relamain, and that I sleep nowhere but here—for all the comfort that gets me." His voice lost none of its cutting edge.

"There's no reason for you to come back here every night."

Outrage, shame, and a profound sense of despair waged war within her. She tried to keep her voice low and even, and was grateful for her hair. "No one would know you came from the forest, or that you don't remember. You don't *need* a shepherd for anything."

Dart made the situation worse by giving the question serious and honest thought. "I am my lady's champion," he concluded. "Now that I have something to remember, even a little, I can see her hand reaching out to me, giving me aid when I have been in need—"

There was more in Dart's mind, but it was lost as outrage won the war for Berika's voice. "Darkwater take your lady!" Darkwater, as opposed to Brightwater, did not exist—could not exist if all mankind's learning about life and magic led to the truth. As an epithet, then, it was meaningful but without risk to the user. "You'd still be crawling on your hands and knees looking for the harp if I hadn't found you."

"I'd still be with my lady in her forest if I hadn't met you at the stream."

"So! Now it's my fault. I should have known that sooner or later you'd find a path to make everything my fault."

Dart shook his head and attempted to bring the conversation back to its beginning. "I'll sell the boots back to the cobbler. . . ." A desperate attempt, and doomed to failure.

"A barefoot nobleman! Oh, that's a rare one."

Agreeing with her, Dart took the breeches from the pile, and when those laces were dangling at his hips, he pulled the boots over them. He gave the loose uppers a thoughtless flip; the mud-cuff formed perfectly just below his knee. Then he clawed Indon's best shirt over his head and tossed it on the bed. "You're right, Berika. Without knowing or meaning, you're right once again. A nobleman cannot be barefoot, and I cannot pretend to be what I'm not."

The sleeves of Dart's secondhand linen shirt descended past his wrists like sausage casings. He shook his hands free and reached for his purse. The cloth immediately engulfed the leather sack. Scowling, Dart scrunched the material above his elbows and began counting out coins. "There is one thing I must do before I can leave for Eyerlon. If I succeed, there will be more than enough for both of us to ride like Donitors; if I fail, we'll be no worse off than we were before."

Dart snatched Berika's hand and pulled it toward him. "This is how I began." He poured three whole marks and a smattering of flakes and grit into her hand. There were fewer coins than had rested in the hollow post, but neither Ingolde nor her husband had ever had an uncut mark. "It will take you back to Gorse, if that's what you wish. If you're frugal, it might get you all the way to Eyerlon, or you can wait for me."

The coins were icy. She had no purse, only the large scrip she'd used to carry their food. It didn't seem right to carry silver with the grease and crumbs, so she tried to knot them into a corner of her apron. Her fingers trembled and the coins bounced loudly across the floor. Berika dropped to her knees. She plucked up all the coins she could see and stared at them. It was one thing to count sheep, which were all alike, but something else to make one counting of the many kinds of coins.

Dart did it so easily.

With a deep sigh Berika sat back on her heels. The coins slipped once again to the floor.

"This thing you must do—Is it dangerous?"

A leather thong dangled from Dart's mouth. He bit it in half before answering her. "I don't know. I think it might be. But I gave my word that I'd be back."

"Like you've given me your word to take me to Eyerlon?"

"Exactly so." Dart tried without success to bind the shirt sleeves at his wrists. Finally he got down on the floor with Berika and placed the entire problem wordlessly in her lap. "A champion's word is more important than any silver or gold. It's pundonor."

The linen was like nothing she'd ever felt before and she could not resist rubbing it between her fingers, even after she'd knotted the thongs snugly over each wrist. "Be careful, Dart," she whispered, stroking the cloth one last time. "You have more to lose than silver or gold."

"Don't worry about me; I won't lose," Dart assured her. He got to his feet and finished dressing with a richly embroidered dalmatic and the feather hat.

"Is that how you've gotten everything? By cheating?" It was a question, not a provocation. Berika thought Dart's eyes were glowing when he turned slowly to face her, though with the rush of her own tears and panic it was impossible to see anything clearly. "I mean—there's nothing wrong with cheating. Anyone who can cheat, does cheat—but don't get caught."

A long moment passed and he said nothing. Berika blinked away her tears. Dart's eyes were not glowing, but he was still dangerously angry. She'd meant to warn him, and, instead, she'd accused him. And successfully accused him, or so she guessed. It wasn't surprising that he cheated—after all, considering the harp and the sword and who his lady was, it was only natural to assume that he had a way with wooden dice. Berika was searching for a safe way to explain this, when Dart swept past her and out of the room.

He won't be back.

She wanted to run after him. She saw the harp and sword in their accustomed places under the bed.

He'll have to come back for those.

She thought she heard his footsteps coming up the stairs. She shivered and hastily plaited her hair.

I don't want him to see me . . . to see him.

She noticed a silver mark lying beside the harp.

It's my money. I can do whatever I want with it.

She began gathering the coins. Since she didn't know how many he'd given her, it took a long time to know that she'd gathered them all. By then, the conflicts and paradoxes had resolved themselves into a narrow path.

Berika knotted the coins into her apron, put on her cloak with the hood raised to conceal her face, and left the room.

CHAPTER

─── 15 ───

Between the tedium of travelling and the delirium of her fever,
Berika had lost count of the days. She worried, as she slipped
unseen from the inn to the street, that it might not be a market
day. Flayne, after all, was nearly as dead as Gorse without
its twice weekly markets. Her plan, raw as it was, required a
market.

Once she had passed through the Knotted Rose's high iron gate,
she realized her problems would not stem from a lack of
opportunity: Every day was market day in Relamain. The streets
were crowded; she was nearly run down by the driver of a huge ox
cart before she'd taken five steps from the iron gate.

"Stay where you belong!" the drover shouted, along with other
insults that made Berika blush and flatten herself against the wall
until the cart was out of sight.

The eaves, Berika quickly discovered, weren't much safer.
While she waited for the cart to pass, a man on the opposite side
of the street was showered with slops heaved out of an upper-story
window. She swayed with indecision: into the street to avoid
falling slops or along the walls to avoid the street traffic?

Fate intervened to help the overwhelmed country shepherd. The
door behind the malodorous, dripping, and cursing man opened

and a woman no older than Berika herself entered the mid-morning light. Her gown was a shiny shade of rose, tightly laced along the sleeves and across the bodice to reveal an embroidered linen smock and a buxom figure. Ash-blond hair was plaited and coiled over the woman's ears. Her face was powdered until it looked as pale as a summer cloud.

"A noble lady . . ." Berika heard herself whisper.

The soles of the lady's wooden shoes rose like carved sails. They lifted the hem of her gown above Relamain's sloppy street. She kept her balance with mincing strides and swaying hips, which drew Berika's eye—and everyone else's—to the jiggle of her breasts against the tight bodice laces. The season was nearly winter, so the noblewoman wore a fur-lined cloak, which Berika judged beautiful but much too short to keep anyone warm; its hem was trimmed with silken tassels that tangled and untangled against her thighs.

Berika was awe-stricken. She forgot the dripping eaves and the noisy carts. She forgot the muddy holes in the street until she planted her foot in one, and then all she felt was envy for those tall shoes. Gallant men appeared from nowhere to carry the noble lady across a lake of mud. The lady laughed and veiled her face with one of the cloak tassels.

The shepherd's heart was close to bursting. She didn't dream that she could own such shoes, much less a flower-colored gown or a tasseled cloak, but Dart had said there were market stalls where commonfolk could buy the soiled, tattered garments noblefolk no longer wished to wear. Berika followed the beautiful lady from one corner to the next, hoping for a glimpse of such a stall.

Luck walked with Berika that morning. She was not run down by oxen, or drowned in slops, and the noble lady minced directly to the open square where clothiers plied their trade. Garments of all descriptions hung from poles and spilled from untidy piles: homespun clothing as drab and shapeless as Berika's own. Men's shirts, dalmatics, and breeches in an array of colors and fabrics. Women's skirts, aprons, and smocks; and, scattered about, laced gowns in bright flower shades. Other traders hawked shoes, belts, and girdles; hats, mittens, and purses of every size and description.

The wonder was too much for one shepherd to appreciate.

Berika wished Embla and Heldey were with her to grasp her hands and share her delight. She couldn't wish or watch for long. The ash-blond woman in the rose-colored gown vanished into the maze of stalls. Berika lingered by the icy fountain at the center of the square, uncertain if she were worthy to enter paradise. The knot of coins that had banged against her knee at every step seemed suddenly small and insignificant. The worth of those shoes must be measured in gold, not silver, and the gowns counted in the gemstones from which they got their color.

Berika was awed, and she was curious. After a few moments, curiosity won the day.

Other women, none quite as splendid as the lady in rose, were eagerly—aggressively—examining the garments hung from poles, overflowing battered chests, and piled on makeshift shelves. They were unwilling to make room for a mousy, downcast country-common shepherd until Berika shyly pointed her finger at a simple, pumpkin-colored gown and asked the critical question in a mousy little voice:

"How much?"

"Two marks, silver."

Two marks! Berika's heart fluttered in her throat. She clasped her hands together and hid her radiant face behind them. Two marks—and she had at least *four* knotted into the corner of her apron. The other, noble ladies in the stall were staring, but she didn't care.

Berika jumped as a hand closed firmly over her shoulder, and a woman's throaty whisper warmed her ear.

"*Ayy*—now. Ain' that be just what you left behind?"

She had her wits about her when she turned, and lost them again when she looked at the pale face, the dressed ash-blond hair, and the brilliant rose gown.

Long fingernails speared the loose weave of Berika's smock and twisted it into a point. "When there's only one dye-pot for the whole stinking village, you don't have a choice. But when you have a choice . . . eh? Won't do anything for your hair, love."

The noble lady was talking to her! Berika swallowed her astonishment. The gown Berika had selected was clearer in color than her smock or skirt had been when they were new, but she had been drawn to it because it was familiar. She couldn't make a choice among the brighter, unfamiliar colors.

"Which would you choose, my lady?"

The stall erupted in laughter. Berika turned crimson, her embarrassment made more acute because she could not guess what she had done. But the lady in rose smiled rather than laughed.

"I wouldn't choose *anything* that Portul had for sale, love. He sells nothing that hasn't been sold many times before. Come along." With her fingernail still twisted in Berika's smock, she led the shepherd deeper into the maze until they came to a merchant with gowns as fine as the one she herself wore. "Neron, you have a customer." She shoved aside skirts and breeches as if they were a curtain.

"Teashia!" he replied with a grin.

Neron was a round man—round bald head, round brown eyes, round ruddy cheeks, and round protruding belly. His arms and legs all but disappeared in the roundness, but he was quick to do the blond lady's bidding. Wonderment was piled upon wonderment as he laid his goods on the bench.

While the lady gushed and cooed, Berika—who was, after all, the daughter of a weaver whose cloth was bought for noblefolks—began to notice flaws in this paradise. Even the shiny rose gown showed clumsy mending on every seam, and a grease blot from the wrist to the elbow of one sleeve. Dart's new clothes were worn, but not filthy. Somewhere else there was another, grander paradise. . . .

She purged the thought from her mind.

"Neron! How long have you been hiding this?" The lady's voice ascended to a grating trill. "It's just per-r-r-fect! Love . . . look at this one, will you! It's just your color."

The gown was red. It had a band of dark embroidery at the cuffs, but the overwhelming impression was *red*. It was redder than Rimp's hands after slaughtering the hogs. It also had a huge, greasy blotch on the front. Berika didn't want to seem ungrateful—certainly not to a noble lady who was being kind to her—but if this was her color, she was in big trouble. The cloth slid from her limp fingers, revealing the penultimate gown of Neron's display.

The gown wasn't shiny or shimmery; it was a soft wool, spun and woven but never dyed. The eye said grey, and then noticed the golds, whites, and browns. It reminded Berika of Dart's hair. She pushed the mounds of red cloth aside.

"*Strewth*—that one's got no color at all, love."

But Neron understood. He swept the red gown from the bench to a heap in the corner. "Merrisat," he whispered, spreading the skirt to its fullest extent.

Berika nodded. Among shepherds the brindle sheep of Merrisat were the stuff of legend. Although the legend Berika had, herself, been most impressed by held that Merrisat sheep would, of their own accord, always return to the meadow where they'd been lambed. Brindle wool might be pretty, but *intelligent* sheep? That was truly a shepherd's legend.

There were no ornate orphrey bands bound over the hems, only a simple casing of Merrisat wool spun to gold rather than grey. The laces were tightly twisted cords of Merrisat fleece. Berika wanted to believe the gown was perfect, but she couldn't help noticing that Neron kept one sleeve folded. He glowered when she pulled it out. It was worse than a stain. Some previous owner must have caught her arm in a candle's flame. The hole was rewoven with a lusterless grey.

Berika let the sleeve fall with a sigh.

Neron saw his morning's sale slipping away. "They say Lady Rani barMeklan wore this at Prince Rinchen's majority last winter in Eyerlon. She wore a girdle of spun gold over it and caught herself a husband without half trying." He ransacked an open chest for a length of silk which he laid across the gown, covering the sleeve completely. "Now I don't have *that* girdle, but I've got this. . . ."

The rose lady trilled again. "Strewth!—now that makes all the difference in the world, love."

Berika bit her lip—she'd be polite even if it hurt—but the yellow-green silk overwhelmed the subtle Merrisat wool. "It certainly does," she admitted, trying to brush the sash aside, trying to imagine the soft wool against her skin.

"Oh, and this too." The lady leaned across the gown, past Neron, to grab an embroidered linen smock from the shelves. She loosened the gown's lacing and pulled tufts of the pink embroidery through the gaps. "Now it's got some *life*, love."

"My name is Berika."

"Strewth! That's not a city name. You must be fresh from some Weychawood village."

The air in Neron's stall became as thick as porridge. "I've come from the assart of Gorse, where we answer only to King Manal himself," said Berika archly. It was the first time she'd ever defended Gorse, but it was also the first time she'd ever heard her home dismissed out of hand by a stranger.

"An assart? Not a lord or lady in sight—no wonder you left. I thought there was nothing in Dunfall, but an *assart!* No wonder you thought I was a lady—Strewth!"

Berika studied the colors of the Merrisat gown. Had she truly believed the braying girl in the threadbare gown was noble? Had she believed that Dart was a demon shaped from her dreams? The answer to both questions was yes, and once again Berika's judgment had failed her.

"Strewth, Berika! How did you get this far from an *assart?*"

"I travelled with . . . a friend."

Teashia was not a lady. Teashia could not say anything without turning Mother Cathe's truth into a single grating sound. But Teashia knew Relamain, and for that reason Berika crooked her desire to run away.

"Just like a man—brought you this far, did he? and then he left. Strewth, it's a good thing you latched onto me, Berika. You'd get eaten alive—"

"Ladies . . . " Neron interjected. "Take your tongues outside, if that's all you're wagging." He folded the Merrisat gown.

"Your travelling friend, what's his name? Man shouldn't think he can change his horses so easy once he gets to Relamain. Get the red one, love, and dance yourself around him. He'll crawl back through a gutter to you."

Neron respected Teashia enough to retrieve the red gown, allowing Berika to gather the Merrisat wool into a tightly clutched bundle. "Canter ruCanter isn't one to crawl in any gutter."

"*Strewth!*" Teashia stretched the syllable from high to low and back again. "You came to Relamain with Canter ruCanter barKethmeron?" She whistled through her teeth and shook her head.

For her life, Berika didn't know what possessed her to use ruCanter's name. She was as bad as Dart. RuCanter was a nobleman, the only true and honest nobleman she'd ever spoken to. She'd wanted to improve her standing in Teashia's eyes; she'd accomplished *that* at least. Teashia's expression had gone from disdain to awe.

Berika began to hedge. "Well, he didn't come all the way to

Relamain, but he arranged for me to stay at the Knotted Rose—"

Now Neron wrinkled his brow and exchanged a meaningful glance with Teashia. "If ruCanter bedded her up in the Rose, she'd be better off with the Merrisat. They don't go for doxies there."

Berika cursed herself up and down for being country-common and blind. The tight laces and face paint fairly screamed Teashia's profession. "I'm looking for the beguinage," she insisted hastily. "RuCanter said he'd find a way to waive King Manal's proclamation." A few more lies couldn't possibly make her position worse than it already was. Then Berika told the truth: "I'm not like you."

Teashia's lips twisted into a snarl. There was nothing wrong with her teeth, and she looked about ready to use them on Berika's neck. "Better'n me 'cause some old noblefolk goat puts you to bed in the Rose?"

Berika was truly frightened, and painfully aware how weak her illness had left her. She was gasping, and each shallow breath felt like a fist slamming between her breasts. She started to cough. Teashia's gown turned grey, as did everything else, and suddenly there was nothing more important filling her lungs.

Grey became black. Berika lost her balance. She clawed the Merrisat dress and everything else on Neron's table in a frantic effort to stay upright, to stay conscious. The battle was lost before it began. Berika hit the cobblestones like a poll-axed ox. Neron lunged for the Merrisat wool as it flowed over the edge of his table. The stitches exploded one by one and he was left holding a lace in each hand.

When Berika awoke she faced a strange ceiling and a cluster of stranger faces. They restrained her when she tried to rise, but not before she'd gotten a look at the walls and knew for certain that she was neither in the Knotted Rose nor Neron's shop. The pain was gone, but the strangers had no trouble keeping her where she was. Then Teashia was among the strangers looking down at her.

"Let me out of here!"

Teashia nodded; Berika was allowed to sit.

"Where am I? Where've you taken me?" Berika studied the closed and sturdy door.

"Grateful bumflower bitch, isn't she?" Teashia said to her

companions as Berika shoved her aside. "Not so fast, love." She put herself between Berika and the door. When Berika shoved again, Teashia was braced and they were flat against each other, breathing in each other's face. "There's a matter of debts owing," Teashia hissed without a hint of friendliness.

Berika became aware that her apron hung evenly from her waist; there was no tug from the corner where she'd knotted up her wealth. "My money!"

"Gone for your gown, love,"

The Merrisat gown was, indeed, hanging from a peg, the mended sleeve and open seams in plain view. "I had at least four marks," Berika protested, once she'd gulped down her surprise.

"Four and a half, love. The gown was eight-and-two. *I* paid Neron the rest, so you owe me, not him."

"Eight marks! I could buy a flock of sheep for eight whole silver marks. You can keep the gown."

Berika put her head down and charged the door with the single-minded determination she'd learned from the sheep. She stiff-armed Teashia and eluded another pair of hands. Glancing left as she cleared the doorway, she saw a broken window and a tangle of ropes and rooftops, none of which looked like escape to a rustic shepherd, so she went the other way, down the dark, narrow stairs and headlong into the hairiest arms and hardest chest she'd ever met.

The brute lifted Berika off her feet and threw her against the wall. Her eyes said *man*, her heart said *beast*, and the combination was Hirmin without the hellfire scars. He roared curses that had never been heard in Gorse, but his anger focused on Teashia, who crouched in terror on the landing. For a fleeting moment Berika thought he might storm past her. She tensed her legs and shifted her balance.

"Stay there!" His arm ended a good two feet away from her face, but Berika flattened against the wall as if she'd been struck.

Teashia was not so fortunate. The back of his hand sent her sprawling against the wall with the broken window. Then he hauled her to her feet and shoved her through the doorway. Teashia screamed and Berika clenched her fists so tight they hurt. She met the eyes of the other doxies who had gathered around her pallet and who now crowded onto the landing.

Berika knew sheep when she saw them, and looked away. The stairs angled down to another landing, and another. She could have run; the flock on the landing wouldn't stop her, but even if she could find her way out of the building, she'd just be alone on the streets.

There was a saying for times like this—even in assarts like Gorse: out of the pot and into the flame. Berika knew by then that things could always get worse, and usually would if she fought long and hard enough. Trees fell, but the grass kept growing and sheep survived.

Berika closed her eyes and sought the empty place on the other side of hope and fear, where she hid whenever Hirmin caught her. She'd rooted herself there when the stairs creaked under the brute's weight. He called her name and she opened her eyes. Teashia stood beside him, cradling one arm beneath her breasts. Her face was dry except for the blood trickling from her swelling lip. When the women looked at each other, no emotion passed between them.

"Teash says you got a noble fish on the line at the Knotted Rose?"

The expression was unfamiliar, but Berika understood it nonetheless. She shook her head. RuCanter had been a lie from the start and Dart was part of a world already lost and forgotten.

"You answer me when I ask you something."

The brute jabbed Berika with his boot; she got the message.

"It's over. He left this morning. I got no one and"—she shot another look at Teashia, but they were both part of the same flock now—"no money either."

He quizzed Berika about the Rose until he was satisfied that despite her plain features and ragged shepherd's clothes, she had indeed met its landlady and, more important, Canter ruCanter barKethmeron.

"Maybe you're worth keepin'," he decided and told her that henceforth she could call him master, as the other doxies in his string did.

Berika bowed her head. "Yes, master." The words came from the empty place within her.

"Teash can't work tonight," the master said with a nod in Teashia's direction. "So you'll take her place. Seems she forgot she don't have nothing at all 'less I give it to her. Seems she gave my money away for you and one of Neron's gowns. Everything goes well tonight an' neither one of you has to pay me back." He opened his hand; Berika placed hers within it and he pulled her to her feet. "You learn quick." He had a leering smile as he traced the outline of her face with a thick finger and pinched her cheek hard enough to make her wince. "You'll fit in just fine."

His hand dropped to his side, and in that gesture Berika saw a flash of silver around his neck. The master caught her just as she looked away. The quiet, empty place shattered around her.

"We don't have any secrets here, do we?"

"No, master," Berika whispered as her hands wove an ineffective barrier over her neck.

Berika didn't want to look at the dark, bearded, and brutal man who'd seized control of her fate, but she had little choice in the matter. She could have fought the waves of compulsion, but if she'd had a prayer of winning, she'd be wearing a sorcerer's torque herself. As she raised her head, she could hear Mag's voice.

Everyone's got a little basi. *You've got more than most, but you haven't got enough to pull down the Web. You'll never work sorcery. None of us will.*

Sorcery couldn't cause pain—that would violate the Compact—so Berika felt fear instead. She could not tell if the master drew upon the Web as he stared, or if he'd already done so, or if *basi* was the furthest thing from his mind as he stared at her with that evil little grin twisting his lips.

Evil sorcerers cropped up from time to time in the winter tales: men and women who set aside the Compact and were vanquished by their powerful peers. The evil sorcerers of the tales were evil through and through; Berika had never considered the possibility that evil, like *basi* itself, was infinitely varied.

Until now.

"So you've got a little charm," the master said. His brows pulled together and he twisted the black wire of his beard into points.

Berika imagined that her arms were wings. She couldn't fly away—escape was impossible—but she could spread them and hide herself behind—

The half-formed image shattered. Berika received an abject lesson in the powers of sorcery that did not quite violate the Compact. The master would never have to strike her as he struck Teashia and the other girls.

"No secrets," he reminded Berika. The wedge of pressure

receded. "Now, go along and get dressed. Teashia will help, won't you, Teash?"

Teashia proclaimed her obedience in all things and followed Berika up the stairs.

"Don't hate me." The ash-blond girl closed the door and leaned against it.

"Why not?" The room was night-dark and unfamiliar. Berika stubbed her toe on her first step and refused to take another. "Where's the lamp?"

"On the shelf."

"What shelf?"

With a sarcastic sigh, Teashia clomped across the room. Her next sigh was far more sincere and followed by the clatter of the lamp striking the floor. Fire was a greater danger than the dark. Berika hurried to the sound and got the lamp righted before all the oil spilled out. Then she lit the wick with the flint-and-steel knotted into her belt.

Teashia was swaying from side to side. Her face was contorted into a silent, endless scream. Her arm was twisted in a way that made Berika nauseous. She set the lamp back on the shelf lest she drop it again.

"He broke your arm!"

Teashia gave no sign that she heard or cared about anything other than her pain.

"The bastard broke your arm." Berika's shepherd's nature rose to the fore. She could curse the sheep while she rescued them, but she could never abandon them. "He's got to get it splinted." She took a stride toward the door, then halted when Teashia implored her with her good hand. "It's got to be done. He's got to understand *that*."

"He'll come up later," Teashia said in a hoarse whisper. "He'll mend it."

Berika rocked back on her heels. "The—He's a *mender*?" Mending was the most precious of sorcerers talents. Menders were honored, and loved, wherever they travelled. Berika could scarcely imagine the brutish master and mending in the same thought, but when she did, another piece of the puzzle fell into place. "He beats you, and then he mends you. . . ."

Color flared in Teashia's cheeks as she twisted away from Berika's stare. "It's no worse here than anywhere else," she said weakly. "Better, maybe, once you're used to it."

"How could you get used to it? He's a demon—" The word froze on Berika's tongue; Dart's face hovered in her mind's eye. "—beast," she finished slowly, closing her eyes and wishing his image away.

Berika kicked off her boots and loosened her apron strings.

CHAPTER
—— 16 ——

A drop of Brightwater liquor large enough to see but too small to swallow swirled around the uneven bottom of Dart's faience mug. It was all that remained from a bone-dry pitcher sitting at the center of his table, and it appeared to have his undivided attention. Dart himself appeared no different from a handful of men sitting apathetically at half-empty two-chair tables with empty mugs and pitchers for companionship.

Every doxy working the Golden Cockerel knew he was different.

The carefully groomed young man was on the porch when the morning taverner arrived. He ordered his pitcher and threw back the first mug like a well-practiced drunk. The early doxies expected him to grow careless with his money as the day progressed. That was the usual way with men who came to the Cockerel before the noon bells—unless they came wrapped in darkness and violence, in which case the master took care of them himself.

But this young man, freshly razored and shorn, with his suede dalmatic snug across his shoulders and his high leather boots sat on that one miserable pitcher. His hands never went back to the sizable purse weighing down his belt.

Not that the doxies didn't try their best to loosen him. By turns they were flirting, seductive, compassionate, and teasing. They were only doing their job under their master's watchful eye. There was no law against a man spending his day with a single small pitcher, nor was there any profit.

"Buy me a mug?" a girl with smudged eyes and a mis-laced gown said as she sat down. "Misery loves company."

Dart stared blankly at her. He had not been back to the Gold Cockerel since the young nobleman labelled him a bumflower, but doxies were doxies wherever they worked. Most of them were haggard, worn, and missing not a few teeth. He hadn't gone after them the way the other men did, because of Berika in the little room under the eaves at the Knotted Rose.

The Cockerel's doxies were younger and healthier than most Dart had seen in the city. But Berika was gone—he didn't expect her to be in the little room when he returned—and he didn't want to be reminded of anything.

"Come on, love. You look like you been whipped. Ain't no good thinking about it." She picked up the pitcher. "Let me get you another, and then you can tell me all about it."

Dart's hand clamped over the doxy's wrist; the pitcher struck the table with a hollow thud. The muzzy, drunken look drained from his face, and what remained wasn't friendly. "Leave it."

The frightened girl splayed her fingers from the handle. "Yes, Midons." He let go and her arm shot back as if she'd held hot coals in her fist. "I was only trying to be friendly." She looked across the room to the bar where the master waited. "I didn't mean no harm—"

"Neither did I. Now just go away." Dart picked up his empty mug and poured his thoughts back into it.

"He's a scary one," the doxy assured the master once she'd scurried close to him. "He's got mean eyes. Shifty, too." The last was an embellishment. The girl hadn't gotten a good look at Dart's eyes. She hadn't gotten a good look at his hair, either. Its parti-colors were dulled to a uniform light brown by the brim of the feathered hat.

The master of the Golden Cockerel reached idly beneath the collar of his shirt. "He going to be trouble?" He scratched idly while glowering in Dart's direction.

"Don't know, master," the girl answered, though the question had not been directed at her.

"Me neither." The master rested both hands on the ancient wood of the bar. "Tell the other girls to leave him alone for a while."

That was an order the girl could obey with enthusiasm.

Clouds swallowed the sun long before it passed to the other side of the Golden Cockerel. The early, middle, and late afternoon hours flowed seamlessly. The squiggle of liquor in Dart's mug evaporated. He remained alone and silent at his table. At sunset, the bells of the sorMeklan tower rang the official warning to Relamain's citizens: Legitimate mercantile trade and the great gates were ready to close for the night. Unofficially, the sunset peal signalled the start of less legitimate activities in the Golden Cockerel and similar establishments all over the city.

The Golden Cockerel's regulars began arriving before the streets were dark. The high-roofed hall echoed their rowdy greetings and demands. Doxies worked up a sweat delivering pitchers of dark beer, amber cider, and, of course, powerful Brightwater liquor. The master was everywhere: beside the huge kegs filling pitchers; at select tables giving his personal greeting to the Cockerel's most valued clients; at the door barring those whose credit was overextended; and in the shallow clay-lined ring where the fights from which his establishment took its name were ready to begin.

The last day of each week brought the best birds and the biggest wagers, but there were good matches on the ninth day as well, when ambitious breeders from the outlying manors sought to catch a patron's eye. A cheer went up from every corner of the room when the master lifted the cages of two country-raised cocks. Touts moved swiftly and smoothly through the customers, calling out the house odds and collecting the wagers.

The master climbed out of the ring with a smile on his face. He glanced toward Dart and the smile faded. Dart was no longer playing with his mug or tracing the woodgrain of the table; he was watching the door, giving each customer a thorough, impassive onceover as he came in. The master stroked his beard and slipped his fingers beneath the collar of his shirt. His smile vanished completely.

The jut of Dart's chin proclaimed his intensity. He should have been shedding enough *basi* to rouse the dead. There should have been something in the air for a sorcerer and his water to detect. A sorcerer of the master's calibre should have been able to pluck the fact Dart sought from the surface of his thoughts. But though the room fairly shouted hope, lust, greed, and a dozen other mortal empathies, the young man in the deep-brimmed hat sat in an aura of unnatural quiet.

The master of the Golden Cockerel reached under the bar where the most powerful spirits were kept. He knew the bottle he wanted by its dusty cork and the lightning tingle it sent up his arm. He put a shot into a mug and covered it with liquor of a more ordinary sort, then snapped his fingers at the nearest girl.

"Take this to the one yonder by himself. Tell him it's on the house, as our games do not amuse him."

The master pounded the bar with his fist when Dart calmly accepted the mug and then set it down without wetting his lips. He left his table to mingle with the raucous men crowding the cock ring.

"He says thank you," the doxy said when she got back to the bar with a clutch of empty pitchers in each hand. The master cuffed her on the cheek.

Dart had been tempted by the free spirits, but not in the way the master had intended. He'd come to the Gold Cockerel for one purpose—to reclaim his honor from the nobleman who had stolen it—never thinking that young man might not make himself available. As the hours dragged by, he'd grown hungry and thirsty, and more determined to be ready when his nemesis walked through the door. Dart knew what Brightwater liquor could do to an empty stomach. He would not have refused a plate of sausage, and thought of ordering one—the few grit wouldn't make a difference in the game he intended to play. Then he imagined himself sitting with grease on his hands when the nobleman came through the door.

Dart's thoughts were wandering when he joined the crowd. He didn't look up when the stewards displayed the victor, and he didn't step aside when the vanquished bird was thrown from the ring. The bleeding mass struck his thigh and fell at his feet. Dart stared at the feebly twitching thing, unable, for a moment, to fit a name over its shape. When recognition struck, it hit his gut first and he was grateful for the nearest post.

He no longer welcomed the flashes from the abyss. The man he'd once been had revelled in a variety of debauched entertainments, none of which the man he'd become retained the stomach for. It was almost enough to make him question the need to satisfy a pundonor with someone who was, doubtlessly, a mirror of his blighted former self.

A man whose sum of experience stretched back to the seventh day of Greater Gleaning should have little need for honor and less for revenge. He'd be wiser to take his hoard of silver and buy a deck passage down the river to Eyerlon before winter froze the boats at their piers. With Berika, if she remained in the room. Without her? If she had flown, should he look for her or accept the fate that had parted them?

Dart shuddered at the memory of how he'd left her.

"I prefer the blue myself— What are you seeing that I'm not?"

While his back was to the door, his quarry had entered and been drawn to him.

Dart's thoughts returned to the Golden Cockerel like a whip cracking. During his idyll, he'd moved away from the post and rejoined the crowd at the ring as two more cocks were displayed by their handlers.

"Nothing, nothing at all."

They did not separate from the crowd, but studied each other's profile with casual directness. The nobleman blinked first; Dart braced for a challenge.

"I don't believe I know you. Are you just come to Relamain?"

"Recently."

"Tell me your name."

"Ean."

The nobleman's nostrils flared. "Your family. Your honor. Tell me who you are, one man to another."

Dart relaxed; he'd worried that his quarry might remember him from the previous week. "I've left my family and honor behind. My lady mother watched my father and elder brothers go off to war with Hazard; they sleep in unmarked graves. When King Manal exempted sole surviving sons from the muster, she bound me with promises and kept me at her side until she herself died. I kept my promises until the war was over; now I've come in search of my fate and fortune. Call me Ean ruNo-man sorNo-family—and tell me that you've been luckier with your own." He extended an open hand.

Dart gleaned his tale from a dozen overheard conversations. It plucked at the fear of every young nobleman: a famine of opportunity to gain glory and honor for himself and his name. His quarry grimaced in sympathy. Dart basked in the glow of self-satisfaction as they clasped their hands together in friendship.

"I'm Driskolt ruEan barRelamain sorMeklan, Sidon of all Fenklare."

Dart fought to contain his wide-eyed amazement. The young man grasping his hand—the object upon whom he intended vengeance—had proclaimed himself to be the son and confirmed heir of Ean sorMeklan, lord of this city and Donitor of Fenklare. Fortunately for Dart, Driskolt took astonishment in stride.

"—And a fine thorn in my fine father's side, you may be sure. So, Ean, will you bet on the blue with me, or be my father's namesake and bet against me?"

A lump had formed in Dart's throat. His mind was slow choosing words, and his tongue was slower yet in forming them. "I . . . No . . . Cockfighting . . ." He shrugged and felt like an utter fool.

"A mark on the blue. Come on, put your money with mine. Where better to start a friendship?"

Friendship was the last of what Dart wanted with this young man, but he needed a measure of Driskolt's trust. Trust was worth a silver mark. Dart reached into his scrip without revealing its weight. He handed Driskolt the silver coin. "A mark where you wish it," he said with a smooth, challenging smile. "But, I'd rather forge a friendship over iron-in-the-fire."

The Donitor's son returned the smile. "You flatter yourself with the dice, then?" He raised his hand and snapped his fingers. The sound got lost in the din, but not the light flashing off his signet ring. A tout swam upstream to collect the bet. "On the left-side blue." Driskolt poured a half-dozen marks into the other man's hand and dug into the tout's left-side pouch for his chits.

Even Dart knew that the tout was supposed to count the chits. The poor man's eyes widened, but he said nothing. The master of the Golden Cockerel might challenge the behavior of Ean sorMeklan's heir, but not a simple tout. He retreated, glancing nervously at the bar where the master was not to be seen.

"Don't you trust me?" Driskolt asked pointedly, gripping the tout's shoulder. "I trust *you*. Bring my winnings—if winnings there are—to the tables. I'm going to show my new friend here how we forge iron in Relamain."

"Yes, midons Sidon." The tout bowed from the waist, but not before deceit lit his eyes.

Dart expected the worst—if he could see the tout's mind

working, then surely Driskolt sorMeklan could. But the sorMeklan heir only laughed as he towed Dart across the room.

The rules of iron-in-the-fire were pretty much the same throughout Relamain and Walensor; the rituals varied. And nowhere were they more complex than at a gaming-house where noblefolk came to play, a house like the Golden Cockerel. Here they could even play a public game where the very-busy touts would collect side-action wagers. Driskolt chose against that by seating himself at a small raked table near the bar, where the master himself would tend to any other need they might have.

Dart had no objection and sat in the other chair. His mark joined Driskolt's in the pit to buy the table for the night. The master came around to collect them.

"Playing for blood?" the burly, bearded taverner asked without betraying a jot of interest.

Driskolt nodded, but Dart shook his head. Blood was jargon for a game in which the players declared their intent to empty each others purses before the first forge was begun. The house provided the dice, the cup, and a referee.

"I doubt I could play the Sidon for blood," Dart said with an ingratiating smile—though that, and more, was precisely his intent. He looked straight into Driskolt's eyes. "Let's play for honor instead."

In jargon, honor meant the stakes would stay so low that the house could ignore them. Dart did want to be ignored. The Sidon hesitated for a hare's breath; he blinked as he studied his opposition. Dart had hidden his hair and his eyes as best he could with the hat. Driskolt might not want to forge with a man whose eyes he could not see.

The Sidon flicked his tongue along his upper lip and made his decision. "Honor it is—unless we raise the stakes, eh?"

"We can *always* raise the stakes," Dart agreed.

They played with house dice in a house cup. The cup was clear crystal and the dice were chips of carnelian and obsidian. The Golden Cockerel cosseted its most noble customers. Driskolt threw first, casting a point that was barely worth the ante. Dart's throw was easier still, and they were playing for honor whether they willed it or not.

"Cider here," Driskolt shouted when they'd pushed the same flakes around for the fifth or sixth time. "And livelier stones, if you please."

Dart was ready for new dice, and he'd drink the cider—though he'd rather see Driskolt drinking Brightwater liquor. But the Sidon played more cautiously than he spoke.

A girl brought over the pitcher, two mugs, and five fresh dice sealed in a wax matrix. The girl stared at Dart; he stared back. She was plainly dressed in a grey-gold wool, with none of the gewgaws the gaming-house doxies usually wore to steal a man's attention from his wager. Her face was caked with paint and the gown was just as tight in the waist and loose around the breasts as any other doxy's. She was still staring, when Driskolt pinched her from behind. Her shriek turned every head in the room.

"An apple that's never been pressed," the Sidon opined as the girl ran back to the bar and the glowering master of the Golden Cockerel. "There's few enough of them in Relamain anymore."

The master snarled at her and she scurried back to the table. Her duties included melting the wax around the dice over the flame in the table lamp, and the master would see that she performed her duties no matter how much, or how often, his customers interfered. The Sidon toyed with the laces on the side of her gown. She looked at Dart, and he looked away. He felt her misery like a cold rain, but he was playing for his own honor.

"You fancy her?" Driskolt asked when the dice were free and the girl had vanished.

Dart shook his head. "Not tonight." The cider turned to vinegar in his stomach. He was alone . . . for the first time in memory.

Without thinking, Dart reached for the cup, bumping Driskolt's hand as he did. Their eyes met, and the Sidon's were icy. Dart remembered he'd thrown last and the nobleman had called for the new dice. It wasn't his turn; his carelessness rattled him.

Driskolt threw. He declared his point to be a cold-iron seven and announced his intention to throw again with both black dice. Dart dropped a mark into the pit before his mind cleared enough to see that two flakes would have been sufficient. His fingers twitched, betraying his desire to retrieve the mark. Driskolt dropped his own mark in the pit and scooped up two dice with a flourish. Iron-in-the-fire was as much a game of intimidation as it was of luck, and Dart, with two gaffes in quick succession, was suddenly and precipitously losing it.

The Sidon threw a pair of fours; he could empty the pot or throw again, trying for eight or better, rather than seven. With Dart looking nervous, Driskolt chose to throw again. The rules said

Dart could put any amount in the pit, but ritual said he had to go better than he had on the previous throw. He separated a mark and a flake from his hoard and pushed them into the pit.

"I think you fancy her after all," Driskolt drily observed as he evened the pit. "We could throw her in on top. . . ."

Dart's wardrobe was testament to the odd things that wound up in a dice pit, but he wasn't ready to place the girl or her maidenhead there. "When the silver's gone," he replied noncommittally.

"You've only brought silver?"

They were past honor and moving toward blood.

Driskolt covered the eight with a six and a four, and promptly announced that he'd throw for the ten point. The game was starting to get interesting, and in a world where every living creature possessed some *basi* sensitivity an interesting game raised heads around the room. Dart added two marks to the coins already in the pit; Driskolt glowered.

"My gods are smiling on me. I feel lucky," he insisted, and exercised the shooter's little-used prerogative of raising the bet at the end of a round. A flake-sized golden mark glittered in the pit.

Gold was not alive. It had no intrinsic *basi*, but its value was such that it attracted *basi* as a flower attracts honeybees. Heads-up interest became an audience. Dart's scrip contained only a few of the tiny gold coins. His fingers were numb when he evened the pit.

Driskolt invoked his smiling gods as he rattled the dice in the cup. They shot across the table, and the quick-sighted could see he'd missed his point with a five and a two, then the two-up struck the lip of the table and bounded back as a five. The gods *were* smiling on sorMeklan's heir.

Dart tasted panic at the back of his throat, especially when Driskolt declared he'd try another toss. Dart could have bowed right then, or played two silver marks and a flake; he chose instead to jump the stakes substantially, and skidded a large, loud, silver memor into the pit. Memors were favored by those who believed wealth should feel substantial. Merchants used them; Driskolt sorMeklan, Sidon, carried none. The nobleman scowled, but he was not bluffed. He counted out four marks of gold and laid them on top of the huge silver coin.

The laws of chance were on Dart's side, but the gods remained with Driskolt. He threw two sixes and scooped the coins from the

pit into a pile on his side of the table, thereby ending his forge.
Dart had lost half his money in one forge. He could feel his
shoulders knotting up.

"Your forge, Ean." The nobleman was uncommonly pleasant
as he passed the cup across the table. Their audience had not
dispersed.

Dart wiped his forehead on his sleeve and called for new
dice—if only to give him a moment's respite. The same girl came
over. She gaped when she saw the coins between Driskolt's hands.
The wax matrix cracked in her trembling hands, spilling the dice
onto the floor. One of the audience put a warding hand on her
shoulder when she tried to retrieve them.

"None o'that."

So she had to go back to the master for another set, and a cuff
on either side of her head for her clumsiness. Didn't she know, the
master bellowed, that the fane charged a silver mark to verify the
dice and set them in that matrix? And as if that weren't bad
enough, the set she'd dropped were the last stone set the Golden
Cockerel had, and now the Sidon must play with wooden dice,
like a commoner. The terrified girl apologized profusely and took
such care releasing the wooden dice that the crowd got bored.
Finally she dropped the five dice into the cup.

The wooden dice had a softer sound as they knocked against
each other and the side of the cup—a sound that halted Dart's slide
into panic and restored his faith in himself. He released the dice
with an easy sweep of his arm, then watched with horror as the
counter-die showed its all-black face and the black dice showed
six and six.

"High iron," Driskolt observed for the benefit of those who'd
wandered away. "Pass?"

CHAPTER

——17——

High iron was not the most difficult point in the game; sparking aces, the singleton pair of fire, was equally difficult. They were both a thrower's nightmare. The logic of experience advised the thrower to pass the cup quickly, in a head-to-head game. It would come right back and he'd lose no more than his ante. Driskolt extended his hand for the cup.

Dart shook his head. The onlookers gasped as Driskolt separated one of the gold marks from his winnings and shot it into the pit.

"Gold says you can't make it."

That gasp became a steady murmur of side action as the stranger rummaged through his scrip and hid the gold mark with another memor.

"You're a damned fool," the Sidon said with genuine regret, but he evened the pit and Dart scooped up the dice for his throw.

Nothing louder than a mouse's squeak would have fit through Dart's throat at that moment. He managed a smile that was more enigmatic than confident and the dice fell out of the cup. Driskolt's fist slammed the table making everything jump, but it was too late: Everyone had seen the double sixes. The Sidon slumped back in his chair as Dart bought himself some breathing room.

"Blood, Ean. My forge and we're throwing for blood."

Dart unhooked his purse and dropped it on the table. It made a satisfying sound, for all that it was mostly filled with grit and flakes. "Blood, if you like, midons—but it's *not* your forge."

The Sidon was muttering like an ox drover as he slammed his own purse onto the table. "Damn your eyes," he swore before looking across the room to the bar. "It's blood!" he shouted.

They needed a referee and touts to collect the side action. The master came running right behind the girl in the grey-gold wool gown.

Five dice—one showing black and four showing sixes—challenged the room while the master counted each player's tabled wealth. Dart had more coins; Driskolt had more gold. There was more money on the table than had been in Gorse in all the years since its founding, and Driskolt had more than twice as much as Dart. The Sidon bet two gold marks; Dart countered with his last memor. The pit was evened and the black dice disappeared back into the cup.

The master's fingers disappeared beneath the collar of his shirt. The girl clenched and unclenched her fists. Driskolt caught her hand while it was open. She closed her fingers tightly, unmindfully, over his and did not move them again. But no one watched the master, or the girl, or the Sidon; they watched the cup as Dart tipped it forward, and the dice as they bounced to their rest.

"High iron again . . . Three in a row—!"

The forging was over. Dart's purse wouldn't cover another round of blood betting, but a man could outfit himself and a horse for war with the precious metal on the table and live comfortably for several months off the change. The doxy squealed with excitement. She tried to bring her hands together, and was surprised to find that one was confined. Her expression grew more puzzled when she landed on the Sidon's knee.

"You've done yourself proud, Ean ruNo-man," Driskolt conceded. "You've got blood." His free hand slid around the doxy's waist. It settled on her thigh. "But you'd never throw a fourth."

Dart leaned forward, studying the pit. This was not the ending he'd anticipated. He'd had an incredible forging, won blood by default, but he hadn't humbled the man who'd dishonored him, not in the least.

"I can throw a fourth," he drawled, still scowling at the dice. "I know I can. I just can't prove it to you." He transferred the scowl to his pathetic reserve of silver and grit.

Pushing the doxy from his lap, Driskolt met Dart at blinking distance above the table. "You said you're the surviving son. You've got birthrights—land and rents. If your demesne wasn't on the wrong side of Tremontin," he whispered. "I'll accept your pledge with witnesses."

"I've no land on the wrong side of Tremontin," Dart asserted with perfect honesty. "My birthrights are pledged to you from now—all of them." He had, of course, nothing to lose.

Driskolt pushed his entire pile to the pit, then called for parchment, pen, and ink. The room remained quiet while the master himself went to the bar. There was clinking and shuffling; then he returned carrying a carefully arranged tray. He spat on the ink to make a workable puddle. Dart waited for a much-needed burst of recognition.

"Mark your name," the master snarled, gesturing toward the pen. "You've already given your word. No time for second thoughts."

Dart wasn't having second thoughts. Recognition didn't hit until he picked up the pen—he simply hadn't known what else to do—but the thin bristle-tipped pen was as familiar as a sword. Dart had not questioned his knowledge of swordsmanship when he needed it; he did not question his penmanship either. He made two flowing designs on the parchment; then, with anxiety tickling the back of his neck, he measured the reaction in the crowd around him.

The doxy looked relieved. Driskolt looked smug. The master didn't look at all; he was melting wax and heating the Cockerel's seals in the flame of the table lamp. Everyone else seemed content, and Dart silently expelled the breath he'd been holding. The master rolled the parchment into a tube and shook a dollop of black wax onto the covering edge. Driskolt flattened the parchment when he slammed the seal into the wax.

"Square," Driskolt said as he pulled the doxy to his lap again and tightened his arm around her waist. "Forge on." Then he moaned as the dice fell from the cup in an altogether too familiar pattern.

"That's it," the master announced, reaching for the cup.

"He took my pledge," Dart said, halting the master. "I'll take his—if he's willing to give it."

"You're empty. What do you have to match *my* birthrights?" Driskolt demanded. His tone, however, made it clear that he would welcome a way to keep the forge alive for one more throw of the dice.

"I have gifts from a lady of the forest. Gifts that will dazzle the basilidans of Eyerlon when I take them there—If I get them there."

The girl on Driskolt's knee gasped. She covered her face with her hands. Dart glanced up and saw wide, familiar eyes peeking through the spread fingers. A torrent of confused questions washed over him. For a moment Berika was all he knew or recognized, but he was no longer the man he'd been at sunrise.

"They're worth more than my birthrights or all the gold in the world—to the right man," he concluded. "Shall we go another round? Do you truly think you can lose?"

Driskolt snatched the pen and parchment. His face contorted with childish concentration; his awkward strokes mashed the bristles and when he was done there was ink on his fingertips, which he quickly transferred to the front of Berika's gown. One had to hope the swordsmanship of the Sidon of Fenklare was better than his penmanship.

"Everything," he declared. "Everything I've got from my majority, and my future rights too. You *can't* roll high iron five times running. It's never been done."

"If it's never been done, it's because *I* never tried."

Dart sealed the Sidon's pledge and made a second of his own. He scooped up the dice. The master openly rubbed the torque around his neck. No one looked happy. Dart gave the cup a short swirl and cocked it above the table—

"New dice!" Driskolt barked.

The master caught the dice before they struck the table. He slipped them into the waistband of his breeches. "Mind your time," he scolded the nobleman while snapping his fingers at the bar. "Don't waste your luck on my hands."

A pocked youth with a wayward eye shouldered his way to the table with sealed dice. He stood on tiptoe to whisper in the master's ear—but his revelation carried across the hushed room: "There's no more in wax after this—"

The master shrugged. This forging would be over with the next throw. Displaying the dexterity of four decades' experience, the master scored the wax and heated it in the flame. The cloudy surface became slick and shiny; the slit widened like ripe fruit. The master of the Golden Cockerel closed his fist and squeezed. There was no tension on his face; he never dropped a die. It was unthinkable that all five wooden cubes would explode from his grasp.

But they did.

They clattered to the table: One showed smoothly black; the rest showed sixes.

Driskolt would not believe what his eyes saw. "New dice!"

Grooves formed between the master's brows; there were no more sealed dice. There were unsealed dice by the handful, but no one would, or should, trust them in a forge gone this far into blood.

"Send to the fane for new dice!" Driskolt insisted when the master did not move.

The master glanced at the hour candle burning steadily in its glass tower. It was halfway through the blue. He weighed his options, and their costs: the time for his men to get to the fane. The time for that man to find a sorcerer willing to certify the weight and measure of each cube, to purge them of any *basi* they might have acquired from past forges. The time for him to return. An ordinary man—even an ordinary nobleman—would endure the wait, but the Sidon sorMeklan was not an ordinary man.

Nor was the master of the Golden Cockerel. He didn't need to send someone begging for sorcery at the fane.

He put the dice in the cup himself and swirled it loudly. He shot the dice with authority, and kenned them to be completely fair as they fell. They struck the lip of the table and bounced back to the middle where they revealed a middling spread: a total of five on the red, eight on the black, red and black split on the smooth-surfaced die.

"The dice are square," he said.

"Again."

The master obliged, and the spread was equally mediocre.

"Square," he repeated, replacing the dice in the cup and handing it to Dart.

"So say you."

That roused the master's ire. He put two hard fists on the table and leaned nose-to-nose with the heir of the lord of his city and province. "So I say." He stressed each word equally. "You have a problem with that? You think I spook my own dice?"

Driskolt gave his head a nervous little shake. Dart took the cup. He was as cool as he'd been at the beginning: no beaded sweat on his forehead, no unintentional spasms to shake the cup, and just the faintest trace of a smile surfacing on his lips as the dice came out.

The master called the spread: "High iron. Thrower makes his point. Thrower wins the forge. Thrower takes the pit."

Flies could have walked on Sidon Driskolt's eyes or set up housekeeping in his open mouth. The master removed Dart's pledges from the pit, broke their seals, and cast them to the floor. Dart's smile became a toothy grin as he picked up two of the gold coins.

Victory was sweet; vengeance sweeter.

Driskolt stared sourly at his feet and, after a moment, at Dart's discarded pledges. Another moment passed before what he saw overcame what he felt. He shoved Berika from his knee and grabbed the scraps of parchment. His eyes widened; rage clogged his throat and made his voice shrill as any woman's. "This is *my* signet!" He threw the parchment squares on the table. "Iser's fist and sword! You white-blooded cheat!" He wrapped his hand around the knife hilt at his belt, but looked at the master before drawing it. "I call him a cheat, a fraud, and a liar. I demand my rights of satisfaction. Pundonor!"

The onus settled on the master. It was his obligation to keep his games honest, and he'd done so for two decades, making the Golden Cockerel the most respected gaming-house in Relamain. The only place where men like the Sidon, whose purse was never truly empty, came calling. In Driskolt's smoldering resentment the master could see the destruction of the only thing he held dear. He grabbed Dart's shirt and pulled him upright.

"Account for yourself!"

The cloth was tight around Dart's throat. "I threw high iron five times running. I won . . ."

Dart's voice trailed off to a whisper as the master's face grew dangerously livid. The question did not arise from the dice, which were guaranteed, but from the pledges which the master brandished with his free hand.

"What's the meaning of this, you misbegotten fool!" He shook his fist until Dart's teeth clashed; then he threw him backward.

Dart hit the floor hard enough to drive the breath from his lungs and the panic from his heart. "The pledges don't count," he insisted, sitting up slowly. "The dice were square. I won square with five high iron." He didn't particularly like the whiny echo his voice left in his ears, but it and the words themselves were coming out of the abyss.

"It's not the gods-rotted iron," the master said with a menacing lilt. He took a stride forward. Dart looked straight up to see his face. "It's the lie you've made for name!"

Dart tried to wriggle free, but the master stood on the hem of his dalmatic. The flickering light from the oil lamps was painfully bright. His temples began to throb in counterpoint to his heartbeat. The searing pain he had felt when Berika first asked that question—a pain which he had repressed—returned.

"Your name! Who are you? None of this ruNo-man. Who's your father? What's your family? What right do you have to your name!"

Though Dart did not believe it at that moment, the master of the Golden Cockerel was not his enemy. Indeed, none of those crowded around his misery hoped more sincerely for a simple refutation of the Sidon's charges.

"Give me a good account of yourself and I'll warrant your iron and your pit to the gods and back!"

Somewhere in the darkness of his past, long before his fateful encounter with his lady, Dart had learned to obey another man's commands. He wiped the glaze of pain from his eyes and pressed his fingers into his temples to ease the throbbing for a moment.

"Dart."

"Dart! Dart—that's no man's name!" the master snarled, not adding that it could be a basilidan's name, and basilidans were the only sorcerers expressly prohibited from trying their luck in a licensed gaming-house.

The respite which finger pressure had brought ended with a bolt of agony that left Dart ashen. Like a stillborn child, he folded his arms and pressed his forehead against his knees. The onlookers silently shared the realization that something out of the ordinary was taking place.

The master's sorcery was as subtle as it was strong. Berika was looking straight at him when his brows and lips tightened, but she felt nothing beneath his understandable consternation. Dart felt something like the mist of a cool waterfall wrap around him, dulling the worst of the pain. He recognized it as kin to Ingolde's hedge-sorcery and Yagrin's intimidations, but of far greater strength. Filling his lungs with a calming breath, he could imagine only one possible source.

"My lady . . ." he whispered as he opened his eyes, half-expecting to see her and seeing Berika's anxious face instead. He looked for the pieces of the name she'd given him. "Ean . . . Ean . . . ruEan . . . Driskolt . . ." His lips moved but no one could hear his words.

The master of the Golden Cockerel brandished one of Dart's pledges. "Your name—it's a simple question, man. Who are you? Where do you come from, and"—the master's voice turned cold and deadly—"by what right do you come gaming in my house?" He hauled Dart back to his feet.

Dart stared at the parchment. The writing he'd made so confidently bore little resemblance to the letters carved on signboards and price lists. There were two black designs, one larger than the other. The larger was curved like trees bending in the wind, the smaller was a maze of quick angles, and neither was meaningful now.

The comforting mist dissipated; the pain rushed back. A spasm twisted Dart's neck until his ear pressed against his shoulder. The deep-brimmed hat dropped to the floor. "I have no name," he gasped.

The overwhelmed expression on Dart's face was familiar to one man in the room, and so was the parti-colored hair, though it had been cleaned and cut since he last saw it.

"You're no nobleman!" Driskolt snarled as he surged between Dart and the master. "You're that reeking mad bumflower who came in here and wouldn't leave last week—You thought to make a fool of me. My pledges. What were you going to try to do with my pledges!"

Driskolt's punch dropped Dart to the floor. His skull hit the wood planks like a stone, and he lay still. Driskolt shifted his weight to one side, but the master intervened before he could drive his boot into Dart's side.

"He makes your signet better than you yourself." The master dropped Dart's marker on the table, where it lay beside Driskolt's. The difference was obvious even to a wide-eyed and illiterate country-common shepherd.

"Whoever, or whatever he is, midons Sidon, he's no bumflower." The master deflected Driskolt's wrath with logic and a subtle wedge of *basi*. "Bring him around," the master continued, issuing commands to his massed touts. "We'll have the truth from him yet."

A pitcher of cider and another of flat ale splashed Dart's face. He groaned and covered his face with his hands. The master readied his powers; he'd have the truth this time.

The master of the Golden Cockerel, despite his temperament, was a mender by talent, not an inquist. He'd left the Eyerlon classrooms when he found he could not breach the defenses of the most ordinary mind. As the years passed, and his *basi* compounded, he'd mastered what might be described as brutal persuasion. It hadn't failed him in a long time, but against Dart it vanished like rain on the ocean. Then it became a matter of pundonor—not intelligence.

"Every man has a name!" the master thundered.

The room was silent, except for Driskolt, who dared the silence: "Unless he's dishonored it."

The master scowled. "Honor means nothing to me. It's his name, and I'll have it from him." He brought his scowl and his sorcery to bear on Dart. "Whatever wrong you've done," he warned, "it's no way as bad as lying now."

Pain narrowed Dart's vision to the heaviest greys and the sharpest brights. It locked each muscle and bone. He had neither the desire nor the strength to resist the master of the Golden Cockerel, but his name, his true name given to him at his birth, remained hidden.

"Dart. My lady called me her dart against hazard."

Dart had no recourse against the master's onslaught. He retreated from his three-week hoard of experience. He cast out such memories and secrets as he had accumulated. They vanished in the searing wind. There was nothing left but the abyss from which he'd emerged, to which he returned. It swallowed the pain. Dart smiled, and then it swallowed him.

The master recoiled. He blinked his eyes rapidly, scarcely believing that he stood on the firm floor of the Golden Cockerel. Nothing in his experience could explain what had happened—or how he had escaped with his life intact.

"He's said he has no name since he came out of Weychawood," Berika said in a soft voice. She'd felt the master's *basi* vanish into the abyss. "He doesn't remember anything before that. He *can't* remember. We were going to go to Eyerlon. He thought maybe they could help."

"Is he dead?" someone asked from the depths of the crowd. "He's not moving at all."

"He's still breathing."

"Straighten his arms and legs," another man pleaded. "It hurts just to look at him."

Driskolt sorMeklan was the only member of the crowd willing to approach the unconscious man—and he was willing simply because the master was not. He nudged Dart with his boot; but that wasn't enough and the Sidon had to kneel before he could get enough leverage to free Dart's twisted limbs. Driskolt had one hand lifting Dart's shoulder and the other beneath his back groping for the end of his sleeve when a tremor passed through the unconscious man's body.

Afterward, no one was sure exactly what happened, it happened so fast, but everyone was sure of one thing: Dart's eyes opened and they seethed with angry color. Sheer terror gave Driskolt all the strength he needed to free his hand and spring backward to his feet.

"Hellfire!" the Sidon gasped, barely retaining his balance.

Hellfire—the essence of conjury—the magic of the Arrizi, the antithesis of Walensor's Brightwater sorcery. Hazard's magic, which turned Kasserine into a molten cauldron and scarred the likes of Hirmin. Berika's gut sank; not once in all the time she'd been with him and wondered if he were a man or a demon, had she considered Arrizan treachery, Arrizan conjury.

The man standing beside her drew a knife. "Arrizi bastard!"

Walensor claimed victory, but the destruction of the Arrizan army in Tremontin had not, in the minds of many Walenfolk, settled the accounts.

The glint of steel cleared the master's mind. His two years in the Basilica hadn't taught him much about conjury, but he knew it didn't feel anything like the abyss underneath Dart's paltry memories. He spun the knife-wielding man around, and became the target of his wrath.

"I'm going to kill the Arrizi bastard!"

The master dodged the wild slashes easily. The outraged man was no threat to an experienced brawler, but he was also beyond the reach of logic or persuasion. The master knocked him out with a well-aimed punch.

"I'm taking him to the inquists at the fane," he said coldly. "He's no good to 'em dead. Any argument?" He let his assailant crumple. There were no other objections.

Driskolt eased up on the master's good side. "I'm going with you." He caught the eye of another well-dressed youth. "Go up to the tower gates. Tell them what's happened. Make sure my father hears."

There was a brief discussion of the best way to get Dart to the fane, which the master ended by grabbing Dart's shirt and slugging him on the chin. "That'll keep him quiet till we get him there. Get me some ropes and a blindfold—" He looked at one of the doxies. "No sense taking chances."

Dart was bound hand and foot. A strip of softened leather was tied tightly over his eyes, and a sack pulled over his head. He was slung on a pole, and there was no shortage of volunteers to carry him to the inquists' mercies. Berika was one of the few who did not join the throng headed for the fane. She sat in Dart's place at the gaming table, too numb to move. Driskolt lingered as well, his eye on Dart's untouched winnings.

"You still owe me seventeen marks—gold," the master said softly, taking the coins. "Five silver marks and seven grit."

Driskolt shrugged. "I always pay up." He started for the door.

"And you always lose again." The master poured the coins into his purse before following Driskolt into the street.

CHAPTER
——18——

The master of the Golden Cockerel and the youthful Sidon of Fenklare were leaders, not followers. They did not remain behind the mob for long, but wove their separate ways to the front. Although it was often complained that no debauchery or rowdiness was foreign to Relamain's twisted streets, rumors that a stranger—a foreigner—spewed hellfire at the Golden Cockerel and was, at that very moment, trussed beneath a pole, headed for an inquist's sacram at the fane penetrated the darkest alleys faster than dawn light.

The Golden Cockerel's assembly swelled with ordinary citizens, a good number of whom were convinced the prisoner at the front of their parade was Hazard of Arrizan himself. They were as frightened as they were angry. It wasn't long before someone shouted for Arrizi blood.

For Dart, drifting in and out of consciousness, life had become an incomprehensible horror, a dream from which he struggled to wake. He writhed like the demon many thought he was, and aided by the jostling, the sack over his head came loose and vanished on the streets. The blindfold was not so easily dealt with. Dart pitted the feeble strength of his eyelids against the knotted leather.

Translucent globes of amber and green replaced his blindness.

They had their own life; they grew within his skull, crowding each other, seeking escape. Dart had not been gagged; nothing blocked his scream as the globes exploded and his world became a fiery, bloody crimson.

"Demon's eyes! Hellfire!"

Waves of hate and terror crashed over the helpless man. In ridding himself of the blindfold, Dart had made what would likely be a fatal mistake. He closed his eyes and swallowed the pain, but by then it was too late. The marchers took aim with the ammunition beneath their feet, heaving cobblestones and worse. Dart's bearers were struck before he was. They began to run, and when that did not protect them from the crowd's wrath, they simply dropped the pole and fled.

The boldest of the marchers approached the motionless prisoner in the street. She threw her stone. When Dart groaned like any other man, she ran up to kick him once before retreating. When hellfire did not consume her, another woman separated from the crowd. A man was behind her, and another behind him. None of them retreated.

The master waded into the mob. Driskolt sorMeklan unsheathed his sword and screamed his family's war cry. The master loomed over Dart like a mountain lion guarding its kill. The mob had no stomach for a fight. He hoisted the pole without turning his back.

"He goes to the inquists."

Driskolt put his free hand on the pole and lifted. They put one pace and then another between themselves and the vengeance-hungry mob. It was risky, and it failed. While they stood and fought, the mob would not attack, but when Driskolt and the master retreated, the mob surged after them. The burdened men ran to the next corner, and a few steps beyond it before the mob was at their heels again.

Those few steps were enough. Driskolt had entered the verge between Relamain's streets and the fane. The Brightwater fountain at the center of the plaza flared lightning bright as the mob poured onto the verge. Everyone blinked, and when their vision cleared, a robed sorcerer stood at the top of the fane steps. The mob retreated and even Driskolt stopped in midstride.

The master pushed Dart's pole into the Sidon's back like a lance. "Shadow's fall," he hissed, a common invocation of the thieves' god, Fethis. "Keep moving!"

The sorcerer was short and more than plump, with long pale hair whipping in the cold wind. Driskolt looked up into her round face from the bottom of the stairs and went no further. Other sorcerers, all of them looking like they were half asleep, formed a ragged crescent behind her.

"There had better be a good reason for all this, Charl," she said in a voice that carried to the bottom of the stairs but no further.

The master's feet scuffed through the gravel. "There is, Lurma."

Driskolt cocked his head to one side. The master of the Golden Cockerel had always gone to great lengths to keep his given name a secret, yet he seemed to be well-known to Relamain's inquist. Driskolt's father, the donitor, would find this tidbit interesting—maybe even interesting enough to overlook the rest of this night's misadventures.

"Lucky for you, *I* don't shirk the tasks I'm fitted for." The inquist extended her arms horizontally, then raised them slowly above her head. Black disks covered her palms. "Go home. All of you—shoo!"

The mob on the verge huddled together, hoping they could hide their thoughts as easily as they hid their faces. They did not leave. Lurma scowled and exhaled loudly. She stared at the pole and the man-shape hanging beneath it.

"Oh, it's a fine lot of trouble you've brought this time, Charl."

"I'm sorry," the master of the Golden Cockerel replied.

Lurma closed her eyes. The sorcerous crescent behind her raised their arms; their palms were empty. Lurma was the only inquist in Relamain. She stood on her toes, her fingers stretched toward the rooftops.

"All will be tended to. We thank you for your help, but now you must GO HOME!"

Her stringy hair lashed her face. Luminous mist boiled out of the fountain and, at last, the crowd began to disperse. When she was satisfied that it would not re-form, Lurma descended the stairs. The water in the fountain flowed normally again. Driskolt tried to keep his eyes on her face, but by the time she stood beside him, he was staring at the ground between his feet.

"Ashamed of yourself, midons Sidon?"

The Sidon looked the other way, but he had to answer her. "It was pundonor, Inquist. I could not back down."

Lurma was the resident inquist of Relamain, and one of the best of her discipline in Walensor. She was magga rank within her discipline—she should have served at Eyerlon—but she chose to live in the town where she was born. No one—not King Manal or Feladon, the magga sorcerer herself—could compel an inquist. With a well-practiced gesture she spun her obsidian touchstones to the backs of her hands. She touched Dart's wrist through the bindings.

"There was no need for this. *This* shook the Web like a thousand madmen dying. You could have simply waited at the Golden Cockerel," she scolded the man she called Charl. "None of this would have happened if you'd waited. You could have been killed carrying this through the streets the way you did."

"I didn't think."

"Well now, that's always been true enough, hasn't it?"

"I suppose it has."

"Take him on inside. You've carried him this far, you may as well carry him the rest of the way. You know where my sacram is."

The master of the Golden Cockerel managed to look squarely into Lurma's eyes before walking past her with his burden. The inquist shook her head and fell in behind them.

The discipline of inquiry, like all the other sorcerous disciplines, was open to anyone who had the knack for it. In practice, however, the inquists were the most homogeneous discipline: all women, all mothers, and almost all of them grandmothers before they found their true calling.

An inquist could not unreel thoughts like so much silk; she could not compel by main force. An inquist's *basi* touched the helpless infant hidden in every adult. It awakened and used a child's desperate need to please its mother. Lurma honed her skills raising six children. She rarely raised her voice or threatened, and she was proud that she had never yet resorted to force.

Never yet.

Charl, the master of the Golden Cockerel and a string of doxies, for all his failings, was no fool. He knew what happened to renegades who strayed too far from the path. He was careful where and how he abused his mender's *basi* lest the Web take note of his activities. But tonight something had scared him witless, and he'd come running through the Web to the fane like a homing pigeon.

Lurma and her comrades hadn't known what to expect, but it

certainly wasn't a young man hanging from a pole like a gutted stag. Following the two men, she led her fellow sorcerers down the public aisles of the fane and into the narrow corridors of the cloisters where Relamain's sorcerers lived and worked. One by one the sleepy sorcerers left the silent parade until Lurma, Driskolt, the master, and, of course, Dart were alone at the top of a spiral stairway which descended to the sacrams.

Moss covered the walls of Lurma's sacram, making it quiet, cool, and damp. The floor was tilted slightly; a trickle of shimmering water moved along the base of the walls to a little pool in the corner opposite the door. Her only furniture was a carved stone stool in the middle of the floor. There were no lamps. The moss was sustained by Brightwater and provided all the light the inquist needed to do her work. Charl's sullen expression did not change when the door closed. Driskolt tried to conceal a sudden surge of guilt and terror.

"Unbind him," the inquist said sternly when she stopped smiling to herself.

The master of the Golden Cockerel balked. "He's dangerous. He's got *basi* like hellfire."

Lurma knelt down to saw on the knots with her own knife. When people balked in her presence their beliefs and fears were in harmony—and not to be ignored lightly. "This is my sacram. Hellfire's no danger here," she explained patiently. Dart's feet were free; she helped him straighten his legs.

Charl shoved his knife into the ropes over Dart's wrists. "It's not hellfire." He yanked the blade through the knot. "It's not like anything I remember. It's dark and empty. But it's *bad*, like hellfire." He got his arms beneath Dart's and hauled him onto the stone stool.

Dart listed sideways on the stool. He had one arm pressed tight against his ribs; the knuckles of the other hand touched the floor. Lurma found nothing about him to inspire fear. His clothes, his face, and his hair were filthy. His eyes were closed. He moaned a little with each reluctant breath. Lurma dipped her sleeve into the pool of shimmering water. She wiped a particularly offensive smear from Dart's cheek.

"I could almost wish for a lamp," she mused, tilting his chin from one side to the other.

There was something unusual about his hair, but in the misty light of her sacram, even without the street-dirt matting it, Lurma would have been hard pressed to say what it was. The scrapes and bruises she could see were not serious enough to forestall an interrogation, but Lurma could not see *within*; only menders had that talent. She stared at the ceiling, thinking of the Web, and her own carelessness. She should have had the prisoner examined before they brought him down to the sacram. It was the sort of detail the Inquist of Relamain did not usually overlook. Lurma doubted she had overlooked it.

Charl was right about the young man: He was empty; he created forgetfulness.

"You're reaching. I can save you the trouble." Charl shrugged as he spoke. "He's got a few cracked ribs, nothing more. The rest is what I was trying to tell you about."

Lurma got unsteadily to her feet. She rinsed her sleeve in the well, and splashed Brightwater on her face. Her mind cleared. She whirled the obsidian to the palms of her hands and held them equidistant from Dart's ears.

"Who are you?"

Dart sagged backward. The master of the Golden Cockerel kept him from falling. "That's the very question that started the problem."

The inquist stuck her moist fingertips gently, but firmly, into the hollow behind Dart's jaw and brought him upright on the stool. "Your name. All that lives has a name. What is yours—?" She found the nexus between body and soul and compressed it; Dart was paralyzed from the place that her fingers touched, down to his toes. "What is the name your mother chose when she took you from Mother Cathe's breast?" The nexus throbbed against her touch. "Answer me. Answer your stepmother!"

"No mother." Dart writhed as he spoke. He nearly escaped Lurma's clutch—nearly, but not quite. "Taken, not given. Changed. Forgotten. No mother. Lady."

Lurma's fingers were dry. She released her prisoner to moisten them again at the well, and to consider his answers. The abyss surrounding him was as forbidding as Charl promised. It, and not the young man, was the source of the confusion. The young man was utterly lost within it. Lurma cupped her hands and plunged them into the well. She splashed the excess on his face.

Dart's eyes opened.

"Cathe weeps—" Lurma withdrew, drying her hands on her robe as she did. "Who is the lady?" she demanded quickly, but without her fingers covering the nexus, Dart resisted her. "Where is she?" Lurma said with the fullness of her power.

Where inquiry intervened, noblefolk and commonfolk were very much the same. Notwithstanding his temporal position, Driskolt ruEan sorMeklan, Sidon of Fenklare, was eager to reveal everything he knew. "There was a girl at the Cockerel. She didn't say where she was from, but she said he came out of Wey-chawood. She said they'd travelled together. He said something about taking gifts to the basilidans, but that was *before*; that could be lies."

Both sorcerers craned their necks to study the observer each had forgotten.

"Fetch her," Lurma commanded, without, for a moment, remembering who she commanded. "If you would . . . midons Sidon . . ."

"I would rather know what manner of honor lies between us. He cheated on the forge; I'm sure of it. I want to hear him admit it, so I can call pundonor—if he has honor."

Dart stared impassively at his accuser.

"Inquist," Charl interrupted softly. "Lurma—you don't have to know who he is to know if he cheated the Sidon at iron-in-the-fire." His face, which Driskolt could not see, wore an expression of concern and urgency.

Lurma recovered her sense of purpose. "Yes. Yes, that is true." There was much wisdom in getting the Donitor's heir out of the sacram before unravelling the mystery any further. "Do you see this man in his true form?" she began the formal interrogation.

Dart nodded.

"Is this the man you challenged to a forge?" Lurma glanced at the master to see if she had the right term. "Do you have evidence?" she hissed belatedly. Charl nodded; the pledges were in his scrip.

"He is the man I challenged."

"Did you have cause."

"I had cause."

Driskolt licked his lips. Mistaking a nobleman for a rustic was cause—if this creature *were* a Walensor nobleman—but that seemed highly unlikely.

"He insulted me. I had cause."

"And you challenged the Sidon of Fenklare with a dice forge at a common gaming-house?"

The hackles rose on the master of that gaming-house, but Lurma was watching Dart's star-eyes flare until they were almost smooth and round. "Did you know that you challenged midons Driskolt sorMeklan, Sidon of Fenklare?"

Dart turned from side to side. When he found Driskolt, his head stopped moving and his pupils were round.

Lurma saw that Dart was surprised, but she could not guess what surprised him. She took the scraps of parchment and held them in Dart's line of vision.

"Charl and the Sidon claim you drew his signet as your own to cover your wager."

"I did not." Dart's voice was soft and distracted.

"He has no rights or chattels!" Driskolt exploded. "He made my signet. He was cheating to win, or he hoped to leave me with a worthless pledge. Which was it?"

"Do not interfere with an inquist's work, midons," Lurma snapped, but not before Dart began to answer.

"I did not cheat. I wagered all that I had. I was in the right; I would not lose."

The inquist sighed. This was what came of using writing, not the Web, to seal contracts. If her prisoner believed he told the truth, and he did, then he either was very noble or very stupid. She ignored Driskolt's sputtering. "It voids all right to make another man's signet."

"I made no other man's signet."

"Look at them! Read them! They are the same. Do you deny that you made one of these marks on the parchment? Do you deny that they are the signet of Driskolt sorMeklan?"

Sweat beaded on Dart's dirty lip. He reached for the parchment scraps; Lurma whisked them out of harm's way.

"What say you?"

"They are not the same. The signet I made has a bar in the first quarter, not the second."

Lurma was perplexed, but not Driskolt ruEan barRelamain sorMeklan, Sidon of Fenklare. "Let me see those!"

Charl took advantage of his position to snatch them out of Lurma's nerveless grip. "Not so fast." He held them above his head, where the light was strongest. The Sidon's signet was heavy with blotches, and the other had been made so fast that lines which might have been broken seemed continuous. "I think he might be telling the truth. I think there is a sunwise bar in the first quarter."

"What does a bar mean?" Lurma asked with human, not inquisitorial curiosity.

Driskolt ripped the parchment from Charl's hand. "It makes no difference." His bar was the most prominent part of his signature and it smeared across the entire family crest. "Son or brother. There's only one Driskolt ruEan sorMeklan. My uncle was dead before I was born; I'm named for him. So he put the bar in the wrong place—What do you expect from a lying, cheating bumflower?"

Dart started to rise from the stool. "I am no bumflower!"

The master of the Golden Cockerel laid a heavy hand on Dart's shoulder to keep him in his proper place.

The inquist sought to regain control of her own sacram. "What bar? Will one of you tell me what is the meaning of a bar in the second quarter against one in the first?" She knew that the noblefolk adapted merchants' script to their own ends, but she could not decipher either form of the scribbling. With the Web always within their reach, sorcerers controlled communication without a need for writing.

By necessity, Charl had set aside sorcerous prejudice when he became a taverner. "The Donitor makes a full circle around his crest. His heirs draw a line through the appropriate quarter: collaterals in the first quarter, depending on the degree; descendants in the second. Driskolt inherits the title from his father, but his name—as he pointed out—he got from his late, unlamented uncle."

"Drank himself to death, didn't he?"

"So the story goes. They found his horse one morning but they never found him."

Driskolt interrupted. "It's pundonor then. He abuses the sorMeklan name, if nothing else. I will have my family's honor cleared."

Charl felt the Web around him. He presumed to answer for the distracted inquist. "Honor for the signet, perhaps—not the forge. He didn't cheat."

"He's lying. Gods' butts, Master Charl, you're saying he's hellfired. I'll have my satisfaction and then my father'll have him killed, and you, too, for taking his part in this."

"He can't tell a lie in an inquist's sacram, and I never said he was hellfired—"

"What did you say? Why did we drag him here if he wasn't hellfired?"

"Out! Out! Both of you— OUT!"

Lurma had her obsidian touchstones showing again. She could not allow these two to quarrel here, as they seemed determined to do. The function of her sacram made it inconvenient for ordinary conversation, dangerous for argument. Her desires had the force of Brightwater torrents, and even though they were directed over Dart's head, that young man's eyes began to glow.

"Midons," she said quickly. "That girl you mentioned, the one who claimed to know this man—find her."

"What shall I do with her?"

Dart's eyes were ember-bright. They were affecting the radiant *basi* of Lurma's touchstones. She was going to have to call for help, but not until she got rid of Driskolt. "Take her to your father or bring her here. Whatever you think is best."

The Sidon's hostility ceased pressing against her touchstones. A smile creased his face. "I will, inquist. I will."

Lurma had seen that smile on a hundred other faces—usually the moment before an accused prisoner ceased his denials and began to justify his crime. It was a sick, dangerous expression, and she ought not let anyone, even a Donitor's son, leave her sacram wearing it. She glanced at Dart's eyes again, and could not look away. Were they pulsing? Spinning? Or was that just her own heart?

"What about me?"

"Charl?" The inquist did not look at him. "Go upstairs. Have Sonelen awakened; he should know what we've got here. He should be the one to decide who else knows."

The master of the Golden Cockerel snapped his fingers; Lurma did not blink. He resisted the temptation to peek at Dart's face. "Are you sure you want to be left alone with him."

"I am safe from hellfire danger in my sacram."

"Hellfire's not the only danger in the world," Charl retorted, daring to touch his silver torque.

"Do not argue with *me*!"

Charl was exhausted in mind, body, and—most importantly—in *basi*. At his best he was no match for an inquist with her touchstones bared. "As you wish."

The moss-covered door opened and closed. Lurma wove the Web tightly around her, restoring herself in its strength. She could hear the Brightwater seeping through the walls and trickling slowly toward the well. She was calm again; she had control.

"Twenty-two years ago, Driskolt sorMeklan, second son of Ean, grandson of Benit, vanished and was never seen again. Do you know what happened to him?"

The fire went out of Dart's eyes. "He died alone in the forest."

"How did he die?"

"He got lost. He could not find his way. He wandered until he came to a great tree. Then he lay down and died."

Lurma folded her arms. She'd forgotten her touchstones were active across her palms. Her *basi* closed over itself, becoming an invisible whirlpool. Lurma had never, in all the years she'd been in inquist, done something quite so foolish. It would take an hour or more to untangle herself; in the meantime she was trapped within her own *basi*.

Dart nodded as politely as he could, then limped from the sacram.

CHAPTER

—— 19 ——

The Golden Cockerel was uncommonly quiet, but not quite empty. The doxies and touts, who knew better than to leave the establishment, lounged against walls and tables, waiting for the patrons to return. Berika still sat on Dart's chair at the gaming table where the excitement started. She idled with the dice, bouncing them, one at a time, across the polished wood. Sixes came up no more often than expected; high iron did not show itself at all.

"What are you looking so gloomy for?"

Teashia, her newly mended arm splinted and supported by a bright silk sling, pulled out the other chair. Berika met her eyes briefly, then went back to her dice spinning. She was gloomy because they'd carried Dart away like a wolf for bounty. He was a fetch, a demon; she forced herself to remember the little creature sitting on the far bank of the stream, and the more ominous one who'd struck Hirmin's head off with a wooden sword. He'd proven once again that he wasn't a man—gods knew, he might even be an Arrizi spy. She shouldn't feel bad for him, because of him.

When she'd seen him sitting on this chair she hadn't even recognized him. He'd seemed just like any other man. But he was a demon—her fetch, stolen from a goddess, so probably he wasn't an Arrizi spy—and he didn't belong here. He didn't belong anywhere. Berika wondered if he'd come to his end because they'd parted company.

"He shouldn't have come here," Berika whispered, unaware that her thoughts became words.

"He'll be back. This is the only place he comes."

Against her will, Berika discovered her eyes filled with tears. "Once they find out what he is, they'll send him back where he came—if they can. If they can't—"

Berika shook her head. Demon or not, she cared about him. It was bad enough to care about people, with all the pain they brought, but caring about a demon—that was as bad as caring for a lamb when it got sent to market.

"I must not think about him. He won't be back."

Teashia brayed. "Not think about the midons Sidon? Strewth, why not? You shouldn't be thinking about anything else, love. He's very particular; he likes his doxies fresh and timid." She paused to reflect a moment. When she spoke again her voice was mellow. "He's gone once he's tired, but he's easy with his favors till then."

"Why're you telling me this?" Berika wiped her face and hoped the other girl hadn't noticed the big sloppy tear she'd caught on her sleeve.

" 'Cause I saw him holding on to you. You've got the ways he likes."

Berika tried to recall the Sidon's face, but he was a blur at the edges of memory's vision: The center was Dart. Dart—so cocky throwing the dice. Dart—collapsing under the weight of the master's *basi*. And Dart—taken away like a wolf. Another tear escaped and an uncouth sniffle.

"Stop snivelling. For all you know, he may be coming back here right now—and he'll be in the mood for you, love. He'll want someone to make him feel big and powerful again. So you had best be willing to make him feel that way. I'm still out four silver marks on account of you. You could pay me back tomorrow morning. I'll take you to the changer's. I'll make sure you get a good exchange on your maiden-gift."

Berika shook her head. The Sidon of Fenklare and maiden-gifts! This wasn't good luck or bad; it was simply beyond belief.

"You listening to me, love? The Sidon of Fenklare's going to come in here and he's going to be looking for you."

"I can't—not tonight." Shivers raced up Berika's back. A look of horror remained on her face when they were gone. "Not even for the Sidon of Fenklare." She rose from the chair. "I can't stay here, Teashia. I can't do *that*, not again. The beguines will have to take me. They'll have to make an exception for me. I've got to get out of here—"

Teashia shoved Berika back into the chair. She rolled her eyes upward and appealed to the honey goddess. "As Apice is my witness—what's *wrong* with you? Beguines! This is better than the damned beguines—we get to keep something of what we earn. We've got the hope that someday maybe some man will buy us out and set us up in a little room somewhere. Do you think you'll find the Sidon of Fenklare nosing around the *beguines*? You're so lucky, you don't know how lucky you are. You should get down on your knees and kiss my feet that I brought you here. What do you think would have happened to you? You and your *beguines*! Forget about that old goat Canter; the Sidon of Fenklare will make you a proper woman."

"I— It wasn't Canter ruCanter. I made that up."

"Someone else then? Someone back in your village? It's no trouble; the Sidon won't know."

Berika covered her face with her hands. "He'll know. I had— I'm no maiden. I was never a maiden."

The other chair clattered closer. A gentle arm settled around Berika's shoulder. "Your father? Was you mother dead, an' you the eldest? I was." The last came very softly.

In a heartbeat Berika understood that some bad luck had, indeed, passed her by. She shook her head. "I was betrothed before I was born. He—" The words could not be freed from their prison. She pressed the heels of her hands into her eyes to block the memories. "Never again . . . "

Teashia stroked the shepherd girl's hair. "The Sidon won't be like that, Berika. There's always a few, but the master keeps the worst away."

"He broke your arm."

"An' he mended it." Teashia squeezed her. "He *mended* it, 'cause it was my fault for doing what I did. Do what he says, and it's good here. I swear to you, Berika, you'd do worse at the beguines. Much worse. You can't avoid men and their pleasures—

stay someplace where you can have a few of your own. The Sidon's rich, and generous. Just let him think he's the first and you'll be rich yourself by morning."

A steady trickle of tears left charcoal tracks across the bright rouge on Berika's cheeks. The last bulwarks of her dreams crumbled: How else would a simple girl from the country survive in the towns? "I can't," she sobbed and tried, unsuccessfully, to pull away. "I can't forget. I can't pretend."

"We all pretend. Pretending you're a maid's easiest of all."

Berika stared reproachfully into Teashia's green eyes. "How can you do that? Once it's gone, it's gone."

Painted brows arched with amusement. "Hardly."

Disbelief dried Berika's tears. She thought of Heldey; Heldey and Teashia were fleece off the same sheep. Heldey was the one who should have left. Heldey would know exactly how to make the Sidon of Fenklare happy— In her mind's eye, Berika saw Heldey flirting with the sorMeklan heir and, beyond that, curled in his arms. If she pretended to be Heldey . . . The perspective obligingly began to shift; Berika shivered the scene away before it became too real.

"Why don't *you* make him happy?" she pleaded with Teashia.

Conversation had returned to the Golden Cockerel. The regulars and the curious shared their experiences now that the adventure in the streets was over. Teashia glanced around to see if either the Sidon or the master were back. When she was satisfied that they were not, she took Berika into closer confidence.

"I've already had my time with him. Like I said, he likes his girls fresh and timid. It's your turn. Come on upstairs. I'll show you—"

"Teash! Hustle your worthless butt over here!"

The sharp voice didn't belong to the master, but the ash-blond girl winced all the same. "Gotta get to work." She tugged Berika up after her. "Come *on*. We'll go upstairs later."

A knot of fire seethed in Berika's gut. Her legs seemed too long when she walked. The lamps were too bright. Voices sounded as they might if she'd plunged her head in the rain barrel. The tout pouring ale put a pair of pitchers in her hands and pointed her toward the fighting pit.

"See there—the ones looking at you." He shoved her on her way.

Berika felt they were all looking at her; certainly enough of them hooted at her as she made her way through the jostling. The customers were supposed to pay the touts. Doxies weren't trusted to touch the receipts, just the pitchers. Berika put the pitchers on the table and turned away. She lost her balance when the customer grabbed her, which made it all the easier for him to land her on his lap.

"Got a smile for Lucky Lewin?" He chucked Berika under the chin as if she were a baby—or a dog. "That's it, a little smile—" He dropped a sticky grit coin down the front of her dress. She grimaced, and that, apparently, was close enough to a smile for Lewin. She escaped back to the bar, where Teashia caught up with her.

"There's gonna be trouble," the older girl conceded, "with the master not here."

Touts were watching the stairs, but Teashia knew the Golden Cockerel almost as well as the master himself. She made the excuse that Brightwater liquor was needed from the cellar, then led Berika down a narrow corridor to a dark stairway.

"Mind the third one," Teashia cautioned, taking Berika's hand. "The board's split; you'll go straight to the cellar if you don't get to hell first—"

Berika knew she wasn't the first to hear that warning, and was careful to avoid the third step. The others were more than solid; they were silent. She gripped Teashia's wrist and stayed close to her until they reached the room the doxy called her own.

"You can stay here. You'll have to share anyway—until you're earning enough on your own. An' I'll be with the master. . . ." Teashia's voice trailed off, giving Berika the impression that the older girl had been less than candid about the good life at the Golden Cockerel. When she spoke again, she was sitting on the bed and the doubt was gone from her voice. "Here's the trapdoor—" It opened silently; a pungent odor flooded the bedstead. "*Ugh*—I forgot to empty it from last time."

Teashia emptied the gelid contents into the slop bucket. With much one-handed tossing and inventive cursing she found a packet of red powder amid the disorder of her chests and coffers. Berika picked up a spray of feathers which, though motheaten, were still bright and soft against her skin.

"I got those from Neron, too." Teashia plucked them out of Berika's hand and reburied them in the chest. "He has the *best* things, love. You'll see. Now—I'll tell what to do, but you'll learn best if you do it yourself."

With Teashia's practiced instruction, Berika mixed powdered oxblood, water, and a few drops of oil from the lamp to a semblance of a fresh maidenhead. She secreted the dish and a clean sea sponge behind the trap door in the bedpost, then arranged the pillows and linen.

"Now you must practice. Take off your gown and lie on your back—" Berika's jaw dropped. "Well, he can't very well *catch* you at it—can he?"

Berika loosened the laces at her wrists and the girdle above her hips. Black grit coins clinked and tumbled to the floor at her feet. She let go of her skirt. Tears were flowing down her cheeks again. Teashia tried to be patient—she was in no great hurry to go back downstairs—until amid the noises rising through the house she heard Sidon Driskolt's name.

"Mother's milk—stop snivelling. He's here!" She pulled the gown over Berika's head. "Gods—You're all streaked. Wipe off your face and take down your hair." Teashia dumped the Merrisat wool gown into a chest which she immediately slammed shut. "Let him think he's awakened you. And for gods' sakes— *Practice!*"

The door shut and, not surprisingly, the outer bolt fell. Berika expected that the Golden Cockerel doors locked from the outside if they locked at all. She wasted precious moments looking for a way out. There was a wad of soft, almost clean cloth next to Teashia's paints and scents. Berika sat down and attacked her face, letting her tears do the hardest work. She removed the pins dressing her hair; it fell to the floor around her.

During the afternoon, while Berika endured the first hot bath of her life, the other doxies said she was lucky to have so much hair. She had enough to sell and keep they said. One girl had already offered a memor for it. Teashia rejected the offer on Berika's behalf: "There's enough here for five rats and it's light enough to take to the dyers. Two memors, and not a flake less."

Berika wound a handful of it over her fist. Her thoughts wandered back to Gorse—to Heldey, whose hair was thicker and darker. There was no comfort imagining Heldey at the Golden Cockerel with her hair whacked off. Condemned and hopeless, Berika went to the bed and fumbled with the trapdoor. She stretched across the mattress, noting where her shoulders had to be to reach the panel. She arched her back, raised one leg, and reached beneath her buttocks. It would be more difficult, of course, when she wasn't alone.

She pounded the mattress with her fists until her strength, if not her anger or fear, was gone; then she curled on her side with the blanket pulled over her head. She wished with all her heart that she were dead, but wishing wasn't enough, and Berika was very much alive when the key turned and the bolt slid back.

The trapdoor!

It shut with a barely audible *click* which was lost in the greater creaking of the door as it opened.

"Girl? Girl—I, the Sidon of Fenklare, wish to speak with you."

She knew Driskolt was coming up. She had already sat in his lap. She had heard his voice through the floorboards. But nothing prepared Berika for the Sidon of Fenklare standing beside her bed. If Teashia was right about him, then her squeak of surprise and terror should have made him very happy indeed. She took the blankets to the edge of the mattress, far from the trapdoor.

"Are you afraid of me? There's no reason to be afraid of me." The Sidon's tone of voice was reassuring; the glint in his eye was not. Berika flattened against the wall. "I haven't come here to hurt you."

Driskolt took the blanket firmly. Berika whimpered as it slid through her numbed hands. When it was gone she crossed her arms over her breasts. He dropped the blanket and took her wrist instead.

Berika pried at his fingers. "Please?" The plea had never worked before—except with Dart, who wasn't a man—and it didn't work with the Sidon.

"Come here." He pulled; she came. "There, that wasn't so hard, was it? I won't hurt you. I'm gentle with my birds, horses, and women."

He traced a line across her face, down her neck and arm. It was gentle, as he promised, but when he was done, Berika's shift was below her shoulder on that side. She went to restore it. He said *No* without using his voice and she left the shift where it was.

"There's no need to hide yourself. There's nothing to be afraid of." Driskolt's sword struck the bedboards, startling them both.

The sword was lighter than the one Driskolt carried all summer: a weapon better suited to the confines of city and castle. He could forget he was wearing it. He opened the belt and tucked it

within easy reach beside the bed. The girl stared as if she'd never
seen a sword before, as perhaps she hadn't if she were from a
lord-less assart, as Teash told him when she also told him Berika's
name. Her shift had the unmistakable look of the country-common
and her terror was a palpable force between them.

Driskolt caressed her cheek, noting with satisfaction that she
flinched more slowly this time. It was the same with women as it
was with horses and hawks. The Sidon prided himself that he
could tame the wildest of them.

"Berika, look at me."

He set his finger against her chin. The girl's face rose, almost
of her own will. Driskolt judged her as he would anything else
about to come into his possession. Berika lacked Teashia's
arresting beauty. She was sullen, slump-shouldered, and thin in
the face. He could mend those faults himself and no sorMeklan
man would be ashamed to have her when he was finished. She
would not be the challenge Teashia herself had been. Driskolt
vowed he would tame her all the same, if only because she was
bound to that damnable wretch in the inquist's sacram and he
might get no other satisfaction for this night's insults.

With his hand firmly cupped around Berika's chin, Driskolt
kissed her. She flinched; he expected and ignored that. She dug
her fingernails into the veins of his wrist, and that the Sidon would
not tolerate. Driskolt pinched the delicate flesh beneath the girl's
jaw and twisted it hard before letting go.

"You do not like my kisses?"

Berika caught the deadly denial before she uttered it and said,
"I am not worthy of the Sidon's kisses," instead.

"But are you worthy to reject them?"

Berika imagined Heldey's laugh and Ingolde's exasperated
scowl. A poor country-common shepherd rejecting the Sidon of
Fenklare's advances? Who did she think she was? The nobleman's
smile was crueler than Hirmin at his worst and then it was gone.
Berika's voice failed. She tried to look away, but he made that
impossible.

"Let's try again, shall we?"

The girl was limp. She offered no resistance at all, even when
Driskolt thrust his tongue between her lips and deep into her
mouth. He tasted her fear and knew he could take her right then,
and break her spirit in the bargain. Splitting her shift wide open,
the Sidon yanked it down to her waist. Her breasts were high and

firm; she'd nursed no children. She might even be the maiden Teashia claimed she was.

The dice-cheat name-stealer hadn't made a woman of her—

Berika was stunned when the Sidon suddenly released her. He walked the length of the room and stood at Teashia's paint table with his back to her. She wiped her mouth on her arm, but made no effort to retie her shift.

"How do you know him? What is he to you?"

"He says I am in debt to him, midons," Berika answered, guessing the subject was Master Charl, and guessing wrong. "He is nothing to me except a master I would escape if I can."

"You said he came from your village."

"I know not where he is from, midons. I did not know him at all before today. But he is not from Gorse, midons, I am sure of it. I think he's owned the Gold—"

Driskolt spun on his heels. "The fire-eyed fraud! The cheat you said came from your village. The dice-cheat who steals my name! Tell me everything you know about him."

Berika had not glimpsed that the Sidon of all Fenklare was interested in Dart and not her maidenhead. She gasped at the immensity of her error. "He is not a man, midons. I stole him from the forest goddess with my prayers."

Driskolt sorMeklan bent backward laughing. It was not a reassuring sound. Berika's gut roiled. She ran to the chamber pot and vomited. He waited with a cold hard expression until she finished.

"And you, I suppose, are a barefoot basilidan. You'll have to do better than that, Berika, or I'll have no choice but to turn you over to my father and the inquists."

"Midons, I speak the truth: I prayed and he appeared. But that night, when our hedge-sorcerer tried to place an appeal in the Web, Weycha came. She said I stole him from her." The goddess had said other things as well, but the Sidon was not an inquist and there were some secrets Berika vowed to keep. "Please. I swear—" She slipped to the floor and beseeched him with outflung arms. "I was taking him to the Basilica at Eyerlon. I got sick and we were separated." The half-truths came to Berika from the refuge behind her *basi*. "I *swear* it, midons—"

Driskolt made fists to stop the trembling in his hands. Women lied; commonfolk lied; and common women lied worst of all.

False oaths from the likes of a shepherd girl didn't get under his skin. Something else did.

"You're in this together," the Sidon whispered as a different light dawned through his memories. "He's some by-blow bastard of my father's. . . . To make a fool of me—Dishonor me before my father . . . Gods willing, I'll see you stripped and flayed." He retrieved his sword. "Get dressed. My men will come for you."

The shepherd's mind became sublimely clear: Where flaying was concerned, all alternatives were preferable. She flayed the stillborn lambs each spring for their valuable leather. The sorMeklans of Fenklare flayed the living and called it justice. She threw her arms around the Sidon's legs as he buckled his belt, and pressed her cheek against his thigh.

"Midons—I beg of you— Cathe's mercy—Anything—"

Driskolt freed his legs; she clung to his arms. He could have run her through with his sword; his position as Sidon of Fenklare would shelter him from the consequences of rash violence, but not even his father could have her flayed without the damned Pennaik royalty making pointed inquiries. Berika's hysterics left the Sidon feeling all the more foolish. He cuffed her; she cried out but did not let him go.

"Whatever you wish of me, midons, for my life."

Rash violence grew tempting, but Driskolt had never killed a woman before and his father would demand an explanation. "One thing—and one thing only."

"Anything."

"Betray him."

Berika straightened slowly. Her arms sank to her lap. "Midons?"

"He said he was taking gifts to Eyerlon. Was he lying about that too? Where are they? Give them to me. I will shame him before he shames me."

A knot formed in Berika's throat. She could neither breathe nor swallow. Dart was a demon. Her fetch. He'd come from the forest with strange hair, stranger eyes, and an empty mind. He had no *basi*. The knot loosened. "There is a harp and a sword in a room at the Knotted Rose."

CHAPTER

— 20 —

The hour candles at the Golden Cockerel guttered before Driskolt sorMeklan set out for the Knotted Rose with a tail of five men-at-arms from his father's garrison. Respectable inns like the Rose had been shuttered and barred since the start of the midnight watch. Most of those whose work was less than respectable had either made their assignations or given up and gone home for the night. Wind gusted at every corner, freezing the horses' breath and carrying it swiftly away. The streets belonged to the rats, the cats, the dogs, and the human refuse who competed with them for Relamain's offal. These scattered to the alleys at the first sound of iron-shod hooves. Their eyes reflected the torchlight. The men-at-arms kept a tight circle around their lord and the doxy riding with him.

Berika had begun the short journey from the gaming-house to the inn riding a-pillion behind Driskolt. It was her first encounter with a horse's back. She'd never been so high in the world, and despite the cold and the dark and her own apprehension, she could not contain her curiosity. When the palfrey began to trot, she grabbed the saddle, allowing her cloak to billow behind her. The Sidon was hard-pressed to keep his horse from bolting. He called a halt and Berika found herself swaddled from head to toe in her own cloak and balanced on the Sidon's lap the rest of the way.

The Knotted Rose was locked tight and dark from threshold to eaves. Driskolt's man pounded on the shutters and roused the households on either side before a lamp flickered behind a second-story window.

"Go away. We're closed for the night." Berika recognized the landlady's voice.

"Open for Driskolt ruEan sorMeklan bar Relamain, Sidon Fenklare!"

"*Midons*! Yes, midons. Immediately, midons."

"Immediately" lasted long enough for Driskolt to instruct his men. Two, as always, stayed with the valuable horses. Three others would wait in the hall while he, alone, would go upstairs with Berika.

"What about the doxy, midons? What if she tries something?" one of the armed and mail-armored men asked, and regretted the asking.

The bar was raised, the door opened. The landlady, her husband, and at least three of the servants shivered in their shifts and nightcaps as the cold air swirled around them and their lamps.

"She won't," Driskolt said, passing Berika from the saddle before dismounting himself. "She's sworn her life on it. Haven't you?" He herded her into the inn; the three men followed.

"Yes, midons. What would you have done, midons?" The landlady bowed awkwardly enough to singe wisps of her hair in the lamp flame.

"The lady says she has stayed in a room here."

The landlady was not fooled. "We got no night doxies—"

Driskolt pulled Berika's hood back. "She swears she has been in a room under your eaves the better part of the week."

Berika met the landlady's stare. She was cold and numb from the waist up and ice water from there down.

"Are you in trouble?" Ownin, the landlord, asked guardedly.

"Your swain hasn't returned," the landlady added. Berika felt the Sidon's grip tighten on her elbow.

"He won't return," Driskolt said in a hard-edged tone that made his own men shrink. "Show me his room."

The landlady hesitated—she had some idea what lay under the bed in her least expensive room. Her husband and the Sidon commanded her obedience; she met Ownin's eyes and grimaced.

"We're a respectable inn," she informed one and all as she started up the stairs. "It's quiet here. Them as stay pay for that quiet, you know, and we leave 'em be so long as they pay. These two came with a vouchsafe from your cousin Canter ruCanter, and enough silver for one night. The swain paid in advance each night thereafter—"

She left the stairwell and started down a corridor. Servants of the Rose's other guests, sleeping guard across their masters' doorways, shuffled groggily to their feet. One recognized the Sidon and made the appropriate obeisance; the others were studiously impassive. Impeccable and respectable as it was, the Knotted Rose was an ideal place for a noble husband, wife, son, or daughter to slip the domestic leash. The Sidon had been here himself, although his tastes did not usually require such expensive discretion.

The landlady stopped at the last door. Her keys rattled and the door swung open. She lit the lamp hanging from the center beam. "They was quiet and they paid each day in advance, midons. The room was theirs till tomorrow." The landlady squeezed between the Sidon's men and joined her husband in the corridor, to avoid any taint the room might contain. "I wouldn't open the door till sundown tomorrow, you understand—"

"I understand, goodwife," Driskolt assured her. "A room that's rented belongs to its renter. It is I who should thank you for your understanding." He took the landlady's lamp and encouraged a suddenly reluctant Berika to keep her promises.

The landlady's word was good. The room was exactly as Berika had left it. A steady draft came through the unbolted shutters. Dart's discarded clothes were strewn everywhere. The chamber pot was noticeably ripe. And clearly visible beneath the rope mattress of the box-bed were a straw-wrapped sword and an unspeakably large acorn. They'd already caught the Sidon's eye.

"Leave us," he said to the three men of his escort. "Wait below until I call for you." He turned to Ownin and his wife. "Send your servants back to their beds. Go there yourselves, if you wish. You have my assurance that there will be no trouble."

The landlady obeyed the Donitor's son, but her eyes said she did not believe him. She might send the servants back to their quarters—or at least put them out of sight—but there'd be no sleep for her until the mystery was unravelled and the Sidon departed.

She left the door open and took up position a little distance down the corridor.

"Good night, goodwife. Go back to your bed," Driskolt reminded her as he closed the door. He waited until the stairs creaked before giving his attention to the objects under the bed.

"Where did he get these?" he asked, pulling both out himself.

"The harp he brought with him from the forest. The sword— He reached inside a tree. There was a brilliant light; I hid my eyes. When I looked again, he had a sword and my— A man's head was rolling toward me."

Driskolt ripped the straw from the wooden sword while she spoke. He had no more *basi* than a man his age needed to have to live and breathe. The wooden sword was lifeless in his disappointed grasp. He left it in the straw.

"What harp?"

"In the acorn."

The Sidon snatched the nut and gave it a hearty shaking. Berika's flesh crawled to think the risk the nobleman took. Perhaps it was just as well touchstones did not react to those with insufficient *basi* to use them. She watched him pull on the leather strap with all his strength and strain his fingers against the rim of the cap. He braced the nut between his knees and drew his knife.

Berika interceded. "No, midons!" She dared to lay restraining hands on him. "I'll open it for you." Thumbs against the strap and hands splayed, her fingers found the subtle hollows in the rough-textured cap. She pressed. The cap separated from the cup; the cup split into thirds. Driskolt grabbed the harp.

"It can be played?"

"Yes, midons. He played it several times in the village—"

The Sidon positioned his hands over the strings. He knew more about how the instrument *should* be played than an assart shepherd, but—Berika noted with some satisfaction—the sounds he produced were less satisfactory than her own feeble attempts.

"These strings feel like hairy roots." Driskolt wrinkled his nose and shoved the harp aside.

Berika caught it before it overturned and, ignoring the insect-tingling, made a random, tolerable chord. "They *are* roots. It *grew* like this. A touchstone." She made another chord, then looked up.

"And you can play it?"

Belatedly Berika realized that noblefolk, especially the Sidon of

all Fenklare, would know about touchstones, and their implica-
tions. He knew that hedge-sorcerers had to have touchstones
because they lacked the Eyerlon training to store *basi* within
themselves. And the most powerful sorcerers had touchstones
because they controlled so much more *basi* than even ordinary
sorcerers. He knew, as well, that no hedge-sorcerer would have
such a wondrous harp as a touchstone, which implied certain
things about Berika herself, if she claimed she had mastered its
secrets.

Berika sat on the floor and reassembled the acorn around the
harp. "Not really. An *old* man in the village—he guessed how."

Driskolt appeared satisfied. At least he appeared more interested in the sword, which he examined closely in the lamplight.
Measuring the hilt with his hands, the Sidon found the wooden
sword's balance point. He raised it into a classic guard, being
careful to avoid the open beams of the sloping roof above him.
The blunt polished stick felt more like a weapon than it looked.
Many years ago he'd begun his martial education with a bated
wooden sword.

Without warning, the Sidon slashed the empty air. No practice
weapon had the satisfying heft of this wooden sword. And the girl
looked like she'd seen the dead moving. He slapped the satiny
reddish blade against the palm of his hand. Nothing happened—
except that Berika closed her eyes.

"Is there a trick to this, too?" Driskolt prodded his companion
with the sword tip. She swayed and did not open her eyes. "I said
I wanted his secrets—not just his possessions. Tell me, girl—if
you value your skin."

A gust of wind hit the loose shutter before she could answer. It
banged open; stinging ice swirled into the room. Driskolt lowered
his guard and Berika fled to the open window. She had it bolted,
when the whole inn reverberated to another shutter striking the
wall in a different room. She turned and saw the wooden sword
pointing at her heart.

"It has no point, nor edge either. You would get a nasty bruise,
but unless I reversed it and bashed your head with the hilt, it is
unlikely I would kill you with it. Yet you are frightened. More
than frightened. Why? Tell me his secrets."

Berika was fixed to the spot in front of the window. "He cut
clean through Hirmin's neck. It didn't hardly bleed."

"A man *bleeds*, girl, when his head's struck off—unless his heart was stilled first."

Berika accepted the Sidon's greater knowledge and did not pursue the argument. Driskolt subjected the weapon to a thorough but no more revealing examination. He tried reversing it; the satiny wood of the blade was harder to hold and the balance was terrible. On a whim, he tried to balance it, hilt down, on his palm, like a sword dancer.

Driskolt was dancing a bit himself to keep the sword from falling when the door flew open. He lost his concentration and the wooden sword clattered to the floor.

A dirty hand closed around the black hilt before Driskolt could retrieve it. The Sidon drew his city sword from its scabbard.

Ugly contusions covered one side of the intruder's face. His left eye was swollen shut. There was a cut on his upper lip which oozed onto his chin. He curved his torso to the left and held that arm tight against his ribs. His clothes were crusted with filth.

Berika screamed and looked to the Sidon for protection; she had, after all, remained in the Golden Cockerel and knew nothing of Dart's journey to the fane. Driskolt recognized his nemesis.

"How did you get out of the sacram?"

The advantage should have belonged to the Sidon. He was healthy. His weapon was steel and chosen for the demands of close-quarters combat. He was as good a swordsman as the sorMeklans had produced in a generation, facing a wretch with a fancy tree limb.

Driskolt wasn't a fool; where swords were concerned, he carefully made no assumptions. He studied Dart's posture. The battered man's one good eye wasn't smoldering; it was hard and very sharp. Despite his injuries, the fraud's weight was evenly distributed over his feet. He held the sword with his whole arm, not his wrist, and he held it steady. Dart wasn't acting like a bumflower and if that weapon he held so confidently was a touchstone sword and not a stick, the sorMeklan heir had a fight on his hands.

"How did you get out of the sacram?" Driskolt repeated.

"Walked. The doors weren't locked or guarded."

"They'll be looking for you. They'll come here. I've got my own men waiting downstairs. You might succeed against me, but there's too many of them." Driskolt recalled the second crashing shutter; Dart hadn't come in through the front door and disabled his escort. "You'd better run while you can." Anything to move this confrontation out of the Knotted Rose where bloodshed was certain to raise questions in his father's justice hall.

Dart considered the advice. He tried to smile. One corner of his mouth twitched upward, the other bled. "Would you make a wager on how far I'd get?"

"Take my palfrey."

"The two you left guarding him wouldn't be happy about that."

"I'll tell them myself."

Driskolt lowered his guard. He advanced a half-step before realizing Dart wasn't lowering his. Oil lamps cast more shadows than light; nothing showed its true form after sundown. The wooden sword was pointed at his throat, and in the flickering light both edge and point seemed keen enough. He'd be dead before he got his own sword into any of Dart's vitals, so he left it pointing at the floor.

"You have my word." He retreated. Dart moved with him; the wooden sword remained an easy thrust from his throat.

"I've had that before, thank you. Berika—" She stood on Dart's blind side. He called her name without turning his head. "Gather up the harp. It's time we were travelling again toward Eyerlon." He could not see that she did not move.

"Without my help—" The Sidon's words ended abruptly. The sword tip was against his throat and it felt for all the world like cold, honed steel.

The room was silent. "Berika!" Dart repeated himself.

"Don't do it!" she shouted. She rushed across the room, using the acorn as a shield boss to deflect the wooden sword from the Sidon's throat. The jolt when the acorn touched the sword dropped the shepherd to her knees.

Dart kept his grip on the sword, which he played slowly between them, uncertain for the moment of his target. "I wouldn't kill him, Berika. He might be kin to me."

"What?" She and the Sidon exclaimed together.

"I don't believe it, either. I think it's some notion the inquist tried to plant in my memory. I'll take my chances with the Eyerlon basilidans—just as we planned. Get your cloak." He meant to take her hand, but the pain in his ribs became intolerable when he moved his free arm. "Come on."

Berika pushed the acorn toward him with her feet. "No. I'm not running anymore. I'll take my chances with midons sorMeklan. You should, too."

Dart didn't breathe. The wooden sword's flat arc swept a little closer to Berika, a little farther from the Sidon. Driskolt hadn't expected Berika to switch her loyalties, but he was ready to take advantage of it. He beat Dart's weapon away with his forearm and hammered Dart's weak side with his fist.

Dart's guard melted. He sagged against the roof post, unable to defend himself against the Sidon's relentless battering. The wooden sword was useless in his limp hand. Berika filled her lungs and began to scream.

Once again Dart felt himself spinning toward the abyss which he now knew, courtesy of the inquist Lurma, was his own death. It was his greatest enemy. The punishment Driskolt gave his ribs was trivial compared to the firestorm brewing within his skull. And yet, if he could stop Driskolt, his namesake, he might have the time to conquer the abyss for all time.

Dart found strength to ignore his pain. He raised his sword arm and brought the black-wood pommel hard against the protruding axial bone of the Sidon's neck. Driskolt's fists ceased their pounding.

The Sidon staggered out of harm's way. His whole side was numbed by the blow to his neck. The three men he'd left below, who'd heard Berika screaming, charged into the room. Two men easily overpowered Dart, stripping the wooden sword from his grasp. The third went to his lord's aid. Driskolt waved his man away. He sheathed his sword one-handed and tried to shake the cobwebs from his off-weapon arm.

"Who taught you?" the Sidon of Fenklare demanded. His face and shoulder still twitched from the stunning blow to his neck.

Dart's knees had buckled; he'd be sprawled on the floor but for the sorMeklan's men holding him on either side, awaiting their lord's pleasure. There wasn't a patch of skin or gut that didn't ache in some way, yet he rode above the pain: He'd conquered the fire of the abyss. He was alive; he was a man. Whatever he could not remember he didn't need to know.

He raised his head and forced his eye to focus on the Sidon's face. "Horsten Rockarm."

"Gods will—you lie."

Dart slumped in the grip of his captors. Having won his private war, nothing Driskolt said seemed worth the challenge. "If it was not Horsten, I swear I do not know who taught me. I have no memory for names or faces."

"You struck shield-side. I could have run you through."

Dart tried to shrug his shoulders—a bad idea. A spasm left him gasping for breath. "It was enough, wasn't it?"

"Horsten would strike you sword-side so you'd never forget your mistake."

"Horsten's not here." The words were sharpened by the twisting pains in his gut.

"But he *is* in the garrison—and he never forgets a student."

Contempt and challenge were implicit in the Sidon's tone. Dart would have laughed, if his body had permitted it. He would risk a visit to the sorMeklan stronghold to meet a man who knew, with certainty, who he was. Who he had been.

"I'm ready."

Driskolt ordered his men to stand aside. A grin sprouted in the corner of his mouth when Dart crumpled to his knees; it vanished when his battered nemesis pulled himself erect. He held his breath as Dart took tentative steps toward the door. The men-at-arms stayed beside him until the Sidon waved them back.

The truest test of a man's nobility was not his skill with a sword, but his ability to overcome adversity. The young Sidon had been pounded senseless more than once; he knew the price of standing, walking, turning, and opening the heavy warped door. His identity as a man of the noblefolk rested on the unshakable belief that commonfolk could not pay that price.

Dart's rigid progress down the corridor compelled the Sidon to accept him as a peer. He followed at a respectful distance and kept his men and Berika behind him.

The stairwell was a tight spiral. Each step made its own angle from the wall to the post; each riser had its own height. Hale, sober guests took their chances. Dart had visible misgivings. He splayed his fingers on the wall before easing his right foot over the lip. He found a rhythm: slide, drop, balance, drag, and balance again. His confidence grew.

Driskolt swayed unconsciously to the other man's rhythm. *Too fast!* He'd warn a common man, even one of his own men-at-arms, but he wouldn't warn Dart. *Keep your damned hand ahead of you on the damned wall! Don't look at the bottom—*

A moment's inattention and Dart lost control. His right heel skidded; he leaned too far back in his effort to regain his balance.

There was nothing but angled wood between him and the ground floor. Berika surged forward, but Driskolt's reactions were quicker. He latched onto the girl's neck. His eyes never left Dart's back.

"Defend yourself—" he whispered hoarsely while Berika struggled. "Strike your feet out. Get your arms up." The falling man could not hear him.

Two steps from the bottom, Dart got his feet against the post and his back against the wall. He wedged himself to a stop and began the tortuous process of getting back to his feet. Driskolt came down the stairs before Berika, magnanimously extending his arm.

CHAPTER
——21——

Berika couldn't stop shivering. The Sidon of Fenklare lapped his cloak over hers.

"We're not far from the outer gates. Once we're inside the stronghold, you can sleep by the fire in the upper hall."

Driskolt sorMeklan had become the essence of compassion since leaving the Knotted Rose. He held her gently against his shoulder as his palfrey carried them through deserted streets. He pulled his glove off with his teeth and warmed her cheek with his hand. Berika burrowed against the fur lining of his cloak. Cold wasn't the cause of her shaking; warmth didn't cure it.

Everything had moved so fast in the stairwell. When Dart took Driskolt's hand, the Sidon hadn't pulled a fallen enemy to his feet; he'd pulled him into another world: the noblefolk world. The landlady had called him *midons* and apologized for putting him in a servant's room. If only he had told her his name—There was always a tapestry-hung room available for the Donitor's kin.

Dart had just smiled and said it wasn't her fault.

Berika tried to apologize, too. She'd betrayed him to the Sidon, but things hadn't turned out too badly, had they? She took his hand between hers; they'd been that familiar with each other countless

times since leaving Gorse. Fetch, man, or *midons*, he was Dart
and they were friends, still—weren't they?

Dart freed his hand. He looked down on her—not because he
was taller; Dart had always been taller, but as if she were
something sticky and unpleasant. There was nothing magical
about his eyes. He wasn't a demon and he wasn't a man. Dart was
midons, now, and his friends were not country-common shepherds.

Berika started shivering when Dart turned silently away, and
hadn't yet stopped.

An iced and treacherous cobblestone turned beneath the palfrey's hoof. The horse plunged and snorted. Driskolt let out the
reins and Berika dug past the fur collar to the Sidon's neck for
safety.

"Easy, there—*Easy* . . ."

Berika felt the words form beneath her thumb. The palfrey
regained its footing. Berika could not tell if Driskolt had been
speaking to her or the horse. His free hand, once again encased in
a fine suede glove, slipped beneath her fingers.

"Let me breathe, mistress. You'll have your chance with me
soon enough."

Suddenly as numb within as she was without, Berika left her
hand where Driskolt put it. Her shivering finally stopped.

The week of Lesser Slaughter was beginning; the moon was a
delicate crescent just above the western wall. Neither it nor an
abundance of stars cast much light into the quiet city. The
processional causeway to the sorMeklan stronghold was as dark as
any narrow street. Berika did not realize they were close to their
destination until the drawbridge over the dry moat rang with the
horses' hooves.

"Raise the gate!" Driskolt shouted, confident that his voice
would be recognized.

Berika dared a glance beyond Driskolt's fur-lined cloak. The
passageway between the bridge and the stronghold gate was
steep-walled and sharp-cornered. Torchlight flickered in the
arrow-slit windows and through holes in the wooden floor above
each of the corners as the night guard noted the return of the
Donitor's heir. Stonework magnified the sound of the clanking
ratchets as the gate was raised. Berika knew very little about
strongholds, but the sorMeklans seemed extremely distrustful of
their visitors. She looked up as they left the passageway: Along

the bottom of the gate was a row of spears. She closed her eyes and did not open them again until the palfrey halted. She was pulled from the Sidon's lap.

"Make her a warm place to sleep in the upper hall. And, Denan, see that she stays there—Gods and my father willing, I'll want her fetched to my rooms. Is he awake?"

A voice not belonging to the one who carried Berika replied: "Yes, midons. We received your message. Midons sorMeklan is in his solar. He left orders that—"

Berika was whisked through a doorway in the arms of one of the Donitor's hundred-plus loyal and well-provisioned retainers. There were no torches in the corridor. None were needed; Brightwater moss outlined the arches with sorcery.

"I can walk—"

"I have my orders, girl."

Dart was a guest; Berika understood that she was something altogether different. She was relieved to find herself deposited in a hall echoing with the snores and sighs of countless sleepers. The hearth fire was banked, but the room was blessedly warm. Denan began a recitation of all that was forbidden, but Berika was wrapped in her cloak and fast asleep before he mentioned the consequences of disobedience.

A mender met Dart in a curtained alcove far from the upper hall where Berika slept. He protested that his ribs were sound enough and, especially, that he wanted nothing more of sorcery, but midons mender took orders from the sorMeklans, not patients. Her expression bespoke the consequences of disobedience. Dart stretched himself out on the hard bed, accepting her ministrations with a wary eye. Warmth and relief spread along his side from the small hands she held inches above his shirt. Dart's distrust ebbed in a series of diminishing shudders.

The mender smiled to herself, then scowled.

"The tearing goes deep. The bones have shifted. His lung is damaged—the blood is dark and slowing. There is mending to be done, midons."

She immobilized her patient with a potent gesture, but before fear could form in Dart's mind, she covered him with oblivion.

Pain was reduced to a dull ache when Dart's consciousness returned, and that came as much from the thick linen bandage swaddling his chest as from any injury. His lip no longer throbbed.

Both eyes opened when he willed them to. Sunlight streamed through a high window on the far wall; it was noon at least. Beyond the curtain men were muttering and whispering excitedly. Dart guessed that he was the subject of the unintelligible conversation. He forced himself to relax and to recall all that he remembered of the previous night before confronting whatever waited for him on the other side of the curtain.

A pattern had finally emerged from the abyss.

Driskolt ruEan sorMeklan—not the young Sidon whose laugh he recognized when it rose above the whispers, but a different man. An older man. A man who had died foolishly. *Driskolt ruEan sorMeklan.*

No wonder my lady said my memories were shattered.

A frisson shook him, and he realized that except for the bandage he was naked beneath the blankets. He recalled the mender—a young, attractive woman and noble as well. He sat up despite the ache, searching for his clothes.

There was a neat pile near the foot of the bed, meant for him and secondhand only in the sense that they'd been gleaned from the wardrobes of kin whose names and faces were still lost to the abyss. His boots stood beside the clothing, glistening with fresh oil. He wondered if they'd been recognized. He swung his legs over the edge of the bed and was instantly lightheaded. He stood up before the sensation passed; the room tumbled wildly. The bed reached for him like a lover.

The bandage prevented him from getting a deep breath. He sat down heavily on the thick feather mattress. With his head lolling between his knees, his skin clammy, and his breath coming in tiny, ridiculous breaths, he brought the floor back to its proper place beneath his feet. He pulled the breeches from the bottom of the pile. There were no mishaps when he tried to stand the next time. He looked for the wooden sword, and didn't find it. That wasn't a surprise. He hadn't expected to see it or the acorn waiting for him.

A woman's laughter filtered through the curtain before it was hushed with many deeper whispers. Dart let the linen shirt fall to his lap. He didn't recognize the voice, but it reminded him of Berika; Berika who had betrayed him. It was no thanks to the shepherd girl that his ribs were mended and he knew what he'd been when Weycha found him.

Dart thrust his arms into the shirt. A wedge of pain pierced his side and his memory: Menders worked miracles, but only a body could heal. He was more careful with the padded dalmatic.

Last night he'd turned away from Berika, but now when Dart thought of her, he did not remember the blank, hard face she'd worn when she chose the Sidon over him, nor the layers of paste and paint she'd worn at the Golden Cockerel. He saw her as he first saw her: eyes closed, face upturned to the sun, praying for a little miracle.

Finger-raking his wild hair, Dart parted the curtain. He had a moment or two to absorb the lofty ceiling, the glazed windows, the brilliant tapestries hung one beside the other along the lower wall, and the tight cluster of men near the hearth—then someone noticed him and the Donitor's justice hall became deathly silent. Dart recognized no one but his namesake; their eyes met briefly before another man stepped between them.

They were all noblefolk, even the men-at-arms who lived off the sorMeklan bounty. Their manner, their clothes, and most especially the steel swords each wore below his hip bespoke those accustomed to force and power. A few images gathered from the abyss in an inquist's sacram were not enough to fortify Dart against the doubt and suspicion directed his way. He barely controlled an impulse to flee.

Responding to an unseen signal, the noblefolk separated. A table bearing the wooden sword, the harp, and the disassembled acorn was revealed, and behind that a man whose demeanor proclaimed a lifelong familiarity with power: Ean ruEan sorMeklan, Donitor of Fenklare. And, if the sorcery of the inquist's vault worked true, the elder brother of one Driskolt ruEan sorMeklan, missing these last twenty-odd years.

Dart searched the weathered, battle-scarred face, hoping for a jolt of recognition from the abyss. None came.

Ean sorMeklan wore a long black robe, trimmed with fur and velvet cord. The Donitor's insignia, a gilt baton and a jeweled circlet, waited on a pillow carried by the one woman in the hall—a woman who wore a similar circlet across her brow. She followed her husband around the table. Ean stilled her with a nod, and approached Dart as a man, not a Donitor.

"There is a family resemblance, I suppose. Though he hardly looks like any brother *I* remember. Dris's hair was brown, as I recall. It might have changed by now, but not like this." Ean stopped about five paces from Dart. Another step and they would

have been in sword's-reach—if the Donitor were foolish enough
to allow men of unproven loyalty to wear swords in his hall.
"What do you think, Horsten?"

A second man, a grey-haired, one-eyed man with metal scales
riveted to his dalmatic separated himself from the other retainers.
Dart felt his heart skip a beat. The face was different; he didn't
recognize the face, but the leather band covering a ruined eye and
an equally ruined cheek . . .

"Your brother would be a man past forty." Horsten studied Dart
with a practiced eye. "This one's no older than your son."

"Inquist Lurma says he reeks of death. It has been upwards of
twenty years since my brother disappeared. What if he had *not*
aged?"

"I do not know, midons, I'm no sorcerer. The boy I taught
stood about so tall and broad. He had a face somewhat like that,
but his hair was brown as yours, midons—"

"And mine is now streaked with age; his seems streaked
with—with what . . . sunlight? But where can he have been?
The inquist says she can't imagine—"

"I was in Weychawood with her, my lady." Dart had his fill of
being an object of conversation. "She said my memory was
shattered when she found me, and while it is true that I hardly
know myself, I would rather you spoke *to* me than around me."

The Donitor's eyebrows shot up. "He . . . *You* have something of my absent brother's impertinence. You also have a scar on
your right side. Do you recall how you got it?"

Dart shook his head. "No, midons, I do—" then, in a familiar
burst of recognition's light, he did. "You gave it to me."

"He might be guessing, mi—"

Dart silenced his old teacher with a look. "Here. Here in this
hall. The night of your majority."

Ean's face gave nothing away. Dart—becoming Driskolt—
glanced from one part of the hall to another, gathering clues and
recognition. "It was the vigil before your majority. I was to pray
with you, wait with you, and help you dress at dawn." In his
mind's eye Dart could see Ean of the past; with his open eyes he
recognized the man that Ean had become. Perhaps his elder
brother had mellowed over the years. It was a risk he would have
to take. "I would not kneel to you. You were not yet acknowledged as a man. I need not bow down to another child, even if he
would become Donitor before the next sunset."

"But you did," the Donitor whispered for his brother's ears alone.

"I had no sword." In Dart's mind the moment was as fresh as yesterday. The man he spoke to was twenty-two, not fifty. "Even so you needed to cheat to win."

Ean did not deny the accusation. "And you have no sword now."

"Midonés," Horsten addressed them both. Over the years he'd heard many versions of that vigil, but never this one. This was the first that had a ring of truth to it. *"Midonés, let it be settled between you."*

The Donitor retreated from the conflict. "I could never trust you after that night, Dris. I never saw a curtain but that I wondered who might be waiting behind it. I had my spies all around you: among your servants, your women. Everywhere. You were never far from my eyes, and then you were gone. I confess I had many a nervous moment those first few years. You were always a better swordsman than I. Dris—

"This will become awkward. I honored your memory when my first son was born—to please our mother—She lives yet, not here, but in Cleavershaw. Do you remember Cleavershaw? She must be told. I'll tell our spooks to shake the Web and get the word to her. You left no issue—none we could find, anyway—and she felt the name would be lost. But now we've *two* Driskolt ruEan sorMeklans among the living."

The flashes of recognition ceased. The sense of reliving the past faded. Dart had never known about the spies—and among his women, too. His outrage was dulled by knowledge that twenty years had passed since he'd seen his brother, nearly twenty-five since their vigil-night brawl. Nothing good would come from reliving the past. He'd been better off without it.

"I renounce Driskolt ruEan sorMeklan." Dart had no sword to break over his knee or crest to throw into the fire, so he shoved his fist toward Ean's face instead.

The Donitor froze and in the background several men reached for their swords.

Horsten put his hand over Dart's fist and pulled it aside. "That would not be wise, midons Driskolt. You're in trouble past your eyebrows and you'll need your family's name if you hope to win free of it. The spooks can swallow a nameless man, especially one whose been dead for twenty years and carries a god's gifts."

Dart stared into his teacher's eye. "I was already going to Eyerlon—"

"Aye—they've got your wind," Horsten said. "They've got a boat waiting at the fane wharf. I'm old now, Dris; I can think like a spook if I will it. You're like nothing they've seen or felt before, Dris, and they're like stags in rut waiting for you."

The comparison made Dart's arm weak.

I'll go back to the forest.

He did not speak aloud, but Horsten was, as he said, an old man with a hint of sorcery around him. "You'll never make it."

"Warn him well, Horsten," the Donitor counselled. "The spooks say there's no hint of hellfire to you—and we can be grateful for that—but half my city went to sleep thinking you were Hazard incarnated, the other half will wake up believing it. Relamain can't hold you; Fenklare can't hold you. If you cooperate, the sorMeklan will make a new place for you when your mystery is made clear. But if you don't—we are not forced to believe your wild tale, and the stepmothers do not look kindly on those who have made them seem foolish."

Dart had never been a political animal like his elder brother. He could not think around corners. If the path was not straight, he would not take it. All the paths around him were twisted and dark; he longed for a sword to make them straight. Failing that, he wanted time to think, but that was also impossible.

"An emissary from the fane has been here since dawn, my brother. They are most eager to get you back, but I could not surrender my loyal kin to them. If you were kin. If you are *loyal*."

The carved beams of the ceiling held no clues, nor did the rushes strewn across the floor. The tapestries depicted the sacrifices and triumphs of the sorMeklan myth. Dart could not recognize the winners from the losers. And Ean grew impatient quickly.

"If it is such a difficult choice, perhaps I should make it for you?"

"There's a price, isn't there? There's always a price with you, Ean. What do I have to give you?"

"Why—*loyalty*, what else? Liege and fealty. Give me your oath—without a sword against your ribs. Place yourself willingly in my hands, in my son's hands."

Dart stared at the parchment roll beside the circlet and baton. "There is no choice." He reached for the pen.

Ean snapped his fingers; his wife and son started forward. "You're smarter than you were, Dris."

"Call me Dart, midons. It's easier on my ears."

"Quite a bit smarter." Ean accepted the circlet from his wife's hands. "Let the spooks in. They'll be the witnesses." He adjusted the sleeves and shoulders of his robe before taking the baton. Dart dropped immediately to one knee. "Properly, brother Dart. We must do this absolutely properly."

Servants appeared from nowhere. They worked up a quick sweat preparing for the oath ceremony. Dart's possessions were whisked away for safekeeping, the rushes were kicked aside, and a patterned carpet was laid over the planks. An old, obviously uncomfortable high chair was set in the middle of the carpet and a crimson canopy unfurled around it. Ean ascended the Donitor's throne and his robe was carefully arranged around him. The formal doors at the far end were opened. The hall filled quickly with lesser members of the household and the honored, but unwelcome, witnesses from the fane.

The sorcerers radiated their displeasure, and their helplessness. Dart's persistent doubts about his brother were balanced, if not eased, by the grim expression on inquist Lurma's face. Like the Donitor, she and the others wore their fullest panoply, diminished somewhat by the hours Ean had kept them standing in a sumptuous, but overheated, antechamber. A portly sorcerer with a crystal-capped staff and beaten silver breastplate began the negotiations bluntly:

"Midons Donitor, surrender the fugitive."

"What fugitive? Has my dear brother committed a crime?"

"He killed a man in an assart and attacked a brother sorcerer who sought to question him." The sorcerer modulated his voice for confidence and conspiracy: "Midons, you cannot seriously believe he is truly your brother—"

"He has made a convincing case before me."

The sorcerer pounded the floor with his staff. "He has been tainted. Victim or not, the Compact has been violated. This man was dead—he cannot be a *man* now. His disposal is a matter for the Basilica of Eyerlon, not the Donitor of Fenklare."

A heavy hand crimped Dart's shoulder. He spun on his heel and pulled his punch just before launching it into Driskolt's face. Horsten dropped the dark green bundle he was carrying and put a restraining hand on each of them, lest a mistake become a disaster. The Sidon led the way to the alcove where Dart had slept.

"This is no time for grudges or pundonors," Horsten chided his favorite pupil.

Dart shook his head, but allowed his old teacher to lead him from the hall. They dressed him in the dark green robe. Driskolt removed his own sword belt and wrapped it below his uncle's waist. Dart adjusted the buckle and toyed nervously with the leather-wrapped hilt.

"I'd rather have my own—"

Driskolt twisted a fistful of his uncle's borrowed robe. They were nose-to-nose and the younger Driskolt got his first good look at his uncle's seething eyes. "Godswill," he swore as he let go. "No wonder they want you so badly. But they don't know about the sword—we've kept *that* damned thing from them. Can't you think what would happen if the spooks got a whiff of it?"

Dart considered; Driskolt lowered his arm. "Where is it? And my harp?"

"Behind the treasure wards."

"Hurry—" Horsten held up a heavy brass chain similar to the ones both he and Driskolt wore.

Dart nodded into it and, without thinking, glanced down at the plaque: a white hunting dog with a viciously spiked collar and bleeding wounds. All else receded while he remembered his reasons for making this the symbol of his membership in the sorMeklan clan.

"You remember it?" Driskolt asked innocently.

"Gods—I hated this place. No child hated home more than I—" But that wasn't true. He looked squarely at his nephew. "The girl—Berika. What's become of her? She must not be given to *them*, or returned to her village."

The Sidon smiled, reminding Dart that nothing was truly settled between them. "She gave herself to me, midons. You heard her. I've made her my leman. I like her well enough, I'm thinking of bringing her to Eyerlon with us. I won't keep her forever. Will you want her back?—when I'm finished, of course."

Once again Horsten moved between them. "Enough! Settle this later."

Driskolt readily agreed. "Who knows what may happen in Eyerlon?" he said as the tapestry fluttered behind him.

"Let it go, midons," Horsten advised, his hand still braced

against Dart's chest. "You need your family now more than any doxy."

"She's no doxy, she's—" Dart looked away from the armsmaster's stare. "She's no doxy, that's all." He brushed the tapestry aside and strode to the throne where his brother waited.

CHAPTER

—— 22 ——

The sorcerers of Relamain duly witnessed the moment when the younger—much younger—brother of their Donitor, Ean ruEan sorMeklan, reaffirmed his liege and fealty to the secular hierarchy of Fenklare and Walensor. Ean sorMeklan struck Dart lightly four times with the gilt baton: once as a man, twice as a nobleman, the third time as a kinsman, and the last as a brother. The portly sorcerer doused himself with Brightwater and restored Dart's name, Driskolt ruEan sorMeklan, and his lineage to its place in the Web. Should Ean and his three children die without further issue, the circlet and baton would return to a man who had been dead for over twenty years.

"It is an outrage. It brings shame and dishonor to your clan and kin," the staff-wielding sorcerer proclaimed the moment the ceremony was over.

"It does indeed," the Donitor purred. "Surely the basilidans of Eyerlon will inquire of the gods what must be done? I would not have the sorMeklan tainted with demonry."

Dart felt the flames of fear and distrust rising within him. Now, of all times, was not the moment to fall into one of his fits. He told himself that Ean was as bound by the oaths of liege and fealty as he, himself, was. He concentrated on the sorcerer's sweating, twitching upper lip: The man behaved as if he'd been hoodwinked by the Donitor—but did that guarantee the safety of the Donitor's brother?

There was no one to ask.

The throne was returned to its dusty corner. Trestles, tables, chairs, and benches were brought out from the wall. Dart was seated on the Donitor's right. He shared Ean's plate, and ear. A multicourse feast was brought out from the kitchens with trumpet fanfares and frenetic entertainment. Distant kinfolk made their way to the high table. Most of them were unremembered and easily forgotten. A few, however, stirred recognition.

Dart saw them as they had been, and with the free-flowing wine, soon saw them doubled, as well. He was caught off guard when men-at-arms appeared on either side of his chair.

"The boat is ready," Ean explained. "You'll be half a league down the river before the spooks realize you're gone. My son is going with you. I suggest you remember that your oath binds you to him as it binds you to me. I'll make arrangements for your living when you need it. It won't be easy. The inheritance was divided without you, and the war has left the whole Norivarl without estate. But I'm sure something honorable can be brought together when you return."

"If I return."

"You'll return. I haven't gone to all this trouble to see you swallowed by the spooks."

The escort laid hands on Dart's arms; he shook free. "Am I a prisoner?"

"More a hostage." Ean waved his fingers and the men-at-arms retreated. "You're my brother, Dri—Dart. The question is: What else are you? I forgave my brother his impertinence and his arrogance long ago; I harbor no grudges, whatever you think. I've missed you all these years. I trust my brother, and his oath, but for the rest: You'll be guarded and confined to quarters. The Basilica insists. It's a gentler passage than you'd have had otherwise, I assure you."

"And in Eyerlon? What happens when I get to Eyerlon?"

"You go to the Basilica and the basilidans. I thought that was quite clear."

"No grudges, brother? What welcome should I expect from the Basilica, now that you've slapped them with your gloved hand?"

The Donitor shrugged. "The court knows you're coming, too.

Written messages will confirm that your oath was taken freely. Dris is quite good friends with Prince Alegshorn and his circle. If you come to harm, you'll have brought it on yourself."

The riverboat cabin was tiny, but as comfortable as anything Dart remembered on this side of death. Driskolt, Sidon, came once, the first night out, to repeat his father's warning. The rest of the time Dart was left to himself. He asked for his harp; the request was, not surprisingly, refused. His ribs finished their healing.

Dart squeezed himself onto a shelf below the barred window. As the early winter countryside flowed by, he tried to make sense out of what was happening, what had happened.

The guards in the passageway banged their weapons against the wooden walls, coming to attention. Dart watched the door. It was too early for dinner. He expected Driskolt.

"May I come in, midons?"

"I'm hardly in a condition to say no, am I, Berika?"

She opened the door no wider than necessary to squeeze through, and closed it behind her. A shamed smile twisted her lips as she held out an angular, cloth-wrapped package closed with a drawstring. "I found this in the Sidon's quarters. He said you could have it."

Dart swung his legs down from the window shelf. "You seem to have found a comfortable place for yourself. A protector— that's what you always wanted, wasn't it? A *midons* to take care of you. Not too many demands, I hope?" he said with false neutrality, looking at her and not the tangled drawstring.

Berika wore the same gown she'd worn at the Golden Cockerel, cleaned and darned with Merrisat floss this time. Her dark blond hair was clean and sparkling. There were no other women on the boat, no one to arrange her hair in fashionable loops and curls. She had left it loose rather than bind it in thick, common braids. Her face was pale until she realized Dart was staring at the jeweled pendant in the hollow of her neck. Then she reddened.

"He says I . . . please him, and he is different to Hirmin as night and day—"

" '*As* different from Hirmin as night from day,' Berika."

She winced and wound the tassel ends of her girdle awkwardly around her fingers. Dart was not pleased to find that he enjoyed tormenting her. He turned his attention to the drawstring. The knot yielded. She had brought him a child's harp: a toy with twelve gut strings, three of which split apart when he touched them. Gasping with dismay, Berika tried, and failed, to retrieve it from him.

"I didn't know—"

"You'll learn." Dart returned the harp to its sack. "You learn quickly."

"—about you. I was so convinced you were a demon or my fetch, I never guessed you might be the Donitor's brother."

"But not Sidon. Not his heir while he has a living son. Don't forget that. I'm part of the family again, but not—if you're careful about these things, and you should be—properly midons. I have no land; I hold no one's oath; I cannot pronounce judgments over anyone, not even a shepherd. I could once, before I—*died*." Dart was not quite reconciled to that facet of his existence. "You made the right choice, Berika."

"You hate me now, don't you?"

Dart stared out the window.

Berika lost patience with his brooding silence. "I wasn't the one who challenged Driskolt. I wasn't the one who made a spectacle of myself in a gaming house. We had enough money to get to Eyerlon. You were the one who couldn't leave well enough alone. We could have gone to Eyerlon, and none of *this* would have happened."

She headed for the door. Dart sighed and called her back. "Something else would have." He got in front of her. She would not look at him; he gathered her hands between his instead. "The truth is only the truth. Once I thought when I knew my name all the mysteries would be over, but that truth has solved nothing. I'm Dart sorMeklan—a sheep among wolves.

"You didn't make me what I've become . . . what I've always been. None of this is your fault. I don't hate you. I'm glad you've found your protector— Ingolde was right: I'm trouble coming and pain behind."

Berika stopped struggling. "Ingolde wanted you to take me to Eyerlon." Her voice got very soft. "I wanted my fetch to just go away because I thought I didn't need him anymore."

Dart's hands no longer confined hers. She hugged him; his arms hung limply at his sides. She squeezed tighter until he moved her arm away from his tender ribs.

"You'll see, everything will still work out once we get to

Eyerlon. The basilidans will understand. I'm sure of it. You never failed me; you won't fail your lady."

Dart meant to say: "Fine for you and my lady goddess, what about me?" He said "thank you," instead. He meant to kiss her lightly on the forehead and then guide her to the door, but that didn't happen either.

Berika's hands were beneath Dart's shirt, his were on her laces, when he heard footsteps and thumping in the passageway. In a heartbeat, Dart thrust his love across the cabin, where she wouldn't be seen when the door opened. He raked his hair and wiped his mouth on his sleeve, but his color was high when Driskolt strode into the cabin, and his shirt was bunched above his waist in the back. Dart concocted a handful of evasions and half-truths to protect both himself and Berika, all of which he discarded the moment he saw his kinsman's face.

"I thought you might care to join me on deck," Driskolt began casually. "We're nearing the chain. Eyerlon's quite impressive from the river—it might be your only chance to see it. Berika, too, when I find her. But if you're otherwise engaged—"

Berika stumbled across the cabin and fell to her knees. "Forgive me, midons."

"Is there anything to forgive, pet?" The Sidon smoothed her hair.

Dart answered first. "No. She brought me the harp. I took advantage of her."

"Did he now?" With Driskolt's assistance, Berika rose unsteadily to her feet, shaking her head as she did. He caught her chin firmly in one hand, then looked at Dart. "There seems to be some disagreement here."

Dart took a deep breath. She was better off with Driskolt than she'd be with him. It was his final duty as her fetch, to make sure she stayed there. "Berika is a shepherd, an assart shepherd and easily deceived. She betrayed me for you. I simply meant to return the favor." He couldn't see Berika's face, and didn't want to. "I've satisfied my honor—and I'm certain she's learned the dangers of disloyalty."

He grabbed his cloak from the bed where it doubled as a blanket. He whirled it around his shoulders with shaking hands. It settled with a graceful flourish.

"Eyerlon awaits." Dart gestured for his nephew to lead the way.

Dart started for the door, fairly challenging his kinsman to stop him.

"Horsten always said you were the best he'd seen. Father said you were a rogue."

"Ean knew me best." Dart laughed as he went through the door.

Sleet stiffened their woolen cloaks and struck their faces like needles. Berika hid inside the Sidon's cloak until they reached the monumental chain, when he went below to pay the king's portage tax. Then she scurried away without a word or glance in Dart's direction.

Dart never moved out of the wind. His hair froze to his hood. Ice formed in the stubble of his beard. The Fenklare boatmen stopped looking at the midship railing and made warding gestures each time their duties took them from one end of the boat to the other.

The boat slued to starboard as they came around to the Basilica wharf. Dart moved with it, never losing his balance. A delegation from the Basilica ascended the ramp once they were tied in. They took one look at the ice-slicked steps to the bridge and decided Dart could come to them.

"Midons? Midons Driskolt? You are remanded to our custody. Do you hear me, midons?"

"I'm ready."

Dart's fingers bled when he tore them from the railing.